Not Without A Fight

Rebecca Lange

Published by Rebecca Lange, 2023.

NOT WITHOUT A FIGHT

First edition. June 8, 2023.

ISBN: 978-1957089263

Written by Rebecca Lange.

Table of Contents

...for the people who freely share their opinions on why a period novel is inaccurate. What part of the word FICTION don't you understand? Who are you to tell characters in the 1800s that they can't be playful and flirtatious: "Thou mayest not enjoy your fictional life - go and be depressed"...

1

This isn't Fair

"Pa, you wanted to see me?" Hazel asked as she entered her father's study before stopping in her tracks. "Uncle Ted, what are you doing here?" She jumped into her godfather's arms, and he gave her a loving hug.

"It's so good to see you again, Hazel. You're getting more gorgeous each time I see you," he said as he ran his hand across her cheek. The young woman blushed and stepped back.

Her father moved closer. "Ted is here for legal matters. I asked him to put my Will together, so my family is looked after in case of my passing."

"I don't like it when you talk like that, Pa," Hazel responded while her beautiful lips turned into a pout.

Her father grinned. "I'm not sick, and I'm not planning to die, but I can't avoid this forever. So, why not getting it done now, while I'm healthy as a horse?"

"Hilarious, Pa." Hazel rolled her eyes.

"Let's sit, shall we?" George pointed to the chairs across his desk, and everyone took a seat. "Ted, Helen and I discussed this matter, and we mutually agreed that Hazel should be the one who inherits the ranch. I know I should leave it to a male heir, but since I don't have one, I want Hazel to take over the ranch. She loves this place more than anyone and has been my right-hand helper ever since she learned to walk. She is fair and honest, and my family and ranch will be in excellent hands with Hazel in charge."

"You seriously want me to take over the ranch, Pa?" A beaming smile spread across Hazel's face, and her eyes lit up like the sky during fireworks.

"We all do. Haven has no interest in running a ranch, and Brenna wants to be a school teacher when she finishes school."

"George, may I say something?" Ted interjected while scratching his neck uncomfortably.

"You never have to ask, my friend."

"As much as I would love to put Hazel as your heir into the Will, it isn't possible. The law states that a woman can't own or inherit land or a business. That means any male related to you can fight her on it and would win."

Hazel let out a frustrated gasp and glanced at her godfather with furrowed brows.

"That's not fair!"

"It isn't, I agree, but unfortunately the way it is."

"So what am I supposed to do? Sell my land because I don't have a son?" George crossed his arms, his eyes squinted, a sign that he was not pleased.

"It doesn't have to be a son, just a male relative or even a friend."

"The only living male relative I have is my younger brother Russell, and he doesn't care about my ranch."

"What does Russell do now?"

"He took over my father's bank in Sacramento. I'm sure he would love to get his hands on this place to sell it and make more money. But I didn't work this hard for him to destroy it."

"Don't worry, Pa, I won't let that happen, ever."

"There isn't much you can do, Hazel. A male relative will always come first. Once your father passes away, Russell can sue anyone who inherits this place. As the only living male relative, every judge will agree with his case."

"But I'm Pa's closest relation. I am his daughter and worked with him all my life. I know this ranch inside out, and can run this place just as well as any man can. Isn't there anyone we can fight on this? This isn't right." Hazel pressed her lips together and squinted her eyes. The smile from before was gone.

George smirked to himself, even if it was only for a moment. He was well aware of how headstrong and determined his daughter could be. She was a spitfire by nature, and always stood up and against unfairness of any kind.

"It isn't right, but those who make the laws don't care about fairness or what's right."

"Uncle Russell has no claim to this place. He only visited us once and made it clear that he had no interest in running a ranch or living in the country. There is no way in he—"

"Hazel!" George interrupted with a warning growl in his voice, raising an eyebrow. Ted turned around, hiding his grin.

"Okay, fine, I won't say it, but there's no way I'll let anyone take the ranch away from us. I'm ready to take over. I know everything I need to know about ranching. You taught me how to hunt, shoot a gun, and use a knife, and I'm good at archery. Girl or not, I can run this place."

"I understand you and your feelings, Hazel. I do," Ted replied, offering her an understanding smile. "You might remember my daughter Marianne. She's going through a similar situation right now. She wants nothing more than to follow her dad's and brothers' footsteps in becoming a lawyer. But, no matter how many universities we've contacted, the answer is always the same: She can't do it because she's a woman. Martin and John have tried their hardest to change the law and the mind of those running the universities, but this is a man's world, and women don't have a say in legal matters."

"But why won't they at least give women the chance to do those things? It wouldn't stop them from being women by owning land or getting an occupation they love," Hazel responded pouting.

"The most used excuse currently is that women aren't strong enough to do certain occupations or not smart enough. I believe in general, most men wouldn't have an issue with one or two women trying out new things. However, they are afraid that once they open that door for one person, more women would want to follow their lead and discover that they are smarter than men want them to believe. They want to keep women where they think they belong—in the kitchen and house. I disagree with that wholeheartedly. Marianne is as smart as a whip, and she can out-debate anyone in any circumstance. The same goes for you, Hazel."

"We need to fight for our rights, then. I'm not willing to step aside and let my uncle destroy this ranch and sell it to someone who does not understand and appreciate how much hard work and long hours Pa and Jackson put into this place."

"Fighting isn't as easy as it sounds. I've tried suing for discrimination, so my daughter would have a chance, but I didn't even get the case to court. The judges block everything that has to do with women getting more rights."

George cleared his throat. "I am not giving up that easily. Hazel still needs to learn about business and management, but hopefully, we will find a way for that. I want her to inherit my ranch, and that's it."

Hazel's eyes lit up again, her expression slowly softening. She loved her father more than anyone. He never stood in her way of following her dreams.

George Buchannon and Ted Burton defined genuine friendship. They had grown up on the East Coast in the same neighborhood in New Haven, New England, and had gone to the same schools.

George had rescued Ted as a four-year-old boy from drowning one day, after a few older boys had pushed him into a lake. George didn't know how to swim, but he jumped into the lake, anyway. He held on to a tree branch hanging above the water. He then used his belt as a fishing pole, so Ted could grab it, and George could pull him toward the shore and then out of the water. They have been best friends ever since.

George moved west before the big gold rush, even though his father wanted him to get into the bank business and take over his bank. But George had no interest in that. His dream was to own a ranch and live out in the country. Neil Buchannon was close to disowning his oldest son, but his wife reminded him that he didn't want to take over his father's business either.

When George ended up in the Oregon Territory to follow his dream, his father supported him and moved his family west. They relocated to Sacramento, and Neil Buchannon opened a bank there. Several years later, Russell took over the Buchannon bank. Neil was grateful that he had listened to his wife. She helped him realize that family should always come first, and different ideas and passions shouldn't destroy the loving bonds.

Ted finished his studies at the University of Boston before following George to the West Coast. He opened his office as an attorney in Salem and became George's legal right-hand arm. He always made time for his best friend, no matter how busy he was. When the twins were born, George made Ted Hazel's godfather.

"If you are serious about trying to change the law and make Hazel your heir, we should wait before writing your Will. If I were to write the Will right now, I would be obligated to name your brother as the one inheriting your ranch. Once written, I am bound to contact the person who inherits your land. If you absolutely don't want Russell to get his hands on it, it wouldn't be wise to make it official now."

"But what if something happens to me before the law changes in favor of women?"

"We can write a legal note which will allow me to write the Will as discussed, and we can ask Jackson to be a witness and sign it. Your signature is the most important, though."

George nodded.

"What would happen if I get married before Pa passes away? Can you name me as the heir then?"

"Yes, but your husband will be the one in charge and can do what he pleases with this place."

"You can't be serious?" Hazel burst out with disbelief, her jaw was clenched, and her eyebrows drew closer together. Her father's expression changed to light amusement when he saw the familiar pout return.

"I'm dead serious. Until the law changes, even a widow has no rights. A widow can inherit her husband's land, but as soon as she marries again, everything will fall into her new husband's hands. She can't pass *her* possessions and property on to her children unless she has a son. If she dies and has daughters, they will get nothing, and the property and possessions will get auctioned off."

"Wow. I'm appalled. Is there no justice for women?"

"No. Once a woman marries, her husband is in full control and can do with her as he pleases, before that, her father. Many women get beaten and abused by the men in their life, and nobody is there to protect them. The law does nothing on their behalf," George said and shook his head. Ted nodded in agreement.

"So if you aren't lucky enough to have a wonderful and loving father and later husband, the men in your life can do whatever they want to you?" Hazel was shocked.

"Yes. Most violent fathers marry their daughters off to someone like them, so they will never know the difference." Her father breathed through his teeth. This subject angered him beyond imagination.

"That's horrible. We are human beings too, and should have the same protections and rights as men."

"Yes, you should, but many men don't think that way and believe that women don't deserve to be treated as equal."

"They should reread the bible. God gave Eve to Adam as a helpmeet, not a slave. He created Eve out of Adam's rib so that they could work side by side as equals. Sure, we have different responsibilities and are unalike in several ways, but Eve completed Adam. We're supposed to be companions to our spouses."

"You have a great understanding of the scriptures, Hazel," Ted said now. "That might help you change the world, change the thinking of many." Ted gave her a side-ways hug, and she smiled.

Perhaps her godfather was right. Maybe it was her mission to fight for women's rights and remind everyone that God created men *and* women, and both were on this earth for a reason. Perhaps she was sent to this earth to help people realize that being treated fairly and equally did not mean they were the same. Being different wasn't bad, but being treated differently because of your race or gender was wrong. Hazel knew she could embrace being a woman and loving her role given and still taking over her father's ranch. Now she had to make others see it that way too.

"Hazel, you realize it won't be easy, right? The men out there will not roll out a red carpet, and they will not let you step into their world without a fight," Helen said while squeezing Hazel's hand.

"I am aware of that. I know it will be difficult, perhaps even dangerous, but someone has to step up to the task and change the world, so women and girls get to choose what they want to do in their lives."

"And why does that someone has to be you? You can't even vote, Hazel," her sister interjected while shaking her head.

"So what? Perhaps that will get changed too."

Haven sighed. Her sister was so strong-willed sometimes, it drove her mad.

"We are in this fight together, Hazel. Ted and I will be alongside you, and we'll welcome anyone who wants to join that fight. We also have plenty of time to deal with this issue. I am still fairly young and should live for many more years." George's chest was filled with pride as he looked at his determined daughter.

"But, Pa, what if something happens to Hazel? I don't want to lose my sister." Haven blinked away a few tears and swallowed the lump in her throat.

"Don't worry so much, Haven. Hazel isn't on her own, and we will let no one harm her," Jackson replied as he gave her a quick nod. He loved George's girls just as much as his friend and would protect them with his life.

Jackson was the first cowboy George hired after purchasing the land from Jackson's father, who owned the bank in Willamette Falls. He was a hard worker, and someone George trusted with his life and family. Since George had used his entire inheritance to buy the land, Jackson's father helped him with loans, so the dream could become a reality. George paid the loans back as fast as he could. Jackson's father was nothing but impressed with the young man who had moved from Boston to Oregon to start his own business by building a ranch.

A friendship developed between Jackson, his father, and him, and when Jackson's father died, his younger son Adam took over the bank. Adam differed from Jackson, but was also a hard worker. The bank business continued to bloom. Adam invested in many big and promising projects and was a financial genius. When Hazel and Haven were born, George made Jackson Haven's godfather. It touched him.

2
A New Challenge

Jackson and George were in George's office to plan out the upcoming weeks when Hazel stormed into the room.

"Pa. Todd Holden told me we would get a new veterinary physician, and a new reverend, in the following weeks. He told me that Reverend Mitchell and Dr. Kent are retiring, and two young men will take over their jobs. Do you know anything about that?"

George Buchannon and Jackson Harrison looked up as soon as Hazel entered her father's office. The old vet had reached a good age, and it was time for him to retire, but Reverend Robert Mitchell was in his late forties. He was a little older than George.

"Yes, I do. Robert Mitchell told me last week when he came over for a visit. He said that Dr. Kent is moving to San Francisco to live with his son and that he would leave as well."

"But he can't retire yet. Isn't Reverend Mitchell just a bit older than you are?" Hazel still couldn't believe it.

"Yes, he is only three years older."

"Why on earth would he retire then?"

"He is not retiring, Hazel. Robert is forced to leave and will get transferred to a church in Salem."

"What?" Hazel gave her father a pained stare, her heart was breaking. Reverend Mitchell had a special place in her heart. He not only had been their Reverend for the past sixteen years, but he had been Hazel's school teacher and had helped her through tough times. He was like a second father to her, and she was not happy about the prospect of him leaving.

"How long has he known, and why didn't you say anything?"

"He only found out last week. It is a sudden transfer, and he doesn't yet know why. I didn't tell you because I know how much he means to you, and I wanted to keep this hidden from you for as long as possible."

"They can't send him away. They just can't. He belongs here. He is part of our town, community, and family. Isn't there anything you can do to stop this from happening?" An ache started deep in her stomach, and she turned around as her eyes welled with tears. George Buchannon pulled his daughter into his arms. He exchanged a knowing glance with Jackson before he responded.

"I wish, sweetheart, but he has no choice. Salem's bishop has decided to have him serve there, and he has to listen to him. He is his boss, so to speak."

"Why would they take him away from us? He is doing such a wonderful job here, and everyone loves him."

"One can only guess, peanut. I don't like the decision because Robert has been a wonderful friend to Jackson and me, but we have to accept it."

She shook her head. "I will not accept this. This is wrong. I don't want to lose Reverend Mitchell. He means everything to me." Tears streamed down her face, and George pulled her closer.

"I realize this will be a tough goodbye for you. We invited Robert for supper tonight, so we can say our farewell before he leaves tomorrow morning."

Her sobbing intensified, and she leaned against her father's chest, feeling heartbroken. It felt as if someone tore part of her heart out of her chest, and it took a while before she could stop crying. George held her in his arms, stroked her hair, and waited until she calmed down again. When her sobbing stopped, he lifted her chin and made her look at him.

"Try to be strong tonight, Hazel. It is hard for Robert to leave because this was his home. We need to stay strong to make it easier for him."

Hazel nodded and swallowed the tears that kept coming. She was willing to do her best but couldn't promise because on the inside, she was falling apart. She gave her father a thankful hug, kissed his cheek, nodded to Jackson, and left the room.

Jackson turned to his friend. "It hurts my heart to see Hazel so upset. Tonight will be a real challenge for her."

George nodded as he put his hand on Jackson's shoulder. "I know, Jackson, but it will be a challenge for Robert as well. He loves Hazel more than anyone, and the memories they share, make this situation even worse."

After her fiancé and his good friend David Johnson died in a mine collapse, George Buchannon married the twin's mother, Abigail. It was a marriage of convenience because Abigail was poor, and George had promised his friend David he would marry and look after her if anything would ever happen to him.

Abigail couldn't get over the tragedy of losing her fiancé. Even after the twins were born two years later, she still grieved the loss of David Johnson. Abigail's broken heart prevented her from moving on, even though George tried to be a loving husband to her. No matter how much she wanted to get herself out of that dreary place, she couldn't.

George was grateful for his girls, and from the minute they were born, they were his everything. Abigail never connected with them and neglected them. She couldn't cope with the fact that they looked so much like George. Abigail withdrew herself more and more from her husband and daughters and then left one night and ran off with a doctor from a neighboring town. The twins had just turned six. She divorced George and married the doctor, but never contacted her girls again.

After Abigail left, George's mother moved in with them and looked after the girls. His father had passed away, and the old woman loved her granddaughters. When it was getting harder for his mother to take care of the children and the house, George hired a housekeeper.

Helen brought her niece, who was living with her after her sister- and brother-in-law had died in a fire. George fell in love with Helen. Before his mother died, and right before the twin's tenth birthday, they got married.

Although Haven struggled for a while after their mom left, Hazel's heart was broken. She couldn't understand why a mother would do something like that to her flesh and blood.

It was Robert Mitchell who helped her get past the first hurt. He held her in his arms when she was unable to stop crying during church or school because she deeply felt the loss of her mother. Robert helped her build a strong faith in God. As she grew older, he helped her understand that trials are part of life, and she was never alone, no matter how hard things were. He taught her that there was a loving Heavenly Father who waited for her to pray to Him so that He could comfort her.

Hazel couldn't have asked for better men in her life. George was the best father anyone could wish for, Jackson was like a loving uncle, and Robert was by Hazel's side whenever she needed a shoulder to lean on, or her father wasn't near her. Taking Reverend Mitchell away from her was like taking air away from her. It was unbearable.

Robert Mitchell arrived just before supper was ready. Helen had created a wonderful meal, and it smelled fantastic. Hazel, however, did not feel hungry. She had felt like crying all day.

The young woman dreaded the evening because she had to say goodbye to someone she loved so much. She paced up and down her room, wondering how she could stay strong and not make matters worse for Reverend Mitchell. There was a knock on the door, and Haven entered the room.

"It is time for supper, Hazel," Haven said as she stepped next to her sister. Hazel nodded, swallowing the tears that tried to enter her eyes, and followed her sister downstairs into the dining room.

Reverend Mitchell sat at the table, but stood as soon as Haven and Hazel entered the room. He glanced at Hazel for a moment, but she avoided eye contact as much as possible. Still, the split-second she looked into his eyes, she saw the sadness, and it became tough for her not to break out in tears. Oh, how she hated this moment. How she hated having to say goodbye to such a wonderful and special person.

Hazel was unusually quiet during the rest of the evening. She knew she could not keep her emotions in check if she wasn't on guard. She kept herself together until supper was over and everyone had moved into the sitting room. The young woman had barely sat down when Reverend Mitchell addressed the family.

"Thank you so much for inviting me, George. I still can't believe I have to leave. Willamette Falls and Beaver Creek mean so much to me, but especially this family."

Hazel felt his eyes on her, and she knew at that moment she had to get out of there and away from him as fast as possible.

When George stood and hugged his friend, Hazel couldn't take it anymore. She jumped to her feet, mumbled: "please excuse me," and left the house. As soon as she was outside and the door closed behind her, she broke out in tears. Hazel hurried to the small lake behind the house. She adored that spot and the view she had from there. That evening, nature's beauty meant nothing to her, though, and she just dropped onto the bench next to her favorite oak tree. As much as she tried to get it under control, her sobbing only intensified.

Why do I have to lose people I love? Why does life seem so unfair sometimes? Hazel had no idea how she could face Reverend Mitchell without making it hard for him. She didn't know how she could go back to the house and pretend everything was okay when she felt as if her heart was being ripped apart. In another burst of tears, the young woman covered her face with her hands.

Suddenly, someone clasped her hands, pulled her up from the bench and into muscular arms. Her sobbing increased as soon as she felt his loving embrace. Reverend Mitchell only pulled her closer to his chest. Not wanting to look up, Hazel leaned against him, her arms firmly around him. She couldn't bear saying goodbye to him.

He lifted her chin when he felt she was calming down and made her look into his eyes. She swallowed hard, but couldn't stop the tears that kept coming.

"Hazel, you mean everything to me. You are the daughter I never had, and I will miss you with all my heart. I have never felt this close to anyone before, but the trust you put in me the moment we met captured my heart. I will never, ever forget you, and I am sure we will see each other again. This isn't a goodbye forever."

Her body trembled as she started sobbing again, and he held her even tighter.

"Oh, Reverend Mitchell, I will miss you so much. You helped me through my most challenging times, and I will always be grateful that you were there for me whenever I needed you. Thank you for being a second father to me. You don't even know the impact you had on my life, and I love you."

Robert had to swallow now too. He kissed her head and walked her back to the house. The rest of the family was waiting for them. He hugged her one last time, nodded to George, and mounted his horse while George pulled his sobbing daughter into his arms.

Reverend Mitchell's gaze swept over the family one last time before he waved his final farewell. Hazel looked up when his eyes rested on her. She tried to be brave and swallow the rest of her tears, but the moment their eyes met, she noticed tears in his eyes. Her fatherly friend quickly turned around and rode off without looking back.

Hazel faced her father again and sobbed against his chest. He held her tight and tried to comfort her as much as possible. He knew how she felt and how hard this was for her. Hazel, however, didn't know how her heart would ever heal from losing such a special friend.

As Robert Mitchell glanced at her one last time and as he turned around to leave, he couldn't hold back his tears any longer. As he rode off, he mumbled: "I love you, too. More than you can ever imagine."

3
The Perfect Fit?

Reverend Jason Clark arrived a few days later. He was a good-looking, tall young man of thirty-two years, with bright-green eyes, dark brown hair, and a smile that made women's and girls' hearts melt. He appeared to be someone who clicked with everyone he met, except Hazel. It was hard for her to go to church, knowing Reverend Mitchell wasn't there anymore.

When Reverend Clark addressed his congregation for the first time, Hazel's heart was aching, and she couldn't help the pained expression that slipped across her face. She missed her fatherly friend, his loving, caring hugs, his deep gentle voice and his touching sermons. Jason Clark came across as nice, but something bothered Hazel about him. She didn't like his arrogance and how he flirted with women of all ages. She was by no means impressed with him.

When she told her father about her thoughts and feelings, he rebuked her and encouraged her to be fair. He insisted on her giving the young clergyman a chance. George was convinced she would like him in no time once she got to know him.

Hazel was not so sure about that. Yes, she was upset that Reverend Mitchell was gone, and that they had transferred her favorite pastor because of this young man, but something deep inside her heart told her to be careful with him and not be that trusting.

Hazel missed Robert Mitchell. He had been the person she had gone to when she needed to talk to someone. He had seen her grow up and had a particular way of knowing when something was bothering her or when she needed a fatherly hug. When her aching heart got to a breaking point, she went to church to pray for comfort and guidance.

It was hard for her to enter the building. Everything reminded her of Reverend Mitchell. She remembered how he had always taught her she wasn't alone and that there was a loving Heavenly Father who wanted to comfort and bless her.

The church was empty, so she sat on a bench and started a silent prayer when suddenly, she was overcome with emotions. She felt peace and comfort, but wished more than anything, her fatherly friend was back. How could she ever get over him when she missed him so dearly?

It startled her when someone pulled her hands from her face. Hazel looked up and saw into Reverend Clark's smiling face. He was close, too close. The moment she felt his touch, she was uncomfortable. His hands didn't feel gentle. His grip was firm, and she could feel his arm muscles tightening. She removed her hands from his in one swift movement and put space between her and the clergyman, before wiping a few tears out of her eyes. Only then did she give him her full attention.

"Reverend Clark, I didn't even hear you coming. Forgive me, but I was looking for much-needed peace and comfort."

"No need to apologize, Miss Buchannon. The church is for times of need, like wanting to feel close to the Lord. May I ask why you were looking for peace and comfort? Is something bothering you?" His eyes bore into hers, which made her nervous.

"I ...well ...no ... I'm just missing a special person, dear to my heart." She blushed as she stammered, trying to find the right words. His smile grew.

"And who is the special person you are missing? Perhaps it will help if you talk about it." He nodded to her encouragingly, but his eyes weren't focused. She felt his intense gaze trailing down her slender figure. A shiver of disgust rushed through her body.

"It doesn't matter who this person is. You wouldn't understand," she snapped as she pulled her shawl tighter around her shoulders. Her mind drifted off as she wondered how she could escape the situation and man.

Jason Clark grabbed her face and made her look at him. He leaned closer—his eyes were darting to her lips and neck.

"I am a Reverend. Who could understand more than I?"

Hazel froze in shock, her thoughts tumbling all over the place. How dare he touched her face and hands without her consent? What nerve this man had. Her temper reached a boiling point and made her angrier by the minute. He was supposed to be a man of God. Hazel wondered whether she should tell him, but his boldness and arrogance needed to be chastised.

"Yes, you are right. You will understand. I am missing Reverend Mitchell. He meant everything to me and was a dear fatherly friend. This church is not the same without him." She realized that the last part must have been a slap in the face to him, but she didn't care.

He hid his true feelings well, but Hazel saw a brief flash of anger appear on his face before his features froze to a serious expression.

"Isn't that man too old for you? I understand older men might allure a teenager, but you should have outgrown those silly feelings by now. That man could be your father. Find someone closer to your age," he scolded her, and the sharpness in his voice surprised her. His chin was tilted as he looked down on her. The uncomfortable warmth from his eyes was gone.

That made Hazel speechless for a moment. She was seriously stunned that he took her admiration, friendship, and love for Reverend Mitchell as romantic love. It made her furious that this clergyman took her openness so out of context. Before she could respond, he was back to his usual smiling self.

"I am here for you, though, Hazel, and you can come to me whenever you need to talk or to be comforted." He patted her knee with his hand to underline what he had said, then rested his hand on her knee. Hazel had enough. She pushed his hand away from her and jumped off the bench.

"How dare you? How dare you touch me without my consent and twist my openness into something sinful and questionable. How dare you treat me with so much disrespect? I don't know what game you are playing, Reverend, but you better stay away from me." She stormed off, slamming the church doors shut behind her.

Hazel was shaking with frustration, disgust, and held-back anger when she reached her horse. Tears shot into her eyes as she took it all in and realized what had just happened. She would never feel comfortable and safe around that man, and wouldn't return to that church by herself.

She knew she couldn't talk to anyone about this incident because nobody would believe her. Everyone was fond of Reverend Clark, and her father would think she made it up because she missed Reverend Mitchell so much.

I'm sure of one thing, she thought as she clenched her fists, her lips turning into a straight, determined line. *I will never let this man touch me again. Next time he does that, he will pay for it.*

She kept the encounter with Reverend Clark a secret, but her dislike for him had grown, and she missed Robert Mitchell more than ever. She wondered what else was wrong with Jason Clark. The experience had shown her that her feelings had been right from the beginning. Now she had to prove to everyone else that he was neither an honorable man nor a man of God.

With Reverend Mitchell gone, and the town unwilling to hire a teacher for the school, George had to hire a private teacher for Brenna. Her fifteenth birthday wasn't for another few months, and he wanted her education to continue until she turned sixteen. Jason Clark had no interest in teaching children, and so George began the search elsewhere.

One evening, while they were eating supper together, Jackson handed an envelope to his boss. Brenna looked up and nervously watched George as he was reading the letter.

"Pa, you made it clear that I only want a female teacher, right?" Brenna asked with darting eyes and held her breath. Jackson and George couldn't hide their smiles.

"It is not that easy, Brenna. Most female teachers prefer to live in bigger towns and cities and not in the middle of nowhere. I didn't mention in my inquiry what my preference was, and so we have to take what we can get."

"But Pa, if she's more comfortable with a female teacher, you should do everything in your power to get her a female teacher," Hazel interjected, frowning. Her furrowed brows and stern glance focused on her father.

"I will see what I can do, but don't get your hopes up. Any teacher will be welcome here, whether male or female." He grinned at Jackson, who glanced at Hazel. She seemed more upset about the possibility of having a male teacher in the house than Brenna did. George put the letter on the table and looked at the two girls.

"This is a person I would consider. He writes—"

"He?" Hazel's face tightened, and she pressed her lips together.

"Yes, he. I told you—"

"I thought you were joking. It isn't a good idea to have a male teacher living here with us."

"And why not, may I dare ask?" George and Jackson appeared a bit surprised. "Why does this seem to be more of an issue for you than for Brenna?"

"Because..." Hazel hesitated as her cheeks turned to a light shade of red. Her thoughts went to Reverend Clark and how he could not be trusted. "... I'm not comfortable having a strange man living with us. Brenna is a teenage girl, and at an age now where she prefers women as teachers, am I right, Bren?"

The girl nodded. "Yes, Pa. Please reconsider."

"Now, let's not jump ahead of ourselves. You know nothing about him, and so how do you know he wouldn't be a suitable fit for our family and situation?"

Hazel and Brenna looked at each other.

"He writes, he is from San Francisco and always wanted to live on a ranch. He has considered moving to Oregon for a while now and would like to have a fresh start somewhere other than San Francisco."

"He wants a fresh start? See, he is in conflict with the law and tries to run away from his problems."

"Hazel!" The rebuking tone in her father's voice didn't go unnoticed.

"Why else would he want to move to an insignificant town like Willamette Falls and live miles outside that tiny town in the middle of nowhere?" Hazel's expression communicated she was ready to argue this out. Her eyes sparkled with stubbornness, and she lifted her chin in defiance but confidence. George watched her, slightly amused.

"Hazel, can you be any more ridiculous?" Haven asked now while shaking her head as she jumped into the conversation. "You are being overly dramatic."

"Am I? Are you comfortable with a male teacher living here with us?"

Before Haven could respond, George spoke again. "Come on, Hazel, haven't I always been cautious about you girls?" He raised an eyebrow.

"Well, yes, but—"

"No but's, trust me." He caressed her arm. "Listen, if this means so much to you, I have an idea. Jackson and I have to drive 500 horses to San Francisco next week. It was supposed to be a business trip only. How about you follow us on the stagecoach, and we will spend a few days there as a family and can meet the teacher together?"

"Are you serious, Pa?" Hazel's eyes lit up, the stubborn sparkle had been replaced by a bright twinkle.

"Yes, I am serious."

She jumped up and into his arms. Brenna had a smile on her face, and even Haven's eyes lit up with sudden excitement. It would be a refreshing change of scenery for everyone.

All three girls couldn't stop looking around. They had never been to San Francisco before. Compared to Willamette Falls, the town, was impressive. It was even more extensive than Portland or Salem. The hotel they stayed at was vast and elegant. George Buchannon knew his way around, as he had made many business trips to San Francisco over the years.

The first few days kept George and Jackson busy, but as soon as they finished the sale, they took the girls out to the theater, the opera, and sightseeing. Hazel preferred life in the country, but she made great memories.

On their last evening in San Francisco, they wanted to meet the teacher at the hotel's restaurant. Jackson and George met up with him during the afternoon, but they told Helen and the girls to wait in the hotel lobby.

Helen, Haven, and Brenna were still getting ready for the evening, so Hazel went to the lobby by herself. As soon as she had sat down, she felt someone staring at her. Sure enough, when she looked around, she noticed a young man leaning against the staircase, staring at her with a playful grin on his face. He even had the nerve to imply a bow toward her. She looked away as soon as she perceived him, but couldn't stop herself from blushing.

What a rude and impudent person. How dare he stare at me like that? Hazel tried to ignore him, but was getting more and more uncomfortable. She finally stood and went back to her room, using the other set of stairs. She had to admit he was a handsome, good-looking young man, but she hated nothing more than having someone bore into her like that.

She had barely reached her room when there was a knock on her door. Hazel swallowed hard and hoped that this young man had not dared to follow her. She opened her door and stood across from her father.

"Sweetheart, didn't you want to wait in the lobby for us? Helen, Haven, and Brenna are downstairs."

"I was in the lobby waiting for you, but when a young man kept staring at me, I decided it was best to get away from him."

"A young man stared at you?" George seemed surprised.

"Yes, he watched me closely, and when I looked back at him, he even grinned. So rude!" Hazel's face flushed with genuine outrage. Her eyes spat fire.

Her father only smiled. She wasn't used to having young admirers around her, but it showed him how important it was to hire a male teacher. It would help Brenna with her studies, make Haven hopefully more outgoing, and help Hazel feel more comfortable around men. Granted, her two best friends were male, she had no one around her who challenged her romantically. Despite her being twenty years old, she had never been in love and wasn't aware that young men enjoyed looking at beautiful young ladies.

As George and Hazel walked down the stairs, she froze on the spot the moment she noticed her family standing next to the same young man who had gawked at her before. She pulled at her father's arm.

"Pa, who is the man standing next to Jackson?"

George smiled. "That is Alex Camden, who most likely will be Brenna's new teacher." He wanted to continue down the stairs, but Hazel stopped him once again.

"That is the rude person who stared at me earlier when I was waiting for you in the lobby."

Her father continued to smile. "Well, now you know why he stared at you. I did show him a photograph of you girls, and so he probably wanted to inspect one of his future students."

"Excuse me, what? One of his future students? Isn't he supposed to be a teacher for Brenna?" Hazel gasped and stared at her father with wide eyes, thinking she hadn't heard him correctly.

"Yes, he is. However, this afternoon I found out he has the qualifications and the right to instruct and test college students. Since I want you to take over the ranch someday, he can teach you a lot about business, sales, and everything needed to run a ranch."

"I thought you and Jackson would teach me." Hazel was irritated now and pressed her lips together, a sure sign of her disapproval.

"We were, but Alex Camden holds a degree in business and will teach you everything you need to know. Please keep in mind, it will be tough for you as a woman. Education is the key to the business side and will make it easier for you. Plus, you have to take a special examination at the Oregon Institute in Salem, and he can prepare you for that."

"Pa..."

"Give him a chance and get to know him. I am sure you will like him as much as Jackson and I do. He is a fine teacher who will help both of you." He grinned again.

"That's not funny, Pa. How would you even know whether he is a good teacher? Last time I checked, he wasn't my teacher yet, so please stop trying to convince me he will be an excellent fit for us."

"Okay, Hazel, just give the man a chance, and please be polite." He nuzzled her forward until they reached the others. "Alex, may I introduce my daughter Hazel to you? Hazel, this is Alex Camden."

Alex turned around and looked at her kindly. He reached for her hand for the traditional greeting. At first, she was tempted to ignore it, but then she shook his hand because she didn't want him to think she was not polite or had ill manners.

"It is an honor to meet you, Hazel. Your father told me so much about you."

During supper, Jackson, Helen, and George had a lively conversation with Alex about many things, including how to run a ranch. Alex addressed Brenna several times, and it was clear that she liked him very much. Haven was her usual shy, and quiet self, and even Hazel kept quiet. She couldn't deny that he was a charming, handsome young man, but Hazel was determined not to trust or like him.

Her thoughts wandered, and she looked around the restaurant. At a table close to them, she saw a family sitting. Seeing the two girls giggling and whispering made her grateful she had Haven and Brenna in her life. When she noticed how the mother put an arm around the oldest girl, however, her heart ached. She thought about Abigail, her mother, who never seemed to have loved her, yet it had broken her heart into pieces when she left. She still remembered how her mother smelled and what her voice sounded like. Hazel's heart was filled with gratefulness for her father and that he had always been there for them.

Hazel nearly jumped out of her skin when someone touched her arm. She hadn't expected that, so the touch startled her, but she looked at her father.

"Wow, Hazel, you were far away in your thoughts," her father remarked, grinning. "Alex asked you a question."

She felt Alex Camden's penetrating glance and once again blushed.

"Could you please repeat your question?"

The young man gave her a heartwarming smile. "Of course, Miss Buchannon. I asked what your interests and pastimes are. Do you like to go dancing?"

Hazel stared at him for a moment, perplexed and unsure how to go ahead. *My interests?* Why was he interested in her pastimes? Was he trying to invite her to go dancing because he took a fancy to her? This was going too far.

"I have many interests and pastimes, Mister Camden, too many to list them right now."

Alex Camden grinned to himself. Hazel Buchannon seemed to be of the suspicious sort and clearly unwilling to share more information than necessary. He would have fun with that.

Nothing pleased him more than the challenge to break someone's stubborn shell.

"So, how did you two like Alex Camden? Can you see him as your teacher, Brenna?"

The young girl nodded. "Yes, he is a likeable person, and I feel comfortable around him. I mean, you said he would not teach me by myself, right, Pa?"

"Correct. Oliver, Lukas, and Cory will take part in the lessons. I hired them as cowboys, but they have had little schooling and are just a bit older than you are. It will do them good to get further education."

Brenna smiled.

"How did you like him, Hazel?"

"I did not like him at all. He is rude and provocative and probably only wants this job, so he can later kidnap one of us and pressure you for ransom," she shot back dryly, her expression dead serious.

Haven and Brenna started giggling, and George and Jackson burst out laughing.

"Hazel," her father said with a scolding tone in his voice while chuckling.

"Okay, perhaps not that extreme," she acknowledged grinning, with a sassy twinkle in her eyes. Her seriousness returned a moment later. "I don't trust him, though. Didn't you hear how he was asking me about my interests and pastimes? There was a reason for me being so reserved and guarded. It sounded as if he wanted to ask me out dancing."

"Sweetheart, be reasonable. Do you think he is such a man? I found him charming and kind, someone who knows how to get young people excited about education. The problem here is that you are not used to having young men around you," Helen commented as she jumped into the conversation.

"I am used to it. We have plenty of young men on the ranch."

"Yes, we do, but you don't interact with them unless it has to do with the ranch. Rob and Namito don't count because they are your friends. Alex is a different type of man, and you should give him a chance. He will be a charming and helpful teacher to you, I promise." George gave her an encouraging nod.

She flashed at her father angrily. "Why do you even ask me if you've decided already?"

George sighed. "There is a good reason why I am so set on Alex Camden. His father is a good old friend of mine, and I've known Alex since he was a child. His father always expected much of him and did not approve of Alex's choice of becoming a teacher. Harry Camden is a well-known and respected lawyer, and he had wished for his son to follow his footsteps."

"Does that mean his father disowned him?" Hazel asked wide-eyed, suddenly feeling sorry for the young teacher.

"No, he didn't disown him, but a separation will be good for both. Alex deserves a chance to do what he loves without being constantly criticized by his father. He will not only teach you two and our young cowboys, but help with ranch work. Alex was always interested in having a ranch, but that is not good enough for his father either." He sighed again.

"Harry denounced my choice of becoming a rancher at first too, but since I made this ranch a booming success, he has long accepted me. Unfortunately, his son is *only* a teacher, and Harry fails to see that as an accomplishment. Can you now understand why I want Alex to be your teacher? I never put an inquiry in the newspapers and sent a telegram to Alex directly since I knew his story and situation." George looked into his daughter's blue eyes, and the young woman nodded.

"Yes, I understand now why you picked him. I will give him a chance, but I don't have to like or trust him." She kissed her father on the cheek and hugged Jackson before she and her sister disappeared into their room. Helen followed with Brenna, and only the two men stayed behind at their table.

"I don't understand what Hazel has against Alex Camden. Why is she so suspicious?" George furrowed his brows. Jackson shrugged.

"Perhaps she is scared to have him around because she fears she might fall in love with him? Besides a few crushes, she hasn't been in love yet, has she? Maybe she is worried she might like him too much."

"You might be right, Jackson. Well, we shall see what happens. I told Alex, he could join us on our way home once we've come to a final decision. Let's get a few hours of sleep before the stagecoach leaves tomorrow morning."

Alex Camden joined them at the hotel for breakfast the following day. Hazel forced herself to be friendlier to him, but she kept her distance, refusing to open up to him. Alex appeared amused by it. Perhaps he was used to having women chase after him, a thought that made Hazel even more determined to avoid him whenever possible.

It was after breakfast when Hazel noticed that Alex had luggage himself. When she went upstairs to grab her bags, she turned to her father, irritation spreading across her face.

"Why didn't you tell me that Alex Camden would come home with us?"

Her father looked surprised. "Why are you asking me that? I thought you were okay with us hiring Alex as your teacher."

She lowered her gaze before she answered. "I was, but I didn't think he would join us on our journey home. I figured he would follow in a few weeks."

"It is best if he joins us right away. That way, we can get to know one another before he teaches Brenna and you. Now, accept this decision and give him a chance. You won't regret it." George grabbed her bags and hurried down the stairs before she could say anything else. Hazel scrunched up her nose, but followed her father right away.

4

Life on the Buchannon Ranch

As soon as they got home, Hazel disappeared into her room. After spending three days in the same stagecoach, only stopping for brief breaks and spending the nights at small hotels along the way, she needed to get away from Alex Camden.

It was late afternoon, when she went outside to check on her horse and greet her two best friends, whom she had not seen in almost a fortnight. Alex Camden stepped out of the house the moment Rob twirled Hazel around before pulling her into his muscular arms to give her a big hug.

"I never thought I would miss you so much, Hazel. Two weeks is a long time when you can't tease sassy girls." He winked at her, and she grinned.

"Ha-ha, Rob. I was actually glad to get a break from you two." She stuck out her tongue, and both men smiled. Namito lifted her off the ground now and bear-hugged her.

"That's the sass Rob was talking about, Sidaa."

She grinned again.

Rob McCall and Namito Blake were not only Hazel's best friends, but they also worked for her father as cowboys. Rob grew up in Willamette Falls and was one of the best Broncobusters in the entire Territory of Oregon and the state of California combined. He was twenty-five years old, had dark brown hair, and was six feet tall.

Twenty-three-year-old Namito was a Native American and belonged to the Kalapuya tribe. He grew up on an Indian Reservation. The land of the reservation used to be part of the Buchannon ranch until George gave that land to the chief of the Kalapuya—Namito's father. He had become good friends with the residing Indians in the territory, and wanted to make sure they didn't have to leave, were free to do what they wanted, and didn't get forced into a reservation with different tribes.

After the big greeting ceremony seemed over, Alex stepped closer. The two young men watched him curiously as he walked toward them. Namito pulled Hazel closer so that he could speak with her privately.

"Who is that?" he whispered into her ear. She rolled her eyes, which made him grin.

"That is Brenna's *and* my new teacher!"

"Your new teacher?" Namito looked puzzled.

"Yes, my new teacher. He used to be a professor at the University of San Francisco, and has the right and qualifications to teach me everything I need to know about the ranch business," she said mockingly while attempting to sound like her father. "As soon as Pa found out, he was all for it."

Namito grinned again. Both watched as Rob shook Alex's hand.

"Welcome to our ranch. I am Rob McCall."

"Pleasure to meet you, Rob. I am Alex Camden." It was obvious that the two men liked each other right away.

"Have you been able to look around yet?"

"Not outside so far. I was hoping Hazel could show me everything." The three men turned toward her, and she blushed.

"Sorry, Mr. Camden, but I have a lot to do," she responded. Without batting an eye, she walked back to the house. Namito was stunned speechless for a moment, but rushed after her when Rob offered to give Alex a tour.

"What in the world was that, Hazel?" Namito clasped her arm and stopped her from going any further.

Hazel sighed. "I didn't want him to come and live with us, and I didn't want a male teacher in the house. Unfortunately, Pa has a personal history with him, and so, I didn't stand a chance."

"But he seems like a likeable guy," Namito said, and before Hazel could even respond, he added, "...and a handsome one at that. I bet girls are all over him because of his good looks," he finished saying with a smirk on his face, making it obvious that he enjoyed teasing her.

"Yes, he is a real charmer," Hazel replied and rolled her eyes. "I don't like men like that." She glared at him.

"You should at least give him a chance."

"Give him a chance? Tell me, Namito, does Alex Camden have a magical power that makes all of you fall for his charm?"

Namito laughed heartily and pulled her into his arms. "You shouldn't always be so suspicious. Have you still not learned your lesson? Not everyone you meet is out to get you, and not everyone is trying to hurt you. Think about how unapproachable you were when we met and when Rob came here, and now we are best friends."

"True, but only because you and Rob were so dang stubborn and didn't give up on me, no matter how much I attempted to push you away."

"Alex Camden will be the same way if he wants to get to know the real you, Hazel. He doesn't strike me as a guy who gives up easily." Namito raised an eyebrow, and Hazel lowered her eyes to avoid eye contact with her friend.

"Well, we shall see who is more stubborn. Would you and Rob like to join us for supper tonight?" She knew he would recognize the sudden topic change for what it was, but didn't say anything about it.

"Sure. We've missed having supper with you and your family."

"Wonderful. I'll see you later then. San Francisco was fun, but I will forever prefer the country."

Supper was peaceful and enjoyable. Rob and Namito teased Hazel as if they had to make up for her absence all at ones. Haven and Brenna whispered with each other, and George, Helen, and Jackson discussed the schedules of the next several days.

Alex leaned back, relaxed. He watched everyone and listened in now and then, but kept quiet.

Once supper was over, Rob, Namito, and Hazel stood and decided to go on a horseback ride. Alex got up as well.

"Would it be all right if I joined you?"

Before Hazel could even respond, Namito nudged her arm. She looked up at him, and he unnoticeably shook his head.

"Of course, Alex. You know how to ride a horse, yes?" Rob gave Alex a friendly pat on the back and grinned.

"Yes, I know how to ride a horse. It's been a while, but I don't think I forgot how it is done," the young man shot back in the same playful tone and winked at Hazel. She lowered her eyes and hurried after Namito.

"Hazel. Don't forget to be polite. You have to get used to him either way, so you might as well make the best of the situation."

"But I wanted to go horseback riding with you and Rob. I don't feel like going anymore. I don't want to take him everywhere from now on," she responded pouting. Namito put his arm around her shoulders.

"You can't leave him out, though. Alex is new here and doesn't know anyone. He needs friends."

A death stare hit the young man. "He is supposed to be my teacher, not a friend." Hazel glared at him angrily because that last remark hit a sore spot. "You know what? You can go without me. I am not coming with you anymore." She turned around and walked back to the house. Alex and Rob watched her with a puzzled expression when she walked past them.

"Hazel, where are you going?"

"I should help—." She wasn't able to finish what she was about to say since Namito grabbed her from behind, turned her around, and threw her over his shoulder.

"That can wait, Missy," he laughed and ran back to the barn.

"Namito, are you mad? Put me down this instant."

"Not until you promise that you will come with us," he whispered. Hazel heard Alex and Rob step closer.

"Okay, fine." She sighed dramatically. The young man took her off his shoulder and beamed at her with an enormous grin. She pinched his ribs.

"Ouch."

"Oh, stop whining. You deserved the pinch, so I suggest you take it like a man. You seemed to be manly enough, a few moments ago, when you lost your mind and threw me over your shoulder." She gave him a sassy grin. Before Hazel knew what was happening, he grabbed her again and lifted her in the air. She wiggled around because this was getting embarrassing for her.

"Namito, let go of me and put me on the ground."

It was no secret, that he enjoyed seeing her embarrassed. As if he wanted to make matters worse, he pressed a kiss against her forehead before putting her down with a grin. She felt her cheeks go off in flames when Alex and Rob looked in their direction, but it was dark enough in the barn that they couldn't see her face's color. She was grateful for that.

Hazel directed her focus on saddling her horse. Right before she mounted the animal, she pinched Namito's ribs one more time and burst into laughter when she saw his stunned face. Before he had the chance to retaliate she kicked her horse in the sides, rode out of the barn, and galloped off the ranch yard.

"The first one at Beaver Lake wins," she called out and made sure her horse ran faster and faster because she needed a head start. Rob and Namito followed suit.

Shortly after, the three men were right behind her. Hazel spurred her horse, Tess, to go faster, but Namito passed her a moment later. His lead didn't last for long, though. His horse, which was afraid of water, threw him into a giant mud puddle when he tried to ride through it. Hazel burst into a fit of laughter, but immediately slowed down her horse.

"Are you okay, Namito?"

He jumped to his feet. "Just you wait," he growled at her. Hazel kicked Tess in her sides and made a wide turn around the young man, so, she could escape his revenge for a while longer.

Rob and Alex were right behind her. Then everything happened fast. A bunny jumped out of the bushes and startled Hazel's horse. The horse rose, and Hazel, who had not expected that, flew off Tess's back and landed hard on the ground. For a second, she couldn't breathe, and everything became unclear. Her head was spinning, and she closed her eyes to stop the dizziness from getting worse.

Rob must have seen Alex jumping off his horse to come to her aid because he continued to follow Hazel's horse, which was still running.

Hazel felt as if everything was spinning around her. When she saw that Alex was kneeling next to her, she tried to get up because she didn't want to seem weak. Alex nuzzled her back to the ground.

"Now, now, take it easy, young lady. You most likely have a concussion, and we need to make sure you haven't broken anything before you can get back on your feet."

She closed her eyes again and breathed in and out. Feeling Alex's firm and manly hands on her waist and shoulder made her uneasy, yet she understood that he was truly worried about her. After breathing in and out a few times, and once the dizziness faded a bit, Hazel made another attempt to get up. Alex encouraged her to stay down a little longer, but she refused to listen. He gave up with a silent sigh and aided her by supporting her waist and back with one hand, while holding her hand as she stood. As soon as she was back on her feet, she removed his hands.

"Thank you, Mr. Camden, but I will be okay now."

Hazel was as white as a bedsheet. Her hand was pressed against her forehead, as if this was an effort to steady herself and stop the dizziness she most likely was experiencing.

Alex noticed her trembling, even while she was clearly aiming to hide it. He did not trust her weak attempt of pretending all was well. The young man stayed close and watched every move she made like a hawk.

Her shoulders, back, and neck were in terrible pain because of the fall, and everything around her continued to spin. Hazel felt darkness closing in on her, but ignored it. She was determined to push past it and continue as if nothing ever happened. Not wanting to realize how serious the situation truly was, she stepped forward. An intense gushing sound rushed through her eyes and she could feel the blood drain from her face before everything went black.

Alex, who had expected her to faint, caught her and lifted her off her feet. As he walked toward his horse, she regained consciousness.

When Hazel realized she was in her teacher's arms, her heart started pounding. She began wiggling, hoping he would put her back on the ground, but he only pulled her tighter to his chest.

"It's okay, Hazel, I've got you." His warm, deep voice, did help calm her a little, but knowing he was carrying her, drove heat into her cheeks. She closed her eyes, so she wouldn't have to look at him. Her head was still spinning, causing her to feel sick to her stomach, but she managed to control her queasy stomach enough, to not vomit.

Rob and Namito reached them a moment later. Rob led his and Hazel's horse by the reins, and Namito did the same with Alex's horse.

"Is she okay?" Both men looked and sounded worried.

"Yes, she should be. She probably has a concussion, but because she didn't stay down as I suggested, she fainted."

"That is typical for Hazel. No matter what, she wants to show how tough she is." Namito shook his head. Hazel opened her eyes and glanced at her best friend.

"It is okay to have weak moments, Hazel. Nobody can be strong all the time," he scolded her, and a brief smile spread across her lips, before Alex pulled her closer to his body so that she could rest her head on his chest. She looked up, and Alex smiled down on her, causing her to blush. She closed her eyes again.

Alex Camden carried her all the way home. George, Jackson, and Helen bombarded the three men with questions when they arrived at the house. Namito and Rob reassured them she would be okay.

George wanted to take Hazel from Alex, but he shook his head and carried her upstairs into her room. He lifted her onto her bed, and Helen and Haven were by her side at once. George sent one of his cowboys into town to get the doctor.

Hazel had not opened her eyes again until she was lying on her bed. Not only was she still embarrassed about having her teacher carry her for so long, but the spinning in her head was better when she had her eyes closed. As soon as her head hit the pillow, she looked up. Rob, Namito, and Alex stood next to her bed, smiling at her. She gave them a weak half-smile before focusing on Alex.

"Thank you. Thank you for bringing me home."

He squeezed her hand. George and Helen sat next to her bed, and Haven and Jackson stood on the other side. Everyone looked worried. She nearly rolled her eyes.

"Why the concerned faces? You all know I'll be okay. I only feel dizzy, and everything around me is spinning, but that won't last forever." She winked at her sister and closed her eyes again. "Remember, *bad weeds grow tall.*"

The quiet chuckles following her little speech, indicated, that the tension in the room began to disappear. Someone leaned over her and pressed a kiss to her forehead. Her father.

Doctor Gordon Harper arrived an hour later. He sent everyone out of the room so that he could examine her. He checked her back, neck, and head, and even though she was in much pain, he found nothing too concerning.

"You were lucky, Hazel. This accident could have ended much worse. You should be more careful next time, or better yet, don't let the boys challenge you to a race." He winked at her, and she grinned.

"Well, it was me who did the challenging."

He chuckled. "That doesn't surprise me, young lady. I know you quite well. Try to get rest now. Nothing seems to be broken, but you have a concussion and should stay in bed for the next few days."

She nodded. She didn't feel like getting up, anyway. "Thanks, Doc."

"No problem, Hazel." He squeezed her hand and gave her a warm smile before leaving the room.

Helen, George, and Jackson waited outside Hazel's door. Helen was next to the doctor as soon as he stepped out.

"Is she okay? Did she break anything? Will she be back on her feet soon? How bad is it? What can we do to help her?"

Her nonstop talking made him smile. He grabbed her by her arms and looked into her eyes. "Relax, Helen, relax. Hazel is fine and only has a concussion. The only thing that needs to happen now is to make sure that she stays in bed for a few days. I will check on her in three days-time, and she should only get up when I give her permission to do so."

Helen sighed, relieved, and looked embarrassed that she had attacked the doctor with so many questions at once. Gordon knew her and understood why she was so concerned. He also knew Hazel well.

He had seen her grow up, and knew that she was an unstoppable whirlwind sometimes. So, it hadn't surprised him when he found out she had been the one starting the race. He knew that she would go back to her normal activities as soon as she felt a little better if nobody was watching her.

Jackson brought the doc back to his chaise. Helen and George went into Hazel's room. She looked at them, but the next moment was fast asleep.

5

The Pain is Deeper Than you Think

As soon as Hazel had recovered from her concussion, Alex started teaching. He had created a schedule to teach the three young cowboys and Brenna in the morning while Hazel worked on her own. After lunch, he sat down with her and gave her assignments and examinations.

Hazel was still not happy that Alex was teaching her. She tried to talk her father out of it, but he was set on his decision. She had become friendlier toward the young teacher, but was still reserved and continued to be on guard and did not open up. Alex tried his best to learn more about her, but she was not willing to share. So, he gave her a homework assignment.

"Hazel, I want you to write an essay about yourself. Picture yourself writing an article for a newspaper and sharing everything important about you. Think of your readers and what they would want to know about you. Be open and honest and share what readers might find interesting about you."

Hazel listened to his instructions, but she tensed up as soon as he mentioned she had to write about herself. Alex saw in her eyes that she was unwilling to do this assignment and would fight him on it.

"I am sorry, Mr. Camden, but this essay has nothing to do with running a ranch. You are supposed to teach me business, agriculture, and ranch work theories and not how I should introduce myself. I know what you are trying to do. You are trying to pry information out of me, information I don't feel comfortable sharing. With you living here, I believe you know me well enough."

"No, Hazel, I don't know you well. I don't know you much at all. You are so reserved toward me that I am wondering what I did to offend you." He studied her eyes and face with a serious yet curious look.

"You are my teacher, nothing more. You only need to worry about my studies and how I am doing with my education, not my life outside of school." She stubbornly pressed her lips together, a sign that she would not budge from her point of view.

"Why don't you want me to be part of your life outside of school? Am I that disagreeable to you?" His brown eyes searched her face, hoping to understand why she resisted him so much. Hazel blushed a dark crimson.

The young woman was at a loss of words at first and didn't know how to respond. Why couldn't he leave her alone?

"I don't dislike you, Mr. Camden. I have nothing against you. I am just a private person and wish for you to respect that."

Her lips turned into a fine line. "I will not write what you want me to write. Please give me a different essay assignment."

He looked at her, flabbergasted. Never in his life, as a teacher, had a student flatly refused to do a task. He knew he had to stand up against her stubbornness and formulate that this was not acceptable.

"I will not do such a thing. I am the teacher and decide what assignments you have to do. Where would we be if we allowed students to pick their tasks? The assignment is set, and you have until Friday to finish it. Refusing to do the work will leave me no choice but to grade you accordingly, and I am sure your father would want to be informed." He stared at her with a firm expression.

"Are you threatening me?" Her blue eyes locked with his, glowing irritation glancing back at him.

"No, but actions have consequences, and I just informed you what the consequences would be if you decide a certain way."

Hazel narrowed her eyes, her lips were pressed together in an angry pout. It was clear that she was outraged. Without saying another word, however, she got up, and left the room. Alex shook his head, still trying to get over her hard-headed refusal, yet he grinned, amused. She was a piece of work for sure.

That same day, after dinner, Hazel decided it was time to have a serious conversation with her father. She had to let him know what she thought of Alex Camden, his rudeness, and how he treated her. Hazel had reached her father's office when she heard voices from inside the room. Since the door was not fully closed, she leaned closer to eavesdrop.

"So, Alex, how are Brenna and the boys doing?"

"Brenna is doing very well. She is an intelligent and bright student and way ahead of the boys. They are doing well enough, too, though, and it won't take too long before they catch up with her."

"I am glad to hear it. And how about Hazel? How are things going with her? Is she opening up to you?"

Hazel held her breath. Was he going to tell on her? She heard Alex let out a long sigh.

"Hazel is as smart as a whip, and from what I have seen so far, she is quite knowledgeable about business and how to run a ranch. She is quick to know the answers to questions, and it is easy to see that she had exceptional teachers in the past. That said, nothing I try makes her warm up to me. I don't know what I did to her that made her dislike me so much." Alex's frustration was showing, but her father patted his back.

"I don't think she dislikes you as a person. Hazel doesn't like that she has a teacher now and can't work on her own anymore."

"I gave her an essay assignment today so that she would tell me more about herself. She refused, and I informed her that this was unacceptable and that I would grade her accordingly. She was not pleased."

Hazel heard enough. She breathed through her teeth as disappointment worked its way to her heart. Alex had ratted her out so quickly, she didn't even have a chance to write that blasted essay. And her father was on his side, of course. She needed time for herself. The young woman left the house and went into the stable to saddle her horse. Fresh air and time alone always made her feel better.

"She is not opening up and refuses to tell me anything personal. Never in my years of teaching have I seen a student so guarded and unapproachable. Hazel will tell me anything that comes from the books, but as soon as I try to ask her something private, she blocks the attempt."

"I am not surprised about the blocking part. Hazel is stubborn, just like her mother was. I am worried, though. She has withdrawn from me as well since we returned to Willamette Falls, and I don't get it. It has to be possible to break that hard shell. She was open and outgoing as a young child, but for many years now, she has times when she locks her heart away."

"Something is bothering her. She must have gotten hurt in the past, and it seems as if she is deliberately trying to push people away. I don't know what the reason could be, though." Alex furrowed his brows.

George sighed. "I'll make sure she writes that essay. With a little bit of luck, she'll open up enough to give us some clues."

"Where do you think you're going, Hazel?" Namito raised an eyebrow when she came out of the stable on horseback, and Rob watched her, just as stunned.

"What do you think I am doing? I am going on a ride-out." Irritation spread across her face, her eyes were distant and cold.

"But not by yourself, young lady. It will be dark soon."

"So what? I am not a baby anymore and know what I am doing," she snapped, which made the two men even more astonished since that wasn't like her.

"Wait, we are coming with you."

"No, thank you. I want to be alone, and I am in no need of two babysitters." With that, she kicked her horse into the sides and galloped off the ranch yard. Rob and Namito watched her, stunned, for a moment, before they sprinted into the stable, saddled their horses, and pursued after her.

Hazel was fuming when she saw that they were following her. She longed for peace and quiet, yet every man on the ranch seemed to see her as a child. She was done with all of this.

"Hazel, wait," Rob shouted after her, but she only kept pushing her horse to run faster.

"Just go away. I don't want to see anyone right now, and I don't want to talk to you." As upset as she was, she enjoyed this quick ride through the fresh evening air. The red on her cheeks brightened into a healthy glow, and her eyes sparkled with excitement. The moon was out, and the sky darkened.

"Hazel Rae Buchannon, stop your horse at once," Namito yelled, and she nearly grinned when she pictured his expression change to irritation for not listening to him. She didn't care, though, and continued her fast ride without looking back or responding.

"What in the world is wrong with Hazel?" Rob looked at his best friend and shook his head.

"That's something I would like to know too. I am certain she heard me."

"Of course, she did."

They continued to go after her, but it took them another few minutes to catch up with her. Namito grabbed her, pulled her off her saddle, and put her on the ground. Hazel didn't even stop and continued on foot. Namito followed her, jumped off his horse, and embraced her with his muscular arms. She tried to get out of his hold, but he was too strong.

"What's all this about, Namito? Let go of me." She continued to fight him, but had no chance. He turned her around, so she had to face him.

"Can you tell me what's wrong with you, Hazel? Did we offend you?"

She shook her head and glanced down at her feet. She obviously didn't want to look at him.

"No, you didn't offend me. I want to be alone, that's all. I don't want to talk about it to anyone."

Rob stepped closer. "What do you not want to talk about, Hazel?"

She rolled her eyes. "Why do men have to know everything? Maybe it is none of your business."

She tried to sound calm, but was still too agitated. Namito lifted her chin higher and looked deep into her blue eyes.

"Perhaps it is none of our business, and we need not know everything, but we can sense that something is bothering you. You are beyond irritated, and that's not like you." He kept staring at her, and she glanced into his dark eyes, knowing that he wouldn't leave her alone until he knew everything.

"You are so annoying, sometimes. Don't you realize that every person has a time when they have to deal with problems by themselves?"

He nodded, grinning down at her. "Yes, I realize that, Sidaa. But we are your best friends, and you will tell us eventually anyway, so you might as well tell us right now." His fake arrogance made her smile. She looked at him and elbowed him in his stomach. He sat on a fallen tree and pulled her next to him.

"It isn't anything serious. I am mad at Pa and Alex Camden."

Namito nodded. He had figured it was something like that. Rob appeared to be confused.

"Why? What's the problem with your father and Alex Camden?"

"They are getting involved in things that are none of their business and trying to force me to share information I am not willing to share," she burst out.

"What?"

"Mr. Camden gave me an assignment today. He wants me to write an essay about myself, to introduce myself and share what I like and who I am."

"So?" Rob couldn't quite follow. Namito's expression turned to confusion now, too. What was she on about?

"So? Why does he care so much? Why does he need to know personal stuff? My private life has nothing to do with him. He is my teacher, not a close friend, there is no need for him to know anything personal about me." She breathed through her teeth. Namito and Rob exchanged a brief look.

"Hazel, he needs to know personal stuff too. First, it will help him discover your strengths and weaknesses, and second, he lives with your family now. He will be part of your personal life, whether you like it." Namito had a serious expression on his face, but she only flashed him a sideways glance.

"I disagree, Namito. He doesn't need to be part of my personal life. He is my teacher, and that's it."

"Okay, and why are you angry with your father?"

"Because he talked to Alex about me already, and Alex told him that I refused to write that essay. They try to force me to do something, I don't want to do."

"How do you know your Pa, and Alex, talked about you? Did you eavesdrop?" Namito raised an eyebrow, and an amused smile appeared on his face. The young woman blushed.

"What if I have? It is nothing to you." She stood, and Rob and Namito followed her example. They mounted their horses and rode back to the ranch at a slow pace.

Namito cleared his throat. "Please don't take this the wrong way, Hazel, but I think you unconsciously still suffer from what you saw happen on the Indian reservation and because your mom left you. You push people away, so you won't get hurt again. You are scared to like Alex Camden. Not only that, but you tell yourself better not get too personal with those who might leave again, than to like someone and feel the loss when that person departs from your life. There are always times when everything is fine, and you are open and approachable. But as soon as someone new comes into your life, someone who could leave again, those feelings of not wanting to get hurt come up, and you are reserved, withdrawn, and stand-offish. Even to us." Namito looked at her, and he saw how her features froze. Her eyes communicated she didn't agree with him.

"That is nonsense, Namito, and you know that."

"That is not nonsense, Hazel, and I encourage you to think about my words. The pain of those terrible childhood memories is worse than you are admitting."

She shook her head wildly. "You don't even know what you are talking about. Now, leave me alone." They had reached the stable, and she dismounted and hurried into the house.

"Don't you think that was too direct, Namito?" Rob watched as Hazel disappeared.

"No. I know undoubtedly that this is her problem. She will continue to deny it for a while, but she will think about my words and recognize the truth. She is so scared to like someone that she will do what it takes to keep that person away from her. If she didn't fight it so much, she would like Alex Camden in no time." Namito looked at his best friend, and Rob nodded. Namito was right.

George visited with Hazel that same evening and left no doubt behind, that she was to write that essay. She had expected the conversation and took it relatively calmly.

"Hazel, you are not to refuse tasks Alex assigns to you. Every teacher wants to get to know their students beyond the classroom, especially in settings like we have, where the teacher lives with us. Alex is not doing this to make things hard for you. He wants to get to know you, so he can be a better teacher and perhaps help you with whatever is bothering you. You trusted Reverend Mitchell as a teacher, so why not Alex Camden?"

"Reverend Mitchell and Alex Camden are two very different people. Nobody will ever take Reverend Mitchell's place, and it isn't fair to compare Alex to him." She glanced at her father, her lips a fine line. George realized that the raw vulnerability in her eyes and voice communicated that she was still not over Robert's transfer, and so he took himself back.

"Okay, fine, Hazel. I see you are still upset with me about hiring Alex, but it won't change my decision, so please try to get along with him. The assignment is set in stone. Just give me your paper once you finish it." He hugged her and left her room.

Hazel thought about everything that had happened that day, including what Namito had said to her. She still didn't see how her disliking Alex Camden had anything to do with her mother leaving. Namito didn't know what Reverend Mitchell meant to her and what she had experienced with Jason Clark. Naturally, she was reserved and careful with any man who entered her life, and if he knew what kept her at a distance, he would understand.

On Thursday evening, Hazel handed her father a few pages of paper. Alex Camden was also in the room, and she knew he was aware of what she gave to her dad, but she ignored him.

"Please leave it on my desk once you are finished reading it, Pa. I still want to go horseback riding."

"Okay, but please take Rob or Namito with you."

"Yes, yes." She couldn't get out of the house fast enough because she was worried her teacher would want to come too.

Alex wasn't planning on joining them, though. He was too interested in Hazel's essay. George must have noticed the intense interest.

"Do you want me to read it out loud, Alex?"

"Yes, please. I can't wait to hear what Hazel wrote about herself."

George smiled and started reading. The beginning was as expected. She wrote reserved and mentioned everything asked of her, but not more than necessary. However, they found a paragraph that made both prick up their ears.

> *"I still can't believe that my mother left Haven and me when we were only six years old. I am so grateful that Pa has always been there for us. Mother knew we were in excellent hands with him. I don't remember her much, but the fact that she left us at such a young age shows that she only cared about being free.*
>
> *I love Pa, and even though my mother never showed much love and affection, it hurt deeply when she left. Even to this day, I think about her. Whenever a person knocks on our door, or I see a woman step out of the stagecoach in town, I wonder if she has returned. She destroyed a lot of trust in me, and I find it difficult to trust and believe people because of it. My biggest fear is that Pa will leave us too. That thought paralyzes me and makes it hard for me to stay positive."*

George and Alex exchanged a look. Both were stunned and surprised and remained silent for a while. Alex hadn't even known that Abigail had left her family. He had assumed that she had died when the twins were young.

"I can't believe it. I had no idea Hazel was still so hurt from her mother leaving her. Haven was upset in the beginning, but she talked about it and worked through her pain. Come to think of it, Hazel never did that. She kept her feelings trapped, always trying to be strong. She even comforted her sister when Haven was overcome with emotion." George shook his head.

Alex nodded. "This is her problem. The pain of being left by someone who was supposed to care for her is deep. It keeps her unconsciousness always on guard. That's why she pushes people away. That's why she is so cold and reserved to anyone who comes into her life and could leave again. She is only so resistant to protect herself from getting hurt. Hazel always seems strong and as if nothing could ever defeat her, but she has a vulnerable, sensitive, and delicate heart. I don't think she fully realizes yet that she pushes people away because of her past. That gives us an advantage, though, and hopefully helps us get to her and heal her broken heart. If I was to take a guess, Namito and Rob must have figured this out already, and Helen probably has too." Alex looked at the older man. Hope and understanding spread across his face.

George nodded, still stunned. "Yes, I have no doubt in my mind that Helen knows, or at least assumes, what Hazel's struggles are. She, too, was left by her mom, when she was a teenager, so Helen knows the feelings of a broken heart. Helen came to us two years after Abigail left. My mother had moved in with us right after it happened, but I hired Helen when Ma couldn't do the work by herself anymore. It didn't take long until Haven and Hazel accepted Helen as their substitute mother." He gasped.

"Now I know why Hazel accepted Helen so quickly. Helen has a wonderful stepmom and did what she could to be one too. Whenever Helen was off and visited friends or relatives, she told Hazel where she would be, how long she would be gone for, and how she could be reached. That was my mistake. I should have done the same thing."

"How did Hazel take it when your mother died?"

"It was hard for her, but easier to accept since my mother had been old. She can handle it when someone old passes on, but when younger people leave or worse, die, it is a challenge for her. She fought long against the friendship with Rob and Namito, but their stubbornness paid off in the end. The same goes for Reverend Mitchell. He, too, figured her out and realized fast what a soft heart she has. That's why she is so attached to him and why she can't let him go. He is part of her heart, and she feels the loss of him deeply."

George finally understood why Hazel missed Reverend Mitchell so much. He had always known that they had a special bond and shared crucial memories, but he never thought about why their relationship was special. What an eye-opening experience. Who knew that an essay could make such a difference?

"I will figure out a way as well. I need to be patient and persistent with her. She loves you and is thankful you love her, but the worry of you leaving her is still there."

Before Alex started school with Brenna and the young cowboys, Hazel handed in her assignment. Her feeling told her that Alex had read it the night before, though.

That afternoon, when he walked into the sitting room to start Hazel's lesson, he greeted her with a warm smile.

"Hazel, I am happy and pleased with your essay. I know how hard it was for you to be so open and honest and that you didn't want to share all that. I am proud of you for doing it, anyway." Alex glanced into her eyes, and she blushed. He noticed that she nearly smiled at his compliment, but quickly took herself back, as if she forbade herself to express that emotion.

The young man chuckled to himself. She was a beauty, especially when she was embarrassed.

"Thank you, Mr. Camden."

As soon as Hazel had finished her studies for the day, she joined Namito, Rob, and Haven outside, but was far away in her thoughts. Was Namito right? Was she scared to like people and have them be part of her life because she didn't want to get hurt again? She had to admit, it made sense. The thought of her mother leaving her was still painful.

Hazel didn't want to admit it, but she was afraid that people, she cared about, would push her away if she opened her heart. Her heart had discovered right away that Alex Camden was a fine young man, but her mind kept warning her.

No, she couldn't allow him to break down the barriers she had so carefully built. She had to stick to her guns, or it would hurt too much when he left in less than two years. Rob and Namito had only succeeded to gain her trust because they had been so persistent and never gave up on her until they had worn her down. Would Alex do the same thing?

One person she had no trouble trusting was her twin sister Haven. They had been in the same boat and had experienced the same things. Although they had distinct personalities, they were there for each other and always had each other's backs.

6

Introducing Dr. Dave Tucker

Fall had changed the trees' green leaves into beautiful shining red, yellow, and brown colors. Hazel and Haven were sitting outside on the front porch waiting for Namito and Rob to go on a horseback ride together. Haven didn't go riding often, but she was always grateful when the group included her.

Hazel loved autumn. It was her favorite season, and she was excited to spend it with her friends. George Buchannon stepped out of the house and walked toward his daughters. He was waiting for the veterinarian physician who had taken over Dr. Kent's practice.

"Everything okay with you, two?"

"Just splendid, Pa," Hazel responded with a twinkle in her eyes. "Do you happen to know where Rob and Namito are? We want to go horseback riding, but I haven't seen them yet."

"They should be back in a short while. They had to finish a few last-minute tasks." He grinned, and as if that were their cue, the two young men came around the corner.

George made his way to the stables when a tall young man rode into the ranch yard. George walked up to him and shook his hand. Hazel was already joking around with her best friends when Haven stood. Her eyes were clued to her father exchanging a few words with the new vet before they disappeared into the stables.

"Shall we go, Haven?" Hazel asked, looking at her sister expectantly.

Haven shook her head absentmindedly. "Leave without me. I'll follow later," she mumbled before heading to the stables.

Rob and Namito stared after her, stunned. Only moments ago, Haven had told them that she was looking forward to their outing, and now she walked away?

"What in the world is going on with Haven?" Rob appeared to be quite shocked about the sudden mood change of the young woman and followed her with his eyes until she disappeared in the building.

"I am not certain," Hazel responded, but it didn't take long before it all made sense to her. She grinned, but nearly jumped out of her skin when Alex stepped next to them.

"Would it be okay if I joined you on your horseback ride? Being out in the fresh air will be good for me as well."

Hazel winced briefly, but didn't say a word. She had become friendlier toward him, but still kept her distance. When both Namito and Rob nodded, Alex saddled his horse, and the group rode off together.

Haven had reached the doors of the stable, but didn't know how she could get any closer to the new vet without making it awkward. Luckily, her father helped her without him realizing it. He stepped out of a horsebox and saw her.

"Oh, Haven, I am glad you are here right now. Dr. Tucker needs assistance treating the horses, and I need to get back to work. Could you lend him a hand, please?"

"Sure, Pa." She stepped closer.

"Dave, may I introduce my daughter Haven to you? Haven, this here is Dave Tucker."

Dave stood, smiled at the young woman, and shook her hand. George nodded to them and left.

Haven looked bashfully to the ground when Dave glanced at her. He was a handsome young man. She guessed him to be in his mid-twenties. He was tall, most likely around six-two, muscular, had dark-blonde hair, and a smile that gave her butterflies. He was bursting with confidence, but had a gentle kindness about him too.

Haven's heart beat like a drum. There was something about him that made her pulse trip. Never in her life had she believed in love at first sight, but that had changed rather quickly.

"Haven," he interrupted her thoughts, his masculine voice now all business. "Please do me a favor and hold this horse by his halter. Don't let him get up, while I am treating him."

She nodded, trying her hardest to focus on the animal, but couldn't keep her eyes off the handsome young man next to her. This would prove itself harder than she had imagined.

"I would like to know what hit Haven earlier." Rob was still thinking about Haven's strange behavior. Hazel giggled.

"Wasn't it quite obvious?" She raised an eyebrow, but the three men looked at her, puzzled. "Oh my, all three of you? Really? How can one be so slow-witted? Let me explain it to you then. A handsome young vet arrives. Haven is suddenly almost unresponsive and doesn't want to join us on our horseback ride anymore, even though she had been for it moments before." Hazel paused and grinned when the expressions of the three young men changed to thinking. Namito clicked first.

"...she fell head over heels for that young man."

"Correct." Hazel smirked as she watched Rob, who still looked confused.

"How did you come to that conclusion by her strange behavior?"

"Seriously, Rob? One would think I am the older one of us two," she remarked cheekily, winking at Namito, whose dark eyes were full of mirth. "It is clear to me that you know nothing about women," she added, sass and excitement in her eyes. Namito and Alex let out a hearty laugh.

"Hey, what's that supposed to mean?" Rob's voice was full of fake outrage, and he gave her a playful nudge on her arm. Hazel wiggled her eyebrows at him.

"I don't know, Rob. What could I mean by it?"

Dave Tucker and Haven stepped out of the stable the moment the other four dismounted their horses. Haven's face was flushed, her eyes sparkled like stars. The two of them had a lively conversation going on, and so Hazel waited until they reached her.

"Welcome to our ranch, Dr. Tucker. It is a pleasure meeting you. I am Hazel Buchannon."

He shook her hand and smiled at her. "Nice to meet you too, Miss Buchannon. Your father has told me much about you, but please call me Dave."

"I will do that, but then you have to call me Hazel. Being called Miss Buchannon makes me feel old." She winked at him, and he laughed. He was certainly a handsome fellow and nearly as tall as Alex was, but he wasn't her type, and so she didn't feel shy or bashful around him.

"Would you like to stay for supper, Dave?"

"I would love that, thank you. Is there anywhere where I can wash my hands before supper?"

"Oh, sure, Rob can show you," she replied, smiling while waving her friend over to them. Dave nodded to her, then turned to Haven again.

"Thank you for your help, Miss Haven. It is always easier to treat animals when there is a second person who can keep them calm." He squeezed her hand and followed Rob into the house. Alex and Namito took the horses back to the stable and unsaddled them. Hazel slipped to her sister's side.

"Wow, Haven, I have never seen you like this. You are captivated by Dr. Tucker."

"I know, but he is so attractive and handsome and kind. I couldn't help it. We seem to have a lot of the same interests," she replied with a beaming smile. Hazel watched her with a grin.

"Nothing will ever come out of it, though. A guy like him will never fall in love with shy me." Haven's beaming smile changed to a look of disappointment.

"Don't think that way, Haven. You never know. If he is the right one for you, and I can see you two as a couple, things will happen when the time is right." She nudged her sister. "Let's enjoy supper with that handsome fellow. Is there anything you want me to find out about him?"

"Hazel, please," Haven tried to shush her sister as she blushed deep red. She briefly glanced around to make sure nobody was near them.

"What?" Hazel asked innocently, and Haven chuckled. "I'll ask him whatever you want me to ask." She looked into her sister's green eyes.

"Okay, well, maybe you can try to find out if he has a woman in his life, but please do it in a way that doesn't make it obvious." The young woman appeared to be quite uncomfortable, and so Hazel rolled her eyes.

"Whatever do you mean? Are you saying that I couldn't get information out of people without them knowing what I am up to? Ha. You haven't seen my acting talent yet, my darling." She smirked at her sister, and Haven giggled.

They had an enjoyable time with Dave. He was a funny guy and made everyone laugh. Hazel already liked him like an older brother. After supper, they moved the conversation to the sitting room, while Helen served tea and cookies. Haven had been shy during the evening, but she kept watching her sister. Hazel smiled to herself, but the right time to ask more personal things had finally arrived.

"Dave, where are you from?" Hazel asked as she observed him with curiosity.

Alex turned his full attention to Hazel. It amazed him how relaxed and outgoing she was around the young vet, yet not much had changed between him and her. Why was she acting like that?

He came to the conclusion that his theory had been right the entire time. Hazel obviously made a difference between those leaving again and those she believed would stay. Dr. Kent had served in Willamette Falls and Beaver Creek his entire work-life. She clearly expected Dave to do the same now that he had taken over the practice of Dr. Kent.

"I am from Australia. I was born and raised there, but my family immigrated to the United States when I was fifteen. Since then, our home has been San Francisco."

"Australia? My goodness, that must have been quite the journey, but it certainly explains your accent." She winked at him, and he smiled back. It was George who addressed the young man next.

"Where do you live now?"

"I rented a room in Willamette Falls, but will try to find something permanent once I have settled."

"I have an idea," George responded. "How about you move in with us and live here? I have the biggest ranch in the area and will need your help the most. You could always visit other farms along Beaver Creek from here whenever someone needs your services. Willamette Falls rarely needs a vet, but the farmers and ranchers in the country do. You can stay here as long as you want, at least until you get married."

Dave seemed to like the idea. Hazel used her father's last words as a cue to ask more about his personal life.

"I didn't know you were getting married," she remarked with an innocent expression and surprise in her voice. "Is your bride in town or will she follow you later?"

"I am not getting married. I am not even courting anyone right now. Your father meant that for the future."

"Oh, yes, that makes sense." Hazel nodded with understanding. Dave returned his attention to George again.

"Are you sure it won't be too much trouble?"

"I'm sure. We have an unused furnished room in the apartment attachment of our house and can get that ready for you in a heartbeat."

"Sounds wonderful. In that case, I'll accept your offer. I'll return to town tonight, but will come back first thing in the morning. That way, I can bring my belongings with me."

Dave moved in the following day. He settled in quickly, and was soon another family member.

7
When Tragedy Hits

The end of November came, and it had gotten cold. Everyone was busy getting the barn and enclosures ready. Fences needed fixing, fence posts were replaced with new ones, so they were prepared for the long winter ahead. Alex gave his students a few days off because it required everyone to herd the cattle and transfer them to enclosures around the ranch house. The ranch hands fixed the cattle shelters, filled water and hay troughs, and made everything as safe as possible.

Even Haven and Helen assisted in every way possible. Everyone was happy to pitch in because they knew things would be quieter during the winter.

After finishing the most intense work, they rewarded themselves with a visit to Willamette Falls. The cowboys hit the saloon for drinks and poker games, and everyone else did what they had come to do. Only Brenna and Haven had stayed home. Brenna was sick with a cold and Haven was around in case Brenna needed something.

George and Jackson visited the bank first. They had paperwork to fill out due to the sales they had made throughout the year. Hazel and Helen went to the store to buy supplies, since they didn't know if they could come to Willamette Falls again once winter hit. Heavy snow always made it impossible to leave the ranch, so they prepared for the worst.

Dave and Alex had gone to the post office. Alex to pick up a few new schoolbooks, and Dave to get medication supplies he had ordered. He also had to write several telegrams to family and friends, and that took time.

Rob had joined the rest of the cowboys at the saloon. He wasn't interested in alcohol, but enjoyed a friendly poker game. Namito stayed with Hazel and Helen and helped them load the wagon with the many supplies they had bought. Once finished, Helen walked over to the bank to warm up and inform George that they were ready to leave.

Alex stood next to Namito and Hazel, who tried hard to keep themselves warm. The wind was icy, and the temperatures kept dropping. When Namito saw George and Helen step out of the bank, he hurried over to the saloon to let Rob know that they would leave soon.

Hazel tensed up the moment she noticed Reverend Clark approaching them. He greeted Alex first before stepping next to Hazel. The young woman was on guard at once, despite having her teacher near them, as well as many potential witnesses if Reverend Clark was to become inappropriate. She didn't trust the young clergyman.

Thinking, he wouldn't dare get out of line with the entire town around, she accepted a handshake from him, but pulled her hand back when he tried to drag her closer. Jason's eyes were on her mercilessly, yet his gaze kept drifting to her lips.

Hazel felt trapped, but made sure she kept a safe distance from the man. He ogled her so obviously, that it sent a chilling shiver down her spine. How did nobody notice what he was doing to her? Hazel watched him out of the corner of her eyes and realized he was looking for a reason to touch her again. Without hesitation, she stepped around him and began heading toward her father and stepmother.

Namito had almost reached the saloon when Rob came out. A drunk and older man staggered after him, cursing at the young cowboy. Hazel stopped in her tracks, her shoulders tensed up. She glanced over to Alex, and he appeared to be on guard. There was a warning feeling in the air.

"I told you I won fair and square. Now go home and sober up, Craig." Rob turned away from the older guy and continued walking.

"You are not getting away," the man shouted and pulled his gun out of its holster, pointing it directly at the young man.

"Rob, watch out," Hazel called out, her eyes wide with fear and worry. Rob turned around and reached for his own gun, but before he could do anything, the other guy pulled the trigger and fired several shots.

Everything started spinning around Hazel, and she heard herself scream in pain. She was about to run to her best friend when Jason Clark grabbed her hand and pulled her backward. She fought him, freed her hand, made a few steps, and was held back again. Alex embraced her with both of his arms, and no matter how much she tried to get away from him, he wouldn't let go.

Namito had watched everything in complete shock, but jumped into action to rescue a child and took it to safety because the older guy kept firing shots. Two more people got injured before a few men overpowered the shooter. The sheriff handcuffed the guy, and Dr. Harper took care of the injuries of those wounded. He checked on Rob first, but shook his head when he observed Namito's hopeful expression.

A sharp pain pierced his heart when the young man's mind recognized that his best friend laid dead in front of him and there was nothing anyone could do about it. He gasped for air, as the agony took his breath away.

Gordon Harper was close to tears. It didn't happen often that he got emotional. As a doctor, he was used to death and loss, but this hit him hard. Rob had been the first baby he had delivered as a young physician, so it was difficult for him to keep his emotions in check. He patted Namito's back in hope to give him some comfort and hurried to the other people who required medical attention.

As soon as Dr. Harper was gone, Namito sank to his knees and pulled the lifeless body of his friend into his arms, while taking a few steadying breaths.

Everyone around was shocked beyond imagination, and it took the rest of the cowboys a while before they felt capable of putting a blanket over Rob and moving him out of the way.

Hazel continued to fight Alex until she saw Namito pulling their best friend into his arms. The intense pain on the young Indian's face undid her, and she turned around and buried her face against Alex's chest. Hard sobs broke out of her, but she managed to mumble something.

"Please, Alex, let me go to Rob and Namito." Her voice was so faint Alex could hardly hear her. But his arms were firmly around her in an attempt to give her some comfort.

"No, I can't let you go. Keep Rob in your memories the way you knew him." Alex was fighting his own emotions, but she needed him to remain strong. She held on to him as if her life depended on it, and he tried to be there for her. He knew exactly how she felt and was grateful that she didn't push him away again.

George, Jackson, and Helen rushed over to them as soon as their body allowed them to move. The witnessed tragedy shook all three of them, especially when they took in that Hazel and Namito had watched the entire thing.

When Helen saw that Alex took care of Hazel already, she walked over to Namito first and hugged him. He was thankful for her sweet kindness, but all he wanted now was to be alone.

As soon as Helen released him from her embrace, Namito approached Alex and Hazel. He turned the young woman around and pulled her into his muscular arms, holding her close. Hazel couldn't stop her heartbreaking crying.

Namito struggled greatly to control his own emotions when he saw and felt her raw pain, but he forced himself to comfort her for several minutes, saying nothing. When the torment within him got to a breaking point, he kissed her forehead, removed her arms from around him, and stepped next to his horse before mounting. Not allowing anyone to stop him he dashed out of town without looking back.

Emptiness embraced Hazel as soon as Namito had let go of her. She watched him disappear, with more and more tears clouding her vision. Despite her attempts of calming herself, nothing worked. As another gush of tears hit her and the sobbing began to spiral out of control, Hazel crouched down, wrapping her arms around herself. She was certain that her heart had never hurt like this before.

Dave had finished sending his telegrams and stepped out of the post office. With one look around, he knew something bad had happened. As he walked back to the wagon, he noticed Hazel breaking down crying, hugging herself, so he stepped next to her, pulled her back to her feet and into his arms. She was crying so hard her entire body was shaking, and that got Dave even more worried.

"What happened?"

Alex explained in a few words what had occurred. Dave's worried expression changed to shock, unbelief, and anguish. The young vet had not expected something like that and had to process the news first. He had become good friends with Rob, so the thought of him being dead was difficult to accept. He knew, though, that he had to stay strong for Hazel and that she would need the comfort and support from him and Alex. It was clear to Dave that Namito could not be there for her, since he had to cope with his own pain and grief.

Dave tried his best to comfort Hazel, but she was inconsolable. It broke his heart to see her so emotional, but there was nothing he could do except hold her close and let her know he was there for her.

Reverend Jason Clark had watched the whole incident with the same horror as everyone else in town, yet his compassion was short-lived when he realized that this was his chance to pull Hazel into his arms. He had tried to make it look as if he attempted to pull Hazel away from the danger, but when she became hysterical, he released her to get a better grip on her.

Unfortunately, Alex Camden had been faster. Jealousy and disdain boiled in him as he watched the young teacher comfort Hazel. After Namito's hasty departure, Jason was determined to step in again, to comfort Hazel, but once again he wasn't fast enough. He watched Dave with an icy fire.

Shortly after, he noticed that the Buchannons were preparing to leave, and Reverend Clark stepped next to Hazel.

"I am truly sorry, Miss Buchannon. I know your friend meant a lot to you." He made his voice sound warm and caring, but she didn't even acknowledge him. Jason was about to hand her up to the coach box, but she pushed his hand away, hitting him with a look of death. He had no doubt in his mind that she would cause a scene if he were to force himself on her, and attention like that was not what he wanted.

The young man stepped to the side and allowed Dave to hand her up, while everyone else settled on the carriage, the wagon or the horses. He watched them ride off.

As soon as they arrived back on the ranch, Hazel hurried to the stables, saddled her horse, and rode off shortly after. She wanted to be alone, so she could let her feelings out without holding back.

George looked at Alex and Dave, and they understood right away. They mounted their horses again, and followed the young woman, but kept an ample space between her and them to give her privacy. George stared after them. He was deeply worried about his daughter.

Hazel knew that Alex and Dave followed her, but she was grateful they stayed away from her and kept their distance. Her heart was broken into pieces. Hazel yelled her pain into the air to get the pressure off her chest. She missed Rob, and it was unbearable to think she would never see him again, and he wouldn't make her laugh anymore.

A thought hit her, stabbing her heart once more. Namito would stay away from her during the following weeks, and that hurt more than she thought possible. She felt lonely and lost and didn't know what she could do to make her heart heal. She made her horse go into a trot and could have enjoyed this ride with the beautiful winter landscape around her if this day hadn't turned so dreadful.

Alex and Dave were lost in their thoughts, mourning Rob's death, but they kept a close eye on Hazel. They knew she could snap at any moment.

Suddenly, a horse tore past them. The rider didn't look left or right, just forced his horse to go faster and faster. Although, he was gone in a blur, they had recognized him almost right away.

When Hazel heard the clatter of hoofs coming closer, she looked around to see who was behind her. Her eyes lit up for a brief moment.

"Namito?" she called after him. "Namito, wait, please!" Her voice cracked, and her sobbing took over again. The young man glanced over his shoulder, but continued his fast ride through the woods. Hazel's sobbing turned into a crying fit, and her entire body began trembling. Everything around her was spinning, and she panicked when her breathing became unsteady, which caused her to hyperventilate.

Dave and Alex realized right away what was happening and caught up with her, reaching for her horse's reins to slow down the animal. Hazel gasped for air.

The young vet jumped off his horse the moment she collapsed. He caught her and carried her to a nearby fallen tree. She gained consciousness once he sat down with her. Alex was by their side, and both men talked to her soothingly until her breathing returned to normal. Dave held her tight in his arms and let her cry.

Alex left the comforting to Dave. He was still Hazel's teacher and didn't want to ruin the trust she had put in him.

Although, Hazel didn't say anything, they knew this would only make her withdraw from everyone again, if they didn't find a way to reach her heart.

"Hazel," Dave said now, his voice raspy. "We are here for you, and you can lean on us at any time, especially while Namito is consumed by grief. I am aware that this loss shattered your heart into pieces, but you aren't alone and Namito will be back by your side before you know it."

Haven came down the stairs when George, Jackson, and Helen entered the house. Their concerned and sad expressions alarmed her.

"What happened, and where are Hazel and the others?"

George tried to give her a reassuring smile, but he was still too upset himself. The awful turnaround of the day had left a trace on everyone's heart, and it pained him to have to share such horrible news with his oldest daughter.

"Hazel went on a horseback ride. Rob got shot and killed today, and Hazel watched the whole incident."

Haven's eyes widened with utter shock, and she started crying. George pulled her into his arms and held her until she calmed down again.

"We need to be loving and understanding now. Hazel will fall into a deep depression, and it will become almost impossible to reach her heart. You all know she is a fighter and usually recovers quickly from trials and hard times, but losing someone she cares about, someone she loves so much, will hit her hard. Losing Rob will bring back the pain from when your mother left, and she will try to push us away to protect herself from getting hurt more. We need to be patient with her, or we will lose her for good. Haven, try to be understanding because she might push you away too."

Haven nodded with tears still dripping down her face. Jackson and Helen also nodded. They remembered Hazel, from her younger years, and how losing someone she loved tore her apart.

George and Jackson went into the kitchen, and Helen followed. She was going to boil water to make hot tea. They all needed the calming warmth of a cup of tea at that moment. Haven sat on the couch, still shocked that Rob was dead.

Hazel, Alex, and Dave entered the house a short while later. Hazel's expression was indifferent, with no emotions on her face. Haven stood and embraced her sister, but Hazel gently pushed her sister aside and disappeared into their room. Haven started to tear up again. It hurt to be driven away by her twin, and it hurt, even more, to see her in so much pain. Haven was about to follow Hazel when Dave stepped next to her and put his arm around Haven's shoulders.

"Leave her be. She is too upset and might just lash out at you. Her heart is shattered into a million pieces, and she has no clue how to put it back together again. We need to love her and be there for her, no matter how much she tries to ignore and avoid us. She will need us more than ever because Namito is in no state to comfort her as he is grieving himself. Both of them watched what happened, and so they are beyond crushed."

Haven nodded again, swallowing her tears. She was heartbroken herself because she had always liked Rob, but she was never as close to him as Hazel had been.

Dave was right, though. Hazel would push them away. She always wanted to appear tough and strong and refused to share her emotions and feelings, yet she was there for everyone who needed comfort. Oh, how she loved her sister.

Hazel appeared to be asleep when Haven entered their bedroom that night, but Haven knew her sister was still awake. She said goodnight but got no response. Haven wanted to help her sister so badly, but had to give her space. Hazel had never been someone who could be pushed. She had to open up herself. Otherwise, she would shut down completely.

Haven waited for her sister to say something, but everything was quiet. After a while, she closed her eyes and drifted off into a restless sleep.

Hazel relaxed when she heard her sister's deep breathing. She tried hard to get her thoughts under control again, but couldn't shake the image of Rob getting shot. Sobs burst out of her, and she pressed her face into her pillow so she wouldn't wake up her sister. Hazel cried until sleep overtook her.

Rob's funeral was only a few days later. Hazel had cried so much over the past few days that her eyes were red and swollen. Her heart was still aching, but she kept her emotions in check. She had let no one come close to her, and any attempt to comfort her was pushed aside. Only Dave had given her a quick hug whenever their paths crossed.

Hazel knew her family was beyond worried about her, but she wasn't ready to talk about her feelings and emotions. Losing someone so close to her was more than she could bear, and her heart was fractured and cracked.

She managed to stay strong during the funeral and even gave her condolences to Rob's parents and sisters. Rob's mother pulled the young woman so tight against her chest that Hazel could hardly breathe.

"Thank you for everything you did for our son, Hazel. He loved you more than anyone and cared about you," she sobbed and held on to Hazel as if her life depended on her.

Hazel had to swallow several times, not to lose it at that moment. She could only imagine what this woman felt by losing her only son. It was Rob's father who seemed to notice how hard it was getting for Hazel, and he pulled his wife away and into his arms.

"He was my best friend, and I will miss him. Thank you for bringing such a wonderful young man into this world," Hazel heard herself saying before she turned around and walked away from the family.

"Namito, can you not at least talk to her for a few minutes? Her heart is so broken, I am afraid it can never be mended. Alex and I tried to comfort and reach her, but she is inconsolable." Dave stood next to the young man.

"Try to understand, Dave. I can't. I really can't. Right now, I need distance from her and everyone else because losing my best friend is hard on me too. I can't offer the comfort she needs because I need it myself."

Hazel stood further away but had heard the conversation. She turned around to walk over to the two men, but Haven and Alex held her back. She hadn't even noticed them.

"Hazel, no, leave him be. He needs his space right now." Haven embraced her sister, but Hazel freed herself.

"I have to comfort him. He needs me. He really needs me." Hazel hyperventilated, and everything around her became blurry before her legs gave out and everything went black.

Alex jumped into action and caught her before she hit the ground. She regained consciousness at once and tried to push him away from her, but he didn't let go.

"Hazel, breathe slowly, and no, I won't let go of you. You are not stable right now."

She nodded, still white as a bedsheet. Dave and Namito looked over with a worried expression on their faces, but Reverend Clark started his funeral sermon now, and so they stayed where they were.

After everyone had left the graveyard, Hazel stood in front of Rob's grave with tears rolling down her cheeks. She sank to her knees and covered her face with her hands, and anyone seeing her like that would have wanted to take the pain away from her.

Hazel was so lost in her grieving, that she was terribly startled, when someone grabbed her hand and pulled her up and into his arms.

"It is okay, Hazel. I am here. Just let it out."

Everything froze in her when she recognized his voice and felt his touch. He stroked her back and held her close, no matter how hard she tried to push him away from her. His hand on her back moved lower and lower until she grabbed it with all the anger she felt and forced his hand to stop. Disgusted, she shoved the young man away from her.

"Get away from me, this instant, you morally corrupt blackguard," she snapped furiously, her eyes burning with an icy fire. "I swear I will yell for help if you don't leave me be. And if you ever step that close to me again, or touch me in such inappropriate ways, I'll report you to the sheriff."

Jason Clark laughed in her face. "And on what grounds? It is my word against yours, and nobody will believe you."

She scoffed, turned around, and was about to walk away when he grabbed her hand and pulled her closer again.

"Let me be clear with you today," he whispered into her ear, and she felt his warm breath on her neck, which made her shiver with disgust. "I always get what I want. You can either choose the easy way or the hard way, but you will be mine in the end."

"I will never be yours, trust me. Now let go of me." She tried to get out of his hold, but he only pressed himself closer to her, breathing in the scent of her hair while tracing her neck with his finger.

Hazel panicked. She wasn't strong enough to fight him off alone. How she hated him. How she hated men like him who only saw women as a pleasurable toy.

He grabbed her chin to pull her closer for a kiss. The young woman tried to struggle free, but his longing eyes were focused on her lips, an intense fire in his eyes.

"Mr. Clark, let me go or—"

"Or what? Call for your daddy? Call for your friends?"

"She doesn't need to do that."

Both shot around in surprise when they heard the deep voice behind them. Hazel's eyes lit up, and Clark dropped his hands. The young woman stepped away from her tormentor and threw herself into the open arms of Robert Mitchell. Her fatherly friend felt her shivering, and he only held her closer. He stared at Reverend Clark with a murderous glare.

"Reverend Mitchell, what a pleasant surprise," Jason Clark sneered. "Back to get your beautiful young bride? Bold move, considering you are nearly thirty years her senior, but I guess if you still want children at your age, you need a young wife."

"You have a filthy imagination, Clark. Keep your immoral thoughts to yourself, nobody wants to hear that," Robert

Mitchell growled aggressively. "Also, let's stop with this fake politeness. We both know you aren't happy to see me here."

"Fine, let's drop the polite tone, shall we? What are you doing here, Mitchell? This isn't your congregation anymore. You are not welcome here, and I suggest you leave me be, as I am attending to the needs of one of my church members." Jason Clark looked at him, his eyes full of hate and anger. Robert Mitchell was not faced or intimidated by it. He scoffed.

"Some needs. I'll stay here for as long as I like. And since you are so fond of threats, let me remind you that the people of Willamette Falls and Beaver Creek had me as their pastor for many years and like me a great deal. Trying to spread lies about me will not work." Reverend Mitchell snapped, putting the younger man firmly in his place.

Jason scoffed, disgusted. He was about to walk past the older reverend when Reverend Mitchell held his hand out to stop him.

"A word of warning, Clark. If you ever approach Hazel Buchannon or any other girl in such an inappropriate way again—if you dare to threaten Hazel like this a second time—you'll have to answer to me. Remember, I am in Salem, and our superiors, and I, will take any complaint against you seriously." He gave the younger man another icy look before Jason walked away and disappeared into the church.

Robert Mitchell sighed. He took and released several slow breaths in an attempt to calm himself. His anger was close to the explosion point, and only a vast amount of self-control stopped him from going after the other man.

Instead, he focused on the young woman in his arms and led Hazel to a bench nearby, sat down and pulled her next to him. She was still trembling, but with the threat not being near her anymore, she burst out in tears. Reverend Mitchell said nothing, just held her close. Seeing her so upset and shaken made his blood boil, but he had to stay calm for her sake.

He had always admired Hazel for keeping her emotions in check until the threat was over, and she was by herself or around a rescuer. She was terrified and scared on the inside, but had enough pride in her, not to give the other person more power than they already had. She stayed as confident as she possibly could in those difficult and harrowing moments and kept a cool head despite the intense trauma surrounding her.

After several minutes, she calmed down again. Robert Mitchell lifted her chin, so he could look into her eyes.

"Are you feeling better?"

She nodded, still swallowing tears. "What are you doing here? Did they transfer you back?" Her glance became hopeful, but he only shook his head.

"Sadly, no. I was on my way back to Salem when I heard of Rob's death and his funeral. I was granted permission to stop here for the funeral and then continue my travels. The stagecoach was late, and so I missed the funeral services, but maybe it was meant to be." He looked deep into her eyes, and she knew what he was trying to say.

"Hazel, has Jason Clark ever threatened you like this before?"

"No."

"Has he touched you inappropriately before this day?"

"He has once." She hesitated for a brief moment, but then it all blurted out. Robert's demeanor changed from worry to outrage.

"Did you tell anyone about that experience?"

She shook her head again. "No. I've told Pa I don't like him and that I don't feel comfortable in Reverend Clark's presence, but he brushed it aside. He asked me to give him a chance. Pa assumed I was still upset that you had left. I was upset, that's true, but the moment I met Mr. Clark I felt that I shouldn't trust him. Something was off, and the way he flirts with women and young girls is despicable, especially for a clergyman. Everyone thinks so highly of him since he can be charming and compassionate, but he is not like that toward me."

Robert Mitchell nodded, lost in thought. "Do you want me to talk to your father? So, he can keep an eye on you?"

"No, better not, Reverend Mitchell. Pa will think I got to you now. Nobody here will believe what Jason Clark's true colors are." She lowered her head, worry and concern returning to her voice. "I fear him," she admitted. "I don't trust him. The way he threatened me today was frightening. What if he gets Pa to marry me off without my consent?"

"Hazel, your father, would never do that, and if he does, I will come back at once and give him a piece of my mind. Is there anyone we can warn about Jason Clark, someone who will believe us and who will keep an eye on you?"

"Maybe Dave Tucker and Alex Camden. Dave is our new vet and lives with us, and Alex Camden is Brenna's and my teacher. Can you not come back and send Jason Clark somewhere else?"

"I wish I could, but there is not enough proof against him. Only I heard the threat he made to you, and he will twist it into something questionable."

Hazel nodded, defeated. She knew it was true. Never in her life had she been afraid of someone. She had always been careful around men, but wasn't scared. Jason Clark's words weren't an empty threat, though, and he meant what he said. How could she feel safe with that man around?

"I have avoided him from the beginning, but I can't go near him anymore, not by myself, at least. Why would a pastor, someone you are supposed to trust, treat me in such a degrading and disrespectful way?" Hazel looked up, and her blue eyes seemed to search for an answer in Reverend Mitchell's face.

Robert squeezed her hand. "I wish I had an answer for you, but I don't. It does show, though, that no matter what status, title, or calling a person has, he can still be evil and dishonest."

"But he is supposed to be a man of God. How can that man live with himself?"

"Once you stop listening to the still small voice, things go downhill. All we can do is hope and pray he will change his ways."

"Hazel, where have you been? We have been looking all over for you and are worried sick." Dave Tucker and Alex Camden stepped into the graveyard. Their eyes expressed concern.

The reminder, why she was in the graveyard, hit her hard. Rob's death had slipped her mind during the encounter with Jason Clark, but now it was back, full force, and her expression froze. She stood and walked back to Rob's grave without saying a word.

The three men watched her for a moment. Robert Mitchell nearly sighed when he recognized something he had seen time and time again. Hazel shut herself off, whenever she felt she had to protect herself. He had witnessed it many times during the years of him being her teacher and reverend. He turned to the two young men next to him.

"Excuse me, may I have a word with you two? I am Pastor Robert Mitchell." Dave and Alex nodded and stepped closer. He shared everything that had happened earlier and what Hazel had experienced with Jason Clark when they first met. Both men were shocked beyond imagination, and it made them speechless for a moment.

"Hazel said nobody would believe her. She says everyone thinks Clark is a saint."

Dave found his voice first. "She is right. Jason Clark is well-liked and respected in Willamette Falls, and nobody will suspect him of doing something so wrong."

Robert Mitchell let out a frustrated sigh. "Please promise me you look after Hazel and not let her be alone with that man. I wish we could do more, but my hands are tied since I was the only witness, and we have no proof. If we call him out, he will deny everything and even accuse me of something questionable. I don't want to put Hazel through that, but I also don't want her to deal with this by herself."

"We will do what we can to protect her. There is no way we'll let that evil man torture and frighten her. Hazel is good at standing up for herself, but she won't be able to fight this person off. How a man like that can become a pastor is beyond me."

"It is about lying and deceiving those around him. He might fool us humans, but he will have to answer to God in the end."

Robert stepped closer to Hazel and pulled her into his arms. Tears entered her eyes when she realized he was leaving again, and this was another farewell. He held her for a few minutes and then pushed her into Dave's arms. Reverend Mitchell smiled at her one last time, before he turned around and walked back into town. Hazel's heart ached ...again.

8

Broken Hearts Can Heal

After Rob's death and the incident with Jason Clark in the cemetery, Hazel withdrew from everyone. She threw herself into the ranch work and did what she could to ensure that the barns, stables, and land were ready for winter. As soon as she got home at night, she either disappeared into the barn or locked herself into the library.

Jackson hired Caleb Norton in Rob's place. He was a kind young man from Willamette Falls and a childhood friend of Haven and Hazel. He was a serious person but a hard-working cowboy, and he had always liked the twins.

Caleb's heart was long attached to Haven. Because of their personalities, they had a special connection. Hazel was too confident and wild for his taste, but he had clicked right away with Haven.

Haven hadn't seen him in several years as he had worked in Portland, but accepted the job offer when Jackson met him and extended it to him. Caleb and Haven continued with their friendship, and Caleb did everything in his power to comfort her in the current sad and challenging situation. He knew how hard it was for her to see her sister in so much pain.

Haven and Brenna missed their sister, and the entire household wanted nothing more than to have Hazel back to her usual cheerful, sassy, happy self. Hazel avoided family meals and refused to talk about her emotions and her broken heart. She felt as if her heart would never heal again.

Namito had left the ranch and had returned to his family. Hazel missed him, but was at a point of not wanting to be close to anyone anymore. It was best to live her life without getting attached to anyone because she was certain another person would be taken away from her soon.

She told herself the pain and heartache would get better if she continued to withdraw herself from her loved ones, but every time she closed her eyes, she saw the image of Rob getting shot. It was burned into her brain and made it impossible for her heart to heal.

When it started snowing, she was confined to the house and couldn't go outside much anymore. Within a few days, they were snowed in, making it hard for her to avoid her family.

A few days before Christmas, Alex decided it was time for a serious conversation with Hazel. She couldn't go on like that. Hazel was ill-looking and thin, and the entire family wanted their old Hazel back. She had forgotten to lock the library door that day, and so he entered the room.

Hazel sat in the big armchair in front of the window and watched the snowfall. Everything outside was beautiful, but Hazel didn't see that. She thought about Rob and Namito, and tears entered her eyes. She buried her head into her arms and sobbed.

Alex watched her for a moment. He wasn't sure if he should approach her, but there was never an agreeable time to speak to her. He stepped closer and touched her hand. She winced as she had not heard him come in and wiped the tears out of her eyes before she looked up at him.

"I am sorry, Hazel. I did not mean to startle you."

She glanced at him for a second and then stared at the snow again. "Hazel, I want to talk to you."

"Alex, please don't." She swallowed hard because she had not expected a conversation, nor did she wish for it.

"Please, Hazel, listen to me. I know how you feel, I know how hard Rob's death is for you."

"Why are you mentioning this? Why can't you leave me alone?" She jumped up, tears streaming down her face. She wanted to rush out of the room, but Alex grabbed her by her arms and wouldn't let go.

"I know what you are going through because I had a similar experience a few years back."

She looked up, and he continued.

"I was courting a young woman a few years ago, and we got along great. As time passed, I realized that although she had become my best friend, I didn't have romantic feelings for her. Unfortunately, she had fallen in love with me, and when I told her how I felt, she got upset and stormed off, away from me. A bank robber came out of the bank, and she was in his way. He gunned her down, no questions asked. I tried to keep her alive, but it was no use. She died in my arms."

Alex stared out of the window, lost in thought. He had let go of Hazel's arms. Her gaze was on him, her heart and eyes full of compassion.

"Her parents and my father blamed me for what happened, which made me feel worse because I felt guilty enough. I avoided everyone and stopped talking about my feelings. That went on for a few weeks until my mom had a heart-to-heart conversation with me. She couldn't bear seeing me like that. *Alex*, she said to me, *you can't keep shutting yourself away from everyone. You shouldn't push away those who love you because something bad has happened. Yes, Sarah's death was tragic, but it is part of life. We experience good and hard times. Life is constantly moving, and people come and go from our life. We have to be grateful for our time with them, but we shouldn't let ourselves go when things don't go as planned. You need to learn to accept that terrible things happen, that you will lose people you love and care about. However, be grateful for those who are still there for you.*"

Hazel knew instantly what he was trying to say. It hit her hard, but she couldn't deny that his words were what she needed to hear. She had done the same thing and had done this in the past too. It was her coping mechanism and a way to protect herself, but it wasn't right, and she was the only one who could change this.

Suddenly, she saw Alex with different eyes. She had to accept him as part of her life and couldn't deny him her friendship any longer. He cared about her and only wanted what was best for her. She needed to stop herself from pushing people away just because they could leave again. It wasn't fair to anyone who tried to reach out to her.

Alex had watched her and recognized a change in her expression. She squeezed his hand. "Thank you, Alex. Thank you for making me realize what a mistake it is to push people away because awful things happen. Your mom is right. I need to learn to let go and not shut myself away. Being vulnerable is the hardest thing for me, but I will try to do better." Her blue eyes filled with tears again, but she did not lower her gaze.

Both of them stared at each other for a moment, not sure how to continue. Alex wanted to pull her into his arms, so he could comfort her more, but didn't want to overstep the boundaries. Hazel wanted to hug him too, to show him how grateful she was, but she couldn't make herself do it.

A loud knock interrupted the awkwardness between Alex and Hazel, and George Buchannon entered the room.

"Hazel, you've got a visitor."

Before Hazel could even respond, Jason Clark walked into the library, followed by Dave. Hazel tensed up and froze on the spot. She locked eyes with Alex, and Dave and Alex stepped behind her.

"Miss Buchannon, how are you? I heard how much you are hurting and came by to share my condolences with you. I am always here if you need me." He grabbed her hand and held it. Jason looked at her with a kind smile, but his eyes told her why he was there. His fake kindness made her even more uneasy, and she pulled her hand back.

Alex put his hands on her shoulders to signal her, she wasn't alone. Jason Clark clearly noticed it as he didn't look pleased. Hazel ignored the reverend and focused on her father.

"What is he doing here? We are snowed in. How did he get to our ranch?"

George was deeply embarrassed by Hazel's rudeness. He was about to scold her when Jason responded to the young woman.

"Dr. Harper has a sleigh, so he can visit patients during the winter. He invited me to join him for his weekly visit to your ranch."

"So, Dr. Harper is here too?" Hazel asked, looking directly at her father and ignoring once again the reverend. George gave her a disappointed glance but nodded.

"Mr. Buchannon, would it be possible to have a few minutes alone with your daughter?"

Hazel turned as white as a bedsheet, but Dave stepped next to her and gave her hand another squeeze.

Before George could even reply, Hazel snapped.

"No! Whatever you have to say, you can say in front of everyone."

Jason was taken aback, and irritation spread across his face. George stared at his daughter, stunned. He had never seen her so rude and disrespectful before, and it wasn't like her, either. Ignoring his daughter's reply, he turned to Dave and Alex.

"Let's give Reverend Clark and Hazel privacy."

Hazel's expression changed to horror. The two young men saw the fear in her eyes, even though she hit it from the reverend. Alex and Dave shook their heads to let her know they would not leave her with that man.

"Thank you, Mr. Buchannon."

"Are you two coming?" George asked impatiently.

"No, sorry, George. We promised Reverend Mitchell we would keep an eye on her after someone in town cornered her inappropriately on the day of Rob's funeral." Alex said it calmly, watching the young reverend intensely. Jason Clark winced.

Alex's gaze did not leave Jason's face. He wanted the young clergyman to know that Hazel was not left to herself, and someone watched over her.

George's face froze in deep shock, and he turned his full attention to Hazel. "You had an inappropriate encounter? Did someone touch you?"

She nodded.

"Who? Did you let Todd know?"

"No, I didn't, and let's not talk about this, okay? Reverend Mitchell interfered in time, and I want to forget about it." Despite having her eyes on her father, she felt the suspicious glance Jason Clark gave her.

"Hazel, we can't just drop it. Don't protect the culprit. Anyone who messes with my daughter is messing with me."

"Pa, please."

"Does Robert know who?"

"Pa, Reverend Mitchell dealt with the situation and has taken action. Please..."

"Did Hazel tell you two who tormented her?" George interrupted her pleas to change the subject, her father's gaze now on the other two men in the room. Alex and Dave shook their heads. It wasn't a lie, since Robert Mitchell had told them, not Hazel.

"Reverend Clark, you need to investigate this and maybe get the sheriff involved. No woman or girl should feel unsafe in our town," George continued, now addressing Jason Clark.

Hazel rolled her eyes. How ironic that the person causing the problems was supposed to investigate. If her father only knew.

"Of course, Sir. I will look into it when I get back to town."

"Good." George Buchannon finally calmed down again, squeezed his daughter's hand, and left the room, so Jason Clark could speak with Hazel. He didn't even try again to have Alex and Dave leave with him. Hazel clearly wanted them around.

As soon as the door closed behind George, Jason's demeanor changed. "I know what game you are playing, Hazel, and you won't win it. You can tell everyone those lies about me all you want, but only fools will believe it." He aggressively stared at Alex and Dave as he walked toward Hazel. Both stepped in front of the young woman, shielding her from the reverend.

"Listen, Clark," Dave snapped. "You keep your filthy hands off Hazel and any other girl in this town. We might not have proof to show the people of Willamette Falls what a blackguard you are, but you can't hide it forever."

"...and once George Buchannon finds out you were after his daughter, he will make it his mission to destroy you. He won't hesitate to have you get punished for the rest of your life," Alex added, glowering at the reverend.

Jason looked from one to the other, but neither Alex nor Dave flinched. He scoffed, disgusted, turned around, and left the room.

Hazel let out a relieved sigh. She had held her breath ever since her father had left the room, but now her body relaxed again.

"Are you okay?" The two young men looked at her, worried. She nodded, still shaken. Dave pulled her into his arms and held her.

"Why does he keep doing that? Why does he keep threatening me?"

Alex and Dave exchanged a glance. "He is trying to get to you. Men like him will do anything to intimidate women because it makes them feel powerful and superior. You are prey to him, something he can pursue and take down in the end. Men like Jason Clark are obsessed with gaining such power, but it rarely ends well for them. The best way to deal with it is to stay strong and not give in to his threats and intimidation."

"But he is getting to me. I fear him, and I am worried he will threaten Haven or Brenna if he doesn't get what he wants." Hazel lowered her eyes, despair coloring her voice. Dave lifted her chin and made her look at him.

"We will not let him hurt you, and we promise we will keep an eye on Haven and Brenna. I don't think your sisters have to worry about him, though. He wants you and *only* you. The way he continues to remind you of his presence and keeps threatening you, tells me you are his target."

"But why is he targeting me? What did I do to him that makes him so persistent?"

"For starters, you didn't fall for his charm and saw from the beginning that his kindness is fake. You are beautiful, confident, strong-willed and determined, and that makes you so appealing to him. Men like Jason Clark want to own women like you. They wish to be in charge and tame you."

Hazel's worried expression turned to fear.

"We will not leave you alone with him, Hazel. Thanks to Reverend Mitchell, we know what he did to you, and we are taking it seriously. We will protect you from him and will fight him if we have to. No matter how much he tries to catch you alone, we will not allow that to happen."

Alex nodded in agreement, and Hazel smiled for a split-second. She wrapped her arms around Dave to thank him when once again someone knocked on the door. Hazel's blood froze, and she tensed up at once.

"Come in, please." Alex stepped forward and opened the door.

"Dr. Harper," Hazel exclaimed, relieved, and let go of Dave to greet the physician.

"Please excuse the intrusion, but your father asked me to check on you since you haven't been well for a few weeks."

"We'll be downstairs," Dave replied with a smile. He nodded to the doctor, and both he and Alex walked out of the room.

That evening, Hazel joined her family for supper for the first time in weeks. She apologized for her behavior and thanked them for always being there for her, even when she pushed them away. They hugged her and told her how much they loved her and how much she meant to everyone.

When Hazel laid in bed that night, she looked over at her sister. Haven had been quiet that evening, more than usual, and she knew why.

"I am sorry, Haven. I know I hurt your feelings by my pushing you away, but it wasn't personal. It is difficult for me to share my feelings with others. I should be more open with you, and I will try to get better at it. I hope you can forgive me." No response.

"How are things with you and Dave? Has he fallen madly in love with you yet?" Hazel knew that this would get her sister talking, and sure enough, she was right. Her sister let out a long sigh.

"I wish. He sees me as a good friend, if not a younger sister. I am too shy and quiet. I don't think he will ever have romantic feelings for me," Haven said, pouting.

"Give it time. Dave enjoys his freedom too much. He will see your beauty and wonderful heart before you know it, and then he will go down on one knee and ask you to be his bride."

"Hazel," Haven rebuked her sister, giggling.

"Just calling it how I see it."

"I definitely missed your sense of humor, Hazel. Love you to the moon and back," Haven replied, smiling.

"Love you too. Sweet dreams."

Hazel was almost back to her usual self. She joked around again, and the entire household perked up by seeing her radiant smile. Hazel still had moments of sadness because she missed Rob and Namito, but she tried hard to break down the wall she had built around herself.

She studied hard and put her energy and time into the lessons with Alex, so come spring, she could take her last exam and start her life in the business world. Her relationship with Alex Camden had improved. She counted him as one of her dearest friends and was grateful that he had taken the trouble of addressing her depression in a way that made her realize something had to change.

Christmas Eve was a celebration full of love and gratefulness. It was still snowing, and the wind was howling, but it was comfortable inside the house.

The cowboys shoveled paths to the barn and animal shelters whenever necessary. But other than that, there wasn't much to do. The woodshed behind the house was filled to the brink, so they had enough wood to keep the fireplaces going. Their storage room had enough flour and other necessities to make it through a long winter.

They now kept their chickens in part of the barn, surrounded by stacked up straw. It kept the birds happy and warm, and so they had plenty of fresh eggs each day. They got fresh milk from the cows, and their earth cellar, which was built into a rock behind the barn, was full of meat and other foods that had to be stored in a cold place.

Helen and Haven made a delicious Christmas Eve dinner. They sang Christmas carols, ate cookies and far too much cake, and George read the Christmas story from the bible. Hazel's heart was bursting with happiness, but she also felt sad. She had hoped that Namito would have returned at this point, but it was almost impossible with the snow out there.

After everyone had gone to bed, Hazel was still on the sofa in the living room. She stared out the window as the snowflakes kept falling.

Hazel snuggled herself into a blanket, took the cup of hot chocolate she had made for herself, and let her mind wander. The fire was still burning, and she listened to the crackling firewood while breathing in the smell of the Christmas tree. She felt peaceful and calm.

Hazel sipped her hot chocolate and thought about the Christmas story her father had read earlier and had read every year since she could remember. She was grateful that God had sent His son to this earth, so He would sacrifice Himself to atone for humanity's sins. She thought about Christ's mother, Mary, and all she had gone through to give birth to the Savior.

Hazel felt a strong, warm feeling that testified to her all of this was true. She was grateful and amazed at how humble Jesus's life had been and how much love He had for everyone. A powerful desire filled her heart, hoping that there was life after death and that she would see God and Jesus Christ again, and thank them for everything they had done for her. She also hoped she would see those who had passed on again. Oh, how she longed for a hug from Rob. Tears entered her eyes, and she closed them to remember her best friend a little longer. At that moment, she missed Namito terribly.

Something inside her told her she would see Rob again, that there was life after this life, and that death wasn't the end. Even though she continued to sob, she felt comforted. A moment later, she heard someone walk down the stairs, so she wiped away her tears before turning her head.

"Hazel, what are you still doing up? It is nearly midnight." George Buchannon was stunned to see her still awake.

"I wanted to enjoy the fire and tree by myself and couldn't make myself go upstairs to my room since it is so warm and comfortable down here." She smiled at him, and he sat next to her.

"I have to ask you for a favor and share a surprise I have for Helen with you," he blurted out as the excitement about the upcoming surprise made him giddy.

"What is it, Pa?" Curious, Hazel snuggled up to her father, and he put his arm around her shoulders.

"Helen's stepmom and brother moved to Willamette Falls."

"Really? Grandma Rosemary and Uncle Warren are in Willamette Falls? Right now?"

"Yes. Warren bought the hotel, and they will live here now. Helen has no idea, though. Adam Harrison will join us too. Because of the snow, I've asked Dr. Harper to bring them over for Christmas dinner, and he is invited as well. Since Helen doesn't know, we have to make sure we prepare enough food. How can we pull that off without her getting suspicious?"

Hazel grinned. "How can *we* pull that off, Pa? Or do you mean how Haven and I can pull that off?" She gave him a sassy look, and he nudged her.

"Touché. How will you two pull that off?"

"Helen will get up early and start preparing food, right?" George nodded. "Well, when Haven and I get up, we can kick her out of the kitchen and tell her we want to finish dinner for her as a Christmas gift. You need to make sure she doesn't come back to the kitchen. It will be your job to keep her distracted."

"Right. Brilliant idea, peanut. That should work." He winked at his daughter.

"Helen plans to make pumpkin and apple pie, and Haven wanted to make blackberry pie for ages. That should be plenty of pie for everyone."

"What else is Helen planning on making?"

"Turkey, potatoes, gravy, and she serves vegetables. She already made Raspberry Tart and Orange pudding. I don't think anyone will go hungry, but we need a second turkey."

"Jackson shot one yesterday, and we hid it in the barn. I better head back to bed now that that's sorted. Sweet dreams, Hazel." He kissed the top of her head, stood, and walked toward the stairs.

"Sweet dreams, Pa." Hazel watched her father as he headed to the second floor, but she didn't feel like leaving the comfortable sofa and following him. Instead, she snuggled herself into her blanket and watched the fire a little longer before her eyes grew heavy, and she fell into a deep, restful sleep.

Christmas morning started with a big breakfast. Helen had outdone herself as usual. After breakfast, they gathered in the sitting room to exchange gifts. Hazel had an exceptional talent for giving the perfect present. She watched her loved ones throughout the year and made a note of whatever they seemed to like. If they hadn't gotten it before Christmas, she got it for them.

Hazel was happy that everyone enjoyed her gifts, but she kept looking toward the Christmas tree, where Namito's gift laid still untouched. Melancholy settled in, so she was grateful that it was time to start with dinner preparations. She and Haven had discussed the surprise for Helen and were eager to get started. They forbade Helen to come even near the kitchen, and she was touched.

As soon as the two young women were alone in the kitchen, they got the second turkey ready, peeled extra potatoes, and Haven made her blackberry pie.

Everything turned out great. In the early afternoon, they baked the pie and then put the turkeys in the oven. It would take a while before the birds were ready, and so Haven and Hazel went back into the living room and joined the rest of the family.

Jackson and Dave were playing chess together, Alex was reading one of his new books, and Haven sat next to Brenna.

Hazel was sitting on the sofa, lost in thought, staring into the crackling fire when Namito stepped through the kitchen door. Brenna noticed him first and wanted to jump up to greet him, but he put his finger on his mouth to keep her quiet.

Her eyes sparkled, and so everyone turned around to see what she was looking at and saw him standing there — everyone but Hazel, who was still glued to the fire.

"Sure looks like I have been missed," he remarked and rolled his eyes, but with an enormous smile on his face. "Everyone is enjoying this fine Christmas day and doesn't waste a tiny thought on me."

Hazel turned toward him the moment she heard his voice. A beaming smile appeared on her face when she saw him standing there. She jumped up and threw herself into his now open arms.

"I can't believe you are back," she mumbled. "I missed you so much."

"Did you? It didn't look that way," he teased her with a smirk. She nudged him, but he only pulled her closer and held her. "I missed you too, Sidaa. I needed the time away, but you have no idea how much I thought of you."

"How did you get here in this weather?"

"I used my snowshoes and left early this morning."

She stepped back so everyone else could greet him as well, and then handed him his Christmas present. Namito gave her a gift as well, and when she opened it, a picture frame greeted her with a picture of her, Rob, and Namito. The photograph was from their trip to Portland during the fall, but she had never seen it, since Namito always had an excuse whenever she asked about it. She swallowed hard and embraced her best friend.

"Thank you, Namito." She looked up at him with tears in her eyes, and he touched her face before the rest of the family bombarded him with their presents. Hazel stepped away, put on her coat, and hurried into the barn to have a few minutes to herself.

She couldn't stop looking at the photograph, but her heart began to ache when she thought of Rob and how he wasn't around anymore to make her laugh.

"Hazel, try not to be so sad. Rob would want us to be happy."

The young woman looked up and saw Namito standing right next to her. "I just miss him so much, but I am glad you are back."

Namito pulled her into his arms and gave her another hug. "Did Alex and Dave look after you? I asked them before I left, since I knew how hard this would be for you."

"Yes, they were there for me. I don't even know how I deserve you." Hazel's thoughts wandered again, and she lowered her head. Namito lifted her chin and looked into her blue eyes.

"We love you for the person you are. You are such a caring girl and usually a happy young woman, and we like that. We can tease you and have fun with you without having to worry about offending you. But most importantly, you are not as dramatic as most girls. That makes it easy to get along with you. And the few times you get angry and upset, don't last long."

Hazel smiled bashfully, and they both wandered out of the barn.

They had barely walked three steps when two snowballs came flying in their direction. Hazel ducked in time, but the snowball for Namito hit him right in the face. Hazel giggled, but then she noticed Alex and Dave coming for them, so the young woman had no choice but to run back into the barn. She was about to climb up the ladder to the hayloft when Dave grabbed her and threw her over his shoulder.

"Dave, let me go. This isn't fair. I did nothing to you," she scolded him. He only laughed at her. As soon as they were outside, he took her off his shoulder.

Namito and Alex were in the middle of a snowball fight. Hazel gave Dave a push, and he landed in a gigantic pile of snow. His stunned face caused her to burst out laughing, but before she could escape, he was back on his feet and grabbed her again. This time it was her turn to fall into the snow.

After he had avenged his manly pride, Dave pulled Hazel back on her feet and hugged her. That was the moment Haven stepped out of the house.

Haven stopped almost right away and didn't dare go any closer. She knew what these young men were capable of and how fast they could turn against her. Sure enough, as soon as Dave noticed her, he formed a snowball and threw it in her direction. Haven, who had seen this coming, jumped to the side. The snowball flew past her through the open door and into the house.

Hazel grinned when she heard Jackson's outraged voice and saw him appear a moment later. He growled at them, intimidating, even though his eyes twinkled with mirth.

"Who threw the snowball at me?"

Dave pulled Hazel in front of him. "Hazel. Who else would do something so sassy?"

"Sure, it was me, you coward," she replied and raised an eyebrow. "How about you act like a proper man and own up to your shenanigans?" Hazel winked at Jackson, gave Dave another push, and hurried toward the front porch before Dave was back on his feet.

"Just you wait," he growled at her, and sprinted after her, but before he could grab her again, Jackson stepped in front of Hazel.

"Well, that was more than deserved. You've been begging for that kind of attention for quite some time." Jackson grinned and winked at Hazel and Haven.

Hazel stuck her tongue out at Dave, and he tried to clasp her hand, but she was faster and disappeared into the house.

Since he couldn't get Hazel, he pulled a surprised Haven into his arms and lifted her off her feet. Haven didn't even know what was happening to her.

"Dave, don't you dare," she gasped, shocked, her eyes wide.

"Oh, you bet I will dare. I have to defend my hurt pride somehow," he responded with an enormous grin on his face. That was the moment Hazel poked her head out again.

"Dave, I am shocked and disappointed in you. Threatening this poor girl just because you can't get me?" Hazel looked at him with playful seriousness, shaking her head. "You should be ashamed of yourself."

Alex, Jackson, and Namito burst out laughing. Dave grinned before he put Haven back on the ground.

"Lucky for you, you were saved this time." He winked at the two girls and went back into the house.

Haven was on cloud nine for the rest of the day. Her heart had beaten like crazy while Dave held her in his arms, and his good smelling after-shave sure didn't make her be any less in love with him.

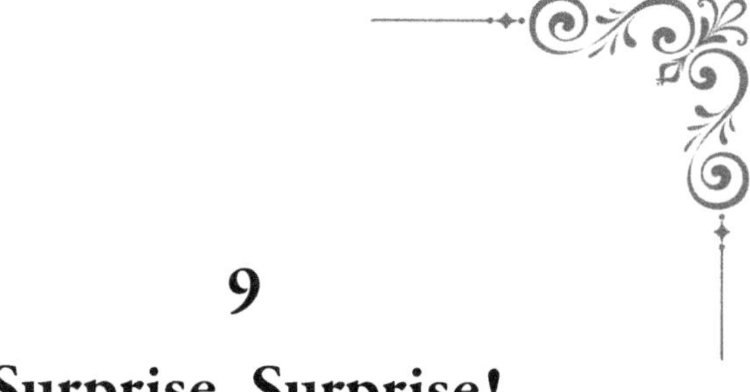

9
Surprise, Surprise!

Everyone had barely put on dry clothes when they heard sleigh bells in front of the house. Before Haven and Hazel had reached the kitchen door, they heard the excited squeals from Helen and Brenna. The twins smiled at each other. That meant Dr. Harper had just arrived, and with him, their surprise guests.

"Mom, Warren? What are you doing here?" Helen had a big smile on her face when she saw her stepmother and brother climb out of the sleigh, and she wrapped both of them into an enormous hug.

Rosemary smiled. "Warren bought the hotel in Willamette Falls, and we moved here. I am so excited to have both my children close to me again."

Brenna threw herself into her uncle's arms, and he twirled around with her. She then greeted her grandmother and the rest of the guests.

After everyone had greeted everyone, they went inside, and Haven and Hazel served dinner. Helen was stunned when she saw the extra food, but it touched her that her husband and daughters had created such a pleasant surprise for her.

While they were eating, the snow picked up and turned into a massive blizzard. None of their guests could leave that night, maybe not for a few days. Helen and the twins prepared beds and rooms for their guests.

When Alex came to the ranch after becoming their teacher, and Dave started as a vet, the two young men moved into the apartment attachment. George had it built when Helen became their housekeeper. It used to be a two-bedroom apartment with a kitchen and living room, but after George and Helen were married, they turned the kitchen into another bedroom. Now it was a guesthouse, even though the apartment part was attached to the actual house.

After the rooms were prepared and everyone had settled in, they met in the sitting room to catch up, eat cookies, and sing Christmas carols.

It was quiet in the house. Everyone had gone to their beds, so Hazel wrapped herself in her dressing gown, snuck downstairs, made herself a cup of hot chocolate, and threw more wood on the fire, so it started crackling. She then sat on the couch and snuggled herself into a blanket. Her heart was whole, and Hazel felt happy that night. It had been a beautiful and exciting day, and she was grateful for every minute.

Hazel stared into the flames when she heard someone come into the room. She turned her head and saw Adam approaching her.

"Hazel, what are you doing up, still?" He looked at her, surprised, but grinned. She smiled back.

"I love sitting here by myself, listening to the fire, and letting my mind wander. It is so peaceful."

He nodded and sat next to her.

Adam Harrison was fifteen years younger than his brother Jackson. They had three sisters between them, but all of them had moved away because of marriage. Two of their sisters lived in Reno, and one had moved to Boston with her husband and their children. Hazel liked Adam. He was like an older brother to her. Adam was a kind and quiet young man and a wonderful, caring friend.

He squeezed Hazel's hand after he seated himself. "I am glad we have a few minutes alone because there is something I want to ask you." Hazel looked at him, puzzled. "I spoke to your father earlier, and he told me you were inappropriately approached in town a while ago. Is that true?" His brown eyes looked at her, curious yet worried, and she nodded.

"I am sorry if this is hard for you to talk about, but I live in Willamette Falls and may be able to help and hopefully stop the culprit altogether. Besides your dad, two fathers told me that their daughters had upsetting and unseemly encounters, which is unacceptable. Willamette Falls has always been a safe town, and that should not change because of the account of one or two men."

"I am sorry to hear that happened to other girls. Did they report it to Sheriff Holden?"

"No. It happened with no witnesses around. The fathers were outraged and upset, but nobody was around when it happened. The guy, who did it, almost kidnapped one girl, luckily, someone intervened in time."

"Who tried to abduct the girl?" Hazel's eyes were wide and fearful. Was Jason Clark more dangerous than she thought?

"Someone new in town. He disappeared right after the attempted kidnapping. Todd Holden and his men are looking for him, but haven't found him yet. His name was Gabriel McKellar."

"Never heard that name before."

"So, he wasn't the one who harassed you?" Adam gave her a concerned side look. Hazel shook her head.

"Then who did?"

"It doesn't matter. You wouldn't believe it, anyway," she responded quickly, before attempting to change the subject. "Did the father of the girl intervene?"

"It wasn't the father. Lucky for her, Reverend Clark was nearby and stepped in before the girl was taken."

Hearing his name made Hazel cringe. *Of course, he continues to be the good guy for everyone else*, she thought. It made her situation so much worse. Nobody in town would ever believe her.

"Hazel, please tell me who did this to you," Adam begged as he grabbed her hand. "I promise I will believe you."

"No, you won't. Nobody in town will believe me, and that's why I never told Pa about it. The only people who believe me are Dave, Alex. Reverend Mitchell witnessed one of the encounters, but he is over forty miles away from here. He heard the threat the guy made to me and even told him to stop, or he would face serious consequences. Did it stop him? No, he continues to threaten me and will continue to get away with it until he gets what he wants because he is a man."

"Hazel—"

"Just leave it, Adam. I fear him, and I am even more scared that he might use Haven or Brenna to get to me." She jumped to her feet and turned away from him to leave the room when he pulled her back into his arms. She wasn't crying, but he could sense how upset she was, so he held her.

"I am so sorry, Hazel, I really am. I didn't mean to cause you any distress or worsen your fear. But please let me know who did this, so we can at least keep an eye on him. The sheriff needs to know."

Hazel looked up and into his eyes. He nodded in encouragement, and Hazel took a deep breath.

"Promise you won't tell Pa?"

"I can't promise that, Hazel."

The young woman sighed again. She was confident she would regret confiding in Adam, but there was still a chance he would surprise her in a good way, so she took another deep breath.

"It was Reverend Clark," she mumbled and lowered her eyes. Adam gasped in shock before he lifted her chin again.

"Are you serious?" Hazel nodded. "I can't believe it. That scoundrel rescues a girl from kidnapping and has the nerve to approach you inappropriately? I will report him to the sheriff."

"Adam, Todd Holden can't do anything. There are no witnesses except Reverend Mitchell."

"He might not be able to arrest him, but he can keep a close eye on Clark, which should make that evil blackguard more careful," he responded, outrage and fury in his eyes. "I want to murder that swine."

"Adam!" Hazel scolded him, even though she was relieved that he believed her and took this threat seriously.

"Sorry," he apologized, "but he is a lowlife vermin, and I hope he ends up in prison for the rest of his miserable life."

"He won't get punished. His charming nature protects him. Everyone here thinks he is a saint."

"I promise, I'll inform the sheriff as soon as I am back in town."

"Thank you, Adam. Thank you for believing me." She kissed him on the cheek, turned around, and made her way back to her room. He continued to watch her until she had reached the end of the stairs. Only then did he head to his own room, still shaking his head about the news he had received.

The blizzard stopped two days later. As much as they had enjoyed the time together, everyone was glad that things were back to normal again. Their visitors looked forward to their own homes.

Hazel couldn't wait for the snow to melt, so she could ride her horse again. She spent the next several weeks learning and studying to be ready for the examination she would have to take during the spring. Hazel was nervous yet excited, but Alex assured her she would be fine. They had sent in the paperwork for her to attend the examination. Not long after, she received a letter telling her that she was expected at the Oregon Institute early on the morning of May second.

In the middle of February, the family went to town for the first time since Rob had been shot. The snow was mostly gone, and everyone was eager to leave the ranch. They split up at first since each family member had places they wanted to go to, but they would return home together.

Hazel had left the library and was heading to the café when she noticed she was being followed. She had walked past the saloon, and three guys had seen her. They called for her to stop, but she hurried along. Before long, they had caught up with her. Hazel had almost reached Dr. Harper's clinic when one of them grabbed her and pulled her into a small alley next to the building. She tried her best to fight them off, but three against one was not a fair fight.

"Well, beautiful," one of them sneered and pushed her against the wall, covering her mouth with one hand. She used her heel and stomped on his foot with all the strength she had. He started cursing in pain, but let go of her. She tried to get away, but the second guy pulled her into his arms with a creepy smile on his face.

Hazel panicked. She couldn't believe this kept happening to her. She had always felt safe and protected in Willamette Falls and couldn't understand why she was such a target suddenly. What had changed?

The guy holding her started kissing her neck and pushed her further and further into the alley when someone grabbed him from behind and pulled him away from her.

Hazel was beyond frightened, and her entire body was shaking. Jason Clark stepped closer after pulling the other guy off her, but she moved backward, away from him.

"Don't you dare touch me," she snapped, her voice shaking. Jason tried to calm her, but she was hysterical now and pushed him away from her. A moment later, two of the men grabbed the young reverend, and one of them put his gun to Jason's head, ready to pull the trigger. Hazel started yelling for help, but the third guy seized her again and covered her mouth with his hand.

Dave stepped out of the bank, watching in horror how three men attacked Hazel. As he was heading across the street to come to her rescue, he stopped a young boy and told him to get the sheriff.

Everything spun when Hazel hyperventilated. The guy kept choking her, and she gasped for air. She tried to remove his hands from her throat, but to no avail. Her face turned purple. Blackness surrounded her already, and it wouldn't be long before she lost consciousness.

Not taking in her surroundings any longer, Hazel noticed a man sweeping in, and giving the guy's head such a forceful blow with the butt of his rifle that the attacker toppled over and blacked out.

The sheriff and deputy were already handcuffing the other two men and Todd Holden called for more men, who helped carry the third attacker to the sheriff's office.

As soon as Hazel was free, she tried to breathe in as much air at once as she could. Tears welled up in her eyes, and she broke out in sobs. Her entire body tensed up, and Dave lifted her arms into the air and talked to her until her breathing slowed, and she relaxed.

Jason Clark left the scene in a fury. He had wanted to be Hazel's hero, yet one of her protectors had beat him to it once again. The young man cursed to himself as he rushed toward the church. He was determined to be faster next time. Hazel would be his and nobody would stop him for long.

Dave pulled the distressed young woman tight into his arms and held her. When her crying stopped, he lifted her chin and looked into her eyes.

"Thank you, Dave," Hazel whispered, and he kissed her forehead, grateful that he had been able to intervene in time.

Haven watched the entire scene with burning eyes. She couldn't believe that her sister would do something like that to her. Yet, here they were, hiding in an alley, so they could share their affections in private.

When Dave lifted Hazel's chin and leaned down, Haven turned on her heels. She grabbed the reins from Dave's horse, pulled herself into the saddle, and galloped out of the town. Tears shot into her eyes as she dashed toward the ranch. Dave had just kissed Hazel.

Alex and Namito came out of the café when Haven kicked her heels into the sides of Dave's horse. Both stared after her, puzzled. A moment later, Dave led Hazel out of the alley and into Dr. Harper's office. Alex and Namito followed. They had seen the frightened expression on Hazel's face, as well as the uneasiness in Dave's eyes.

Dr. Harper looked up, alarmed. Hazel's eyes were swollen, the blood drained from her face. "What happened?"

"Three guys attacked her and pulled her into the alley next to your clinic. One guy choked her hard until I stepped in and prevented worse. I believe they wanted to kidnap her."

"Who did that?" Namito snapped right away and clenched his fists.

"Todd arrested them," Dave responded calmly, even though he wanted to rip their heads off too.

"Would you, three, please wait outside?" Dr. Harper interjected. "Are her parents in town?" The three young men nodded. "Please let them know what happened, but have them wait outside until I am done examining her."

As soon as he was alone with Hazel, Dr. Harper took her hand and led her to the nearest chair. He could see a bruise forming where she had been choked, and he checked the rest of her throat and neck to make sure she was otherwise unharmed.

"Do you want to talk about it, Hazel?" His warm, caring eyes rested on her face, but she shook her head. "It might be good for you to get it off your chest," he continued, but she couldn't make herself do it.

"I am appalled at what happened to you. I have heard stories from other towns where girls have been abused and kidnapped, and nobody knows what happened to them. I thought Willamette Falls was still safe, and this wouldn't happen here, but the people behind this are working through the country. We need to alert the sheriff and everyone in town to let them know that our daughters and women are in danger, and we have to keep an eye on them."

"You mean there are men out there who kidnap girls and women?"

"Yes. In Boston, girls as young as fourteen disappeared and were never found again. It is like a new evil epidemic is spreading across the country, and there doesn't seem to be a cure."

"So what happened to me today was truly an attempt to kidnap me?"

"It is possible. It could be a coincidence, but the chances are high that this was related to the other incidents."

Hazel was distraught by the news, and she worried about Haven and Brenna. How could anyone feel safe anymore if such evil spread across the country and couldn't be stopped? What if the laws changed, and she inherited her father's ranch? Would that make her and her sisters more of a target?

Terror and fear crept up on her and settled like a dark, gloomy cloud on her mind. For several minutes, it paralyzed her. She heard her parents come in and saw how they spoke with Dr. Harper, but it was as if they were far away and not in the same room. Cold sweat appeared on her forehead and everything around her began to spin.

As soon as the three older adults noticed Hazel's ashen complexion, they rushed over to her. Dr. Harper made her lie on the examination table and told her to breathe slowly, while feeling her pulse.

Helen reached for a towel, poured cold water over it and gently laid it across Hazel's forehead.

Hazel closed her eyes for a moment. The awful feeling of dismay and horror ate her from the inside and covered her entire body. The pressure she felt on her chest was unbearable.

Just when the feeling was about to consume her completely, another sense pushed through, and it was as if someone were telling her not to let fear overpower her.

She breathed through her teeth and fought off the horror that tried to silence her heart and brain. She would not give in and let fear win. Her fighting spirit kicked in full gear, and she relaxed. Life was still beautiful despite evil lurking around every corner, and she would continue to see the blessings in her life.

10

Just A Misunderstanding

When they left the doctor's office and met to ride home, Haven was nowhere to be found, and Dave's horse had disappeared too.

"Does anyone know where Haven is?" Hazel looked around, her brows furrowed.

"We saw her leave right before you and Dave came out of the alley. She seemed to be in a big hurry and looked upset," Namito responded, and a terrible thought entered Hazel's mind.

What if? No, she couldn't have witnessed that part, or did she? Hazel couldn't get home fast enough. She needed to clear the air because if Haven had seen what Hazel thought she might have seen, it wasn't what her sister thought it was.

Haven arrived home, jumped off Dave's horse, and disappeared into the house. She was unable to get the image of her sister and Dave out of her head and started pacing the sitting room.

Her emotions were all over the place. Deep hurt had settled on her heart, and she felt betrayed and angry. Hazel had promised she had no romantic feelings for the young vet, yet they were sneaking around together?

Haven knew if Dave and Hazel had feelings for each other, she had no chance and would never have a chance with Dave. Hazel, and her, were too different, and she was so much quieter than her sister. Part of her wanted to burst out in tears, but another part was furious, and so Haven clenched her fists and kept pacing. When she heard horses outside, she hurried into her room and locked the door. She was not willing nor interested in facing her sister anytime soon.

As soon as Hazel arrived at the ranch, she climbed off her horse and ran inside to find her sister. She kept calling for her, but no answer. When she reached their room and tried to open the door, it was locked.

"Haven, please open the door. We need to talk." Hazel listened but could hear no sound, and there was no response. She knocked loudly.

"Haven, I know you are in there. Please unlock the door."

"Go away!"

"We need to discuss this."

"So, you know why I am so upset?" Haven asked, mumbling to herself.

"I know what you think you saw, but you are wrong," Hazel replied with an urgent tone in her voice. It was quiet for a moment before she heard the unlocking noise, and Haven opened the door wide.

"How could you? Why would you do this to me?"

"Haven, listen—"

"You know how much he means to me. If your feelings for him have changed, why didn't you say so? Sneaking around, lying to my face?"

"It isn't what you think. Dave and I are—"

"You hurt me, Hazel. How can I ever trust you again?" Haven interrupted once again, pain coloring her voice. She looked at her sister with so much anguish that Hazel stepped to the side. Haven ran down the stairs and out of the house.

Hazel threw herself onto her bed and buried her head into her pillow. Tears were dripping off her face, and she sobbed. She even understood her sister.

Haven ran to the lake behind the house and dropped herself onto the bench next to the large oak tree. Only then did she burst out in tears.

Namito stepped closer. He had come out of the barn and was about to walk around the corner toward the front door when Haven scared the heck out of him by opening and slamming it shut. He watched Haven for a while until she calmed down again.

"What's wrong, Haven?" She looked up but didn't answer. "Do you want to talk about it?"

"No. You wouldn't understand, anyway."

"If it is about your broken heart, I understand."

"How do you know that? Oh, I get it. Hazel shares everything with her best friends, doesn't she?" Haven scoffed, her face tightening. Namito looked at her, surprised. Such an outburst was unusual for the quiet Haven.

"No, Hazel has said nothing to me about you and Dave since the day he arrived. And she only said something then because we kept nagging her about why you acted so weird suddenly. Believe it or not, I have eyes in my head and can tell when you have feelings for someone. I've known you for many years, and even though I am not as close to you as to Hazel, I still know you more than you think." Namito continued to watch her.

Haven remained silent, clearly unsure what to say to him after his brief speech, and so she sighed.

"Do you want me to talk to Dave?"

"What for? There is no point since Dave and Hazel have already started courting."

"What?"

"Don't pretend you didn't know. I bet everyone knows they are a couple and sneaking around, so I won't find out."

"What are you talking about, Haven?"

"Really? Are you still playing dumb? Well, I know now. I saw Dave and Hazel today, holding each other tight, hidden away from the public, and Dave kissed Hazel."

Namito looked at her, stunned for several seconds, not sure how to go ahead. Suddenly, it struck him what she must have seen.

"You saw them kissing?"

"No," she had to admit, "but I saw him leaning down to Hazel and knew what was about to happen."

"Haven, listen, you are getting something wrong here. You should talk to your sister and ask what happened. Dave and Hazel are friends."

"Don't defend her, Namito. I saw what I saw. This is so typical—Hazel is always innocent in your eyes, incapable of making mistakes," she responded, pouting, but he heard the hardness in her voice. Haven was about to walk away when Namito clasped her arm.

"You are judgmental, Haven. Hazel would never do something like that. She is far too honest and open to keep things like that a secret, and she would never hurt her sisters like that. I know that Hazel has faults too, but you are wrong about her and unfair," he snapped.

"For your information, Hazel was attacked in town today and nearly kidnapped. Dave was the one who rescued her, and you probably saw them together afterward when he was trying to comfort her. There is nothing between them except friendship." His eyes were dark with anger, and he glanced at her impatiently.

Haven turned as white as a bedsheet. "Are you serious?"

"Yes. Hazel had a horrible experience in town today and was choked so badly she almost passed out. She had every right to be comforted after such an ordeal." His voice was firm and angry. Haven nodded, her eyes wide with shock and concern. "You owe your sister an apology."

Without replying to his last remark, she hurried back to the house and looked for her twin. Hazel was still in their room, but she had calmed down again.

Haven pulled her into her arms and hugged her. "I am so ashamed, Hazel. I am sorry I misjudged you and that I ever doubted you. How awful that something so dreadful almost happened to you. Namito just gave me a piece of his mind and told me what you went through. I hope you can forgive me."

"It is fine, Haven. I have forgiven you, and I even understood you. If you only saw him comforting me, it must have looked questionable. I can promise you, though, that Dave and I are not in love. He is like an older brother to me."

"Will you be okay, though? I can't even imagine having to go through something so terrifying."

"We need to be careful and should not go places on our own anymore," Hazel remarked and told Haven everything Dr. Harper had told her. Both girls agreed that they would not risk being alone. Hazel loved her independence and didn't want to have a protector by her side all the time. She realized, though, that it would be incredibly stupid if she were to play with the fire just to prove she could survive without a man looking out for her.

Hazel began studying hard for her big test, and Alex did what he could to prepare her for it as well as the reactions from male participants and those who would test her knowledge. They both knew she had to prepare herself for ugly feedback, even rejection, and so she made sure she listened to Alex's instructions.

One day, while Alex and Hazel worked together in the dining room, they heard a loud knock on the front door. Haven and Helen were upstairs cleaning, and her father was somewhere on the ranch, so Hazel stood and answered the door. A young, tall, handsome man stood in front of her and gave her a winning smile.

"What can I do for you, Sir?"

"Is this the Buchannon Ranch? I am looking for Alex Camden."

Before Hazel could even respond, Alex stepped behind her.

"Miles, what are you doing here?" He eased Hazel to the side and gave the strange man a brotherly hug.

"Just came back from Australia and thought I would visit my big brother before returning home," Miles retorted. Hazel looked from one to the other. Alex had never mentioned his brother before, so having him show up at the ranch like that was strange.

"Miles, this is Hazel Buchannon and Hazel, my brother Miles."

Hazel smiled at him, and he enthusiastically shook her hand.

"It's been a long journey, and I am tired and exhausted. I am in desperate need of a nap," he said, while winking at the young woman. "Can I lie down somewhere?"

Alex nodded and led his brother to the empty bedroom in his apartment. They talked for a few minutes, before the young teacher returned to the dining room.

Alex wanted to dive straight back into the lesson, but Hazel was not ready to move on right away.

"So, how come you never mentioned you had a brother?"

Alex sighed. "Miles is not the easiest person to get along with, unfortunately. He has some unpleasant traits and is someone who doesn't see the need for work. He likes his freedom and doesn't want to be trapped. My dad has thrown him out of the house many times in hopes Miles would realize he has to work for his survival. He only takes on jobs for a short time. Then he travels around, visiting relatives or returning home to get his hands on more cash or at least being fed and having a roof over his head. I haven't seen him in three years, and I think he spent most of that time with relatives in Australia. I love my brother, but whenever he shows up, it rarely takes long before he gets into trouble."

Hazel gave Alex an understanding smile. "Maybe Pa can hire him for a while."

"Excellent idea. Miles needs to work for his stay here."

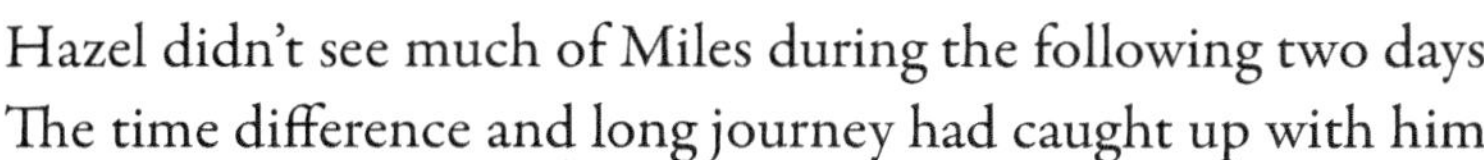

Hazel didn't see much of Miles during the following two days. The time difference and long journey had caught up with him, and so he slept.

Two days after his arrival, Hazel and Haven had a horseback riding date with Namito, Alex, and Dave and were waiting on the front porch for them. Alex and Miles joined the girls first, and Miles greeted Hazel with a big grin on his face.

"It is good to see you again, Miles," Hazel said as she approached him with a kind smile. "Were you able to settle in?"

He nodded, and they exchanged a few words before Namito and Dave showed up. The horses were saddled, and soon they were on their way to a lake not too far from their house. It was the end of March and warm for this time of the year. They soaked in the sun and the smell of spring.

Miles stayed by Hazel's side and immersed her in a lively conversation. Namito and Alex watched the two like hogs and with mixed feelings. Alex knew that his brother thought highly of himself and always assumed that no girl could resist his charm. He also knew about Miles's horrible temper and how offended he got when a girl was not interested in him, so he was concerned. Hazel would not hold back when she was not okay with something, which worried Alex. He wasn't concerned about Hazel, he knew she could stand her ground, but his brother acted embarrassing when he was offended.

Namito didn't like the unspoken bond that seemed to form between Miles and Hazel. He always disliked guys who threw themselves at every girl they met, and Namito was certain Miles was that type of guy.

After a few minutes of watching the two, Namito couldn't handle it anymore. He knew he had to do something.

"Hey Hazel," he yelled with a grin, and when she looked over her shoulder, her serious expression changed into a sassy smile. She knew what Namito wanted to do.

"You will lose," she shot back and sped up her horse. Pretty quickly, the two were head-to-head. Dave and Haven followed suit, and Alex caught up with his brother.

"Miles, stay away from Hazel. She isn't a girl to play around with. The girls here are modest and have high standards and take relationships seriously."

"So what? Hazel and I are getting along, and if she falls in love with me, that's not my fault. There are many out there who can't resist my charm."

"Your arrogance will be your downfall one day. I am giving you a fair warning. Hazel will not hold back if you overstep the boundaries, so don't act offended and hurt when she puts you in your place."

Miles scoffed at his brother. "You are her teacher. You shouldn't be interested in her that way and be jealous just because she might be interested in me."

"I am not jealous. I am trying to give you well-meant advice before you make a fool out of yourself and embarrass me in front of my friends."

"I don't need your advice. I can take care of myself."

Alex shook his head before both of them hurried after the rest of them.

"I won," Hazel cheered and jumped off the back of her horse. "Told ya." She grinned at Namito, and he shook his head at her little celebration. Her childlike excitement always amused him.

"You were lucky," he responded.

"Ha, whatever. That was pure skill," she shot back, before she scooped up water with her hands and splashed it into his face. Hazel burst out laughing when she saw his shocked expression but ran away as fast as she could because Namito wouldn't let that go unpunished.

Sure enough, he was right behind her only moments later, but before he could grab her, she had reached a tree and quickly climbed up a few branches. The rest of the group laughed, and Namito grinned.

"Just you wait. I will get you back."

Haven giggled too but stayed in the background since she had no desire to end up in the lake. The air was nice and warm, but she could imagine how cold the water was. When Dave slipped and nearly fell into the lake, even Haven's giggling turned into laughter. Hazel watched everything from a safe distance.

Miles and Alex both chuckled when Dave walked toward Haven with a deadly stare. She hid behind Namito.

"Please help me, Namito. You laughed at him, too, so, why should I get punished?"

The young man grinned. "Sorry, Haven. If I protect you, I might end up in the lake myself, and I don't feel like that today."

"Traitor," she mumbled. She turned around, looking for a hiding place, but Dave had reached her and lifted her off her feet.

"Please, Dave. Don't do this to me," she begged, but the young man was unmoved. Before Haven could say or do anything else, she flew screaming through the air and into the lake. When she appeared above water again, the four men stood there laughing. Haven just shook her head, but she was relieved that the water wasn't as cold as she thought it would be.

While Dave was busy with Haven, Hazel climbed off the tree and snuck up on the now laughing men. Haven swam out of the way. Before Dave and Namito knew what was happening, Hazel gave them a strong push, and the two men ended up where Dave had thrown Haven. Hazel hid behind Alex and Miles.

"Please, Alex, you need to help me."

"Definitely not. Actions have consequences, and some people beg for the consequences," Alex responded with an amused grin.

"Fine, that works for me too." Hazel gave her teacher and his brother a big shove, and they joined the two other men in the lake. Haven laughed out loud, and Hazel giggled when she saw Namito and Dave hurrying out of the water. Like lightening, she turned around and sprinted back to the tree to get out of reach, but this time Namito was faster. He grabbed her around her waist and handed her over to Dave. The twenty-seven-year-old threw her over his broad shoulder and ran back to the lake.

When they reached the water, Dave took Hazel off his shoulder. He held her upper body, and Namito grabbed her feet. They began swinging her back and forth before they let go. She soared through the air before splashing into the water.

When she emerged and shook her fist at them, Namito and Dave jumped back into the lake. Dave lifted Hazel on his shoulders, and Alex did the same with Namito.

Hazel and Namito tried to push each other from the shoulders of the other person. The young woman burst out giggling when Dave made Alex and Namito fall. She was only a moment longer on Dave's shoulders, though, since Namito swam behind Dave's back and pulled her into the water.

As soon as Hazel had her head above water again, she noticed Haven, sitting on the shore, shivering. She swam over to her sister, climbed out of the lake, ran to Haven's horse, and grabbed a blanket they always had on the saddles. She wrapped the blanket around her sister's shoulders, and Haven gave her a grateful smile for remembering. The young woman was trembling like an aspen leaf.

"That was fun," Dave exclaimed as he climbed out of the water, and Hazel nodded, grinning.

"It was, but if Haven gets sick now, you guys will be in trouble," she scolded Namito and Dave.

"I am not worried," Dave responded, "she is a tough cookie just like you. However, if it helps her, I am more than willing to give her a big wet hug." He stepped closer, and Haven's heart skipped a beat.

"Don't you dare? That girl is wet enough," Hazel responded, and when Dave turned around to grab a blanket from his saddle, Hazel leaned closer to her sister. "...but I bet you would enjoy such a hug."

Haven blushed at once. They noticed now that the sun was going down, and the air wasn't so warm anymore. It was time to return home.

Not long after they started their ride home, Namito spotted Miles, who was trying to get closer to Hazel again. He challenged her to another race, and she responded immediately. Both of them were riding nearly side by side when Namito's horse let out a nervous blow. The young man glanced around and saw a mountain lion on a nearby rock, ready to pounce. Hazel was ahead of him, which meant the animal would get her since they had to pass the lion.

"Hazel, wait," he shouted, trying to put enough urgency into his voice, but she only looked back at him for a split-second and laughed.

"No way, you are trying to trick me, so you can pass me. That will not work, Mister."

Panic struck him, making him to push his horse to speed up. When he was right next to Hazel, he pulled her off her horse, but before he had the chance to put her down, the lion collided with him and dragged them all to the ground. It was a hard landing and Hazel laid still for a moment, not wanting to move. Namito, however, had no time to breathe because the giant cat fought him.

Hazel watched in deep shock what was happening, but quickly recovered, stood and grabbed a big rock. She knew Namito was fighting for his life, so she threw the rock at the mountain lion, which distracted the cat enough to turn away from Namito and toward her instead.

Namito pulled a knife out of his halter. He was about to stab the aggressive animal when a loud shot rang through the air, and the lion sank to the ground. It was dead.

Hazel looked back and saw Dave with his rifle in hand. She ran to Namito and helped him get up. He had a few scratches on his face, arms, and a wound on his shoulder, but seemed to be okay otherwise.

"Are you all right, Hazel?" He glanced at her, worried. She was pale and in shock, but not hurt.

"I am fine—you should worry about yourself. You were the one who the lion attacked." She took off her neckerchief and dabbed the blood off his shoulder.

A moment later, the rest of the group reached them, and Dave and Alex jumped off their horses.

"Are you two okay? Hazel, are you hurt?"

"We are okay, it was a shock, but Namito needs a doctor for his shoulder."

Alex nodded. "I go and get Doc Harper." He mounted his horse again and dashed toward the town. Dave and Hazel assisted Namito in climbing on his horse before they walked to their own horses. Dave clasped Hazel's arm.

"Are you sure you are okay?"

"Yes, thanks, Dave. I am only in shock, that's all."

"I've about had it with those crazy accidents. Every time you do something as a group, someone gets hurt," George scolded

Namito and Hazel when they were back on the ranch. Helen touched his arm.

"They help each other, though, and it isn't on purpose."

"I know," he admitted with a snarl, "but it would be nice if we didn't have to get Doc Harper all the time."

After supper, Hazel went outside and sat next to Namito. Alex and Miles had gone to their rooms, and Dave was playing chess with Jackson.

"Why are you so determined to keep me away from Miles, Namito?"

He looked at her, surprised. "You noticed that?"

"I am not dumb. It was obvious."

"I don't want you to get hurt. I don't want you to have feelings for Miles only to find out he is not serious about what he claims to be feeling for you. My gut tells me he likes to play around with women, but doesn't want to give up his freedom. He sees girls as prey."

Hazel shook her head. "I am touched you look out for me so much, but I am not a child anymore. I have no interest in him romantically, and that will not change. He is not my type, and I am stubborn enough not to let anyone play around with me. If he is like that, I guess he has to learn that there are girls who take relationships seriously and are not interested in games."

"That's why he is after you. He sees you as a challenge."

"He can challenge me all he wants, but that will make no difference to me. I am nice to him because he is Alex's brother, not because I am interested in him."

"Hazel..."

"I am not looking for a relationship right now and aren't drawn to men who are in love with themselves. Please trust me."

"I trust you, Hazel, but I don't trust him."

"Do you think Alex would let him stay here if he was dangerous?"

"He isn't dangerous, but I am concerned about his motives."

"Let's see what happens. I promise you I will be careful and won't let Miles corner me."

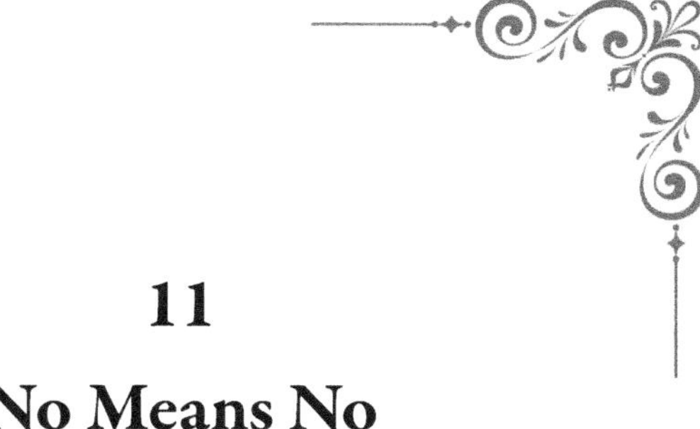

11
No Means No

Hazel kept her promise. Miles tried several times to get alone time with her, but she declined his invitations and advances, even though she stayed friendly. Hazel was sure he would eventually get the message, but her disinterest made it more exciting for him.

When Hazel needed time to herself one evening, she went to her favorite spot, the little lake behind the house. She stood against the fence and closed her eyes for a moment to let her thoughts wander, breathe in the pleasant-smelling evening air, and listen to the crickets. It was heavenly, and Hazel was grateful that this special place on earth was part of her life.

Miles had watched her over the past few weeks and knew that she took these timeouts for herself. When he saw her leave the house that evening, he followed her.

Hazel was greatly startled, when an arm came around her shoulders and she opened her eyes at once, looking up to see who had approached her like that. Miles grinned at her.

"What are you doing out here, Miles?" she asked, even though she didn't want to know the answer. She removed his arm from her shoulders and stepped away from him.

"I want to tell you how much you mean to me," he responded.

"Oh?"

He grabbed her hand. "I have fallen in love with you, Hazel. I know you like me too, so let's give *us* a try."

"Miles..."

"I know you are young and have no experience with love, but I am okay with that. I can teach you."

"No experience?" she mumbled to herself, frowning. Miles stepped closer, and she moved away from him, but couldn't go any further as she had the big oak tree behind her. "You don't understand," she began again, but he continued to interrupt her.

"You need not be afraid of these feelings. Everyone falls in love at one point." He took her head into his hands and was about to kiss her when she shoved him away from her.

"You are going too far, Miles. We hardly know each other and—"

"No matter, this is a way to get to know a person," he interrupted with a grin and pulled her into his arms. She tried to get out of his hold, but he wouldn't let go. When he tried to kiss her a second time, she slapped his face. He looked at her, stunned for a moment, but continued his unwanted advances.

"Oh, you are one of those? You prefer it the rough way." He was about to grab her around her waist when she kicked him against his leg and smacked his hands away. She was furious.

"How dare you? I never allowed you to step that close to me, and I didn't permit you to force your advances on me. If you thought my kindness to be a romantic interest, you are mistaken."

Miles was speechless. So far, it had always been him who ended a relationship or put a girl in her place. Before he could respond, however, she continued.

"Who do you think you are? I don't like it when someone tries to force me to do something I don't want to do, and I am having none of it." Her eyes spat fire, and she was fuming. His expression changed from shock to offense.

"Don't be such a baby. I just wanted to have fun."

"I am not such a girl, Miles. A kiss is something personal and intimate and should be shared with the person you love and not because you want to have *fun*. I try hard to be modest and have high standards, and I expect a man to respect that."

He scoffed. "You are old-fashioned and silly. You won't find a man who will respect you and your prudish behavior."

"We shall see about that," she shot back. "A proper man will respect me if he wants respect in return." She turned around and started walking back to the house.

"I am not running after you, Hazel. If you leave now, it is over between us."

"Nothing can be over if it hasn't even started yet. Your manipulations will not work on me."

"You are stupid and arrogant and will end up as an old spinster." He was getting angrier by the minute, but Hazel only shook her head at his childish behavior.

"I don't care. If a man can't respect me and my wishes, I will gladly turn into a spinster. I refuse to be someone I am not just to please the ego of a man. Men like you have to be reminded that they aren't a God, and women don't have to worship the ground they are walking on," she finished saying before turning the corner toward the house.

Miles was fuming and kicked the oak tree with all the anger he felt.

"How can anyone be such an arrogant, self-centered ratbag? What nerve he has to get offended after me telling him to stop his unwelcomed advances. I can't believe this man," she muttered to herself before running into Namito, who had come outside to look for her.

"Which man can't you believe?"

It startled Hazel when he stood in front of her so suddenly, but she tried to get rid of him as she was still angry.

"Oh, I was talking to myself, everything is okay," she replied without making eye contact and tried to walk past him, but Namito didn't let her go.

"Hazel?"

"Okay, fine," she burst out. "I am upset and furious because Miles followed me to the lake while I was trying to get alone time and attempted to—"

"And attempted to what?" Namito growled, suspicion in his mind.

"He tried to kiss me several times, telling me he was in love with me. I asked him to stop and that we hardly knew each other. He had the nerve to tell me that kissing was a way to get to know a person. I slapped him, kicked his leg, and he was still not getting the message. I mean, can you believe that guy?" She had talked herself into a rage and only stopped for a short breather.

"And then?"

"And then I exploded and told him off. He acted offended and childish as if I were the one overreacting, and he didn't deserve to be put in his place." Hazel repeated the entire incident precisely as it had happened and what she had said to him.

Namito was speechless at first and couldn't believe Miles's bold and shameless advances toward her, but when he pictured her exploding temper and the young man's angry reaction, the young Indian burst into a fit of laughter. Hazel looked at him, stunned.

"May I ask what you find so funny?"

Namito continued to laugh and pulled her with him until they reached the lake and her favorite spot where they sat on the bench. He had barely calmed down when his eyes wandered, and he saw the oak tree. He began laughing again.

"Namito," she scolded him, trying to find out why he was laughing so hard.

"Sorry, Hazel. I just envisioned how you bit his head off, and he got offended in return. I am sure he is pretty hurt now. A male ego like his can't handle rejections well."

She grinned now too, but only for a second before she turned serious. "Do you think I was too harsh with him? Perhaps I shouldn't have been so blunt and direct, but he made me so angry, and I couldn't control my temper any longer."

Namito put his arm around her shoulders. "No, Hazel. You did what you had to do, and that was good. He is the type of man who doesn't get friendly and polite rejections. He will act offended now, though, and will try to hurt you too. That said, your bluntness is refreshing as it isn't used to be mean and cruel, but to make a point. We always know you mean business and are honest. So many women, and men too, set out to manipulate those around them. Sometimes brutal honesty and bluntness make it easier to be around a person. Some people only learn the hard way."

Hazel sighed, but nodded in agreement. Namito was right.

Miles stayed away from her for the next few days, but it didn't bother her. She told Alex the day after the incident what had happened so that he would hear it from her. He apologized for his brother, but Hazel didn't blame him for it. It was Miles's fault.

After a few days, he went to town every day and came back with a girl, probably a girl from the saloon, and positioned himself with her in spots Hazel had to pass. Hazel rolled her eyes when she saw him kissing her. It was pathetic to witness his childish behavior, and she didn't even pay much attention to it.

George put an end to it and told Miles he could meet his girlfriend in town, but he didn't want to see them kissing on the ranch anymore. Miles was not happy about it, but knew he had to follow the rules, or they would send him away. He was not ready yet to give up on Hazel.

Alex was embarrassed, but his younger brother didn't listen, no matter how much he tried to talk sense into him.

Two weeks after the incident, Hazel rode into town to get a few things from the store. She was about to get back on her horse when the girl Miles had kissed stepped next to her.

"Miss Buchannon, may I talk to you?"

Hazel turned to face her and looked at her with a smile. "Of course. What can I do for you?"

The girl glanced around shyly. She never dared to talk to people, and only spoke when someone spoke to her first. A few older ladies stood not too far from Hazel and gave the young woman a disapproving stare-down. However, Hazel was raised to be polite and kind and not judge a person, since outsiders never knew what was happening in someone else's life. She didn't care what the fine ladies of the town thought of her.

"I wanted to ask," the girl began, but stopped when one of the older ladies approached them.

"How dare you talk to someone on the street, especially a lady like Miss Buchannon?" she scolded the young woman, and the girl lowered her eyes, but Hazel hated behavior like that and ignored the older lady.

"You can ask me anything you want," she said in an encouraging tone and smiled at the girl.

"Miss Buchannon, you don't have to talk to people like her. You are a lady, and she is a simple saloon girl. Talking to women of her kind will ruin your reputation." She tried to pull Hazel away from the girl, but that was something Hazel could not stand at all. She pulled her arm free and straightened her back.

Before Hazel could even say anything, a crowd of curious onlookers started forming around them. Not much happened in the tiny town, and so anything exciting was always welcome. The sudden audience made the shy girl nervous, and she was about to hurry back into the saloon when Hazel clasped her arm.

"No, it is okay. Please stay." Hazel kept her eyes on the shy girl and didn't turn away until it was evident she would wait. Only then did Hazel turn her attention to the older lady.

"Mrs. Brenton. As kind as it is that you care about my reputation, I think I am old enough to decide with whom I can have a conversation and which people I should avoid."

The older lady looked offended. "Miss Buchannon, you should follow my counsel and not converse with people like her," she said, pointing her finger at the young woman with a smug expression. That made Hazel angry. She hated arrogant, judgmental behavior like that and would not put up with it.

"Why should I care what other people think of me? None of us is entitled to judge a person by their clothes, work, or how rich or poor they are. We know nothing about their background and situation and don't know why they do something we might disagree with. Nobody has the right to tell me who I can talk to, especially not a bunch of presumptuous women."

Harriet Brenton gasped for air. She was beyond upset now and turned red. A few of the onlookers grinned to themselves. Hazel had said what many thought.

"How dare you talk to me like that? Do you know who I am?" Harriet snapped.

"I know who you are, Mrs. Brenton," Hazel replied sweetly. "Everyone in this town knows who you are."

"I expect an apology from you."

"Excuse me?"

"I don't deserve to be treated like that or spoken to in such a rude manner."

"There is nothing I need to apologize for, Mrs. Brenton. You were the one who rudely interrupted a conversation that had nothing to do with you. It is you who continues to tell people what they can and cannot do or say. You seem to be under the impression you are in charge here, but I can assure you that you are not. I talk to who I want to, and you have no say in it. You are welcome to gossip about me and tell everyone what a naughty girl I am, but I am not faced by it. Please remember to look for the beam in your eye and stay out of my business. Good day, Mrs. Brenton." Hazel turned away from her, but saw out of the corner of her eye how the older lady stormed off.

As soon as the wealthy ladies were out of earshot, everyone around started clapping. Hazel looked around, stunned. She had not expected such a reaction. Before she could address the girl from the saloon again, the general store owner stepped next to her.

"Well done, Hazel. I am glad someone had the guts to put that lady in her place." He patted her shoulder and walked back into his store. Hazel just shook her head.

"I guess that will be the talk of the town for a while," she said, grinning, as she turned back to the saloon girl. "Please don't pay attention to these arrogant ladies. They might influence some people, but you can always talk to me."

Tears entered the eyes of the young woman, and she lowered her gaze. "Thank you, Miss Buchannon. I haven't met many people who are kind to me and would talk to me."

Hazel believed that. People judged saloon girls and women from a brothel harshly and didn't want to be seen with them. Even men, who paid for their services and were regular customers, snuck around in secret as they were worried about their reputation. Of course, some women wanted to do that type of work and enjoyed the sinful life, but most girls who worked in those places were forced to do it by men who owned them.

"I wanted to ask if Miles Camden still lives on the ranch. He was so kind to me in the beginning, and I thought he was interested in me. Then he told me your father doesn't allow saloon girls on his property, and we couldn't meet up anymore.

At first, I believed what he said, but I haven't seen him since and knowing now how kind you are, I think he made it up to get rid of me. Perhaps he wasn't serious about a relationship?" The young woman lowered her gaze again.

"What's your name?"

"Shelly," she responded shyly.

"Shelly, my father is not like that. He didn't tell Miles he couldn't bring you to our ranch because you were a saloon girl, but because he kept kissing you for everyone to see. Miles is one of those men who like enjoy playing around with the hearts of women. He took a fancy to me, and when I rejected him, he was angry and tried to make me jealous by using you."

Shelly sighed. "I was afraid of that. It was too good to be true that a handsome man like Miles was interested in me."

"You deserve better than that, Shelly. No man should use a woman to get to someone else. It is just not right."

"Thank you, Miss Buchannon."

"Please, call me Hazel." Hazel squeezed the hand of the other woman. She was about to climb on her horse when Miles stepped out of the shadow behind the saloon. He had watched and heard everything. Shelly smiled at him, but he ignored her and pushed himself between Shelly and Hazel.

"Miles, why are you so rude to her?"

He shrugged his shoulders. "Shelly is a girl from the saloon and probably doesn't even understand what is going on. Come with me, I want to talk to you." He grabbed her hand and wanted to pull her away from her horse, but Hazel pulled her hand back. She smelled the alcohol coming from him and was disgusted. Shelly stepped away, but Hazel saw how hurt she was, and it made her angry.

"I am not coming with you. If you have something to say, say it here. You owe Shelly an apology. Your impertinent and impolite behavior is embarrassing. You should be ashamed of yourself."

Miles glanced at Shelly before turning back to Hazel.

"She is just a saloon girl. Now back to us. Admit it, you were jealous when I kissed Shelly, weren't you?"

Hazel shook her head. "Definitely not. You are only looking for a shiny new toy, and I told you I am not interested in you. It is time for you to move on and stop using other women hoping to get to me." She was about to turn around when he grabbed her arm and pulled her closer.

"Let go of my arm, Miles," she snapped, trying to get away from him.

"What if I try my luck with your shy twin sister? Perhaps she would enjoy the extra attention." He looked down on her with a nasty grin.

"So because I am rejecting you and your manly pride is hurt, you are now threatening my sister? Let me be clear with you today. My sister is not stupid, and she has no interest in you either. Your childish tantrums are not attractive, and it is time for you to grow up. Leave my sister out of it. If you can't handle girls who don't enjoy playing around, maybe it is time for you to leave." Hazel pulled her arm out of his grip to finally get away from him when he tried to seize her wrist. She slapped his hand away.

"Stop touching me," she barked at him, her eyes dark with anger. "Leave me alone before I call for help."

"You think I feel rejected," he scoffed. "I don't need you or your sister. There are plenty of women out there who will gladly be with me. Let's go, Shelly," he responded with disdain and pulled the girl with him toward the saloon.

Hazel stepped in their way. "You are drunk, Miles. Leave Shelly alone. If you don't leave this instant, I will call the sheriff."

He laughed out loud. "For what? Because I drank too much, or because I am amusing myself with a saloon girl? I bet he does the same thing."

"You are disgusting."

"I can live with that. Shelly?" He was about to pull the shy saloon girl back into his arms when Hazel stepped between them once again.

"You are welcome to take her place if you are so desperate to protect her," he said, grinning, pushed Shelly out of the way, and snatched Hazel by her wrists. For the first time, she felt fear toward him. The situation reminded her too much of the encounters she had with Jason Clark. She knew she had to stand her ground and couldn't show her fear.

"Let go of me before I yell for help."

"You will regret rejecting me, Hazel. I don't take no for an answer. I am going to—"

"Is there a problem, Hazel?" Hank Thompson, the saloon owner, stepped next to her and gave Miles a death stare, and he let go of her arms.

"No, everything is okay. This young man was just about to leave," she responded, feeling relieved that someone had stepped in. Miles looked from one to the other before turning around and walking away from the scene.

"Seems to be an unpleasant fellow. Are you okay?" Hank asked, looking concerned.

She nodded—still a bit shaken.

"I am fine. Miles is unpleasant. Women are only toys to him, and if you reject him, he gets offended." She watched Miles, who had now reached his horse, swung himself over the saddle, and rode away. Hazel wasn't scared of riding home by herself, but she also didn't want to meet him alone, since he wasn't sober. Hank observed her.

"Do you want me to escort you home? He probably won't do anything to you, but just in case?"

"Thank you. I have to admit, I was hoping for that."

"I will get my horse and let my wife know." When he saw Harriet Brenton and her followers, he grinned at Hazel. "Unless, of course, you would rather not ruin your reputation."

"If being escorted by a man who looks out for others ruins my reputation, so be it. They can bad-mouth me all they want."

"Thank you so much, Hazel. Please look after yourself, and if we see each other again, don't feel obligated to greet me. I understand and won't get offended." Shelly gave her a warm smile.

"I am not like that and never will be. One piece of advice, though, stay away from Miles."

12

Judge Not, That Ye Be Not Judged!

"I am impressed with you, Hazel."

"Why?"

"I heard the whole incident and what Mrs. Brenton said to you and about Shelly. Not only did you stand up against that old hag," he said but stopped when Hazel cleared her throat in a rebuking manner, and he grinned.

"Forgive me, but she is one. You not only stood up against her, but showed what's in you. Few people defend a saloon girl, and Shelly is grateful beyond imagination."

"It was nothing. She was mistreated and judged for no reason, and I would always do it again."

"I beg to differ that it was nothing. Shelly had a harsh and horrible life. I met her a few weeks ago in Salem. It was supposed to be a business trip to buy more supplies for the saloon when I came across this secret auction in which they auctioned off women. I couldn't believe my eyes. I have seen much in my life, but that was by far the evilest. If I had enough money, I would have freed them all. Shelly stood out to me because she was so terrified and shy. I knew I had to get her out of there before she ended up in the wrong hands. I reported the auction to the sheriff as soon as I had paid for Shelly. By the time the sheriff made it there, they had disappeared."

Hazel gasped in horror. Why were women treated in such a horrific way?

"My wife Caroline and I took over my father's saloon when he died, but we decided we would not use women for the pleasure of men. Every girl who works for us, or has worked for us, was rescued, and we are giving them a home and a way to earn money."

He sighed before he continued. "Shelly is so shy. She is not even a suitable fit to work at the saloon. Unfortunately, nobody will give her a chance because everyone thinks Shelly is immoral and should be avoided. Her mother died when she was a baby, and she grew up with a violent father who beat and tortured her daily. She is twenty-five years old and has never experienced love. Her father sold her to a man named Gabriel McKellar, and that's how she ended up at the auction."

Hazel winced when she heard the name and swallowed hard. So, he was one of those horrible men who kidnapped or bought girls and women.

"I wish I could find a better place for her, somewhere where she feels safe and can develop her talents without fear."

"Let me talk to my father. Perhaps we can take her in and give her a safe home."

"You have a heart of gold," he said, squeezing her hand, which made her blush.

When they reached the ranch, Hank looked at her with a serious expression. "Please tell your father what the young man did to you today. He should not be around you anymore."

She nodded and watched him ride back to Willamette Falls. She felt bad for Alex, but Hank was right, Miles had to go.

Her father and Alex were sitting in the living room when she entered, and so she told them everything right away. Alex was shocked and went straight to his apartment and asked Miles to leave at once.

Miles finished packing before he asked one of the ranch hands to take him to Willamette Falls, so he could catch the next stagecoach. It was time to pay his parents another visit.

A few days after the incident with Miles, George Buchannon called Hazel into his office. When she opened the door, she noticed that nearly everyone was present.

"What's going on here? Did something happen that you have to have a secret meeting?" Hazel grinned, and a cheerful twinkle appeared in her eyes.

"Helen and I have just returned from town. We had an interesting conversation with Mrs. Brenton." George gave his daughter a stern glance, even though she could see amusement in his features. Hazel only rolled her eyes and sat on a chair. "So? Do you have something to say?"

"Say about what?" she asked innocently as if she did not understand her father's meaning.

"Why didn't you tell us you had an encounter with her?"

Hazel bit her lip. She wanted to burst out laughing because, by now, she had regained her humor.

"I forgot about it. Why? Has Mrs. Brenton complained about me?"

George looked directly into her eyes and noticed a mischievous sparkle. His daughter knew perfectly well, that the older lady wouldn't have let this incident go without making a fuss about it. He hid his grin and continued to stare at her with a straight face.

"Yes, she was furious with you and told me that your behavior was out of control. She said that you were insulting and disrespectful and that I wasn't strict enough with you as a child."

The door opened, and Brenna walked into the room. "What is going on here?"

"I am informing Hazel about something that happened in town today," George commented before turning his full attention back to his daughter.

"Mrs. Brenton said you need a good spanking. She claims a young woman is never too old to get good old discipline from her father, and that I didn't put you over my knee enough." George raised an eyebrow and continued to stare at her without flinching.

Hazel felt the heat creep into her cheeks, and her entire face was in flames instantly. Her father had never spanked her in her life, but he knew how to stare right through her, and she had not expected the conversation to go in such an embarrassing direction, especially with all these witnesses around. If only the floor would open up and swallow her.

Dave, Namito, Alex, Haven, and even Helen had to turn away to stop themselves from laughing. Everyone knew George was enjoying this conversation a little too much, but seeing Hazel's reaction was priceless. Brenna, however, stared at him with wide eyes.

Jackson's expression was just as stern as her father's, which made the young woman even more uneasy and uncomfortable, and she felt guilty, though she had done nothing wrong.

"Perhaps you should entertain the thought of serious discipline, George. If Hazel behaved like that in public, she needs to learn a lesson. As Haven's Godfather, I support that. I mean, she could become a poor influence on her sister."

As if on cue, George stood and walked toward his daughter with a determined expression in his eyes. It caught her off guard, and she wasn't sure how to respond and what to expect. Brenna jumped in front of her.

"Pa, no, please. Whatever Hazel did, I am sure she didn't mean any harm." Brenna looked at the older girl with compassion and empathy.

"Brenna, this is between Hazel and me. Do not make me come after you next," he growled to make it sound more intimidating. Helen and Jackson pulled the younger girl out of the way.

Brenna didn't see the playful sparkle in everyone's eyes, and she didn't notice that Helen and Jackson had a tough time keeping a straight face. She was mortified.

When George clasped Hazel's hand and pulled her out of her chair, she panicked.

"Wait, Pa, please. You can't do something like that to me. I did nothing wrong," she stammered and tried to loosen his grip.

Hazel looked intimidated. It wasn't the punishment that scared her because her father would never hurt her. But being humiliated in front of everyone and treated like a child was too embarrassing for her.

When Brenna saw the distressed expression on Hazel's face, she jumped into action again. "Pa, if you punish Hazel, I'll report you to the sheriff and will never talk to you again." Her lips were pressed together, and she had her eyes unyielding on the man she saw as her father.

George stopped in his tracks. He looked at his step-niece, but didn't let go of Hazel's hand. When Brenna settled down again, he continued moving backward, leaned himself against his desk, and pulled Hazel ...into his arms for a loving hug. Hazel was beyond relieved and sighed.

Brenna looked taken aback at first, but eventually grinned. Everyone else burst out laughing. George lifted his daughter's chin and made her look at him. She was still bright red.

"That was mean, Pa," she said with a bashful yet amused smile.

"Yes, it was," he responded, smirking, and kissed her on her forehead. "I am sorry I scared you, but it was too tempting. I am also sorry you thought I was being serious, Brenna. I couldn't help myself, though." He winked at both of them.

"Did Mrs. Brenton seriously say that?" Hazel's expression was now a mix of mirth and frustration.

"She did. She was upset and angry, but I thought I would hear your version first before believing everything she said. I also asked around town, and when Mr. Bennett told me what he had witnessed, I knew my feelings had been right about Mrs. Brenton. Now, tell me what truly happened."

The room fell silent. They all knew Hazel was too honest to lie about it. She shared the experience and argument word by word. At first, her family was speechless, but soon they started laughing again.

"I thought something like that," George responded after he had calmed down again. "I knew I had raised you better than what Mrs. Brenton claimed, and taught you not to be disrespectful and rude, especially to your elders. Here, the good lady had been begging to be put in her place and receive some serious bluntness."

George didn't like Harriet Brenton either, since she always got involved in everyone's business, but he still believed that everyone deserved respect, and he had taught his girls that very principle.

Harriet Brenton was a woman in her late sixties. She and her late husband William had grown up in Boston. They lived there until they joined the gold rush of 1848 and ended up in California for a year, searching for some promising wealth.

When their oldest son took over their mine and business in California, Mr. and Mrs. Brenton traveled north to find a place for their retirement. One of their stops was Willamette Falls, and they liked it so much that they stayed there and built a big house they could enjoy for the rest of their life.

William passed away two years later. Harriet continued to live her life to the fullest and enjoyed the luxuries her wealth gave her. Her son had inherited everything, but he was kind and giving and ensured that his mother and siblings lacked nothing.

Unfortunately, her wealth made her arrogant, and she considered herself to be better than everyone else. She had high respect for George Buchannon since he was one of the richest men in the territory, but treated everyone else judgmental and poorly.

Hazel told her family about Shelly and what Hank had shared with her, and the life she had. She asked if they could take her in and give her a home and safety.

George, Helen, and Jackson looked at each other with a grateful smile on their faces. Hazel had an enormous heart and would always stand up for those who couldn't stand up for themselves.

"She can live with us. I know what Caroline and Hank are doing for those poor girls, and they should receive credit for it, but they don't want credit. I wish the rest of the town would look past the alcohol and the reputation of a saloon and look behind the facades. If Mrs. Brenton paid attention, she would see that the Thompson's are an outstanding couple. They do what they can to rescue girls from horrible men and evil slavery work."

Helen smiled at her stepdaughter. "I will teach Shelly everything about housekeeping, and if she feels comfortable with it, she can attend school lessons with Brenna and the boys. I am sure you won't mind an extra student?" She looked at the young teacher.

Alex smiled. "I will gladly have her join the lessons."

"She can move into the guest room we still have next to the kitchen, but perhaps you girls can make it more welcoming and give it a homely touch."

Hazel felt happy. She knew she could always count on her family, and her heart jumped for joy when she thought about Shelly and how much her life would change now.

"Wonderful. I will return to town tomorrow to let Shelly know and bring her home with me," Hazel responded.

"Are you sure you should do that so soon?" Namito asked, causing Hazel to stare at him as if he had lost his mind. "I am just saying, Mrs. Brenton might cross your path again."

"So what? I did nothing wrong and only told her to stop meddling in other people's business. I will not act as if I fear her now."

Namito and Hazel went to Willamette Falls together the following day. Helen had given Hazel a shopping list, and Namito wanted to be a first-hand witness if it came to another encounter with the old lady. Plus, he could help with the heavy things they had to buy.

As soon as they entered the town, they saw Mrs. Brenton and her followers further down the road. They stopped at the saloon first, and the ladies watched everything with disapproving expressions on their faces.

Hazel went inside and spoke to Hank and Shelly. After a brief conversation, Shelly agreed and promised to gather her few things and be ready when Hazel was done with her shopping.

When Hazel entered the general store, only the shop owner, James Bennett, was in the large room. Namito had gone to the post office to send off a telegram for George Buchannon, but would join Hazel afterward.

Hazel handed her shopping list to the shop owner and began looking at the dresses in the corner. She liked two of them and thought about asking her parents to get those for her birthday.

While Hazel paid attention to the dresses, Harriet Brenton and her friends entered the general store. Before long, more and more people came in, watching curiously. It was obvious that they waited eagerly for another encounter between Hazel and the old lady.

"Good morning, Mrs. Brenton. Ladies," Hazel said with a polite smile on her face. They responded by nodding in her direction, but nothing else. Harriet Brenton kept glancing at her, and although Hazel was aware of it, she pretended she hadn't noticed. When Hazel didn't acknowledge Harriet's looks, even after several minutes, the older lady couldn't hold herself back any longer.

"Don't you have something to say to me, Miss Buchannon?"

Hazel knew what the old lady was referring to, but continued to act clueless.

"No, I don't think so."

"Your father did not talk to you about the situation?"

"What situation?"

James Bennett grinned. Hazel was a true actress and played her part well. Mrs. Brenton gasped for air.

"What situation? My dear, how can you forget something so serious? I complained to your father about you and your horrible behavior. Didn't he mention the conversation I had with him to you?" Frustration and anger colored her voice. Hazel acted as if it had just clicked.

"Oh, that situation. Yes, my father talked to me about it."

Harriet waited for Hazel to continue, but the young woman stayed silent and scanned the bookshelf now.

"And?" Mrs. Brenton's impatient voice made several people smile.

"And what?" Hazel looked at her, stunned and with an expression of confusion.

"I am still waiting for an apology from you. I am sure your father told you to apologize to me."

"No, he didn't. He only wanted to hear my version of the *situation*." Hazel emphasized the last word purposely, but continued to stare at the shelves. Harriet Brenton looked like a stick of dynamite ready to explode. That was the moment Namito entered the building. All the ladies retreated further into the store and away from the young Indian. Their expressions changed from outrage to disgust.

Namito was no fool. He felt the disdain people felt for him simply because he wasn't white. It didn't bother him anymore that many treated him as an outsider because he was an Indian. He was concerned about Hazel, though. She hated such hateful behavior, so he had to keep his cool to ensure things wouldn't escalate.

"Namito, could you please take these sacks to our wagon?"

"Certainly," he replied and winked at her to keep her calm.

"Thank you, you are an angel," she responded, rose to her tiptoes, and kissed him on his cheek. Outraged mumbling came from the ladies, but Hazel ignored it.

Namito grinned to himself. Hazel only did that to drive these ladies up the wall. She wasn't a cuddly girl and kept hugs short unless she needed to be comforted.

Memories of the beginning of their friendship hit Namito suddenly. It had taken him and Rob a long time before she allowed them to hug and touch her. Showing affection other than words was still hard for her, but she valued her friends and family and tried to show them she loved and cared for them. Through years of hard work, she had learned to accept and enjoy hugs from those she loved, and sometimes even reached out on her own.

George had always shown affection and hugged his girls, but their mother didn't. Hazel grew up thinking she had to be tough like her mom and shouldn't show her feelings and affections. Haven needed her father immensely after the twins' mother left, but Hazel kept most of her hurt inside, and no matter how hard George tried, he couldn't reach her little heart to make her open it up to him.

When Hazel went through more traumatizing experiences a few years later, she repressed her feelings even more whenever she was around others. Luckily, George paid attention to her.

Whenever he found her crying, he pulled her into his arms and gave her the love she so desperately needed. Jackson and Robert Mitchell did the same thing. She grew up with these incredible, loving men in her life and learned at a young age that men were her protectors whenever she needed them, and it comforted her.

Since she didn't have a mother during the first ten years of her life, at least not a mother who cared for her, she relied on those men. It was hard for her to reach out to Helen when she became part of the family. She loved Helen, but until her grandmother had moved in with them, she had only received affection from the men in her life.

Her childhood experiences shaped her into a strong, independent woman, but it also affected her ability to show her feelings. Hazel had a big heart and always cared for those around her. However, being open about her struggles continued to be difficult for her even to this day.

Namito heard Hazel asking him again to take the heavy items outside, and he realized he had been lost in thought. He grabbed a big sack of flour, threw it over his shoulder, and left the store.

Mrs. Brenton had tried to ignore Namito, but one comment still slipped out. She said it to the other ladies in hushed tones, but Hazel heard it.

"Well, as long as she keeps company like that, she won't be able to earn the respect of Willamette Fall's upper class."

"I am okay with that," Hazel shot back loudly. "It wouldn't matter anyway, since I haven't seen an upper class in this town."

Harriet Brenton turned bright red, but Hazel's last remark made her speechless. Everyone around grinned. Namito came back inside, grabbed something else, and left the store. Hazel took a box with smaller items from the store owner and was about to go outside when she heard Mrs. Brenton whisper yet again.

"Someone told me not too long ago that Helen Buchannon isn't even Hazel's and Haven's actual mother. Their father was married to some poor nobody, who left her family and ran off with someone else. You would think he learned his lesson, but Mrs. Buchannon was his housekeeper before they got married. He has no class."

Everyone around held their breath. Hazel turned around, but her expression made it clear that she was close to losing her temper. Namito had come back inside and heard what Mrs. Brenton said. He clasped Hazel's arm and squeezed it to let her know she needed to stay calm. She would have stayed calm if Harriet hadn't chosen that moment to yell at the young man.

"How dare you come in here and touch a white girl? Go back to your reservation and stay out of my town. You have no business here."

Outraged mumbling went through the entire store. Namito was fuming, but he bit his tongue because anyone could see that Hazel's blood was boiling, and she was ready to snap.

"How dare you, Mrs. Brenton? This young man here is my best friend, and he can touch me whenever he wants. You have no right to boss him or anyone around. We have every reason to be nice to the Indians. They were here first, and when the greedy white man came, they took everything away from them. So many were killed, and the rest of them get jammed into reservations where they have to live with other tribes and do and eat what the white man tells them. They lost their land and homes, and freedom. That is nothing we should be proud of," she said seething.

"Now, about my family, please keep your judgmental comments to yourself. You know nothing about the situations and background, and I am sick and tired of your evil gossip you like to spread around town. Our private life has nothing to do with you, so stay out of it. You have no right to judge anyone. Indians, blacks, saloon girls are humans and deserve to be treated with respect. Stop meddling in other people's affairs." Hazel breathed through her teeth, but before Mrs. Brenton could say anything, the young woman continued.

"One more thing, Willamette Falls is not *your* town. You weren't even here when the town was founded and moved here a few years ago. Hard work, dedication, and love transformed the area of Willamette Falls and Beaver Creek. The town belongs to everyone who made this place what it is, and you were not part of it." Hazel had to breathe again and paused.

Everyone around started clapping, and Harriet's face turned to a darker shade of red.

Every person who had heard Hazel's speech thought about her words and started to see things with her eyes. It was time to change their thinking and be welcoming and less judgmental toward those who were different. The respect for Hazel Buchannon increased, contrary to the feelings toward Mrs. Brenton.

Harriet was fuming and took a deep breath to give the young woman a piece of her mind, but Hazel was faster.

"If you must, you may complain to my father again, but I promise you one thing: I won't give in, and I will not apologize. I am a grown woman and have my thoughts and opinions on certain things, and nobody can change my mind when I am doing the right thing. Perhaps you should start changing your attitude toward those around you. Stop thinking you are better than everyone else." Hazel gave her a firm glance.

"Oh, and before I forget. Since you are so eager to give out parenting advice and kindly suggested that my father give me some good old discipline, your father should have been the one disciplining. The only one who needs a good spanking is you." Hazel raised her eyebrow, her face red with anger. Harriet Brenton scoffed, offense coloring her voice, but she stormed out of the building.

James Bennett put his arm around Hazel's shoulders. "Thank you for being brave and outspoken and calling it as you see it. We learned an important lesson today." Everyone around nodded, and it took Hazel a while before she could join Namito outside.

As soon as she stepped next to her best friend, he pulled her into his arms and twirled around with her. Onlookers watched it with a smile, and nobody found it disgusting and inappropriate anymore.

"You are a wonderful girl, Hazel. You not only stood your ground and said things that needed to be said, but you have a heart of gold. I am so honored to call you my friend. All of us can learn something from you. You are an inspiring person and an incredible example."

13
No Escape

They introduced Shelly to her new home and room and everyone living on the ranch. Helen found out that Shelly was a seamstress and promised they would help her find work.

After Hazel had shown her the house, she took her outside to show her the barn and stables. The two young women were about to enter the stable when Jackson and his brother Adam came from the other side. Shelly, who had expected no one, bumped into Adam and almost lost balance. He grabbed her arm to steady her, and Hazel also jumped into action. All of them looked worried, but Shelly recovered from the shock and smiled shyly.

"Shelly, may I introduce our foreman Jackson to you?" They shook each other's hands. "And this is Adam. He is Jackson's brother and owns the bank in town."

Shelly blushed when she felt his fascinating stare, but shook his hand. Adam could not stop looking at her beautiful face and began a conversation with her. Hazel and Jackson grinned at each other. Cupid had just shot his arrows, and two individual hearts had found one another.

Shelly settled in quickly. She loved her new life and was grateful for the Buchannon family and all they did for her. Adam Harrison showed up regularly now, and they started courting not long after Shelly had moved to the ranch. It was beautiful to watch Shelly blossom, and every day she changed more into a different person.

Hazel's upcoming examination in Salem was just around the corner, so she spent most of her day studying. She wanted to be ready and show everyone that girls were intelligent and capable of doing well in the business world.

The weather was exceptionally warm for this time of the year, and since she loved being outside, she took her books and went to her favorite spot next to the lake. The sky was so blue, it looked unreal. Birds were chirping, the first insects were out and about, and the trees and plants were blooming.

Hazel made herself comfortable on her bench and breathed in the early spring air. Her spot was secluded as the oak tree was growing, and its branches and fresh green leaves hid the bench from the house.

She had been studying for a while when she saw two squirrels chasing each other. She paused for a moment, watched them run up the oak tree, and jump from branch to branch. It put a smile on her face, and she got up and leaned against the fence next to the lake. She closed her eyes, bent her head back, and just let the sun warm her face.

Suddenly, someone grabbed her hand and pulled her into his arms. She opened her eyes, and there stood Jason Clark right in front of her. She felt the blood drain from her face.

"What are you doing here? You are trespassing," she snapped while trying to get out of his hold, but he had her.

"I am here to claim you as my bride," he responded with a sleazy smile on his face. His lips traced down her face and neck, and when she fought him, he grabbed her and threw her over his shoulder. Hazel screamed for help.

He reached his horse and was about to put her on it when her yelling became hysterical, and she kicked and hit him with all the strength she had. Somehow she was able to free herself, and before Jason could seize her again, Hazel gave him a hard shove. He stumbled backward and fell into the lake. Hazel turned around and ran as fast as she could. She ran as if the devil himself was chasing her, and didn't stop running until she came around the corner.

Jackson and Adam had been sitting on the front porch and had just finished bank business when they heard Hazel screaming. They stood at once and rushed toward the sound, but that's when the young woman ran straight into their arms. Adam grabbed her by her arms. He saw how beside herself she was and tried to calm her down, but Hazel did not seem to recognize him as Adam, but as someone who had attacked her.

"*No*, I am not coming with you. Leave me alone," Hazel kept saying, fear and horror coloring her voice.

"I'm Adam, Hazel. I am Adam. It is okay," he repeated in a soothing voice until he felt that his voice was reaching her.

When Hazel realized Adam was holding her and not Jason, she broke down crying. He pulled her into his arms and held her close to his chest. Jackson hurried away.

It took Hazel quite some time before she managed to stop her sobbing. She hyperventilated several times and was shaking with fear and distress, but Adam talked her through it.

George and Jackson came rushing toward them. Her father had been in one of the enclosures, branding new horses with some of his ranch hands, but he had dropped everything as soon as Jackson had called him over. None of them knew yet what had happened, but they realized it was serious.

George pulled his daughter into his arms once he reached her and held her close. He had never seen her so upset and frightened before, and was beyond worried now, but they couldn't bombard her with questions until she was ready to talk.

After more time had passed, she wiped away her tears, but was still shaking. George sat on a bench on the front porch and pulled her next to him, not letting go of her. Jackson sat next to her, squeezing her hand, and Adam pulled a chair closer. Grave concern was written on their faces.

"Hazel, what happened?" her father finally asked. His eyes signaled distress, almost fear and the young woman knew she had to let her father know. This was getting out of hand, she didn't even feel safe at home anymore.

She shared everything that happened to her, including the other times Jason Clark had threatened and harassed her. Jackson and George looked horrified, and Adam listened, but anger spread across his face when she spoke about her experience at the lake. They had to stop that man.

"Why didn't you tell us?" George lifted her chin and made her look at him.

"At first, it was so you wouldn't think I was making stuff up because I was upset that Reverend Mitchell was gone. I told myself it would get better. When Reverend Mitchell heard him threatening me and putting him in his place, I thought he would at least be more careful, but it is getting worse. Clark leaves me alone for the longest time and then shows up out of nowhere. How did he know where to find me?" She didn't even wait for anyone to respond to her and answered her own question as logic replaced her emotions.

"He must have secretly watched us for days. He obviously knew everyone's work schedule, when Alex is teaching, and when Dave goes to visit other ranches and farms."

She shuddered as the realization hit her that he had obviously shadowed her more than she had ever imagined.

"We need to let the sheriff know at once. I will also contact Ted and see if there is anything he can do."

"Nothing can be done, Pa. There are no witnesses. He is so careful and continues to be a saint around everyone but me. I am so scared. What if his next attempt to take me is successful, and he forces me to marry him?"

"We will do what we can to keep you safe. The sheriff needs to know."

"You won't be able to keep me safe. I thought I was safe here, at least, but he even invaded my favorite spot. He is like a horrible, evil shadow, I can't escape. I don't know how much longer I can fight him and the paralyzing fear. The day I was attacked in town, Doc Harper told me about the threat this country faces with girls disappearing and kidnappings everywhere. I felt like a huge heavy dark cloud was smothering me. It was the worst I ever felt. I was close to giving up and letting the cloud take over. I have been fighting despair and darkness ever since. This is a never-ending nightmare, and I can't take this much longer." The horror in her voice was quite pronounced.

"Dave and Alex encouraged me not to let him get to me. But he is getting to me. I am terrified of him and what he can do to me. Each attempt to break me is getting more aggressive and bold. He is tormenting me and always present in the back of my mind." Pure despair was in her eyes, and she looked defeated. George pulled her closer and held her.

It hurt everyone's heart to see her so hopeless, but they were ready to fight for her.

"We will report the incident to Todd Holden and have a little talk with Reverend Clark," George said fiercely, and Jackson nodded.

"Pa, it won't do anything."

"Clark needs to know that he is being watched, even if we can't prove anything right now. He won't be able to get away with it forever. Adam, can you stay here with Hazel and make sure she is looked after until we are back?"

The young man nodded.

"I hate this," Hazel said through gritted teeth as she jumped to her feet. "Because of that man, I have to have a babysitter now and will become a burden to everyone."

Adam pulled her into his arms and looked into her eyes.

"You will never be a burden, Hazel. We love you and want to keep you safe. I promise you we will not let Clark win. I hope that evil piece of—"

"Adam!" the two older men interrupted growling as a warning to not continue his sentence.

"...prairie coal will rot in opposition of heaven," he finished saying, and for a split-second, everyone grinned. Even Hazel forgot the horrible incident for that moment and joined in before she turned serious again.

"Make no promises you can't keep, Adam," she replied with a tired smile on her face. She gave everyone a quick hug and went inside the house. George and Jackson nodded to the young man and mounted their horses to ride into town.

Adam sighed. What that demon-reverend put Hazel through was torture, and he would take him down.

George and Jackson went straight to the sheriff's office when they arrived in Willamette Falls. They told Todd everything Hazel had told them, and he was as shocked as the other two men were. Adam had told him about the cemetery incident, so he kept an eye on the young reverend, but never saw him doing anything questionable.

"I have three other fathers who are beyond angry because their daughters were targeted too and nearly kidnapped. Reverend Clark wasn't doing it, but the fathers feel he is involved in this kidnapping mess," Sheriff Todd Holden commented. The two older men nodded.

"But again, there is no proof. The girls were attacked by someone we don't know, and if they had encounters with Jason Clark, they have said nothing."

"Do you think he is trying to get Hazel for whoever started this entire kidnapping thing, Todd?"

The young sheriff shook his head. "No. From what you told me and what I heard about the danger for our women, Clark is most likely involved with something evil, but he wants Hazel for himself. He is targeting her and is doing what he can to make her fear him."

"You need to arrest him, Todd."

"I am sorry, George, but I can't. I have nothing but Hazel's word, and it is his word against hers. We won't stand a chance. Most judges still don't consider abuse and harassment of women a punishable offense. Unless there is remarkable and sure evidence, they won't even allow it to court. Men still get away with almost everything."

"We need to talk to him, though. He has to know that we know, believe Hazel, and do what we can to stop that filthy swine. I am not letting him destroy my daughter." George was furious. Todd Holden understood him, but his hands were tight.

"I will join you, but realize he will lie through his teeth and make stuff up to rescue his lost soul. He might even make himself the victim, and that Hazel is after him. Remember that, and don't attack him. If you hurt him, I have to arrest you for assault."

George nodded. It would be difficult to keep his temper under control because anyone messing with his children was messing with him.

Jackson and George walked over to the post office to send a telegram to Ted Burton to find out about the legal options. They met Todd Holden thirty minutes later in front of the church.

"Just remember to keep a cool head when we are in there. I don't want to arrest you two for losing your temper," Todd reminded them.

"Clark, where are you?" George shouted as soon as he opened the church door. Jackson and the sheriff followed him. A moment later, they saw Jason Clark come from the back.

"Mr. Buchannon. Mr. Harrison, and Sheriff Holden, what a pleasure to have you visit me," the young reverend welcomed them, but George waved his hand.

"Stop your fake politeness. We only came over for one reason. If you don't keep your filthy hands off my daughter, I will make sure you end up in prison for the rest of your life."

Jason Clark looked at them, stunned. "What are you talking about, Mr. Buchannon?"

"Don't play these stupid games with us, Reverend," Jackson snapped. "You've been after Hazel ever since you got here."

"You are getting something wrong here. I did nothing to Hazel. The first time we met, she told me she missed Reverend Mitchell and that this church was not the same without him. She is probably spreading rumors about me because she misses him and wants him back. They are in love, and because I know of their affection, they try to make you believe I am doing something wrong. I care about the welfare of your daughter, Mr. Buchannon, and would never want to harm her."

George scoffed. "You did more than harm her, and stop with that nonsense about her being in love with Reverend Mitchell. The bond they have and the love they feel for each other is something you will never understand and has nothing to do with romance."

"Whatever you say, Mr. Buchannon."

"Just so we are clear, Mr. Clark," Todd Holden interjected as he jumped into the conversation. "I take the accusations against you seriously and will inform your superiors in Salem. I might not be able to arrest you right now because of missing evidence and witnesses, but I will keep an eye on you for sure."

"I am sorry you have made up your mind about me, but my superiors believe in me and are behind me. I promise you that I have never tried to overstep my boundaries with your daughter. What are you accusing me of?" he asked with an innocent arrogance in his voice, and George had to hold himself back at that point.

"If you EVER come to my ranch again, if you even set foot on any part of my land, I will have you arrested for trespassing."

"The last time I came to your ranch was before Christmas, and Doc Harper was my ride. I had no ill intentions."

"Stop your filthy lies," Jackson barked the very next moment. If he had been any closer to the younger man, he would have planted a facer on him, despite the threat of getting arrested hanging in the air. "You came to the Buchannon ranch today and tried to kidnap Hazel. You are a pathetic excuse of a human being and a coward, but not a man."

"Mr. Harrison, you are mistaken. I just got home from Portland. I had no time to come over to your ranch, and I would never attempt to kidnap a girl."

"And we are supposed to believe that?" George asked, anger coloring his voice.

"You may ask Mrs. Brenton. She was with me on the stagecoach, and one of your cowboys saw me as I helped Mrs. Brenton down the steps after we arrived in Willamette Falls."

"And which cowboy would that be?" Jackson snarled.

"He was one of the newer ones, the one you hired after Rob McCall got killed. Was his name Caleb? Caleb Norton, right?"

"We still don't believe you one bit. You might have your alibis and bought witnesses, but your dishonesty will be your downfall one day," Jackson scoffed.

"I don't have to listen to your accusations. You have no proof that I did anything wrong, and I wasn't even here to do anything to your daughter. My superiors will believe me, and if you try to press charges, I will sue you for slander. Check with your lovely daughter and remind her that lying is a sin."

"Mark my word, Clark. You will pay for this one day, I promise." George gave him another icy glance, and the three men left the church.

"Well, well, well. It looks as if your plan isn't working out, Clark. Didn't I tell you to keep your hands off that girl? I told you the rancher would find out, and he will not rest until you are finished."

"Shut up, McKellar. I haven't lost yet, and that little beast will pay for ratting me out. I still have most of the people of this town on my side."

"But for how long? If you keep threatening Hazel Buchannon, it won't be long before you tick off the rest of the town, and at one point, they will catch you."

"I will stay away from her for a while, but she will still be mine."

"I told you from the beginning, you should focus on the families who mistreat their daughters. Those girls are easy targets and cheap to buy and expensive to sell. They make money. Hazel Buchannon has a loving family, and she has friends who will do anything to protect her. Her father and that Reverend Mitchell will kill you before they hand over the girl."

"How do you know so much about her and her family?"

"I have been watching her too. She is a pretty thing, and if I ever get my hands on her, I will do some taming myself," Gabriel said with a sleazy smile on his face.

"Stay away from her. She is mine, and I will get her. I will force her to marry me, and I will do what I please with her. It will be fun to tame her."

"Fine, whatever, Clark. What do you want me to report to our boss?"

"Tell him I have to step into the shadows for a while, and you guys should avoid kidnapping from Willamette Falls at the moment. I admit I created this mess with my fancy for Hazel, but more and more people are getting upset and realizing what is happening, and we need to be careful. Plus, Hank Thompson is rescuing girls, and if we don't watch out, the girls will spill the beans on us. The girl you kidnapped last is now on the Buchannon ranch, so don't show yourself if you don't want to get into trouble."

"Don't worry. Shelly won't see me, and even if she did, it wouldn't bother me. We earned good money with her by making Hank Thompson pay big time, and so we are good now."

"Don't let anyone see you when you leave the church."

Gabriel McKellar nodded, opened the back door, and snuck out.

Jason Clark sat on one of his church benches for a long time. He was worried and knew it was his fault. He had miscalculated and would pay for it if he was not careful. As he watched the night settling in, the church door opened, and he heard someone enter. Jason didn't even turn around to see who was there.

"What took you so long, Adam? You were supposed to be here hours ago."

"And you promised you wouldn't come to their ranch to get her. I had to babysit her these past few hours because her father and my brother know what you are doing, and they will not leave her by herself anymore."

Jason sighed. That made everything so much more complicated.

14
War Council

"Ted? What are you doing here?" George Buchannon exclaimed when he opened the door. His friend gave him a brotherly hug, and George asked him to come inside the house. "Todd, welcome, come on in too."

"I received your telegram about the situation with Hazel, and we need to discuss this in person."

"Sure, let's go into my office."

"Where is Hazel?" Ted looked around the room.

"She is helping to break in the horses, so they are ready for the auction in Salem."

"Is she out there by herself?" Ted's expression changed to concern.

"No, Namito and several of our cowboys are with her. Namito won't let her out of his sight."

"Good."

"George, can you get Jackson, Dave, and Alex too? I need to speak to every male in the house," Todd Holden commented, and George nodded.

"I have to know exactly what happened, everything that happened to Hazel," Ted began as he started the meeting. George and the rest of the group filled him in. Ted thought for a while, not saying anything. "Has Hazel talked about it?"

"Not since Clark's last attack. Hazel blocks every attempt to talk about it. She told us everything after it happened, but has shut down since." George sighed as worry and frustration spread across his face.

"Has she talked to any of you?" Ted asked, but everyone just shook their head.

"What can we do, Ted? What can we do to help her and stop that maniac?" Jackson felt helpless, and it hurt him to see her suffer so much.

"We need to be careful with how we address and handle this. I spoke to Robert Mitchell before I left Salem. He said he was working on the situation but didn't give me any details and said he would let me know when he knew more. He suggested getting someone into Clark's circle and investigating undercover."

"We have someone in there. He is a good fit who has already discovered that Clark is associated with Gabriel McKellar," Todd interjected.

"The guy who tried to kidnap girls from Willamette Falls?"

Todd nodded.

"Great. Can you tell us the name of the undercover person?" Ted glanced over to the sheriff, but Todd shook his head.

"I can't give you a name, but I know him well from my time in Sacramento. He is one of the best sheriffs in the country."

"Great."

"So what can we do, Ted?"

"Don't threaten Clark. Men like him can snap in a heartbeat, which would put Hazel in even more danger, especially if he works with Gabriel McKellar. Make sure Hazel always has a male protector around, even if she complains. I know she hates it. She wants to prove that women can take care of themselves, and she loves her independence, but in cases like these, women need protectors, and there is no shame in it. God created us differently for a reason." Everyone in the room agreed.

"Anything you wish to add, Todd?"

The young sheriff nodded. "I talked to Harriet Brenton, and she confirmed Clark's story about traveling with him on the stagecoach from Portland."

"We asked Caleb about it, and even though he had not seen Clark riding in the stagecoach, he saw him helping Mrs. Brenton just like Clark said."

"Jason Clark is targeting Hazel. He wants her for himself. If the kidnappers wanted her for their dirty business, they might have succeeded by now, but Clark is stopping it."

"Why is he so obsessed with Hazel?" George asked.

"Because she is a beautiful young woman, strong, opinionated, and a fighter, and men like Clark find girls like Hazel a challenging temptation and attractive. They want to own them and break their spirit. It makes them feel powerful. It is a hunting game - an addiction. Clark will not rest until she is his. Jason Clark is a rejected predator, and that makes him dangerous." Todd had a serious expression on his face.

"The best way to help Hazel is giving her space while not leaving her out of your sight. I am grateful you take this threat seriously and believe her. Most women who go through something like that are on their own and end up abused and murdered. Hazel's willingness to fight for more rights for women is more important than you might think." The young sheriff looked at everyone.

"Todd is right. It is disheartening to see how many women suffer and the way they are treated. So many women reached out to me, asking for help, but there isn't much I can do for them. I work with a remarkable team in Salem, and the sheriff and marshal favor more women's rights, but most men in powerful positions don't. A woman asking for help because her husband abuses her most often gets into more trouble if the sheriff and I get involved. We can threaten the husband, but legally can't do anything about it. Hazel is a lucky woman to have so many caring and kind men in her life. I wish more men were like that and stopped treating their wives and daughters as a servant and slaves." Ted's expression was fierce.

Jackson and George looked at each other. It blew their mind that men out there mistreated someone they were supposed to love and protect. Once alcohol was part of it, the torture for those girls and women got even worse.

"Is there anything we can do to stop Clark right now? I mean, Reverend Mitchell threatened him and Alex, and I did, but it changed nothing." Dave wanted nothing more than to stop the torture for Hazel.

"I think the fact that George, Jackson, and I went to him and told him he was being watched will keep him away for a while. He knows he has to be careful, and Clark knows he is playing with fire by targeting a girl like Hazel. She is loved and protected, and he knows the consequences will be severe if he isn't careful. That said, the threat isn't over yet. You might not see him much in the next weeks or months, but he is still there, waiting for his moment," Todd Holden said, looking at the surrounding men.

"He is definitely waiting for his moment," Dave replied. "Clark is like a crocodile. Once it latches onto its prey, it won't let go again. He latched onto Hazel, has torn off parts of her, and is getting ready for the death roll."

"He will not have my daughter. I don't care what I have to do to stop him, but I will do what it takes. I love that girl with all my heart, and I will not have that evil demon destroy her beautiful soul."

"I promise you, George, none of us will let that happen. Jason Clark will not win this war. He has targeted the wrong family." Jackson was determined and serious. Nobody would hurt Hazel Buchannon and not pay for it.

"Jason Clark aside, I hope Reverend Mitchell is working with other reverends and church leaders to bring down this whole evil kidnapping scheme," Alex said, jumping into the conversation.

"I can't tell you much, but my father, who is a US Marshal, is working hard with the other marshals and countless sheriffs. They want to destroy it once and for all. My father told me they were even considering bringing the army into this, but it isn't an army issue where our soldiers storm a town and wipe out evil. It is hidden everywhere, and only a small group of men spreading it across our nation. According to my father, this fast-expanding evil is complex because it has advanced into churches and law enforcement. They have to look into everything and make sure they work with people who will help them and not the predators."

"Have they named this horrible evil yet?" Jackson asked.

"Yes," Todd replied. "The term used within law enforcement is *white slavery*, since the methods are like the methods for slavery. Women and children are being abducted and kidnapped, forced into prostitution or marriage, sold to be a slave to men, and have to obey every command and fulfill their owner's fantasies and perversions. It is disgusting. Disobedience gets punished harshly, and many of the women get killed."

"Jason Clark is part of that?"

"He is involved to a point. He wants to enslave Hazel to himself, driven by immoral thoughts and sinful fantasies, but as a reverend, he knows the members of his church. He can point out girls and women to the abductors working for who knows who. They infiltrated the church in several areas for that reason." Todd's eyes narrowed as frustration crept onto his face.

"That is outrageous. These men are supposed to be men of God, and they should protect their church sheep and not hand them over to the wolves." George was fuming now.

"I agree, but you can buy even those who work for the Lord if they are not committed and like to make pacts with the devil," Todd replied sarcastically.

"Beware of false prophets, which come to you in sheep's clothing, but inwardly they are ravening wolves." [i]

"Exactly, Dave. Clark is a wolf in sheep's clothing. We have to expose him like that and protect Hazel and other girls and women in this town and country from that dangerous man and the rest of those criminals."

"Would it help if we boycotted his church services? I mean, we've done our service here at home before, and I don't see Clark as a pastor, but a criminal hypocrite," Jackson blurted out.

"It would send a coherent message to his superiors in Salem," George responded. "Maybe that's a thought we should consider. We need to keep Hazel away from that awful man."

"What's the plan for you and having Hazel take over the business?" Ted asked, guiding the conversation in a different direction.

"I am sending her to Salem to the big horse auction next week. I want her to get firsthand experience with selling horses and what it is like to have nothing but cowboys and ranchers around."

"You are not sending her by herself with a bunch of cowboys, right?" Ted raised an eyebrow.

"No, of course not. Jackson and Dave will go with her, but I want her to try registering for the auction herself. It will help her see what she will have to deal with when taking on this men-powered world."

"Excellent plan. When is Hazel taking the exam for her business certification?"

"Next month. That will be another challenge for Hazel. I am sure they will put up a fight about her being a girl."

"Don't they know her name?"

"No. The application form only asks for your first name initial, and full last name. So far, they had no one challenge the rule, since only men take that exam. I am certain that even if they let her take the examination, they will change the application forms afterward."

"I like it," Ted replied with a grin. "Who is taking Hazel to the exam?"

"It will be Alex and me. She'll need moral support from her teacher, and we will be her backup if the board of examination gives her a hard time. I am sure Robert Mitchell will join us, too."

"Wonderful, I see you have excellent distractions in place for Hazel. That should get her mind off Jason Clark for a bit, at least."

"Don't forget the big cattle drive to San Francisco, George."

"Right. Hazel will join us for that as well, and we asked Haven to come too, so Hazel isn't the only girl on that trip."

"Okay, great. I will keep you updated with everything I find out about the Clark situation. Please keep me posted too, and Todd, make sure you step in as soon as you have proof."

"Sure thing, Ted," the young sheriff replied.

"Thank you so much for coming and discussing this in person. We know now that we should not underestimate the threat to Hazel or this country."

15
Mental Torment

Hazel never found out about the special meeting the men of the ranch had with Ted Burton and Todd Holden. Nobody wanted to worry her more than she was. Dave and Alex informed Namito about everything they had discussed, but they agreed that Hazel only needed to know they cared about her and would look out for her.

"*Dave*? Dave, where are you?" Hazel called out and opened his bedroom door. "Oh my goodness, you are still asleep? Wake up, sleepyhead."

"What's wrong, Hazel?" he mumbled, still mostly asleep.

"You overslept, Jackson is fuming, and we have to leave for Willamette Falls in ten minutes," she replied and hurried out of the room again.

"What?" He jumped out of bed and rushed through his morning routine. When he checked his pocket watch, he saw that it was only five o'clock in the morning.

"HAZEL," he yelled and went looking for her.

"What are you doing up already?" Jackson asked when Dave stepped out of the house.

"Hazel stormed into my room, woke me up, and told me I overslept," he replied dramatically, causing Jackson to let out a hearty laugh. "Very funny. Have you seen Hazel by any chance? She is in big trouble."

"Perhaps she went back to bed?" Jackson chuckled.

"Ha, Ha. That girl was wide awake, and she knows what will happen once I find her." Dave grinned now too. He had a good sense of humor, but was looking forward to getting back at Hazel.

"Good luck with the search. I hope you find her before we have to leave." Jackson winked at him and continued on his path to the stables.

Dave sat on the steps to the front porch and thought hard. Were there spots Hazel liked to hide?

"Good morning, Dave," Namito said in a surprised voice when he saw him. "Not tired anymore?"

"Oh, I am tired. Hazel played a trick on me and woke me up by making me believe I overslept." Namito grinned. "You wouldn't happen to know where she is, would you?"

"I might," Namito responded with a twinkle in his eyes.

"And?"

"You think I would rat out my best friend?"

"Yes."

"Hmm. You don't know me as well as you thought," the young Indian replied and started to walk away.

"Namito!? Seriously?"

"Fine, since you are asking me so nicely, last time I saw her, she was in the barn collecting eggs. Knowing her, she got distracted by the hatched chicks, is sitting on a bale of straw, and watching them."

Hazel sat on a bale of straw and watched the tiny chicks, just like Namito thought she would. She adored baby chicks and loved their cute little peeping. She was so engrossed in her chick watching activity that she didn't hear Dave entering the barn.

"Hazel *Rae* Buchannon," he roared with an angry tone in his voice. Hazel froze for a moment, then jumped up, turning around to face him.

"Dave, please...," she began saying before the young man grabbed her and threw her over his shoulder.

"You want to bet that you will never do something like that again?" he asked, not holding back a sinister grin.

"I thought you had a sense of humor."

"I do, but actions have consequences, and your early morning action is begging for serious punishment."

"What do you mean?" she asked with a worried expression on her face. They had left the barn and Dave was now walking straight toward the lake. She squirmed and hit his back with her fists.

"No, no, Dave. Please don't do that. I promise I won't do that again," she stammered, but he didn't respond, nor did he acknowledge her attempt of trying to free herself. When he reached the lake, he took her off his shoulder but held her tight to his body. She grabbed onto his shirt.

"Please, don't do this," she begged with her best puppy dog face and looked at him.

Dave stared back at her for several seconds, not saying anything. Suddenly, he picked her up, stepped closer to the shore, and threw her in the air. Hazel started screaming. He caught her a second later.

When she realized she was in his arms again, she sighed. Dave gave her a winning smile, and she kissed him on his cheek before he put her back on her feet. He put his arm around her shoulders, and they walked back to the house.

"Just so you know, next time you wake me up and give me a heart attack, you'll end up in the lake. I promise you that."

The stagecoach came to a halt, and Jackson and Dave jumped onto the street after the driver had opened the carriage door, then helped Hazel down the steps. Hazel looked around. She hadn't seen Robert Mitchell since Rob's funeral, and she couldn't wait to see him again.

Dave took Hazel's bag when he saw Robert Mitchell standing off to the side.

"Hazel," he said and pointed in Reverend Mitchell's direction. Hazel's face lit up, and she ran with childlike joy toward him and jumped into his outstretched arms. He caught her and twirled around with her until she pleaded for him to put her down. Onlookers smiled at the pair and kept on walking. Robert pulled Hazel into his arms and hugged her.

"It is so good to see you again, Reverend Mitchell. I missed you." Her beautiful blue eyes looked up at him, and he kissed her head.

"I missed you too. I am so glad I have you three in town with me for a few days," Robert responded and greeted Jackson with a warm hug and shook Dave's hand. As they walked toward the hotel, Robert and Jackson began a lively conversation.

Robert Mitchell still had an arm around Hazel's shoulders when Hazel noticed how many people gave them disapproving looks. The people and smiles from before had disappeared, and everyone who passed them seemed to judge them.

Why were people always so quick to judge? Why was it questionable to others that she had a loving and close relationship with this remarkable man, and they both shared their father-daughter affections for each other? What happened to humanity? Why were innocence and pureness taken out of everything and replaced by something inappropriate and even sinful?

Hazel felt uncomfortable, and it made her angry that the looks surrounding her suggested she should be ashamed of her attachment to Reverend Mitchell. Her feelings for Robert Mitchell were natural and innocent. She had no romantic feelings for him, and he didn't have inappropriate feelings for her, either.

Her heart told her she wasn't doing anything wrong.

Satan twisted everything, and that included happy and healthy relationships. Couldn't people mind their own business and give everyone the benefit of the doubt before making up their minds about other humans and situations? She didn't want to feel ashamed of loving this man, and she didn't want this relationship made into something evil when it wasn't.

Why is everything so complicated now? Yes, she was a young woman and not a child anymore, but why did that mean she had to stop showing affection for those she cared about? She admired Robert Mitchell and loved him. Was it so wrong to express childlike joy and love even as an adult?

"Hazel, is everything okay? Hazel?"

She looked up, still far away in her thoughts. She realized Robert was talking to her, and so she looked into his eyes.

"I am fine, sorry," she responded. "I was just thinking."

"You look upset, though. Do you want to talk about it?" He looked down at her with a worried expression on his face. Dave and Jackson seemed just as concerned.

"Not here. Can we go somewhere where we can talk?"

"How about we drop off your luggage at the hotel, get you settled, and then go to my church office?"

Hazel nodded, and the four of them hurried across the street into the big hotel, asked for their keys, and went upstairs to check out their rooms. Dave and Jackson gave Hazel the room in the middle, so they could interfere if something happened to her.

Robert Mitchell's office was comfortable yet simple. He had a settee and two armchairs in one corner, and so they took a seat.

"What was the matter with you earlier?" Robert looked deep into her blue eyes, searching for an answer. She blushed, but told them her thoughts from earlier.

"Is it wrong that I show my admiration and love for you, Reverend Mitchell?" Her simple question's innocence made it clear that she didn't want to be forced into someone, she was not.

"No, it isn't. Strangers don't understand, and they don't know us. They judge by the things they can see. To them, it is outrageous that a reverend, not to mention a reverend of my age, is taking a fancy to such a young and beautiful girl. They don't know our hearts, Hazel, but God does. He knows that the love we have for each other is not questionable, but real. Technically, we are brother and sister, at least our spirits are, and I see nothing wrong with siblings showing their love for each other." He winked at her, and she smiled.

"More people should show their non-romantic affections, so the ridiculous judging stops. Society is teaching something unreal, and once we become an adult, proper behavior and respectful manners are expected, which forbids showing your feelings for another person in public. People seem to have forgotten that God created us the way we are and that He loves us, and we are supposed to love each other. Satan is trying to turn natural and normal feelings into something questionable, and it shouldn't be. Romantic affection is intimate and should be treated as such, but showing that you love and care for a person should be encouraged. It might be contagious and spread around, so they judge only the things that are wrong and inappropriate." Dave smiled at Hazel and squeezed her hand.

Namito and Rob had told him how hard it was for Hazel to learn to show affection and feelings. Making her ashamed and uncomfortable for such tedious reasons was wrong.

"What's the plan for the rest of the day, Jackson?" Hazel asked, not sure what to expect. Jackson looked at Robert and nodded.

"We are invited to dinner," Robert replied with a smile.

"Who invited us?"

"Marshal Sterling Holden and his wife Katherine."

"Todd's father invited us to dinner? Why?"

"He wants to meet you and wants to hear firsthand what Jason Clark did to you."

Hazel's smile faded at once, and fear entered her eyes. She did not want to think about that man. She had not spoken to anyone about him since his last attack, and she was confident Robert didn't even know about it yet. Hazel stood.

"I am sorry, but I won't be joining you tonight," she responded calmly yet firm. The three men stood as well.

"Why not?" Robert didn't trust her sudden mood change and looked into her eyes, but she lowered her gaze.

"I am not feeling well and should lie down and rest. Pleasant day, Reverend Mitchell." She nodded to Dave and Jackson, who looked at her, stunned. Hazel was about to walk out of the room when Robert clasped her arm.

"What is going on, Hazel?"

"Nothing, I just need time to myself." Her look was cold and distant. She tried to get out of his hold, but Robert Mitchell didn't let go.

"You can't keep shutting yourself off, Hazel. I realize that talking about your tormentor is hard and brings back horrible memories, but you have to face those feelings. You can't run away from it." His expression communicated understanding but unyielding firmness.

Hazel panicked. She didn't feel capable of talking about the horrible experiences with that man, and didn't even want to be reminded of him. When her father had approached her about going to Salem for the auction, Hazel had agreed to it because that would get her away from everything for a few days. She felt everyone's eyes on her, but she couldn't look at them. She was close to tears now.

"I am sorry, but I can't," she muttered, avoiding eye contact with Robert. "Please excuse me." She removed his hand from her arm, but he clasped her hand and pulled her closer.

She didn't want to look at him. It would come bursting out, and she was trying so hard to forget. Why would he, of all people, mention it?

"Reverend Mitchell, please let me go. I need time to myself now," she tried again, not looking at him. He lifted her chin, but as soon as their eyes met, she burst into tears. She tried to get away from him, but he pulled her into his arms and held her.

"Hazel, let it out. You need to talk about it."

"No, I don't. I need to move on and forget it ever happened. Just let me go," Hazel sobbed as she tried to pull herself out of his embrace.

"Marshal Holden is on our side, Hazel. He is working hard, so you and many other girls can feel safe again."

"You don't understand," Hazel said, despair and horror coloring her voice. "He won't leave me alone. He keeps coming after me and gets more aggressive and bolder each time. I can't stand it anymore. This constant fear is breaking me."

"Has he come after you even after I threatened him to stay away from you?" Robert's eyes were full of anger and fire. Hazel nodded. "What did he do?"

"I don't want to talk about it right now."

"Okay, I understand," he replied, trying to calm himself. "We will win this. I promise you, he will get arrested and punished for everything he ever did to you. Be brave. Marshal Holden is a fine and compassionate man. He wants to help you, but you have to tell him everything. We will not be the only guests there. Bishop Steven McDonald, Territorial Governor Joseph Lane, [i] and his deputy Wayne Reeves will also join us. They will help us solve this. I have been working with them ever since we found out about the threat to our girls and women. We will continue to fight it, so *white slavery* will hopefully only be a term at one point."

"But isn't Governor Lane a supporter of slavery?" Dave asked, concern coloring his voice.

"Yes, he is. His North Carolina upbringing is very much a part of him, but he doesn't condone *white slavery* and wants to know where that evil is coming from, so it can be stopped."

Jackson and Dave exchanged a glance.

"I know what you are thinking," Robert Mitchell said as he watched the two men. "He isn't the most promising help with his political and personal views, but we still need him to fight this. We hope that hearing Hazel's story will open his heart and mind to a much-needed change. Steven McDonald and Marshal Holden are the most important in this case, and they are caring and wonderful men."

Since dinner at the Holden's was a formal occasion, everyone dressed accordingly. Hazel had wondered why Jackson and Dave had asked her to bring her evening gown. She thought they were only going to a livestock auction and would spend time with Robert Mitchell, now she knew.

Hazel looked stunning in her dark green dress. Her hair was pinned up, and the long white gloves complimented her entire outfit. It rarely happened that she had to dress so formally, and so she felt like a princess. When she stepped out of her room and came down the stairs, the three men looked at her, fascinated.

She was beautiful. Dave offered her his arm, and she tucked her arm under his. She had to say, all three of them looked attractive and handsome in their evening attire, and she felt honored to be associated with these wonderful men. An open carriage was waiting for them in front of the hotel, and Dave was a complete gentleman and helped her up the steps.

It was chilly, and she was only wearing a shawl. Robert noticed that she was shivering, took off his jacket, and put it over her shoulders. She gave him a thankful smile. The three men chatted quietly. Hazel leaned back and watched buildings and people as they passed by. As they reached their destination and were getting ready to leave the carriage, Robert pulled Hazel into his arms.

"It will be okay, Hazel. Marshal Holden will wait until after dinner before he asks questions. You will like him, I promise."

A servant opened the door and asked everyone to enter. Hazel was unusually shy, but Dave put his arm around her shoulders to show his support. A tall man with dark brown hair, several gray highlights, and broad shoulders approached them.

"Welcome to my home. Robert, good to see you again," he said, smiling, and they shook each other's hands. Marshal Holden then greeted Jackson and Dave before he stood in front of Hazel. He looked kindly at her and took her hand into his.

"It is such a pleasure to meet you, Miss Buchannon. I have heard so many wonderful things about you." He gave her a big smile, which made Hazel feel more at ease. Reverend Mitchell had been right again. She liked Sterling Holden.

He led her into the dining room, and two men stood up and greeted her with a bow, the same kindness on their faces, the same pleasing manners. Hazel relaxed. Governor Lane greeted her kindly, but she could sense hostility from him. However, after what she had learned about him earlier in the day, she understood.

During dinner, she was seated next to Marshal Holden and Dave. Across from her sat Robert Mitchell, next to him, Katherine Holden, and Governor Deputy Reeves. Bishop Steven McDonald, Governor Lane, and Jackson, finished the round of dinner guests.

The food was delicious, and Hazel enjoyed herself. Dave was his pleasant self, and Katherine Holden was an elegant lady.

"Miss Buchannon," Marshal Holden said as he turned to her. "I heard so many incredible things about you, but one struck me the most. Robert told me you are here in Salem to take part in the livestock auction?"

"Yes, I am, Sir," she replied.

"I have to say, I am impressed. The livestock auction has the toughest cowboys and ranchers of the West Coast in attendance, so the conversations and interactions are rough. I am uncertain whether it is the right place for a lady like you," he said with a grin on his face.

"My father would like to leave his ranch to me when he passes on, and well, that means I have to learn to deal with rough men."

"They won't make it easy for you, though. Many men still believe women aren't smart enough to run a ranch and do things men do. They will put up a fight."

"One has to step up to the task, and it looks like Miss Buchannon will be the one," Bishop McDonald said and gave her an encouraging nod.

"You will meet a bull in an arena, Miss Buchannon. Russell Montgomery is one of the richest guys in the country. He buys livestock and sells them again and even ships them to England. He is traditional and doesn't believe a woman should have a say in anything. The auction tent is off-limits for ladies, even if they only want to watch."

"Does he have a wife and a daughter?"

"He had a wife, but she died two years ago. He has two daughters and three sons."

"And does he mistreat them?"

"Nobody knows. He keeps his family out of the public eye. He lives in San Francisco, but travels the country a lot because of his work. His children are married now, except the youngest son."

"So, do you think the laws will change if I convince him that women deserve better treatment and more rights?"

"You would get a fighting chance if you have a man like him on your side," Reverend Mitchell commented.

"If I didn't have to travel again tomorrow, I would offer you my protection, Miss Buchannon."

Hazel smiled. "Thank you, Marshal Holden, but that would make things even more complicated. I have to do this on my own. If I want men to take me seriously, I can't hide behind men."

"Jackson and I will be close by and can get involved if things get out of hand," Dave assured everyone.

"Besides," Warren Reeves interjected, "most cowboys try to behave better when a beautiful young lady is present. They might whistle and try getting her attention, but I have high hopes they will leave her alone."

"Robert and I will be on the grounds too," Bishop McDonald promised and smiled at Hazel. "There is no way we will feed you to the wolves by yourself."

"Thank you. I appreciate it." Hazel was touched. Apart from Dave, the men present that evening were between forty-five and fifty-five years old, and besides Governor Lane, seemed genuine, caring, and plain sweet. Perhaps they could save her from Jason Clark.

"Let's move into the sitting room, shall we?" Marshal Holden stood, and everyone followed his example.

After everyone had found a seat, Marshal Holden looked at Hazel. She was seated next to Dave and Robert Mitchell and was getting uneasy since she knew what was coming now.

"Miss Buchannon, you know what I am about to ask you, right?"

She nodded, anxiety kicking in. Her heart beat so fast, she was sure it would jump out of her chest. Dave put his arm around her shoulders and pulled her closer.

"I realize this won't be easy for you, but to stop that man and the whole white slavery threat, we need to know everything you can tell us."

Robert Mitchell squeezed her hand.

Katherine Holden was amazed by how sweet, and gentle everyone was with this young woman. Her husband was a strict and rigid guy, but she knew his soft side. He knew how to approach delicate and challenging subjects and not make someone more uncomfortable.

She realized Dave Tucker and Robert Mitchell were fond of Hazel and loved her. Katherine also noticed that the Bishop and Governor Deputy Reeves took a shine to her. She couldn't tell what Governor Lane was thinking, but his eyes told her he, too, was impressed by Hazel. There was something special about that beautiful girl, and Katherine was determined to know her better.

"Since I am now conducting official marshal business, I have to ask you questions formally. Miss Buchannon, is it true that Reverend Jason Clark has harassed, threatened, and attacked you?"

She nodded.

"Has he attempted to touch you inappropriately without your consent and even against your wishes?"

Hazel nodded again.

"Has Jason Clark tried to abduct you to force you into a marriage with him?"

The young woman lowered her eyes, fear creeping up on her, but she nodded. Robert looked at her, shocked.

"Miss Buchannon, please tell us everything you experienced with Reverend Jason Clark. Every detail, every insignificant thing you remember, is important."

Hazel made eye contact with Dave, and he gave her an encouraging nod. Marshal Holden felt the turmoil in her and took her hand in his.

"Hazel," he said, and she noticed how he used her first name now, trying to connect with her on a personal level. "Take your time. If you have to stop, we can take a break. If you get emotional, let it out. We will not judge you, but we understand. You went through terrifying ordeals in just a few months, and we want you to be safe again."

Tears entered her eyes, and she had to swallow hard. None of these men rushed her, just looked at her with compassion and understanding. She shared her first encounter with Reverend Clark. It was silent in the room, and she didn't look at anyone but shared her feelings and what had happened. She told them about the moment he cornered her in the cemetery and the threat he made to her. When Katherine heard the threat, she gasped in shock, but fully controlled her emotions right away.

Hazel stopped for a moment. She could still feel his warm breath on her skin and the fear she felt when he told her she would be his.

Hazel continued, and told them about the near-kidnapping attack during the town visit after winter. She lowered her gaze when she spoke about being choked, and Dave pulled her closer. Hazel felt how Robert Mitchell was now on the edge of his seat and kept clenching his fists.

Dave spoke of his experience, how he saw the attack, and how distressed she was afterward. Everyone in the room shook their head in disbelief and shock.

Hazel's heart raced in fear and horror when she thought about the last encounter she had with Jason Clark and how close it had been. She tried to talk about it, but her breathing became more and more unsteady until she was hyperventilating. She jumped up and gasped for air. Robert Mitchell, Dave, and Marshal Holden stood at once and calmly talked to her. Dave lifted her arms in the air and held her hand.

When she didn't manage to calm her breathing, she panicked. "I can't ...I can't do this," she mumbled. Everything around her spun, and she gasped for air several times before everything turned black.

Robert Mitchell caught her when she collapsed and put her on the settee behind them. Katherine Holden ordered a servant to bring water and a washcloth.

"That poor girl. What for a devil would torment such a beautiful girl?" Katherine was outraged.

"Someone who is selfish and works with the devil," Dave answered. "He has done nothing but torture her."

When Hazel opened her eyes, she was exhausted and tired. She had a cold, wet cloth on her forehead, and Katherine used another cloth to cool her burning face. At first, Hazel remembered nothing, but when she saw Marshal Holden standing next to her and Robert Mitchell next to him, it came back quickly. Fear and panic returned, and she wanted to jump up, but they held her back.

"It is okay, Hazel. Just breathe slowly. It is okay."

She closed her eyes again and tried to relax and calm her breathing.

"Perhaps she shouldn't continue and rest now," Katherine remarked as she caressed Hazel's face.

"It is best for her to get it out tonight. If she has to come back another time, she will go through the emotions again," Sterling Holden replied, and the rest of the men nodded in agreement. "Hazel, listen to me. Take the time you need. If it is easier for you to talk about it lying down and with your eyes closed, that is fine too."

The young woman swallowed hard. How a marshal could be so kind and understanding was beyond her. He was right, though. She had to get it done and over with because she didn't want to go through this again.

"I can sit up," she replied and was about to lift her body when Dave's hands clasped her waist, lifted her in the air, and sat her next to him. She smiled for a split second.

"I was sitting outside, studying, when I saw two squirrels chasing each other up and down the oak tree. I got up and watched them, leaned against the fence behind me, and closed my eyes to enjoy the warm sun. Reverend Clark snuck up on me, stepped next to me, and pulled me into his arms. When I opened my eyes and tried to get away from him, he began kissing my neck and face. He told me he was there to claim his bride."

Robert Mitchell was now fuming, and he breathed in and out because he was ready to snap. Hazel's eyes welled with tears when she thought about the next part.

She covered her face with her hands and sobbed. Nobody said anything, they waited for her to be ready.

"...I fought him, and he grabbed me and threw me over his shoulder. I screamed for help," she continued as her body shook and her heart raced. She had to finish, though.

"...he tried to put me on his horse. He tried to kidnap me," Hazel said, horror and despair returning to her voice. "I was able to get myself out of his hold and pushed him away from me. He tumbled into the lake, and I ran. I am so scared of him. What if he comes back for me?"

Robert Mitchell stood and pulled her into his arms, just holding her close. Tears were still streaming down her face, and even though she tried to get her shaking under control, she couldn't. Hazel leaned against Robert's chest and cried. When she calmed down again, Marshal Holden clasped her hands.

"Thank you, Hazel. Thank you for being brave and letting us know what he has been doing to you."

She tried to smile, but was still too upset.

"If you ask me, someone should shoot that man," Katherine blurted out. "What an evil creature to cause so much pain and fear to this poor girl."

"Katherine," Sterling remarked reproachfully, gently scolding his wife, even though he wholeheartedly agreed.

"I am only saying. I am appalled that someone who is supposed to be a man of God is obsessed with torturing and hurting a girl. He is supposed to look after his church members. What an evil creature." Everyone in the room nodded.

Hazel looked sad and defeated. Katherine's heart was hurting for her, and so she pulled her into her arms.

"How are you feeling, honey?" she asked, holding the girl close to her.

"I am tired. Sometimes I think it would be best if I gave myself up to Clark, so I wouldn't have that constant fear and horror pressed on my chest."

"You will not give yourself up to him, Hazel." Marshal Holden spoke gentle but firm. "That's what he wants. Clark is trying to break your spirit. He tries to make you think things will be easier and better for you if you give up and surrender yourself to him, but it won't. He will torment and abuse you in ways you can't even imagine, and you will pay with your life for it."

"But what if he threatens or even hurts someone I love? What if he uses his connection with the white slavery movement to kidnap my sisters or hurt and kill one of you guys?"

"Hazel," Marshal Holden spoke again. "It is my job to protect the people of this country, and that means there are countless risks involved. Now, everyone who cares about you and willingly puts themselves on the line to protect you does that for a reason. They love you and want to keep you as safe as possible, especially under the current circumstances. Let me ask you a question. Would you give your life for someone you love and care about?"

"Absolutely," she replied without skipping a beat.

"See? Mr. Tucker, Mr. Harrison, your father, Reverend Mitchell, and the other people in your life would do it too. Genuine love, and I don't just mean romantic love, means give and take, and that means you will die for someone else so that person can live."

Grateful tears entered her eyes, and Robert Mitchell pulled her into his arms again.

"Perhaps we should start thinking about the set-up of an arranged marriage. Wouldn't this girl make a fine wife for Todd?" Marshal Holden asked with a smirk, and everyone grinned. Hazel blushed.

"She would," Katherine agreed and squeezed Hazel's hand. "Having you as our new daughter would be a dream come true."

Hazel smiled. Marshal Holden was trying to lighten things up again, but she felt that they both meant what they said.

"It is time for us to return to the hotel," Jackson said now. "We have a long day ahead of us."

"Thank you for having us in your home and for such a delicious dinner," Hazel said with a smile, and Katherine gave her a warm hug.

"Please don't be a stranger. You are welcome to visit us whenever you are in Salem."

The young woman nodded.

"May I give you a hug, Hazel?" Marshal Holden asked, and she nodded again. He pulled her into his muscular arms and gave her a fatherly Papa Bear hug. She smiled up at him, and after everyone said their farewells, they left the house.

Sterling sighed. "This isn't over yet."

16

Salem Livestock Auction

Hazel did not sleep well that night. She kept waking up in a cold sweat and was exhausted when it was time to get up and ready. It was an important day, though, and she knew she had to prepare herself for some ugly drama.

Dave and Jackson waited for her in front of her room. She looked, once again, beautiful. She was wearing her dark brown riding outfit, which complimented her blue eyes, and her hair was up in a ponytail.

They had a quick breakfast and then left the hotel. Jackson had rented them three horses, and a bellboy waited outside, holding them. Hazel preferred riding a regular saddle, but here she had to ride sideways like a lady. Dave helped her on her horse, and the three of them took off toward the livestock auction.

The livestock auction was outside of Salem. They had to ride for a while before they got there. The sight was overwhelming. Hundreds of horses, cattle, and cowboys covered the area. They stopped in front of the tent where they had to register. Dave jumped off his horse and came to her aid.

He grabbed her around her waist and lifted her off her horse. She gave him a beaming smile.

The cowboys around stared at her curiously and enviously at Dave. Seeing a beautiful young lady in this environment was a rare sight.

Dave gave her a quick hug, a few instructions and watched her go into the tent.

As soon as she was inside, all eyes were on her. The first whistles came from one corner. She pushed herself through the masses until she reached the registration table. An older gentleman gave her a judgmental, grumpy glance.

"Ladies are not allowed in here," he said curtly.

"I am not a lady, and I am here to register our horses for the auction."

His mouth dropped. "Women aren't allowed to sell horses."

"Why not?"

"Listen, young lady, the law is the law, and we don't do business with women. Now, if your husband, brother, or father are here, they can come in, and we will serve them."

"I am not married," she replied, and the cowboys nearby looked her up and down, which made her uncomfortable. "My father asked me to come to this auction to sell our horses, and here I am."

"Are you here by yourself?"

Hazel noticed the looks from the surrounding men and shook her head. "I am not."

"Miss, I am sorry, but you are wasting your time."

"How am I wasting my time? I understand that I can't inherit my father's ranch yet, but nowhere does it say I can't sell my father's horses in his name."

The young men around her looked stunned.

"Is there a problem, Walter?"

"Mr. Montgomery, Sir," the older man replied. "No problem, this young lady was about to leave."

"No, I wasn't," she disagreed and looked at Russell Montgomery now.

"Women have no business in here."

"I am doing business for my father," she replied, unimpressed. Russell studied her carefully.

"If your father wants to sell his livestock, he has to come in here himself," Russell responded.

"Mr. Montgomery, as I told your employee. I am aware that it is against the law for a woman to own land. However, nowhere does it say I can't sell livestock in my father's name." She gave him a determined look, and that made him speechless for a moment.

"Who is your father?"

"George Buchannon."

"George Buchannon?" he replied, impressed. "He has the best horses and cattle in the country."

"Yes, he does, Sir. And he wants me to sell some of his finest horses. Now, to not waste any more of your time, would you please register our livestock?"

"Sweetheart, you will not sell anything here. Now, you are welcome to send in your foreman or brother or whoever came with you, and we will make a deal with him."

"Sweetheart? Sir, I am not a child and would like to be treated with respect. I can handle business just as well as our foreman can."

"I highly doubt it," Russell said with a grin, clearly amused by this conversation. "Find a reverend and marry one of these young fellows here, then you can come back with your husband."

Loud cheering was the answer. Hazel straightened her back.

"I marry you, darling. We can go to a reverend right now," one cowboy replied with a big grin on his face.

"Perhaps she has better taste than that," someone else shouted, and everyone laughed.

"I tell you what. Since you put up a good fight and amused me, I will buy your horses for ten dollars each. Is that a deal?" Russell's expression was full of mirth.

"No, it isn't. You haven't even looked at our horses, for starters, and you said yourself that my father has the best animals in the country. Are you trying to insult my intelligence with such a ridiculous offer? I will not sell something when it is worth four or five times as much."

Some young cowboys let out impressed whistles. That girl undeniably had fire and courage.

Russell looked at her, confounded for a moment. He, too, was impressed by her, but he had to stick to his guns. If he gave in now, nobody would take him seriously anymore. He nodded to one of the young men next to him and walked away.

The young man stepped forward before Hazel could call Russell back, grabbed her, and threw her over his shoulder.

"Hey, put me down," she argued and squirmed around, but he held her firm and carried her out of the tent. Whistling and jeering followed her until they were in front of the canvas. The young man took her off his shoulder.

"I am sorry, Hazel, but Russell Montgomery is my boss."

"How do you know my name?" She looked at him, surprised.

"You probably don't remember me, but I worked for your father for five years. I think you were ten when I left."

Hazel thought long and hard and studied his face. "Aaron Cooper?"

"That's right, so you do remember me?" he said with an enormous grin.

"Of course. You always lifted me on your shoulders, so I could see better when my dad and the other cowboys worked with the horses."

"I did."

"Looks like you're still lifting me on your shoulder," she sarcastically referred to him carrying her out. He let out a hearty laugh.

"I also caught your sister once when she fell off a fence."

"I am surprised you remembered me," Hazel said now.

"Well, I did not recognize you right away. You are a beautiful young lady now and not a child anymore, but it clicked when I heard you speak about your father." He squeezed her hand and she smiled at him. “Listen, I know you are not happy that I carried you outside, but Mr. Montgomery is strict about his rules.”

She pouted. “So it seems.”

“It was a miracle you were able to stay inside as long as you did. He won’t admit it, but I believe he was impressed with you, and your fighting spirit amused him. Keep impressing him like that, and you will win him over in no time. I have never seen him take a shine to any lady before, and so you must be doing something right.” Aaron grinned at her, and she smiled.

“Aaron?”

“Jackson. So good to see you again.” The two men greeted each other warmly. Dave came around the corner a moment later.

“There you are, Hazel. I was getting worried. I waited in front of the tent, but when I didn’t see you come out, I went around it and began looking for you.”

“I am fine. I got an offer for our horses from Mr. Montgomery. Not an offer I could accept, but that’s still good, right?”

“Good? That is incredible. You were in there for a while, so I take that as a good sign.”

Jackson followed Aaron inside to register their livestock for the big auction later in the day. Since there was nothing else for Hazel to do, she asked Dave if he wanted to join her on a ride around the lake behind the many horse enclosures. He agreed. He helped her on her horse, and they both trotted along toward the lake. It was a beautiful day, and the water sparkled in the sunshine.

The path around the lake was perfect for a ride, but they passed many people on foot. Hazel soaked in the air and listened to the sounds surrounding them.

When they had reached their original path back toward the enclosures, Hazel gave Dave a playful smile.

"Let's race back," she said, and he looked at her in disbelief.

"Are you sure you want to do that? This isn't your horse, and you are riding side-saddle." Dave's amused expression changed to concern.

"I can handle it, I promise."

He grinned. "Okay."

They stood side by side, both leaned forward, and when Dave nodded to her, they both kicked their horses in their sides. It was a tight race, but Hazel felt free and happy. For the first time in a long time, she forgot her problems.

A few of the cowboys watched them. Hazel had a bright smile on her face, her hair was blowing in the wind, and her cheeks were glowing with happiness. She looked beautiful.

Russell Montgomery stepped out of the tent's back exit when Dave and Hazel were on their last stretch. He was fascinated and couldn't stop looking at Hazel. Never had he met a girl so full of life, energy, determination, and stubbornness. Something told him he hadn't seen the last of her. He was looking forward to seeing her again and wondered what life held in store for her.

Hazel reached the fenced area first and stopped her horse. Childlike joy was on her face. "I won," she cheered, and her eyes sparkled in the sunlight. Dave grinned.

"Yes, you won," a deep voice called from behind them. Hazel turned her horse around, and there stood Robert Mitchell and Bishop Steven McDonald. They had watched their entire race and had amused smiles on their faces.

"Let me help you," Reverend Mitchell said. He lifted her out of the saddle and put her on the ground. She smiled at him and greeted him with a hug before she turned around and shook the hand of the bishop.

"Looks like you enjoyed yourself," Bishop McDonald remarked, and she nodded.

"It was heavenly," Hazel replied enthusiastically.

She felt happy when they were on their way home the following day. She hadn't sold horses yet, but had made a big step in the right direction. As they came closer and closer to Willamette Falls, her smile faded. She was excited to be back home, but home meant she eventually had to face Jason Clark again.

17

Diploma for Hazel Rae Buchannon?

Reverend Clark did not show himself on the ranch again, and the Buchannon's stayed away from Willamette Falls as much as possible. Hazel was now in the end phase of preparing for the final exam to earn a business and agriculture diploma. Since the study focused on farm and ranch work, most students didn't go to a university but studied it at home. They only took their exams at school. Hazel was lucky to have an actual teacher at home, so she only had to go to the final exam.

George, Haven, and Alex came with her this time. George and Alex were Hazel's emotional support and backup, and Haven wanted to be with her sister for such a special event.

Robert Mitchell did not meet them this time, and so they went straight to the hotel after they arrived. Hazel shared a room with her sister, and George and Alex slept in a room on each side. They met downstairs for a quick supper and went back to their rooms for an early night. The examination the following day was scheduled for eight am sharp. Since they were expecting difficulties, they wanted to be there as early as possible.

Haven fell asleep quickly, but Hazel was too nervous. She got up again, put on her dressing-gown, and kept pacing the room. After a while, she sat in a chair and tried to read, but she couldn't concentrate.

Suddenly, she heard someone attempting to open the door. Her blood froze, but she immediately thought of her sister. Hazel woke up Haven and told her to hide in the closet. Haven looked terrified but did as her sister told her. Hazel knew they wouldn't both fit in there, and she wanted her sister to be safe.

Whoever was at the door tried to get the key out of the door lock. Hazel grabbed a stocking and was about to squeeze it in the hole to stop the key from falling out when the key dropped. She rushed to hide behind a thick velvet curtain in front of the window and held her breath.

Alex Camden woke up, and a strange but strong feeling urged him to check on Hazel and Haven. At first, he tried to ignore it, but the sensation only got worse. He got up and listened at the door. It was quiet, and he couldn't hear anything. Alex unlocked the door and carefully opened it. When he glanced into the dark hallway, he saw two shadows standing in front of Hazel's room. Alex tip-toed back to his bed, grabbed his gun from his night desk, and went back to his door.

Hazel heard steps coming inside, and someone closed the door. Her heart was beating so loud, she was sure the intruders could hear it. One of them lit a candle and held it up to light up different corners in the room. Hazel squeezed herself as tight to the wall behind her as she could.

Now that there was light in the room, her shadow reflected from behind the curtain. One of the trespassers pulled a gun, pointed at the shadow, and fired a shot.

Haven almost passed out when she heard the gunshot. She wanted to burst out and check on her sister, but didn't know what was happening in the room. She kept listening with tears streaming down her face and prayed that her sister was okay.

The door flew open with a loud bang, and Alex Camden, the sheriff, two of the sheriff's deputies, and Robert Mitchell burst into the room, followed by George Buchannon. All of them had their guns drawn. Before the two intruders could react, Alex and one deputy had thrown themselves on them and knocked them to the floor. The sheriff and his second deputy handcuffed them and led them out of the room.

"Haven? Hazel?" George called out, his voice filled with worry and fear. Haven burst out of the closet and threw herself into the arms of her father. Her entire body was shaking with horror and fright, yet she kept looking around the room for her sister.

"Hazel? Where are you? Please be okay," she sobbed.

"I am here," Hazel replied quietly, and both Reverend Mitchell and Alex reacted quickly. Alex pulled the curtain back, and there she stood, white as a bedsheet but alive.

Robert Mitchell grabbed her and wanted to pull her into his arms when she cringed and moaned in pain. She had blood on her upper arm.

Her body collapsed when he tried to pick her up, so he caught her, lifted her, and put her on her bed. Haven lost it when she saw her sister so lifeless and knelt next to her, trying to keep her crying under control. Alex left at once to get a doctor.

"A grazing shot hit her. I cleaned her wound, added ointment and a bandage, and told her she needed to rest," Dr. Brendon Hinckley said when he came out of Hazel's hotel room. He was a young man of thirty years and a good friend of Todd Holden. George thanked him before everyone went into Hazel's room again.

The young woman was lying on her bed, staring out of the window. She glanced at her family when they walked in and gave them a weak smile. She was still pale, but her face showed no emotions.

"How are you feeling, Hazel?" Haven asked, her voice trembling.

"Okay, I guess, just tired."

"Do you want to talk about it, peanut?" George looked at her, worried. She only shook her head. A knock at the door made Haven jump up in fear, and Hazel tensed up, bracing herself. George opened the door, and in front of him stood Marshal Holden.

"Marshal, come on in," George said, and the other man stepped through the door frame. Hazel gave him a friendly nod. That was it.

"Hazel, how are you?" he asked, but could tell by her pale face that she was not doing well.

Robert Mitchell addressed him now. "Did you interrogate them?" Sterling Holden nodded. "Did they cooperate?"

"No. Both were not willing to speak."

"So, who were the intruders?" George asked.

"One was the concierge of this hotel," he responded. Alex, George, and even Reverend Mitchell gasped. Hazel didn't even look faced.

"And the other one?"

"Kendrick Carlton Mason... US Marshal." Sterling Holden was fuming.

"The young man you promoted last year?" Robert Mitchell asked, shocked. Sterling nodded.

"How did you even know about tonight's attack?" Alex still tried to grasp the events of the night.

"We've been working with our telegraphist, and he has been keeping us updated on everything that sounded suspicious. This evening, a wire came in for the hotel's concierge, and we knew we had to follow that one."

"Where did the wire come from, Sterling?"

"Willamette Falls."

Hazel, who had listened lifelessly to the entire conversation, sat up. Panic spread across her face and body. Her pale face turned even whiter.

"Was it from—?"

"We don't know yet. The telegraphist in Willamette Fall responded to our telegram and said he didn't know the person who sent it. Todd is now investigating, and he is trying to get in touch with our contact undercover. I understand that this is frightening, Hazel, but you need to stay calm. It might have nothing to do with Clark." Sterling Holden tried to soothe her, but he saw in her eyes it wasn't working. He even understood her.

They watched her out of the corner out of their eyes because she could snap at any moment. She stood and walked toward the window, just staring out into the darkness.

"I don't think we will hear from Todd during the night. Please go back to sleep, and we will let you know as soon as we have additional information."

George nodded and thanked Marshal Holden and Robert Mitchell gratefully. The two men leaving said goodnight to Haven, George, and Alex and hugged Hazel. She remained unresponsive. She acknowledged them going, but that was it.

George scanned the room before he cleared his throat. "We shouldn't let the girls sleep alone, not after this last attack. Let's move the furniture around, and then we can go to our rooms to get our mattresses and everything else we need."

Alex nodded in agreement. They moved the girl's beds to the furthest corner of the room, away from the door. Alex got his stuff first. Once he was back, George went to his room to collect his things. He was worried about Hazel. Just like after her mom left, she closed herself off and was unapproachable. It would come crashing down on her, eventually. At the same time, he was grateful and touched. Hazel had once again shown what a strong and incredible woman she was. Instead of losing it, she ensured that her sister was hidden and protected before thinking about her own safety.

They said goodnight to each other and went to sleep. George had his mattress directly in front of the door, so anyone coming in had to go through him.

Hazel couldn't sleep. Her wound was burning, and she couldn't stop thinking about yet another attack. She waited until everyone sounded asleep. Only then did she get up and walked back to the window. She stood there for quite some time until the tears came, and she broke out in quiet sobs. She covered her face and let her emotions run wild. Her heart hurt so much, she wanted to scream. Would she ever feel safe again? She didn't know how much more of this she could take. It was a never-ending horror nightmare. She had reached the end of her rope.

As she stood there crying, she suddenly felt an arm around her shoulders. It startled her at first, but when she looked up, Alex stood next to her, compassion and understanding on his face. He pulled her into his muscular arms, and she leaned against him, terrified and heartbroken, yet his presence comforted her.

Alex held her until she calmed down again and was ready to go to sleep. Hazel squeezed his hand with gratefulness. He put his hand on her warm cheek and communicated to her, she could always count on him.

That brief gesture gave her hope. Everyone around her fought along with her. She couldn't give up and had to stay strong. She promised herself she would fight until she had nothing left in her. Hazel was grateful for everyone who helped her go on when she felt like she couldn't anymore. She knew God had blessed her with remarkable people in her life.

Hazel did not look well when they met for breakfast the following morning. Her arm was still in pain, and she was pale but tried to appear cheerful. Nervousness kicked in, and it wasn't because of the exam. She endeavored to calm herself, though, because she needed to concentrate if she wanted to succeed.

A few young men were outside the Institute, waiting for the exam to start. They watched Haven and Hazel with great curiosity but stared at Hazel, stunned, when she stepped to the sign-in table. The secretary didn't even look up.

"Initials and last name," he said casually.

"H. R. Buchannon."

He looked through his papers and found her exam application right away.

"What's your full name?"

"Hazel Rae Buchannon," she replied, and for the first time, he looked at her.

"Is this a joke?" He glanced at her with a raised eyebrow.

"Why would this be a joke," she responded. "You are holding my application, don't you?"

"Yes, but women aren't allowed to take this exam."

"Says who?"

"The application states," he began, but Hazel cut him off.

"The application states nothing about gender and who can take part. I studied it before I signed it, and everything is as requested. I sent you my former exams and test results, and you accepted my application, which means I am entitled to take part."

A few of the young men let out an impressed whistle. The secretary was confused and speechless and didn't know what to do. He looked through the application, and sure enough, it said nothing about who could take part.

"Excuse me for a moment, Miss Buchannon," he said, more polite than before, and disappeared into the building.

It seemed like a long time until he came out again. Hazel was a nervous wreck at that point, but she kept a cool head.

"Please follow me, Miss Buchannon."

She nodded, and he led her into the building, into a large room full of tables. At the front of the room was a long table with six men behind it — the examination board. She scanned them as she walked closer, and nearly rolled her eyes when she recognized the last one at the table.

Great, she thought. *That's what I need today, an encounter with Russell Montgomery.* Why was he on the board of examination?

He recognized her too, but his eyes looked kindly at her and not judgmental. Perhaps he was willing to give her a chance.

"Miss Buchannon, I am sorry to inform you, but you can't take part in the exam," one examiner said.

"Why not?"

"You don't have the qualifications and ability," the examiner began, but she interrupted him.

"You mean I don't have the preferred gender, Sir. Let's at least call it by the right name," she said firmly, and saw an amused twinkle in Russell's eyes.

"Miss Buchannon," the examiner began again.

"This isn't fair or acceptable," she continued, standing her ground. "I worked hard for this. You received my application, saw my test and exam results, and accepted me. I traveled here at substantial lengths, and deserve a chance."

"You can't do anything with a diploma if you pass," another examiner interjected.

"I am aware of that, Sir. As of right now, I may not own land and put my knowledge to work, but perhaps someday I will. My father wants me to take over his ranch, and this is the first step in that direction."

"Miss Buchannon," Russell Montgomery said now. "What makes you think you've got what it takes to earn a degree and certificate in business and agriculture? What makes you think any woman can take on that task?"

Hazel looked into his eyes. He wasn't mocking her, he wasn't trying to make things difficult. He was genuinely interested in an answer.

"The answer is easy," she replied. "I love our ranch. I have been learning to run it ever since I could walk. My heart belongs to that place, and I will never give it up without a fight. It is overdue that women get more rights and respect." Her eyes were unyielding on him, willing to argue this out.

"We are not allowed to vote or own land and make our own decisions, yet we are expected to help run the farms and ranches our fathers or husbands own. Men can't do it alone. If a family doesn't have enough money to hire help, the entire family must do the work to survive. It isn't just the father and his sons working outside. Every hand is needed, especially during harvest. Women and daughters work in the fields, help with the livestock, and do many jobs men normally do. We can do the work, and we do it, but we don't get credit for it. Now, I was fortunate enough to grow up with a father who worked hard and had the means to hire help, but I still learned and did the work on our ranch. I learned how to break in a wild horse, have done plenty of cattle work, learned how to fix fences and other things, and have learned everything about the business side."

"...yet, you didn't learn to be a lady," one of the examiner's interjected. "Your father turned you into a son. It is a woman's job to take care of the house and, later, children." He looked at her with a stern expression, clearly thinking he had made an important point. Hazel wasn't intimidated.

"Do I look like a boy to you?" she retorted, and he had to shake his head. "I can do housework. I might not be the best at it, but I still know how to do it. And not being good at it has little to do with me not knowing how, but not being interested in it. Besides, who says I can't run a ranch and take care of my children and the house simultaneously? Why can't we, as women, do the things we enjoy doing? We are partners to our husbands and should be treated as such. We do our share of work and would not stop being women just because we are doing jobs men do. Not every woman wants to do things in a man-run world. Those who like a challenge should be able to do that, though. And to be fair, there are jobs out there we won't be able to do because we are not strong enough. That is okay too. Men claim that we aren't smart enough to do these things, yet many teachers are women. If we aren't smart enough, how come you allow us to teach your sons what they need to know to be successful in life?"

"All right, all right," Russell Montgomery said with an enormous grin on his face. "You made your point. I say we let her take the exam. Are you sure you want to take an exam for business and agriculture and not law?" he joked, and Hazel gave him a beaming smile.

"I am confident," she replied and winked at him.

"Let's put it to a vote, all in favor of letting her take the exam, raise your hand."

Hazel held her breath. The other five examiners still looked shocked. She had won over Mr. Montgomery, but were these men worse than him? No, they weren't. They gave Hazel a yes vote. She was so excited about this victory that she twirled herself around before leaving the room. They watched her amused and felt like they had just crowned her. What a beautiful whirlwind she was.

18

Choked into Unconsciousness

"And?" her father asked when she came out of the building. A few of the young men waiting stepped closer. She looked at her hands and let out a long sigh before her lips turned into a pout.

"Oh, Hazel, I am so sorry," Haven remarked before her sister's face changed into a beaming smile.

"I am in. They voted yes for me to take part," she replied and threw herself into the arms of her father.

Haven embraced her sister next, and the pair of them twirled around for a moment. Their excitement and happiness were contagious, and a smile spread across everyone's faces.

Alex pulled her into his arms when Hazel took a little breather from twirling and showed her how excited and proud he was of her.

"Congratulations, Miss Buchannon," one of the young men said and shook her hand with enthusiasm. "We were rooting for you." He pointed at four more young men and gave her a beaming smile.

"Thank you," Hazel replied, her cheeks reddening under his fascinated look.

"You probably didn't notice me last time you were in Salem, but I was in the tent when you tried to register your livestock for the auction. My name is Stewart Montgomery."

Hazel looked at him, surprised. "As in Russell Montgomery's son?"

"The very same," he responded with another big smile. "He might not have shown it, and he most likely will never admit it, but you impressed him that day."

"Really?" She glanced at him, an amused twinkle in her eyes.

"Really," he replied.

"Thank you, Mr. Montgomery."

"Please call me, Stew. Mr. Montgomery is my father. May I call you Hazel?"

She nodded.

"Well, Miss Buchannon," another young man said as he stepped closer, "not everyone rooted for you."

Stewart and his friends gave that young man a death stare. "Keep your comments to yourself, Philip," Stewart snapped, but Philip wasn't impressed.

"Why should I? Miss Buchannon should know that most men still believe women only have two functions. They exist to serve their husbands, or fathers if unmarried, and to share their bed with their husbands or other men if men so desire." He gave her a nasty smile and came close to her ear. "... I would gladly share my bed with you," Philip whispered into her ear while licking his lips and trailing a finger down her arm. Hazel turned around and slapped him.

"You are disgusting and have a filthy imagination."

Philip only laughed. Stewart, Alex, and even her father had intended to step in when he so indecently approached Hazel, but when she slapped him, they stayed back.

"Truth's hurts, honey."

"Nothing is true about the things you said. I would be surprised if you will ever find a wife with your tedious attitude."

"I don't have to find a wife," he responded with an arrogant smirk on his face. "I am married."

"She must not have known what you were like when she accepted your proposal."

"I didn't propose," he scoffed with disdain. "Her father told her to marry me, and that was that. She gets the things done I need her for, and that's what matters. She might not be the prettiest person, but hey, if I need someone pretty for something special, there are ways." Philip gave her another nasty smile. She only shook her head.

"An arranged marriage was the only way to get a wife, huh?" Hazel shot back, letting her quick wit shine. The men around them, chuckled. Philip turned red with anger, before he could say something in return, however, Hazel continued.

"Your poor wife. Having such a husband must be devastating. Nobody deserves such a punishment."

"You arrogant little beast," he began and grabbed her wrists.

"Let go of my daughter," George barked at once as he seized the young man by his shirt and pushed him backward. Alex's arm came around Hazel's waist, and he pulled her away from Philip Mason.

Stewart and his friends placed themselves between the young woman and the rude troublemaker.

"If you ever put hands on my daughter again, I'll make sure you'll regret that for the rest of your life." Her father was still seething.

"She insulted me," Philip erupted with an offended tone in his voice.

"You have done nothing but insult her from the moment you stepped next to her. You are lucky her father didn't step in until now." Stewart was fuming.

"You should be ashamed of yourself for being such a coward," another young man commented. "First, you disrespect and insult her in every possible way, and then you get upset when she puts you in your place?" He shook his head with disdain.

Philip stepped back. "I am not done with you," he spat out, contempt and hate in his voice.

"Yes, you are, Mr. Mason."

Russell Montgomery stood in the wide open doors, outrage and fierceness on his face. "If you get out of line around this young lady, or any lady, again, we will call the sheriff, *and* you'll get expelled from this Institute and exam."

"You can't do that," Philip snapped.

"Actually, we can and will," another examiner said and stepped past Russell. "You may have your opinion on things, but you have no right to attack a young lady in such an inappropriate and rude manner. Your behavior is way out of line, Mason, and if she had been my daughter, your mother wouldn't recognize you anymore," the examiner continued, held-back anger coloring his voice.

"You are fortunate that her father is in control of his feelings and emotions. You deserve much more than a slap across your face."

Philip couldn't believe what was happening. Where did these examiners come from? How did they know about the encounter he had with Hazel Buchannon? It blew his mind that they stood up for her. Had men not always prided themselves on being the stronger gender and for owning and controlling women? He gave Hazel another dirty look before moving away from her and her protectors and stepping to a group of benches across the schoolyard.

Hazel thought she had done a decent job of defending and standing up for herself. She felt she was in control until Philip grabbed her wrists. It was easy for her to fight with words, but when a man used his strengths against her, the fight became unfair and dangerous.

As soon as her father had taken on Philip Mason and Alex had pulled her backward, her tensed up body began to relax. She stepped off to the side to compose herself.

It got to her, as this attack reminded her once again of Jason Clark. He had the same evil attitude toward women. She realized men used physical attacks and aggression when they lost control in an argument and didn't get what they wanted.

Hazel was touched and thankful when she saw how many of the men around stood up for her. It showed her that chivalry was not dead, and many men were good, honest, and kind. Their fathers and mothers had taught them well.

When Russel Montgomery and his colleague stepped out and got involved, her heart jumped. Thoughts of every threat and attack entered her mind, but she pushed it away from her. As long as Hazel had inspiring and wonderful people in her life, who was she to give up the fight? She would keep fighting, no matter how much someone knocked her to the floor. She would keep fighting until she couldn't stand up anymore, and presently, she had to focus on passing this exam.

After Philip stepped away, everyone turned their attention to Hazel to make sure she was okay. She didn't want them to make such a fuss over her, especially when she noticed that more and more students showed up for the exam.

The students were now let in, and everyone found themselves a table and seat. Since Russell Montgomery and the other examiners had witnessed the encounter between Hazel and Philip Mason, they made sure Philip was on the other side of the room. Stewart and his friends sat around Hazel to give her extra protection.

Russell stood, made a few opening remarks, and explained why Hazel was part of the examination. Most of the young men had a positive and welcoming reaction, and the few who disagreed kept their comments to themselves.

The professors handed out the exams, and the room went quiet. Hazel worked through her papers, concentrated and sufficient. Russell and his colleagues walked through the room and made sure nobody cheated. Every professor stopped next to Hazel at one point and looked over her shoulder. Each one of them stepped away with a smile on their face. Russell even patted her on the shoulder, a sure sign of approval.

After three hours, the first part of the exam was over. Everyone handed in their papers and was released for thirty minutes before the second part began. All the young men rushed outside, and Hazel went to the washroom to freshen up and drink water. Her arm was hurting again, but she tried to ignore it.

When Hazel stepped out of the washroom, the hallway was empty, and it was quiet. She walked toward the front door to join the other students outside when someone grabbed her from behind, turned her around, and pushed her against the wall.

As soon as Philip realized that her arm was hurting, he grabbed her even harder and pressed on it until it started bleeding again.

"Let go of me," she shouted. "You are hurting my arm."

"I know, and I will enjoy every moment," he replied with a sleazy smile on his face. Hazel kicked his leg with such force that he dropped his hands and started cursing at her. She turned around and was about to flee when he seized her again. He slammed her into the wall and started choking her.

"This is for getting my brother into jail, you little witch. All he did was enter your hotel room," he shouted in her face. Hazel tried to loosen his hands, but he only closed his hands more around her throat.

"He shot me," she whispered, her voice full of panic. She frantically gasped for air, and everything started spinning. When he let go of her throat, she collapsed to the floor, hitting her head against a door frame. Everything went black.

Russell Montgomery and two of his colleagues had barely returned from the teacher's lounge when they heard Hazel and Philip's voices in the hallway. They rushed out of the room, only to see Hazel unconscious on the floor. The side of her forehead and her arm were bleeding.

While Russell lifted Hazel, the other two grabbed Philip Mason and held him. The rest of the examiners returned from the teacher's lounge, and one of them hurried outside and asked two students to get the sheriff and doctor at once. Stewart and two of his friends came inside to check on Hazel, and two of the young men rushed away to get her father.

Russell carried Hazel into the teacher's lounge and put her on the settee. That's when Stewart and his friends stormed into the room.

"Father, I am so sorry. I thought Philip was in the schoolyard. We saw him leave the building. I was waiting outside for her, right next to the front doors. I didn't want to invade her privacy and follow her to the washrooms."

"It is okay, Son," Russell replied and patted his son on his shoulders. "This was not your fault. Mason snuck into the building using a different way, so he could catch her alone. I could blame myself too. I thought he wouldn't dare another attack against her, not today, at least, and I was wrong."

"Is there anything we can do to help?" one of Stewart's friends asked.

"Yes. Please stay with the professors to make sure that Philip Mason won't get away. Stewart, grab water and something we can use to stop the bleeding."

The three young men nodded and left the room. Russell grabbed a chair and sat next to Hazel. He looked at her and felt guilty. Even though he had never put his hands on a woman, he had been plenty harsh to women like Hazel.

His arrogance had given him the reputation he had now, and this remarkable girl had to come along to open his eyes. He could have changed women's lives by standing up for them and giving them a chance instead of judging them. Maybe this wake-up call had to happen, so he would do something he should have done all along? He promised himself he would not stand back and let Hazel fight this war alone. He was ready and willing to do his part.

Hazel started moving her head and opened her eyes. When she saw Russell sitting next to her, she thought of Philip Mason. Hazel began lifting herself, but a stabbing pain in the forehead made her lay down again. She closed her eyes.

"What happened?"

"Philip choked you unconscious, and you fell to the floor and hit your head on a door frame," Russell replied. Hazel was about to touch her wound, but he stopped her hand.

"Don't. It is still bleeding."

The door opened, and Stewart came inside with a bowl of water and washcloths. The young woman gave him a weak smile.

"How are you feeling, Hazel?"

"Tired," she replied. The two men were about to clean the wound on her head when the door opened, and the sheriff, Dr. Hinckley, George Buchannon, and Haven stormed into the room. As soon as Haven saw her sister, she started crying. Dr. Hinckley sent everyone out of the room, so he could attend to Hazel's wounds. Haven was the only one allowed to stay.

Alex was in front of the teacher's lounge waiting when the Montgomery's, the sheriff, and George stepped out again.

"Where is the person who did that to her," the sheriff asked with anger in his voice. Stewart and Russell led him into a small classroom, where Stewart's friends and the other teachers still held Philip. George and Alex followed.

George had always been someone who was in full control of his emotions. But when he saw the young man who had attacked his daughter, sitting on a chair with a smug grin on his face, he had to hold himself back to not plant a facer on him.

"Philip Mason," one of the examiner's roared, "you are expelled from this school and the exam. The board of this Institute will decide if we let you come back after the summer or if we expel you for good."

"Headmaster Walden, my father will cut off financial support for the school if you kick me out."

"He may do that if he wishes to do so. We don't condone this behavior at our school. You insulted and attacked a young woman who was a fellow student. If her father wishes to press charges, we will provide the evidence and witnesses needed."

Philip's face dropped.

"I am pressing charges. You won't get away with this," George promised him with a deep growl in his voice.

"Let's get you out of here, Mason," the sheriff said and moved him out of the room.

"What is happening to Hazel?" Alex asked, shocked. "It is as if Satan himself is after her."

"He probably is," Russell responded. "From what I have seen so far, she is a strong and determined young woman, and he wants to see people like her broken."

After the doctor finished treating Hazel's wounds, he called everyone back into the room. Headmaster Walden went outside to inform the other students that they would postpone the rest of the exam to the following day.

Hazel was still lying on the settee, her wounds covered with bandages, but she looked better. Haven was sitting next to her, the shock written on her face. She couldn't believe what her poor sister had to go through.

"It is important she stays off her feet for the rest of the day. She needs to take it easy during the next few days. Her body has gone through much agony these past two days, and her mind is constantly working," Dr. Hinckley said, and George nodded. "She needs and deserves to be spoiled," the young doctor added and smiled at Hazel.

"I agree," Russell Montgomery commented. "Let's get this girl so many flowers that she won't know what to do with it." He winked at her but nodded to his son, and Stewart left the room. Hazel blushed but smiled. She was about to sit up when the doctor stopped her in her tracks.

"No way, Miss Buchannon. You are not ready to get up yet. When I feel you are ready to go home, one of these gentlemen here will carry you."

There was a knock on the door, and a moment later, Reverend Robert Mitchell and Marshal Sterling Holden came into the room.

"We just heard," Marshal Holden said.

"Oh, Hazel," Reverend Mitchell uttered when he looked at her face. She gave him a weak smile.

"Hazel," Russell Montgomery said now, "don't you worry about the second half of the exam. We postponed it to tomorrow, and if you don't feel well enough, you can take it another time."

"Thank you, Mr. Montgomery."

He squeezed her hand. Hazel looked at him for a moment before, she closed her eyes.

"Let's let her sleep for a while. I'll stay and watch her, and Miss Haven can keep us company," Dr. Hinckley said, and Haven nodded. "Please wait in the hallway. I'll let you know when she is ready to return to the hotel."

"Have you found out anything about yesterday's attack?" George asked when they stepped into the classroom next door.

"What attack?" Russell Montgomery glanced around with wide eyes. Everyone stared at him, stunned. They had forgotten that Russell was new in the picture and had no idea what Hazel had gone through during the past few months. Since he had been so attentive to Hazel, and they knew he was a law-abiding citizen, they filled him in.

It hit home for him when they spoke about the almost abductions. His youngest daughter had barely escaped a kidnapping the year before. It was prevented by her now-husband, his son Stewart, and their friends. He was grateful for their heroic actions, and he knew she was married to an outstanding man.

"That is horrific. I can't even imagine what that poor girl has gone through, and from the sound of it, it isn't even over yet."

"No, it isn't," Marshal Holden replied. "We have been able to make several arrests, but many of those evil vermin are still free and continue to harass and threaten our female community. Hazel is especially targeted because that low-life reverend of theirs is such a filthy demon."

"Why hasn't he been arrested yet?" Russell asked.

Marshal Holden sighed. "Not enough evidence. It is his word against hers. Reverend Mitchell saw one encounter between that scumbag and Hazel, but if we use Mitchell as the only witness, Clark will twist it into something questionable. We have people working undercover and are searching for more witnesses against him."

"Have you found out who was behind yesterday's attack?" George asked, his expression serious.

"Our contact in Willamette Falls sent a telegram informing us that he couldn't find anything on Clark. However, when Todd showed the telegraphist a sketch of Gabriel McKellar, he recognized him as the person who sent the telegram to our two intruders in Hazel's hotel room."

"McKellar is still in or around Willamette Falls?" Alex asked as he jumped into the conversation.

"Yes. Todd has been trying hard to find that coward, but with no luck so far. Nobody has seen him. He keeps showing up and then disappears again." Marshal Holden was seething.

"I wouldn't be surprised if Clark still had something to do with yesterday's attack," Robert Mitchell remarked, and his eyes had a dangerous sparkle. The rest of the group nodded.

"What will happen now?"

"We will continue as we have. My men are all over the country. With the arrests, we have made so far, we have prevented several kidnappings. We still haven't found the person who started it, and until we get him, the evil will continue to spread. Meanwhile, we can only do so much to protect Hazel." Sterling Holden looked at the other men.

"That's true. We try to be around Hazel as much as possible, but we can't take away her privacy. If we keep invading her personal space, she will feel like we are trying to take away her air to breathe. She likes her independence and does not want to give up her freedom," George responded.

"She strikes me as a strong and determined young woman," Russell repeated his thoughts from before. "I am surprised, though, that these terrible incidents haven't broken her spirit yet."

"It has been close, but she keeps pushing herself back up. I think knowing that we believe her and are doing what we can to keep her safe and want this to stop as much as she does, helps her to keep fighting."

19

A Reason to Celebrate

"Hazel is awake, and you can take her home now," Dr. Hinckley said as he stepped into the classroom. "Please ensure she stays in bed and keeps her physical activity to a minimum. I will check on her this evening."

George went into the teacher's lounge, lifted his daughter, and everyone followed him to the hotel.

Hazel was stunned when George opened the door and carried her inside their room. Not only was this a different room, but the room was filled with flowers. Stewart stood there with a grin and handed Hazel a single red rose. She blushed.

After her father laid her on her bed, she glanced around again. A beautiful smile appeared on her face, and she looked at Russell Montgomery.

"Thank you."

"This is from all of us," he responded. "I was hoping it would bring a smile to your face. May we call on you tonight?"

Hazel nodded, still overwhelmed by the sight of so many flowers.

"Why are we in this room, Pa?"

"The hotel owner heard what happened and was very sorry. He arranged for us to move into this room as an apology. It is much bigger and has a small washroom behind that door. Alex and I will continue to stay with you, and so the owner ordered his employees to set up this thick velvet curtain so you two have privacy."

"That is so kind of the hotel manager," Haven said with a smile.

"He also hired two of the sheriff's deputies to stand watch in front of our room during the night."

Hazel closed her eyes, and tears streamed down her face. She was touched and grateful. What did Reverend Mitchell teach in church? *For verily I say unto you, blessed is he that keeps my commandments, whether in life or in death, and he that is faithful in tribulation, the reward of the same is greater in the kingdom of heaven...' 'For after much tribulation come the blessings....'*

Heavenly Father loved her, and he had sent these wonderful people into her life to bless her. Trials were part of life, but these past few months had pushed her to her limit, and it wasn't over yet. It was the blessings of kindness and love that kept her going and made life beautiful again.

Marshal Holden and Reverend Mitchell said their goodbyes, but promised they would be back that evening. Hazel smiled at everyone, closed her eyes, and was fast asleep.

George watched her for a while. What a day. She won over the professors and had done the first part of the exam. Philip

Mason had verbally attacked and then physically assaulted her. His beautiful daughter went from one hell to another, yet she continued to fight and kept seeing the blessings in her life. He was beyond grateful for this incredible girl, her strength, and her striking example.

Since George knew their old and new friends intended to visit that evening, he arranged with the hotel to set up dinner in their room, so Hazel could take part. He wanted to show everyone his thankfulness and celebrate the blessings of the day.

He closed the curtain toward the girl's part of the room. The hotel employees set up the rest of the room as a dining room. They pushed the other two beds against the walls, turned them into sofas, and placed tables in front of it. More chairs were brought in, and the hotel staff put another big table in one corner to serve as a buffet table. When they were done setting up, the room was difficult to recognize.

Hazel slept most of the day. After the little sleep of the previous night and the many excitements she went through, she had to catch up on well-deserved rest. Her sister stayed by her side the entire time. Knowing that Hazel had almost been choked to death made Haven not want to leave her.

Dr. Hinckley showed up first. He checked Hazel's wounds, but everything looked much better. George invited him to stay for dinner, and he accepted. He also asked him if Hazel could join them at the table. Brendon Hinckley agreed, but he made Hazel promise to continue to be careful.

Reverend Mitchell came next. He greeted Hazel with a smile and kissed her on her head before greeting the rest of the family. Russell Montgomery, his son Stewart and two of Stewart's friends called on her next, and everyone accepted the spontaneous dinner invitation. Last but not least, Marshal Holden came as promised, and he brought his wife with him. She went over to Hazel and hugged her.

"Honey, I am so sorry this keeps happening to you. You must have been quite an angel if Satan is targeting you in such horrific ways." She gently patted Hazel's cheek when her husband stepped next to her.

"She is still quite an angel," he added with a big smile and winked at her. Hazel blushed.

It was a wonderful evening, with excellent food, lots of laughter, and creating friendships they never thought they would have. As bad as it was what Hazel had to go through, meeting, so many caring people along the way was a blessing she would cherish forever.

Before Dr. Hinckley left, he checked on Hazel again. He told her she could participate in the second part of the exam if she promised to rest afterward. She promised.

Everyone was seated by eight am the following day. Stewart assured George Buchannon that he would not let Hazel out of sight, and so he and his friends sat around her again. The principal and other examiner greeted her happily and were relieved to see her so well again.

George and Haven picked her up, walked her back to the hotel, and made sure she relaxed the rest of the day.

Hazel didn't sleep well that night, so many thoughts tumbled through her mind. Did she pass the exam? Would Jason Clark come after her again once she was home? Would her family be in danger? What if they released the Mason brothers, and they came after her too? It was way past midnight when she pushed those thoughts away. She needed to relax. There was no point in stressing over the exam since it was done, and she would get the results within the next twelve hours.

Stewart squeezed Hazel's hand. The tension in the room was unbearable. Everyone looked up when the examiner's walked through the door. It was time to find out whether they had passed this vital test. Stewart Montgomery had failed once before, and so he hoped he had succeeded this time. George, Alex, and Haven waited outside and were just as nervous as Hazel.

Headmaster Walden said a few words before the examiners handed out everyone's exams. The first excited cheers erupted in the classroom, and a moment later, Stewart high-fived his friend next to him. Hazel looked confused since she hadn't gotten her exam back yet, but Russell Montgomery stood and cleared his throat.

"As you know, I am not a professor at this school. That said, since I am well known in the business world for livestock and agriculture, I was asked to help supervise this exam. We want to congratulate you on passing this important test. It is a huge stepping stone into the actual world. Before we release you, though, I would like to ask Miss Hazel Buchannon to join me."

Hazel looked surprised, but stood and went to the teacher's table. Russell put an arm around her shoulders.

"Miss Buchannon not only convinced us she deserved a chance at this exam, but she also passed this test as the only student with 100%."

The young woman blushed, but a beaming smile appeared on her face. She didn't care that she had the best test results. She cared that she had passed and that she had proven that women were smart too.

Loud whistling and cheers erupted in the classroom, and Stewart gave her a thumbs up and an excited grin. All the professors congratulated her and had kind and encouraging words for her.

However, the best part was that each one promised to join her in court when it was her time to fight for a law change. Stewart embraced her and twirled around with her. The professors watched the happiness and excitement with a smile.

"Gentlemen and Miss Buchannon," Headmaster Walden roared to calm everyone down again. "Please join me in the schoolyard outside. The Salem News wants to write an article about the examination results, and they also would like to take a photograph of all the participants and professors. The journalist and photographer are out there waiting for us."

Everyone flooded out of the room and building. George, Alex, and Haven looked for Hazel, and when she came outside, gave her a questioning glance.

"I passed," Hazel burst out, and George and Haven embraced her at the same time. Alex held her a moment later and lifted her in the air, he was that proud of her. Russell Montgomery stepped next to them.

"She didn't just pass. She passed with honors and was the only one with perfect test results."

Alex's mouth dropped, but at the same time, he wasn't surprised.

"Miss Buchannon," Headmaster Walden said with a smile. "Would you do us the honor of joining us for the photograph? We want the world to see that our school not only had a woman take part in this exam, but that this astonishing woman beat her fellow students in the score."

"It would be my pleasure," she responded with a smile, and followed him to join the rest of the graduates. Before Hazel had reached the other students, Stewart grabbed her, and with two of his friends, carefully lifted her on his shoulder. Hazel let out a shocked gasp, as she had not expected that, and everyone around grinned.

"What are you doing, Stew? Put me down."

"No way. You are the honor student here and need to stand out between us men."

He placed himself in the middle of the crowd, and everyone gathered around him. The professors sat on chairs in the front, and the photographer moved the young men around until he had everyone in the picture.

When the photographer was happy with the outcome, one of Stewart's friends lifted her off the young man's shoulder and put her back on the ground. Everyone spread out and said their goodbye's until the schoolyard was empty again.

Stewart stepped next to Hazel. "Both our fathers have been planning a celebration ball for tonight, and it will be at our hotel. Would you do me the honor of accompanying me this evening?" He looked into her blue eyes and gave her a winning smile. Hazel blushed but nodded.

Stewart had asked George Buchannon for permission to ask her, and one of his friends invited Haven.

George and Alex greeted Hazel and Haven with big smiles when the girls stepped through the curtain. The two young women looked lovely. Hazel wore a dark blue gown and her sister a light pink dress. Alex and George both bowed like gentlemen, and the two girls started giggling.

George opened the door. Stewart and Haven's escort were waiting outside and offered them their arms. Hazel tucked her arm under Stewart's, and he led her along the hallway, down the stairs, and into the ballroom.

"You look gorgeous, Hazel," he said and pulled a chair back for her. She sat down, cheeks blushing, but gave him a beaming smile.

"You don't look so bad yourself," she replied with a twinkle in her eyes, and he grinned.

Russell Montgomery stepped next to her now and bowed, taking her gloved hand in his and implied a hand kiss. It made her feel so royal.

Robert Mitchell and Bishop Steve McDonald entered together, and both of them greeted Hazel first. Right after, the two clergymen, Katherine and Sterling Holden, stepped into the ballroom.

"Hazel, you look breathtaking," Katherine called out and made Hazel twirl around herself. "You are the queen of this ball."

"Thank you so much, Mrs. Holden, but I bet your husband would beg to differ with you in the room." Hazel winked at the Marshal, and he grinned.

"Katherine is certainly my queen of the ball," he replied, embraced his wife, and kissed her cheek. Katherine blushed.

Like the rest of the men, Marshal Holden looked incredibly handsome in his evening attire, and when he bowed his head, Hazel dropped into a curtsy. He saw a playful sparkle in her eyes and winked at her.

It was custom for a host to open the ball with a waltz. Since Russell Montgomery and George Buchannon were hosting this event together, both had to find a partner. George wanted to dance the first dance with Hazel since this ball was in her honor, but he knew how shy Haven was. He didn't want her to be uncomfortable if Russell thought about asking her, so George asked Haven to dance.

Russell Montgomery looked around to find Hazel. She wasn't sitting next to his son anymore. He grinned when he saw her in the back of the room and hurried over to her. She had hidden deliberately, since she didn't want to open the ball with everyone staring at her.

Russell had expert eyes, though. He took a bow like a gentleman and gave Hazel a winning smile. "Miss Buchannon, would you do me the honor of this dance?"

She couldn't say no now, and so he took her hand and led her onto the dance floor. She quickly realized what an incredible dance partner he was. He grinned at her, and she couldn't help but smile.

When the waltz was over, and he had brought her back to her table, the ballroom door opened, and in came Helen, Brenna, Dave, Namito, and Jackson.

Hazel's eyes lit up, and she lifted her dress, so she could run over to them and greet them. Jackson, Namito, and Dave wanted to be the first to hug her, but Dave was the fastest. He opened his arms, and Hazel jumped into his embrace. He lifted her in the air, twirled around with her, and pulled her into his arms.

"It is so good to see you again, and I am glad you are mostly okay." He caressed her face before handing her over to Namito, who hugged her just as tight.

"That horrible telegram from your father scared us half to death. I am so glad this last incident wasn't worse."

"What are you doing here?" she asked as Namito was putting her on the floor. Before the young Indian could even respond, Jackson pulled her into his arms.

"Your father invited us as a surprise to celebrate your amazing accomplishment."

"But how did he know I would pass?"

"You might have had your doubts, but none of us doubted you for a moment," Jackson replied with a grin. "Now, for the rest of this trip, I am glad nothing else happened."

She looked into his eyes, and even though there was still a smile on his face, she could see worry and concern. Haven had greeted Helen and Brenna, and Hazel welcomed them now too.

Stewart and his friends had watched the entire greeting ceremony with envy. They had no idea how close Hazel was with her loved ones, and that Dave and Namito were her best buddies and like brothers to her.

Hazel and Haven danced the night away. Hazel had hardly time to eat and breathe, since everyone wanted to dance with her. Dr. Hinckley finally stepped in and told everyone that Hazel could not dance anymore. Doctor's orders.

Stewart was by Hazel's side whenever she wasn't dancing with someone else. As the ball ended, he took her hand in his.

"Hazel, I am in love with you. I don't want to return to San Francisco and forget about you and the past few days. You are such a beautiful girl, and my heart is yours."

Hazel froze in shock. She had not expected a declaration of love from him. She knew that he liked her a great deal and maybe even fancied her, but that was almost a proposal. She didn't know what to say. Stewart waited. He didn't rush her, just sat next to her until she was ready to respond.

"Stewart," she finally said. "I like you, and I am grateful for everything you did for me the past few days, but how would a relationship between us work? You are in San Francisco, I am in Willamette Falls. I can't move away from my family. I belong there, and I can't ask you to come to Oregon. You have dreams and wishes, and so do I."

He nodded, resigned. He had thought the same things and agreed that he was unwilling to leave everything he worked for behind and move away. Hazel's dream was to take over her father's ranch, and the battles she still had to fight would not be easy. It would be unfair of him to ask her to give up everything when he wasn't willing to do the same in return.

"Can we still be friends, and can I call on you whenever I am in Oregon?"

"Of course you can. I will always cherish your friendship."

20
It Isn't Over

"Clark," Adam Harrison called out as he entered the church and looked around to see where the reverend was.

"I am here, Adam," came the reply out of a corner. Jason Clark was sitting there, and next to him was Gabriel McKellar.

"I received a letter from William Mason. He wrote that both his boys accomplished their tasks, but were caught and ended up in prison. They are now waiting for their trial for attempted murder. Mason will not work with us anymore. He said if his boys make it out of this alive, they'll stay out of criminal's way."

Gabriel scoffed. "As if that will happen. If they are tried for attempted murder, they won't make it out alive. Oregon's laws are intense."

"Don't be so smug, McKellar. They could come after us next," Adam snapped. "Mason said in his letter that Marshal Holden and Salem's sheriff found out you wrote the telegram with the instructions on how to attack Hazel Buchannon. They are looking for you everywhere now."

"So the telegraphist in Salem is working with the sheriff and marshal? Big Deal. They will never catch me," he bragged. "They haven't caught me yet and never will. I am good at what I do."

"Arrogance is a person's downfall," Jason Clark interjected.

"You should talk," Gabriel snapped. "You were only supposed to point out girls we can kidnap. After the incident in Salem and your sudden transfer here, I thought you had learned your lesson, but no, you had to go after that Buchannon girl."

"Both of you should finally learn your lessons," Adam snarled as he jumped back into the conversation. "Because of your actions, we are getting fire from all directions. Your sick obsession of wanting to make a girl yours, so you can make your filthy fantasies come to life, is way out of control. If you don't stop harassing her, they will come after you before you know it."

"Speaking of harassing," Jason Clark said, "what was her reaction to our latest attack?"

"I spoke to my brother. He said Russell Montgomery and the Institute's professors stepped in and held Mason until the sheriff arrested him. Hazel won those guys over too. I am telling you, Clark, she gains more believers and protectors each time you have her attacked. Marshal Holden is one of her new admirers."

"Okay, we get it. Clark needs to step back and get his obsession under control, but what about Hazel? Did we at least stop her from taking the exam?"

"No. Kendrick Mason shot her, but she was only hit by a grazing shot, and it only scared the heck out of her and her sister. The doctor took care of it, she pulled herself together and took the first half of the exam the following morning. Philip Mason caused drama before the exam started, but was put in his place by a bunch of Hazel's new admirers. Montgomery Jr. and his friends sat around her during the exam to keep her safe. When Philip attacked her during break and choked her until she fainted, she hit her head against a door frame. They moved the second half of the exam to the following day for everyone. She passed with honors, and they celebrated her and her fellow students that evening with a ball."

"Curse that girl," Jason Clark snapped. "How much more do I have to do before I break her spirit and have her come crawling to me?"

"Stop targeting her for a while, so she can recover from the anguish and stress you are putting on her. She keeps bouncing back because your attacks are so aggressive and constant that everyone who finds out is on her side."

"That is the only reason I am constantly after her. I don't want her to recover. I want her to give up, I want to break her."

"A girl like Hazel will not break easily. You might knock her down, but she will find a way to get back on her feet. Having so many protective men around her makes her a hard target to crack."

"So, we need to kill off the men in her life?" Gabriel McKellar asked with a sick grin on his face.

"If you do that, you might as well bury yourself," Adam seethed. "Can you two idiots not get it into your heads we are being watched? They trust me so far, but it won't be long before they figure it out, and they can't wait to take you down, Clark."

"What do you mean by they can't wait to take me down? They have nothing against me. It is Hazel's word against mine."

"So far, yes, but they still believe her, and everyone she had contact with believes her. Bishop McDonald and Reverend Mitchell are already on your bad side because of what you did in Salem."

"They have no proof."

"Not yet, but they are working on it. They are trying to find witnesses willing to testify against you. The girls in Salem are too scared because of the constant threats they keep getting. If Hazel continues on her path, though, Mitchell will use that against you and take her as an example, so the other girls get the courage they need."

"They wouldn't dare."

"Yes, they will dare. Marshal Holden and his men are all over the country and made several arrests. Once they find out who is behind this, they will arrest everyone."

"So, what are we going to do now?" Gabriel asked.

"After these last unsuccessful attacks, Hazel will have even more protection around her. They won't let her out of her sight."

"She can't be happy with it," Clark sneered, anger coloring his voice.

"No, she isn't, but despite her not giving up, she fears you."

"At least that."

"I suggest you continue to stay away from her and stop hiring other people for a while. Let her feel safe again before you try to put your hands on her once more."

"Maybe my friend Dwight can give her attention while you and I stay in the background, Clark," McKellar said now. "It is time he comes out of hiding."

Back at home, everyone got ready for the big cattle drive. The cowboys rounded up 500 cattle, which they had to drive to San Francisco. They would be gone for at least two weeks, possibly longer, and every hand was needed. Jackson had hired a few more cowboys to help with the drive, since they also required cowboys at home.

The new cowboys were all hard workers, except one. His arrogance and conceit made it unbearable to be around him. Whenever Hazel came outside to help or prepare something for the cattle drive, he was there showing off. He took off his shirt, flaunted his muscles, and tried every possible way to impress her. He kept bragging about himself, and that made him even less attractive to the young woman. She avoided him whenever she could.

The day before the cattle drive, Hazel sat in front of the house with her saddle and fixed it up. She had barely sat on the front porch when Dwight once again approached her. He was not a bad-looking young man, but Hazel had never liked men in love with themselves. When he kept posing, she grabbed her things and went into the house. Dwight followed her.

She sat on the sofa in the living room, and he jumped over it and placed himself right next to her, putting his arm around her shoulders. She moved to the side, he followed. Hazel had enough.

"Mr. Miller, our foreman, didn't hire you to be lazy. Everyone is working hard to be ready by tomorrow, and I would recommend you do the same."

"I want to get to know you better before we leave tomorrow, Hazel. A pretty thing like you and a good-looking guy like me make a wonderful combination." He tried again to put his arm around her shoulders, but she slapped his hand away.

"I am Miss Buchannon to you, and while I am at it, keep your hands away from me. I am not interested in you, so leave me alone," she snapped, but saw in his eyes that he was not accustomed to being rejected.

"You are too good for me, huh? You think you are better than me because I am only a simple cowboy?"

"You being a simple cowboy has nothing to do with this. I have a problem with your arrogant attitude. Now, if you don't want to lose your employment, I suggest you get to work."

"You are not my boss, Hazel Buchannon," he responded aggressively. "Think before rejecting me because I can assure you, you don't want me as your enemy."

"GET OUT!" she yelled.

"You...," he began before a noise above them made them turn around.

"Miller," Alex bellowed as he stood on top of the stairs, staring down on them. His expression was fierce, his fists clenched. "Miss Buchannon has asked you to leave and to stay away from her. If you don't stop threatening her, I'll throw you out myself."

Dwight scoffed, but stood, opened the door, and stormed out, slamming the door shut behind him.

Hazel let out a relieved sigh. “I don’t think it is safe to have him around.”

“I agree,” Alex responded. “He should not come with you tomorrow.”

“Who should not come with us?” George and Jackson stood in the door of George’s office, looking confused. Hazel and Alex shared what had just happened.

“That is outrageous. Another way of getting to you?” George fumed. “Fire him at once, Jackson, and we should let Todd know.”

“We are one man short now,” Jackson reminded his boss.

“That’s true.”

“I can take his place,” Alex reassured them. “Brenna can work on her own for a while, and I am sure she wouldn’t complain about extra time off.”

“Are you certain? Have you ever been on a cattle drive?” Jackson asked with a raised eyebrow.

“No, I haven’t, but I might be of help, right?”

George and Jackson looked at each other, but they had no other choice.

21
Cattle Drive

They left early the following morning. The sun had barely reached the horizon, but it would take them four to five days, at least, and they had a deadline. Haven drove the wagon, and Dave joined her for the first few hours. Having Dave next to her made Haven giddy and happy. Hazel watched her out of the corner of her eye and smiled, amused.

It was exhausting and painful to be in the saddle every single day, but Hazel loved it. It was part of being a rancher, and she enjoyed a good adventure. When they were only a day away from San Francisco, they reached a beautiful valley with a river and lots of green grass.

George and Jackson decided they would stop early and give everyone some well-deserved rest. The ranch hands kept an eye on the herd, and since the animals were calm, Hazel rode into a small grove of trees behind the river. She found a tiny stream and filled her water bottle again. She hadn't adequately washed since they left Willamette Falls, and this water was inviting.

Hazel knelt next to the creek. She was about to shove water in her face when someone grabbed her from behind, pulled her to the ground, and was on top of her a moment later.

"Dwight?"

"That's right. You didn't think firing me would stop me from coming after you? I told you, you don't want me as your enemy."

She fought him and tried to push him off her when he slapped her across the face. Her head hit a big rock right next to her, and she nearly lost consciousness, but she knew she had to keep herself awake.

Hazel began yelling for help when he ripped her dress open. He covered her mouth with his hand when one cowboy stepped into the grove.

"Let her go, Dwight!"

Dwight only pulled his revolver out of the holster and gunned the young cowboy down.

"NOOOOOOOOOOOO." Hazel broke out in hysterics and began hitting him with her fists as hard as she could. When he tried to slap her again, she grabbed a rock from behind her and smashed it into his face. He fell backward, cussing at her. Hazel was on her feet at once, threw herself on her horse, and rode out of the grove.

Dwight followed her. He watched her for a moment before pointing his gun at her horse and pulling the trigger.

Dave, Namito, and Alex jumped up when they heard the shot. They looked around, scanning the area and saw Dwight coming out of the grove of trees. He was following Hazel who was a little ahead of him. The three young men mounted their horses and dashed across the valley.

A bullet hit Hazel's horse, Tess, in one of her back legs. The animal rose, throwing Hazel, but instead of just crashing to the ground, part of her hit the dirt, while Hazel's left foot got stuck in the stirrup. Tess bolted.

Hazel was dragged across rocks and sharp edges, and no matter how much she tried to calm her horse, Tess was out of control. The young woman heard another shot, which knocked the animal off her feet, and Hazel quickly pulled her foot out of the stirrup before the animal crashed.

She crawled next to her horse, tears streaming down her face. Tess was still breathing, but Hazel knew there was no hope for the mare. She put her uninjured arm around her horse's neck and let the tears flow. She didn't care about herself at that moment, but it broke her heart when she realized she was about to lose her favorite companion.

Dwight reached Hazel, pulled her away from her horse, and turned her on her back. Hazel bit her lips. Her entire back, left arm, and leg were covered in cuts and gashes. The pain was unbearable, but she was determined not to show Dwight any sign of weakness.

"You can't get away from me, Hazel Buchannon. Making you mine will be your biggest defeat, and you'll beg me to kill you before I am done with you," he sneered.

"I will never declare myself defeated to a swine like you," she retorted and spat into his face. He was about to backhand her again when someone pulled him away from her.

Hazel rolled back to her stomach and crawled closer to her horse again. She at least wanted to be with Tess until the mare took her last breath.

Dwight tried to fight off Namito and Dave, but Namito punched him in his guts with such force that he doubled over, hit his head on a rock, and passed out. They tied him up, and two cowboys took him with them.

"Hazel," Alex leaned down to her and attempted to pick her up, but she clung to her horse. "Please, we need to treat your wounds. Dave will take care of your horse."

He lifted her, not wanting to hurt her more than she was. Her back burned like fire. She closed her eyes, but couldn't stop the quiet sobs that escaped her lips. He held her close to his body and carried her as carefully as possible.

Dave took a look at Tess and knew he had to relieve the animal. It was in much pain and didn't deserve to suffer any longer.

"Jeremy is over there in the grove of trees. Dwight shot him when he came for my rescue." Hazel's voice was only a whisper, but Namito had understood her and disappeared into the trees to collect the dead cowboy.

"I am so sorry, Hazel," Alex said when he saw the tears running down her cheeks. "Would it be less painful if you walked?"

"Maybe."

He put her on the ground, but held her uninjured hand and steadied her with his body. She stepped forward, but each step ran through her body like fire. Everything around her was spinning, and she was close to losing consciousness.

She fought hard against the blackness that was closing in on her. She moved forward, step by step, when a loud shot echoed through the quiet valley. Hazel collapsed with one last thought on her mind. Tess was dead.

Alex caught her and carried her to camp. Haven covered her face with her hands and burst out in tears as soon as she saw her sister's injuries. George stepped closer, his eyes full of rage yet pain when he stared at his lifeless daughter. Jackson and a few of the cowboys had taken Dwight and were on their way to San Francisco.

Dave and Namito brought the dead cowboy and covered him with a sheet. Dave grabbed his medical bag and asked Alex to put Hazel face down on a blanket.

Her back looked horrific. Her dress and undergarments were soaked in blood, and when Dave removed the torn-up fabric, it looked as if the girl had been brutally flocked.

Haven leaned against her father's chest and kept sobbing. It hurt her heart to see her sister so severely injured.

Hazel regained consciousness when Dave tried to figure out how to treat her wounds best. Her back stung so badly, she felt like screaming.

"Hazel," Dave said to her. "You have deep cuts and gashes on your back, arm, leg, and head. I need to stitch those up, so the bleeding stops, but I don't have chloroform with me, and it will be excruciating."

"It is okay, Dave," Hazel mumbled without looking up. She inhaled sharply as every movement felt as if knives cut into her. "Just do it. I can't take this for much longer."

Dave nodded and caressed her cheek before getting everything ready for the upcoming, painful procedure. George sat next to his daughter and clasped her hand.

"Hazel, if you need to scream, let it out."

She dipped her head to signal him she had heard him before burying her head into her arm. Dave cleaned the wounds, first with water, then with alcohol. He seared some skin and tissue, and it was hard for Hazel to lay still. She moaned and whimpered, but endured it. When he stitched her gashes and wounds, it hurt just as bad. She breathed through her teeth, tears streaming down her face. When he was done, her back felt as if someone was burning her alive. Dave spread healing ointment over a clean cloth and placed it gently on her back to cover the wounds.

They helped her sit up and leaned her against Alex and Namito so that Dave could treat her arm, leg, and head now. Hazel's body tensed up, and as soon as she felt the needle on her arm, she collapsed. The two young men steadied her, and Dave worked quickly to get it done before she woke up again.

When Hazel regained consciousness, her wounds were stitched up and dressed. Her back was still burning, but the healing ointment had improved the pain a little. Exhausted, she leaned with her uninjured side against Alex's shoulder.

"Thank you, Dave."

He put his hand on her cheek, and she grabbed his hand.

For the night, they made Hazel a bed out of blankets and warm jackets. Haven had helped her sister change her dirty, torn-up dress to a skirt and light jacket. Since they had to keep the fire going, one of them always sat next to her.

Namito was watching the fire when Hazel became restless. He tried to wake her because she seemed to have a nightmare, but she kept pushing him away from her until she woke herself up, screaming. She was covered in sweat and didn't know where she was at first.

George, Dave, and Alex jumped up at once. A moment later, Haven crawled out of the wagon. All of them looked worried. Hazel cried, and George pulled her into his arms. One of the wounds on her leg had started bleeding again, so Dave took care of it.

"Why did Dwight do that?" she cried into her father's shoulder. "Why did he have to kill Jeremy and Tess? Wasn't it enough that he attacked me?"

"I wish I had an answer for you, honey, but men like Dwight don't care about anything but themselves. He wanted to get to you and got rid of everything in his way."

Dave finished treating her bleeding wound, and her father put Hazel on her blanket. She fell asleep at once.

She woke up a few hours later. Namito was still watching the fire, but he stood and helped her to her feet, so she could sit next to him. He gave her water, and she smiled at him.

Hazel was exhausted, in pain, and wanted to go back to sleep, but nature called, and she had no idea how to manage that by herself. It embarrassed her to ask Namito for help, so she asked him to wake up Haven, so her sister could assist her.

Namito and Haven took Hazel to a sheltered spot, and he returned to the fire until Haven called him. The young Indian helped Hazel lay down again and watched her sleep for a moment, only one thought was on his mind. *Heaven, help this remarkable girl.*

22

On the Verge Of Death

They packed up before dawn the following morning. The valley provided shelter, food, and water, so George left the rest of his cowboys with the cattle until Jackson returned. Caleb was a hard worker, and George knew he could trust him. They bedded Hazel onto the back of the wagon and stacked blankets and jackets behind her, so she wouldn't roll on her back.

Around lunchtime, they took a quick break, and Dave looked at Hazel's wounds. Despite their precautions, some of her cuts and gashes had broken open again. He cleaned and dressed it.

After a brief discussion, they decided someone would always sit with Hazel to keep her steady and hopefully prevent further bleeding. Namito climbed into the back of the wagon and helped Hazel to sit up and lean against him. He had his arm around her waist.

"Thank you, Namito," she said suddenly. "Thank you for being there for me and helping me through this. Everything is much more bearable because of you."

He kissed her head and brushed some of her hair out of her face. Hazel closed her eyes. He watched her for a while, lost in thought. As he was caressing her face, he noticed how warm her head was.

"Haven?" he called out to the front of the wagon, and Haven turned around.

"Yes?"

"Can you stop the wagon and call Dave, please?"

"Is Hazel getting worse?" Fear and concern colored her voice. Namito nodded.

"We need to get her to a hospital as soon as possible," Dave said after feeling her forehead. "She has a fever now, and that means her wounds are infected, and the body is trying to fight it."

"So, we are not stopping anymore, but will be riding through the night?" George asked, and Dave nodded.

Namito held Hazel tight against his body, but she kept throwing her head back and forth. A sign that she was not well, and the fever took over her body.

"We need to hurry. We are running out of time." Dave's grave expression signaled the severity of the situation.

Hazel's fever rose in the evening. She was unresponsive now, and it was getting harder and harder to keep her calm.

Alex held her while Haven tried to sleep next to him. George drove the wagon, and Namito would switch with him soon.

The young teacher had barely fallen asleep when he noticed how restless Hazel was getting. He grabbed her arms, so she wouldn't start hitting everything around her. He calmly spoke to her and caressed her face, but she fought him more and more. George stopped the wagon, and Dave climbed on. He checked her forehead and saw that she was covered in sweat.

"Her fever is too high, we need to cool her down at once." Everyone grabbed towels and cloths, put them in cold water, and covered her head, arms, and legs with them. They kept repeating it until she felt less hot.

They reached San Francisco the following day around noon. Jackson, and the cowboys who had gone with him, had ridden past them during the night, on their way back to the cattle. He informed them that the sheriff wanted to see Hazel's injuries. Since her condition had worsened, they didn't want to stop and drove straight to the hospital.

George sent Alex to get the sheriff and a judge if available, and Dave mounted his horse to ride ahead to let the hospital staff know that it was urgent. Both men dashed off into different directions.

As soon as Dave reached the hospital, he sounded the alarm and alerted the staff, so they were ready for Hazel. When the Buchannon's arrived some time later, doctors and nurses came rushing out and hurried Hazel into the building and to a treatment room. The door fell shut behind them.

George walked up and down the hallway. Haven sat on a chair, crying. Namito and Dave leaned against the wall, lost in thoughts, but fighting with their emotions. They were dirty and beyond exhausted, but could only think of Hazel.

It took a long time until the door opened again, and a young doctor approached George.

"Are you the father of this young woman?"

"I am."

"We treated her wounds and are trying to get her fever down, but I have to be honest with you, it doesn't look good. She is in critical condition. How long has she been in this fever-unconsciousness?"

George felt like his heart was being ripped apart. He swallowed hard before he responded. "Since last night. Can we see her now?"

"Yes, but please only one at a time and only family."

George stepped into the room, and tears entered his eyes when he saw his lifeless daughter lying on her bed. Two nurses were by her side, changing her compresses every few minutes. When they saw George, they gave him an encouraging smile. Both of them left for a moment—one to get fresh water, the other one to grab ice.

Hazel didn't move, but he still saw the sweat of pain and fever on her forehead. He grabbed a chair and placed it next to her. Her hair was wet from the sweat, and so he brushed it out of her face. When he took her hand in his, he was overcome with emotion.

"Please keep fighting, Hazel," he whispered. "Don't give up now. We love you and don't want to lose you." He heard a nurse come in and wiped his tears away.

"Mr. Buchannon," she said, "Sheriff Baker and Judge Thomas McGregor are outside and would like to see the injuries of your daughter."

George nodded and stood. The nurse left the room, but came back a moment later.

The two men following her had a grave expression on their faces. They had heard a lot about the attack, first from Jackson when he brought Dwight and Alex. The three men greeted each other with a handshake, and then they stepped next to Hazel's bed. The nurse lifted the blanket and bandages.

Both of them were horrified. The wounds, cuts, and gashes looked as if someone had brutally whipped her, and the two men couldn't even imagine the pain and agony she had gone through and was still going through.

Without talking to each other, both knew that Dwight needed to be punished harshly. The outcome of his attack wasn't just a criminal offense. This was pure violence and attempted murder.

Alex took Namito, Haven, and Dave with him to his parents. Haven begged to stay with Hazel, but the doctor only allowed one person to stay, and George wanted to be with his daughter.

Dave sent a quick telegram to Helen to let her know what had happened. Jackson and the cowboys arrived in San Francisco the following day. He stopped by the hospital to see if Hazel was doing any better, but there was no improvement.

The cowboys rode back to Oregon. Jackson, Haven, and the rest of the group took the stagecoach home, knowing that they couldn't do anything else for Hazel at the moment. Helen was desperate to join her husband and stepdaughter at the hospital. Her stepmom moved in with the girls while Helen was gone, so Haven, Shelly, and Brenna weren't alone in the house with a bunch of men.

After Helen arrived in San Francisco, Hazel took a turn for the worse. No matter what the doctors and nurses tried, the fever did not go down. George and Helen had not slept in days. George had not shaved, washed, and bathed since they had arrived at the hospital, and he just sat there in silence, holding his daughter's hand.

Helen was heartbroken too, but George was deeply affected because this was his daughter. She stood behind her husband and wrapped her arms around him when the doctor stepped into the room.

"I am sorry, Mr. and Mrs. Buchannon. We've done everything we could, and she hasn't woken in over a week. You must prepare yourself."

Helen broke out in tears, and George stood, turned around, and pulled her tight into his arms. They both cried now and just held on to each other.

"Mr. Buchannon, Marshal Sterling Holden, and Reverend Robert Mitchell are waiting outside. I talked to the doctor, and he agreed to them staying."

"Please let them come in," George said and stood at once.

"George, how is she?" Marshal Holden said as soon as he walked through the door. George just shook his head, and the Marshal embraced him and gave him a brotherly hug. Robert went over to Hazel and gently caressed her head.

"She hasn't woken up since the day after the attack. The doctor told us earlier they can't do anything else for her." George's voice cracked, and tears streamed down his face.

"Do your loved ones at home know?"

"No."

"I will send a telegram for you," Marshal Holden said compassionately, "and Robert and I will stay with you tonight. You are not alone in this."

"Thank you."

Haven was inconsolable when the telegram arrived and burst out in tears. Dave pulled her into his arms, but he was emotional too.

Namito couldn't believe it. God could not do that to him. He could not take another person he loved so much. That evening, he went to the reservation and told his father about Hazel and what had happened to her. The Kalapuya chief was shocked. He loved that girl, and she would always have a special place in his heart. He called the tribe elders and medicine man for their traditional healing prayer to their Great Spirit.

It was tranquil in the room. George, Helen, and Sterling Holden had fallen asleep on their chairs, but Robert Mitchell couldn't stop looking at that youthful face below him. He kissed her cheek and held her hand.

"I love you, Hazel," he whispered with tears in his eyes. "I always have and always will. You are like a daughter to me, and you have to keep fighting. You mean everything to us, and we want you to stay with us. Your mission on this earth isn't done yet. You still have to fight for respect and more rights for women, and you have to take over your father's ranch. Don't give up. You've come so far, and I know you are on this earth to carry out great things."

The sunlight pushed itself through the curtains of the room and landed on Robert Mitchell's face. He lifted his head and realized he had fallen asleep. Horrified that the young woman might have passed away while he was sleeping, he looked down at Hazel, but she was calmly breathing. He felt her forehead, and her fever had sunk a bit.

Robert sighed with relief and moved his head and shoulders around to get the pain out of his body. He glanced around the room. Helen, George, and Sterling Holden were still asleep.

A young doctor entered and nodded to Reverend Mitchell. When he stepped next to Hazel and Robert stood to get out of the way, the other three woke up. The doctor felt her forehead and pulse, listened to her heart and inspected her wounds. Everyone held their breath.

"She is doing better. Her fever is down a little, and her pulse is steady and normal. She is fighting."

Helen burst out in tears of joy, and the three men smiled and hugged each other before Sterling Holden left to send another telegram to the Buchannon family.

"She is doing better, her fever is lower, and the doctor thinks she has a chance. Sterling Holden."

Dave had accepted the telegram with mixed feelings, but everyone was relieved and grateful when they read it. Finally, some light at the end of the tunnel.

It was late afternoon when Hazel opened her eyes for the first time. Since she was lying on her stomach, she couldn't look around but saw Reverend Mitchell next to her and smiled. As soon as he noticed that she was awake, he took her hand.

"How are you feeling, Hazel?"

"Exhausted," she admitted. "Where am I?"

"You are at the hospital in San Francisco," her father replied as he stepped next to her. "You haven't been awake for over a week, and last night we thought we would lose you." His voice cracked, and he had to swallow several times before he was in control of his emotions again. Hazel smiled.

"I can't give up now. I still have missions to fulfill."

Robert Mitchell squeezed her hand. She had heard him during the night.

Hazel was almost asleep again when Dr. Sanderson entered the room. He had been the doctor treating her, and behind him were a few nurses.

"It is good to see you awake, Miss Buchannon," he said with a kind smile, and checked her forehead and pulse. "How are you feeling?"

"Tired and exhausted, as if I have walked through the desert for days."

The young doctor nodded. "Fever drains the energy and hydration out of you, but it is going down at last. Now that you are awake, we need to make sure we nurse you back to health."

George, Helen, and Reverend Mitchell nodded. Dr. Sanderson turned to the nurses. "She needs plenty of fluids and soup later today."

They nodded, but before anyone could offer her water, she was asleep again.

Marshal Holden stared at the telegram in his hands. He couldn't believe it. *Dwight Miller is not the person he claims to be. His actual name: Gabriel McKellar!*

23

The Ultimate Sacrifice?

"Clark," Adam said when he entered the church, "they caught McKellar."

"What? How did they do that?"

"McKellar went after Hazel. They hired him as a cowboy for the cattle drive, but he threatened Hazel before leaving and got fired. He followed them and attacked her."

"Ha, it looks like I am not the only one obsessed with that girl. It is about time that he pays for his arrogance. What did he do to her?" Jason asked, contempt and outrage in his eyes.

"He tried to ravish her and ambushed her. He is now in jail in San Francisco and is waiting for his trial for attempted murder. Hazel is in the hospital, trying to recover from the severe injuries he caused. Jackson told me McKellar shot at her horse, and Hazel got thrown off. One of her feet was stuck in the stirrup, and she was dragged across rocks and sharp edges until the horse collapsed. My brother said it looked like she had been brutally flocked." Adam shook his head.

"I told McKellar that she is mine and that he needs to stay away from her. If anyone gets to whip her, it is me."

"You would beat her?"

"Sure," he replied. "If Hazel is disobedient. You are getting married to Shelly, right? Wouldn't you do that too if she didn't obey your orders?"

"Not sure if I would beat her, as I am not that type of guy, but she would learn her lesson."

Jason Clark grinned. "A man's command is the law. If a woman doesn't follow that law, there will be consequences."

"Now that McKellar is out of the picture, what is the plan?"

"We need to make sure Hazel doesn't get killed. As much as I want her, there is no use in her if she is dead." He stopped and thought for a moment before he said something Adam had not expected. "I am not the person after her."

"Drop it, Clark. I know you want to blame Reverend Mitchell for this, but he has no inappropriate or ill intentions toward her. Nobody will believe you if you try to make him the offender."

"I am not planning on making him the offender. That was just a farce."

"Clark, you can't be serious. Do you want me to believe that your talk of wanting to own Hazel and making her your wife was just talking?"

"Yes, I want you to believe that. I am not after her. Sure, she is a pretty little thing, but I am doing this for someone else. Someone who wants to own her and wants to own the ranch."

"What are you talking about, Clark? All this time, you've been going on about Hazel and how obsessed you are with her. Now you are claiming you are doing it for someone else?"

"That's right."

"Does McKellar know about it?"

Reverend Clark scoffed. "McKellar knows nothing. He is just a woman hunter, trying to make money and use them for his pleasure. He only showed up when he needed to hide or when he was looking for more girls to kidnap."

"So, he doesn't know who you are working for?" Adam furrowed his brows.

"Of course not. I can't trust McKellar. He is in it only for himself."

"Who are you working for?" Adam made sure, his voice told Clark he didn't believe him.

"I promised him I wouldn't tell. I shouldn't have told you about him in the first place, but oh well. He pays me a lot of money for this, and so we need to make sure we get Hazel to him, and she has to be untouched."

"So, we caught McKellar?" Robert Mitchell asked, shock written on his face. Marshal Holden nodded.

"That's what the telegram said."

"That means Shelly has to come to the trial too, since he was the one who abducted and sold her to Hank Thompson," George commented. "Should we let Hazel know?"

"You shouldn't share anything with Hazel until she is stronger and healthier again," Dr. Sanderson said as he stepped out of Hazel's room. "She has gone through much trauma and still has the trial ahead of her. You must keep worry and fear away from her right now. She is weak, and her body will react severely to anything thrown at her."

"What do you mean?"

"The way she has been targeted and continues to be a target is harrowing her even into her dreams. She has reached her absolute limit. Another attack might put her over the edge, and she will stop fighting. If her body catches another infection, it will most likely kill her."

Now that Hazel was awake again, Dr. Sanderson and his staff did what they could to help her recover. George made preparations for the upcoming trial against Dwight Miller and hired his friend and Alex's father as his lawyer. Harry Camden was an outstanding attorney and well known for his hardworking and honest nature.

When Hazel was well enough to sit up again, he began visiting her in the hospital to prepare her for court and talk about what happened to her. At first, she refused to talk about it, but Harry won her trust and created a father-daughter friendship. It was tough for her to open up, but Harry was patient and never rushed her. She still had to be in the hospital until she was recovered, so they had time to prepare for the trial and get her ready to face her demons.

George sent a telegram to Dave and asked him, Alex, Namito, and Shelly to return to San Francisco as they were witnesses. Haven was eager to join them too, but the telegram instructed her to stay home. She was too fragile and sensitive, and George didn't want her to be traumatized for life. This trial would be emotional and challenging for Hazel.

Reverend Mitchell and Marshal Holden were still in San Francisco. They had a new lead for the white slavery case and worked with church leaders and local law enforcement to rescue abducted girls and women from saloons and brothels.

Hazel missed her friends. Now that she was feeling better, she had too much time to think and needed distractions. Nightmares followed her at night, and she had woken herself up, screaming, more than once.

One afternoon, while Hazel was alone in her room, she got up and opened her window to let the warm air inside. She put on her dressing gown and sat on the window ledge to enjoy the sun and look at the beautiful park behind the hospital.

Hazel was expecting Harry Camden for another trial preparation discussion. Her thoughts wandered off again, and she thought about the terrible things she had experienced. Her heart beat faster, and fear paralyzed her, so she closed her eyes and forced herself to think of the many blessings instead.

Suddenly, she was grabbed from behind. Someone covered her mouth with his hand, pulled her backward, and threw her onto her bed. As soon as she saw who it was, she turned as white as her bedsheet.

"Dwight? How can you be here? You are supposed to be in prison."

"I was, but it is easy to buy law enforcement officers as long as the price is right."

"The sheriff let you out?"

"No, not the sheriff, but one of his deputies. Now let's finish what we started, shall we?"

Hazel froze, but only for a second. The terror she felt took her breath away, but she fought back. Her screaming made him angry, and he brutally backhanded her. Her lip and nose started bleeding, but all she could think of was getting away from the demon.

"Step away from her, McKellar," Robert Mitchell growled, standing in the door frame. Gabriel grinned.

"You think you can help her? You are no threat to me, Mitchell." He pulled out his gun, pointed at the reverend, and fired a shot ...the moment, Hazel threw herself into the arms of Robert Mitchell.

At least the fear and terror will be over when I am dead, and Reverend Mitchell can live, she thought before everything went black.

Hazel had seen the gun in Gabriel McKellar's pocket. She knew what he was about to do. She jumped off her bed and straight into the arms of her fatherly friend and protector. The bullet hit her, and she collapsed the moment Dwight was knocked off his feet by a shot that went straight into his shoulder.

Marshal Holden had been behind Robert the entire time, ready to pull the reverend out of harms way, but they hadn't expected Hazel to interfere, and they also hadn't expected McKellar to have a gun. With the young woman in Robert's arms, Sterling had only seconds to decide what to do next. The shot he fired was precise.

Once McKellar was down, Marshal Holden pushed himself past Robert and Hazel, and turned the criminal to his stomach, so he could handcuff him. Dwight was in the right place for medical attention, and Sterling would be the one to lock him up. This time, his people would watch him. Gabriel would not get back out of prison again. Sterling promised himself that this man would be there for the trial and hopefully get the death sentence, so they could blast his evil brain out of his head.

Robert Mitchell stood there in shock. Holding this lifeless young woman was more than he could bear, and he teared up. He had not expected Hazel to jump into his arms, and his heart sank. He remembered what Doctor Sanderson had told them: another infection and attack would most likely be her death.

Dr. Sanderson, a few other doctors, and nurses rushed into the room and put Hazel back on her bed. They asked everyone to leave at once, as they had to remove the bullet.

The hallway in front of Hazel's room was filled with people. George and Helen Buchannon, Marshal Sterling Holden,

Reverend Robert Mitchell, and Harry Camden. Sheriff Baker joined them right before Dr. Sanderson finished the emergency surgery on Hazel.

When the doctor came out of the operation room, Alex, Namito, and Dave arrived at the hospital. They had just made it to San Francisco, and Alex's mom had told them what had happened.

"Mr. Buchannon. We removed the bullet and stopped the bleeding. Hazel was blessed and must have had several guardian angels by her side. None of the organs got hit, and there was only damage to the shoulder tissue and muscle. However, because she is so weak and still in recovery, this last attack could be deadly. If she falls into a depression and her body gets an infection, there is little we can do."

George nodded, still in shock. Before anyone could say anything else, Dr. Sanderson turned to the sheriff.

"Sheriff Baker," he snapped. "Can you explain to me how a dangerous criminal like Gabriel McKellar can escape the prison unnoticed? Hazel Buchannon barely survived the first attack of that coward, so how is it possible that he can go after her again?" Dr. Sanderson's voice was full of rage, making it obvious, that it blew his mind that the young woman was still targeted and brutally attacked. Sheriff Baker looked uncomfortable and unhappy.

"I am sorry, Mr. Buchannon. One of my deputies worked with McKellar and let him out when I was on one of my rounds. Marshal Holden has taken over, and his men are now watching McKellar around the clock."

"We are," Sterling Holden responded. "He will not see the light of day and will not get close to Hazel again. I give you my promise. I hope that evil brute of a lowlife will get sentenced to death, so we can either shoot or hang him."

"Why is a young woman like Hazel even attacked in such horrible ways?" Dr. Sanderson shook his head.

"Women still don't have much rights. Most men see them as servants and treat them as such. Hazel is lucky and blessed that she has wonderful and caring men in her life who always encouraged her to go for her dreams and not let men mistreat her. Unfortunately, some men will use physical abuse to get what they want. The two men who have done that to her over the past few months are so set on wanting to destroy and hurt her, they don't stop. Gabriel is locked up and will get punished, but we need more evidence on that other piece of prairie coal," Marshal Holden responded through gritted teeth.

"Why are women not better protected against these abusive swine?" Dr. Sanderson was outraged.

"They don't count as equal to men. Many lawmakers, who could make a change, don't want women to be treated better, most likely because they abuse and use them themselves. We need more men to stand up for women, and more women to speak up and not let that happen anymore. Hazel will do that, but McKellar and Clark make her life a living hell. They target her because she is strong and determined."

"What can we do to make a difference?"

"We need to stand behind her. I hope that once the trial starts and newspapers are reporting about McKellar and his evil doings, and once people in this country hear about Hazel and what she's been through, people will realize how wrong some of our laws are. Women deserve as many rights and protections as we do, and nobody deserves to go through the things Hazel has, except maybe the men who do those things to women." Sterling Holden's voice was firm and calm, but everyone could see the held back anger and fierce fire in his eyes.

"Will Hazel be okay, Dr. Sanderson?" Robert Mitchell asked now.

"I don't know. If Hazel has enough courage and spirit left to fight this, she has a chance. If she doesn't, she probably won't make it. Her body is not strong enough to fight this by herself, not after going through so much trauma and terrible abuse."

Nothing changed during the next two days. Hazel did not wake up, but everyone kept visiting her, and George and Helen stayed with her.

At the end of the second day, Hazel turned for the worse. Her fever skyrocketed, and her bullet wound had gotten infected. Dr. Sanderson and his staff tried everything they could for her, but it made no difference.

During that night, everyone wanting to stay with her did so. Hazel was now fighting for her life. Whenever someone talked to her, she had horrible fever-induced seizures, and it took Dr. Sanderson, her father, Reverend Mitchell, and Namito to calm her down again. After each episode, she was drenched in sweat, and everyone had to leave the room, so the nurses could change her bedding and nightgown.

Near the end of the night, Hazel had such an aggressive seizure that they thought it was the end. George pulled her into his arms and just held her with tears streaming down his face.

Her hair was soaked, and she kept gasping for air in between cramps. Everyone in the room watched this heartbreak with tears in their eyes.

"Peanut," George whispered into her ear as he held her tight to his body, "please keep fighting. You can beat this. We are here and love you more than you can ever imagine. Don't give up. We will fight alongside you and will make you safe again, I promise. I love you and don't want to lose you." He kissed her forehead and continued to hold her through the entire seizure.

Suddenly, the seizure stopped, and she laid still. Dr. Sanderson checked her breathing and pulse. Everyone in the room stared at him with fear, while also saying a silent prayer. Before the physician had the chance to say something, Hazel took a deep breath.

"It looks like we have her back," Dr. Sanderson mumbled. "She is willing to fight again."

24
Heartfelt Recovery

When Hazel opened her eyes several hours later, she felt drained and exhausted. She had no energy to move, but she glanced around in the room, and grateful love filled her heart. Everyone was still there, asleep on their chairs.

She thought about the moment Dwight had shown up in her room and attacked her. Fearful shivers ran through her body, but she shifted her thoughts to Dwight's attempt of shooting Reverend Mitchell. This time, anger built up in her, and Hazel clenched her fists.

How could that devil even think she would let him shoot anyone she loved? Her eyes wandered over to her fatherly friend. He was sitting right next to her, breathing deeply. A sign that he was sound asleep. Hazel's heart was whole. No matter how tough life was presently, Heavenly Father still blessed her beyond imagination. She loved Reverend Mitchell and everyone else in the room, and they loved her too.

Tears welled in her eyes when she recalled the beautiful things everyone had said to her during the night, but her father's words had touched her the most. She had no idea how she deserved such outstanding people in her life.

Without meaning, too, she was overcome with emotion. Since she was lying on her stomach, she turned her head around and buried it in her pillow. Despite her best effort to cry as silently as possible, her sobbing woke up Robert Mitchell and her father. As soon as they moved, everyone else woke up too.

Reverend Mitchell took Hazel's hand in his. "What's wrong?"

She heard the worry in his voice, but didn't answer. Someone else stepped next to her and stroked her head.

"Sweetheart, we know something is up. Are you in pain?" Her father's voice was loving and gentle.

Hazel felt everyone's eyes on her, but shook her head. "I am grateful," she mumbled, while facing her father.

"Grateful?" George Buchannon asked with a puzzled look on his face.

She nodded. "For all of you. For being with me and there for me. For loving me. I love you so much and can't ever repay you for everything you have done for me."

"Hazel," her father said, and her eyes scanned his. "You have done nothing but bring joy to us. Your love keeps us on our toes and is what moves us forward. There is nothing to repay. Family and love are a give and take. You don't even realize how much you have given us." He touched her face and caressed her cheek. Hazel smiled at him, closed her eyes, and was asleep again right after.

She woke up when it was late afternoon. Nobody but her father and Helen were in the room. She smiled at them.

"Do you think it is okay for me to sit up? I can't stand lying on my stomach anymore."

Before her father could respond, Dr. Sanderson and a nurse walked into the room.

"It is good to see your smiling face. You've had a few terrifying weeks, and we were worried about you. Now, you may sit as long as it feels comfortable to you, but please be careful, and you should always have a few pillows behind your back. Your first injuries have been healing well, but your bullet wound is fresh."

"Thank you, Dr. Sanderson."

After her parents left, she was by herself for a while. She closed her eyes. Dark and depressive thoughts were weaving their way into her mind when there was a knock at her door. After calling for the visitor to come in, Dave, Namito, and Alex entered the room. A beaming smile appeared on her face.

Namito gave her a gentle hug. "I am so glad you are doing better. The last few weeks have been intense, and it drove me mad, not knowing whether I would see you again."

"What Namito said," Dave commented with a big grin on his face and embraced her with a warm hug.

"I missed you guys too." Hazel winked at them.

When Alex stepped next to her and took her hand in his, she was hit with butterflies. His eyes looked into hers, and her feelings went crazy. She closed her eyes.

I can't fall in love with him. He will leave again once Brenna is done with school. That's the reason I didn't want to open up to him. How can I be around him without letting him know? He can't find out, not like this.

The three young men had concern written on their faces when she suddenly closed her eyes, and her expression changed from smiling to anxious.

Hazel had only one thought in her head. She needed to get out of Alex's presence as soon as possible. She couldn't face him, not until she had her feelings under control again. Hazel opened her eyes and looked at Namito.

"I can't breathe. I need air," she mumbled and jumped out of her bed. The quick and sudden movement was too much for her weak body, and she collapsed.

Alex caught her, lifted her off her feet, and put her back on her bed. Dave left the room to get the doctor.

Hazel regained consciousness only a few moments later. Dr. Sanderson rushed into the room, followed by Dave, and stepped next to her bed.

"Miss Buchannon, what happened?"

Hazel tried to remember. Her head was still spinning, and she couldn't think. She closed her eyes and concentrated.

"I got up too fast," she replied with closed eyes.

"And why did you get up too fast?"

"I was thinking about something that made me panicky, and I felt like I needed air to breathe." Hazel knew everyone would link her panic to the past traumas, and that put her at ease. She didn't want to talk about her current feelings and didn't want to think about them.

Dr. Sanderson, Alex, and Dave seemed satisfied with her answer, but Namito gave her a suspicious glance. She silently sighed. Once again, Namito would make things difficult.

Somehow she made it through their visit, but faked falling asleep in the end to have them leave earlier. After she was alone again, she allowed her thoughts to run wild. She couldn't understand why her feelings of friendship to Alex Camden had changed to something more. Memories with him of the past few months flooded her mind, and she realized he had slowly taken over her heart. Her love for him had been there for a while, but she didn't discover it until seeing him again.

How can I be myself around him now that my feelings have changed? Can I hide my feelings enough, so he won't notice anything? I don't want to lose his friendship.

Hazel usually had no trouble keeping her emotions hidden from the world, but this unexpected development made her feel unsure and overwhelmed. She got up, slowly and with ease this time, and walked over to her window. She opened it wide and breathed in the fresh, rainy air.

"Hazel," Namito said as he stepped into the room, and Hazel turned around, startled.

"Goodness, Namito, why would you sneak up on me like that? And what are you doing back here?" she asked, even though she didn't want an answer from him, "I thought you returned to the hotel." She walked toward her bed, but Namito clasped her arm and looked straight into her eyes. She hated it when he did that.

"What was going on earlier?"

"I don't know what you mean," she responded as she removed his hand from her arm and climbed back into bed. "I already told you."

"I know what you said and that everyone now thinks you were talking about Dwight, but that was not the truth."

"Are you saying that I am lying?" Hazel challenged him and flashed him a determined glance.

"Not lying, since the last few weeks have been traumatizing and could set off panic, but you are hiding something."

"Oh, you think that, do you? Have you considered that it might be none of your business?" she retorted and raised an eyebrow. Namito grinned.

"I have considered that option, but as your best friend, I would still like to know."

"Well, I will not tell you."

"Why not?"

"Because I don't want to talk about it, that's why," she pouted, and her expression changed to serious and stubborn.

He took her chin in his hand and turned her head toward him, so she had to look at him. "Are you going to tell me?"

"No."

"Hazel," he said with a twinkle in his eyes, "we've been through this. You will tell me eventually, so you might as well get it out of the way right now."

"I don't want to talk about it, Namito," she snapped. "Let it go and leave me alone."

"Being in love with someone is not a bad thing."

That caught her off guard, and she cringed. "You don't even know what you are talking about," she replied, trying to sound casual.

"I think I do, and Dave is a good guy. Sometimes friendship turns to more."

"Dave?" She looked at him, surprised. She had not expected that.

"Yes, Dave," he retorted, amused. "I noticed how you reacted when you two greeted each other. Your expression changed right before you could say Hi to Alex. Coincidence? I think not."

Hazel cringed again when he mentioned the young teacher, but he misread that sign too.

"You two would make a great couple. Perhaps he needs more time to see you in the same light."

Hazel felt like laughing. It amused her that he thought her feelings for Dave had changed. Sure, she loved him and would die for him in a heartbeat, but she only felt friendship for him, and she was certain Dave felt the same way.

"Perhaps you are right. Maybe I need to give it time."

"Just promise me something. When you and Dave start courting at one point, please tell your sister first. She deserves to know."

Hazel nodded, but deep inside, she knew she would never do that to her sister. She would never break her heart like that.

25 Trial of Truth

Since Hazel's recovery was going well, Harry Camden started preparing her for the trial again. It wasn't easy for her to open up. Dwight's last attack had left even more impressions and pain, but Harry was patient with her. They worked through it together. Having to face her tormentor in court made her nervous and scared, but there was no way around it.

She was released on the day of the first trial session. Hazel was a nervous wreck, and her anxiety was high. Dr. Sanderson and his staff said their goodbyes, but they would see her again in court since they were witnesses as well.

Her father picked her up and took her to a small café for a light snack before they had to be in court. She wasn't hungry and looked pale and worried. George pulled her into his arms and hugged her.

"I understand that you are scared and worried, Hazel, but I promise you everything will be fine. Marshal Holden and his men are there, and they will not let him come close to you again. Harry Camden is a wonderful lawyer, and he is well-prepared. Dwight will not get away. He will get punished."

She didn't feel reassured. After the attack on the cattle drive, she had thought Dwight wouldn't be able to get to her again, yet he came after her. Dark, paralyzing fear crept through her entire body and made her shiver. Her father lifted her chin and made her look at him.

"I promise we will not leave you alone with him. We will be around you the whole time."

"Is Helen going to be there too?"

George shook his head. "No. She said it would make her too emotional."

Hazel nodded. She wished she could stay away from it too.

When they got to the court building, several of her friends and protectors were already there. Shelly saw her, walked up to her, and embraced her in a warm hug. Hazel was touched. They hadn't seen each other in weeks. Shelly hadn't visited her in the hospital. She had purposely stayed away since everyone else wanted to be with Hazel, and she didn't want to take someone else's chance to be with her. She kept praying for her instead.

Shelly had gone through much hardship herself and was grateful that Hank Thompson and his wife Caroline had rescued her before things would have ended badly for her.

Namito pulled her into his arms next. "It is so good to see you outside the hospital again, Sidaa. We will be back on your dad's ranch before we know it and can forget everything."

Hazel forced herself to smile, even though she didn't think she could ever forget the things that happened to her. Hopefully, she would learn to live with it.

Alex Camden gave her an encouraging smile, which made her heart skip a beat, but she was too distressed to focus on her feelings for him.

Reverend Mitchell, Marshal Holden, and Harry Camden arrived at the same time. As they greeted everyone, Hazel stepped away from the group, trying to collect herself. What she had before her was painful beyond imagination, and it terrified her. She had thought she couldn't be more scared of someone than Jason Clark, but she was wrong. Clark harassed and tormented her, but Dwight Miller had physically attacked and hurt her.

She looked at the building in front of her and burst out in tears. She covered her head in her arms and leaned against the wall, trying to steady herself. Suddenly, two arms embraced her, and she turned around and leaned against his chest.

Dave said nothing, just held her. He understood how she felt and wanted nothing more than to take the pain and worry away from her.

The rest of the group watched her with concerned looks on their faces. This trial would be another massive challenge for her. Dave held her tight to help her calm down again.

"Oh, sweet Hazel in the arms of her protector," Dwight sneered loudly as he was led by three deputies toward the court building. "My lawyer will get me free, and I will come after you and finish what I started. Mark my words."

Hazel tensed up. Terror-related goosebumps spread across her entire body. Marshal Holden turned around furiously, grabbed the other man by his throat, and pushed him against the wall behind them.

"You will never get close to that girl again. Your pathetic threats mean nothing but will be evidence against you. I recommend you keep your filthy mouth shut before my men and I finish you off right here. I don't mind holding a trial on the street because you deserve the death sentence."

Dwight scoffed, but before he could respond, Holden let go of his throat. "Get this demon away from here," he snapped, and his men pushed the prisoner forward.

Hazel had felt the blood drain from her face. She was not willing to be around this evil man anymore. She removed Dave's arms from around her, turned, and was about to rush across the street when Dave and Reverend Mitchell seemed to realize she was about to bolt. Both reacted quickly and clasped her hands.

"Let me go. I don't want to deal with this any longer." Hazel tried to shake them off, but they weren't faced.

"Hazel, listen to me," Reverend Mitchell grabbed her by her arms. "You can't run away from this. I understand that this is painful and hard for you, but you need to keep fighting."

"No, I don't," she snapped. "That man is threatening me even though he is in handcuffs and surrounded by marshals. It doesn't matter what will happen to him after the trial, he will always be there, and he will always come after me." She tried to get out of his hold, but he held her. "Let go of my arms."

"I will not let go of your arms, and I won't let you give up."

"I am not giving up, but I refuse to let him torture me any longer. You can't force me to go against him in court."

"Hazel, facing and testifying against him is the only way to stop him once and for all. If I have to carry you inside, I will. You have made it this far, and you will continue to fight."

George and Marshal Holden glanced at them, concern and worry spreading across their faces. They had never seen Robert Mitchell so stern and forceful before, not toward her, at least.

"You have no right to boss me around, now let me go." She continued her attempts to get out of his hold, but he was firm. It amused him how much she was trying to resist him. It reminded him of the first few times after her mother had left her, and he had tried to reach out to her and comfort her. She had fought him with everything she had, as little as she was.

When he sensed that she was calming down again, he pulled her into his arms.

"Please, let me go, Reverend Mitchell. I can't face him, I just can't," she mumbled, held-back sobs in her voice.

"Yes, you can, Hazel. We are by your side, and he will not touch you. He might attack you verbally with his big mouth, but he cannot come close to you again."

"The best way to respond to him is by ignoring him. Don't look at him, don't respond to any of his threats, and pretend he doesn't exist," Dave interjected, and everyone around nodded.

"He exists, though. He is not only here in person, but he is in my mind and dreams."

"It will get to him, though. Men like him hate nothing more than being ignored. It is okay to be scared and worried. He can't see that. If you don't look into his eyes, he cannot tell how scared you are of him."

They entered the building together, and Hazel took a deep breath. She tried to calm herself, but with each step closer to the doors of the courtroom, her breathing became more and more irregular, and she hyperventilated.

"Dave," she gasped, "I can't breathe. I need air." Everything around her started spinning, and her legs gave out. Dave's arm came around her waist, steadying her. Dr. Sanderson, who had just entered the building, jumped to her side and lifted her arms into the air. He talked to her until she was more herself again.

Hazel closed her eyes for a moment. Dave and Reverend Mitchell were right. The only way to rid herself of that man was pushing through this. As scared as she was of him, she still had pride and determination left not to let Dwight see her distress and fear.

When she stepped into the courtroom, she ignored his presence. She sat behind her father, surrounded by muscly men. Next to her were Reverend Mitchell and Dave, and Dr. Sanderson sat with them as well. The courtroom filled quickly.

Hazel glanced around but continued to ignore Dwight. She noticed that the courtroom had several young women present, and that made her curious. Did Harry Camden find more victims of Dwight, or were those ladies the girls Reverend Mitchell and Marshal Holden had rescued from the *white slavery* scheme?

She felt Dwight's eyes on her, but no matter how nervous that made her, she pretended he didn't exist.

His aggressive movements told her that her behavior was getting to him. She had to admit it felt good because it meant she took some power away from him. Hazel relaxed.

It turned out that the ladies in the room were a combination of girls he had attacked privately and girls he had kidnapped for the white slavery exploitation. It was horrifying to hear their testimonies and what these poor girls had gone through because of that man.

None of these girls had been targeted like Hazel, but they had experienced horrible and evil ordeals, and one girl had even gotten pregnant from his attack. Hazel felt more and more uncomfortable. Dave put his arm around her shoulders, and Reverend Mitchell squeezed her hand.

Harry Camden called Hazel into the witness stand as the last witness of the day. She got up, walked over to the judge, and took her seat. The judge was the same one who had seen her horrible wounds after the attack on the cattle drive, and he gave her a kind and encouraging smile.

"Miss Buchannon," Harry Camden began saying. "Please share with the judge and jury your first encounter with Mr. Dwight Miller, better known under the name Gabriel McKellar."

Hazel looked startled for a moment. In all her conversations with everyone, she didn't recall anyone saying his actual name. Not wanting Dwight to see her confusion, she told the court about him threatening her at their ranch and that it had gotten him fired before the cattle drive.

"So he was supposed to be out of the picture after that, is that correct?"

"Yes."

"What happened next?"

She shared her experience, what injuries were caused, and that her horse and one of their cowboys had been killed.

"Tell the truth, you little wench," Dwight yelled at her. "You lured me into the grove to seduce me."

"Mr. Dean," the judge said as he turned to the defense lawyer, and held-back anger colored his voice. "Please make sure your defendant doesn't interrupt this court's proceedings."

"Yes, Sir." The defense lawyer leaned over to his defendant and snapped at him for his remarks. Dwight was not impressed, nor was he intimidated.

"Maybe you should tell Hazel Buchannon and the other women in this court to shut their mouths. They are only women and shouldn't be allowed to testify against a man."

Outraged mumbling went through the courtroom. Hazel had tensed up as soon as Dwight burst out his first comment, but was in control right away. His second comment only angered her, the same pathetic attitude and opinion as Philip Mason.

Judge McGregor used his gavel several times before the courtroom was quiet again. He looked at Dwight with fire in his eyes.

"Mr. McKellar, let me be clear with you right now. I am not one of those men who think women should be silent and do what men tell them. I don't mistreat and enslave women. In fact, I have high respect for our female population and will do what I can to change the laws in favor of women, so they get the rights and respect they deserve. Women don't deserve to be mistreated. Men who think they are better and more powerful than women are cowards in my eyes."

The attendees began clapping in agreement. Hazel gave the judge a grateful smile, even though her expression was full of concern and worry.

Gabriel gave one of the jury members a quick nod, and before anyone knew what was happening, that man was behind Hazel. He pulled her off her chair, held a knife to her throat, and looked at the judge.

"Let McKellar go, or this one dies right now," he roared, causing everyone in the room to gasp.

Thomas McGregor was shocked but in control of himself. Several marshals were in the room, and the sheriff and his deputies. He wasn't concerned that this man or McKellar would get away, but he was worried about the young lady in front of the jury member.

Hazel felt the sharp edge of the knife and knew one wrong movement would be the end of her. She looked down at the hand below her and noticed a crumbled piece of paper tugged into his shirt sleeve. Something told her to grab it.

Since she was determined not to go down without a fight, she threw her head back and hit him straight in the nose. The guy lowered the knife for a second. Hazel used her hands to pull his arms away from her throat. She only had a split-second to think about her options. To get the paper, she had to let go of his arm with one of her hands. Hazel realized she wasn't strong enough to stop his arm and hand from stabbing her with only one hand holding on to him. She was already struggling as he tried to get out of her hold. Hazel had to decide.

She could either hold on to his arm, hoping he wouldn't injure her, and the marshals would take him down, or focus on getting that piece of paper and risking getting stabbed, even killed. An inner voice kept telling her to grab the paper, and she didn't hesitate anymore, snatched it out of his sleeve, and dropped it into the pocket of her dress.

Not realizing Marshal Holden as well as two of the deputies had their guns pointed at him, the man behind Hazel stabbed her left arm the moment Sterling Holden fired a precise shot. Just as it had been with McKellar, the bullet went straight into the man's shoulder and knocked him off his feet.

Hazel moaned in pain, her pale face turning white. Dwight watched her with a grin. The marshal closest to her leaped to her side. He grabbed her around her waist and pulled her with him, away from the now injured jury member.

Witnesses and the audience were on their feet, watching with horror as Hazel's sleeve turned red where she had been stabbed. She collapsed the moment the marshal had her in safety, with him still holding on to her.

"ORDER, ORDER!" Judge McGregor shouted over the noise, and everyone quieted down at once. "We will adjourn the trial session to tomorrow morning. I am asking everyone to leave this room in an orderly fashion. Sheriff Baker, make sure they get out of here."

The sheriff nodded, and everyone besides those who were with Hazel left the courtroom.

"Marshal Deputies," Judge McGregor said as he looked at several men left in the room, "get these filthy demons out of here and make sure they are locked up and can't escape."

"Yes, Sir." They grabbed McKellar and the injured jury guy and took them to jail.

George and Reverend Mitchell took Hazel from the marshal holding her and bedded her on a bench. Dr. Sanderson jumped to her side, ripped the sleeve off her arm, and looked at the wound.

"Nurse Walton, please bring me my bag from over there," he said to a young woman still in the room. She nodded and handed him his bag a moment later.

"Is it bad, Dr. Sanderson?"

"It isn't as deep as it could have been, but we still have to sew it."

"Marshal Holden, how is it possible that McKellar still has so much help and support? This is outrageous." Thomas McGregor was furious, not with the marshal but with the situation.

"He works with the people behind *white slavery*. We still don't know who started it, but we are assuming men higher up the ladder. Once we know where the threat is coming from, we can destroy it from top to bottom."

"They infiltrated the jury, and that is unacceptable," McGregor continued. "Marshal Holden, from now on, it is your responsibility to make sure that nobody enters the courtroom with a weapon. Only law enforcement may have a gun with them."

Sterling Holden nodded.

"Nurse Walton, please put chloroform on a cloth and hold it over Miss Buchannon's nose. I don't want her to wake up until I am done with treating her wound. She has gone through enough."

"I can't believe Hazel loses consciousness so much at the moment. That can't be healthy for her. She has never fainted in the past." George stood next to the doctor, still in shock.

"Hazel has gone through numerous traumas, pain, and terror in the past few months, and her body is reacting accordingly. This is physical and emotional, and I am sure she has never experienced that before, right?"

"She had traumatic experiences as a child."

"Was it physical as well, or only emotional?"

"Just emotional."

"It is the combination of the two that makes the reaction of her body so extreme. Plus, a child copes with those things differently than an adult."

Hazel woke up fifteen minutes later. Her arm hurt but would hopefully heal quickly, and the worst was over. She sat up.

"How are you feeling?" Dr. Sanderson asked.

"Tired." She moved her healthy arm around and remembered the piece of paper she had taken from the attacker. "I saw this note in the sleeve of my attacker and took it." She handed it to Marshal Holden. He opened and unwrinkled it and read what was on the paper. His jaw dropped.

"You got that from the man who attacked you?"

"Yes. When he had the knife at my throat, it popped out of his sleeve, and something told me to take it from him."

"Judge McGregor, you should see this," Sterling Holden said with an urgent tone in his voice, and the judge stepped closer.

"That is incredible evidence if this paper is legit."

Holden nodded, and now George Buchannon, Reverend Mitchell and the rest of the men gathered around the judge and read it.

Bradley,

> *Once you took Hazel Buchannon hostage and freed McKellar, I need you two to head over to Walnut Creek. The rest of the kidnapped girls are in my old gold mine.*
>
> *Several guys are there, making sure they don't escape, and we need Hazel with them. Her beauty, temper, and good breeding will get us the best price of them. Hire a few more men and get them on their way to San Francisco. 'The Oregon' will take everyone to New York, and from there, we will ship them to England.*

This will be our last big sale, so make sure everything works out. McKellar needs to keep his filthy hands off Hazel Buchannon, or we will kill him ourselves. She needs to be untouched for us to get the best price for her.

If something goes wrong, get in touch with me or the following men: Marlin Jenkins, Mark Moore, Howard Webster, or Gregory Watkins. If I don't hear from you, I will see you in New York in a few weeks.

Everyone went quiet for a moment and looked around in shock. Hazel stood on the bench she was sitting on when nobody moved, and glanced over Marshal Holden's shoulder. She gasped in shock and horror when she saw the signature on the letter. One man involved in the dirty business of white slavery was Oregon's Governor Deputy Wayne Reeves.

"That means four senators are part of this evil spiel."

"Yes, and Governor Deputy Reeves played us as well." Marshal Holden was fuming.

"I don't understand. How does Hazel fit in this scheme? Reeves didn't even know her until we met you and Reverend Mitchell," Dave commented.

"Your guess is as good as mine. Currently, I am leaning toward the following explanation: Jason Clark was instructed to check out the girls in Willamette Falls, but because he was interested in Hazel himself, he tried to keep her away from the men abducting women. When Reeves met her, she became a target for the *white slavery* exploitation, and Clark got under fire for not passing on the information about her."

"Do you think Reverend Clark was only a distraction?" Hazel's expression was concerned but calm.

"Not at first. He was in it for himself, but once Reeves met you, he kept using Clark as a diversion to make us more worried about him than the overall white slavery threat."

"That's why he prevented the kidnapping of the girl in Willamette Falls, and why he showed up in the alley at my attempted abduction."

"Exactly."

"So, what will happen now?" Reverend Mitchell asked.

"I'll tell you what is going to happen. I will contact the marshal headquarters in Washington and Salem and inform my colleagues about this letter. They will arrest these men and then search their homes and offices for every single piece of evidence. Once the evidence has been located, they will organize a massive raid and arrest every one of these prairie coal vermin who work with and for the senators and Reeves. We will bust this entire scheme and restore law and order." Marshal Holden's fists were clenched, but there was a determined sparkle in his eyes.

"After I wired Salem and Washington, I'll grab a few of my men, the sheriff, and his deputies and ride over to Walnut Creek, get the kidnapped girls out of the mine and freed, and arrest the guys who are holding them there."

Thomas McGregor nodded in agreement.

"You mean this will be over soon?" Hazel had a hopeful expression on her face.

"Not quite, but we are getting closer. You still have to finish this trial with McKellar, and we have nothing on Clark yet, but once we busted everyone and put them in jail, Clark will have to be even more careful and will most likely stay away from you."

"That's correct," Thomas McGregor interjected. "We have to move fast before they can notify anyone and help people disappear. The first arrests have to happen tonight before the San Francisco Post gets their newspaper out. Marshal Holden, when you wire the news out, please have the marshal headquarters wire me back as soon as they have made the arrests. We have to stay on top of things, and with you riding to Walnut Creek tonight, you won't be back until tomorrow morning since you have to take a steamboat both ways."

Sterling Holden nodded, his lips tight with anger.

Hazel, her father, and her friends, watched Sterling Holden mount his horse after alerting the marshal headquarters on the east coast and up north. Several of his deputies, the sheriff and his deputies, and a few other men followed him, and they rode out of town.

"Good luck, Marshal Holden," Hazel mumbled to herself. "Please stay safe and come back in one piece."

26
White Slavery Raid

Loud banging on the front door woke up the entire household. It frightened the children out of their minds, and everyone jumped out of bed. The servants also looked scared.

"OPEN UP! THIS IS MARSHAL TIMOTHY GARRETT," a man shouted. "IF YOU DON'T OPEN, WE WILL BREAK IN THE DOOR!"

Marlin Jenkins watched his wife with wide eyes as she put on a dressing gown. Dread and horror crept through his entire body. His wife followed the noise toward the front door. Marlin knew what this visit meant. He had not expected it, nor had he thought this would happen, but as soon as he heard the marshal's voice, he knew the game was over.

He got up and dressed, grabbed his gun, snuck down the stairs and went to the backdoor of the kitchen entrance.

Jenkins looked back one last time before opening the door toward the backyard. Everything was silent, and so he stepped out and closed the door behind him.

"*Stop* right there, Mr. Jenkins," a voice from the darkness yelled. "Surrender, and no harm will come to you."

Jenkins pulled out his gun.

"What can I do for you, Marshal?"

"Please step aside, Mrs. Jenkins. Where is your husband?" Marshal Garrett asked before he and a few of his deputies stepped inside the house.

"He is upstairs. May I ask what is going on?"

Loud shouting and shooting came from the backyard, and Mariah Jenkins froze in terror.

"No, please, don't hurt him," she gasped and was about to hurry toward the back, but Marshal Garrett stopped her.

"No, Ma'am. Stay here. I will check on what is going on."

When he reached the back, the shooting had stopped. He opened the back door and saw Marlin Jenkins dead on the grass in front of the stairs. Garrett looked at his men.

"What happened? I told you to arrest him, not kill him."

"I know, Sir," one deputy responded, "but he opened fire on us. No matter how much we tried to convince him to surrender, he wouldn't do it."

Timothy Garrett nodded with a sigh. Now he had to fill in Jenkins' widow, on what this guy had done.

Mariah Jenkins listened with shaking hands and trembling lips, but she wasn't crying. "Let me show you something," she mumbled after the marshal finished talking. She led him down the hallway, opened a door, and went down a few steps into the basement. She led him into the furthest corner of the room and pointed at a small wooden box.

"I found this yesterday when I was looking for something in the basement. My husband has been very secretive during the past few months, and I have seen him go down to the basement a lot, which he never did before. I have not opened the box because, frankly, I feared what I would find, but this might have some evidence you are looking for."

"May I?"

"Yes, of course," she nodded.

He opened the box and found it filled with letters and different papers. The first one alone was all the evidence he needed, as it was a correspondence between Jenkins and Wayne Reeves.

The same scene repeated itself at the homes of Mark Moore, Howard Webster, Gregory Watkins, and Wayne Reeves. Mark Moore and Howard Webster surrendered, Gregory and Wayne started a shoot-out and lost. Their homes were searched, and the evidence was confiscated.

Marshal Holden and his men reached Walnut Creek long after midnight. It was pitch black out there, but they met a drunken miner, and he told them how to get to the old goldmine of Wayne Reeves.

They left their horses in a grove of trees and insinuated themselves everywhere around the mine. Sterling Holden listened. They had to figure out where the men were and where they kept the girls.

Loud snoring came from one corner of the mine. Holden crept into the tunnel, followed by a backup. Only a small fire was going, but the snoring came from five men sleeping at the entrance to a different passage. Sterling looked into the path and could only make out shadows, but the women seemed to be in there. He pointed at one of his deputies, who went back outside to call for more men. They positioned themselves around the sleeping kidnappers and attacked a moment later. None of the men stood a chance and were handcuffed within minutes.

As soon as the girls heard the commotion and fighting, they whimpered and some started sobbing. Marshal Holden took a few torches, lit them with the fire, and stepped into the passage.

Terror and distress were written in their eyes, and it broke his heart to see them so traumatized. They had been chained to the walls and must have been beaten and tortured, as bruises and wounds covered their thin bodies. Two of the girls didn't even move anymore. He realized they had come at the right time. A little longer in this mine, and these two would have been dead.

He tried to approach them, but they became even more fearful. Sterling told his deputy to bring in the three fathers from San Francisco he had brought with him, hoping their girls were part of these hostages.

As soon as four of the girls recognized their fathers, they burst into tears. The rest of the women relaxed as soon as they realized the men were a rescue party.

The girls were unchained and covered in blankets before the rescuers helped them on the two wagons they had brought with them. Sterling counted twenty girls and women, which had to be taken to the hospital right away. They would have to return to San Francisco at once.

Hazel did not sleep well that night. Elizabeth and Harry Camden had invited her and her family and friends to stay with them and not stay at the hotel, hoping an actual home would help Hazel feel more comfortable. She was fine until it was time for bed.

Every time she closed her eyes, she saw Dwight in front of her. What if the raid hadn't been successful, and they would free her tormentor within the next few days? And even if they arrested everyone important, what if there were still men out there who would help him escape?

He would come after her because of all the girls he had attacked, he had not finished what he wanted to do to her. He had attacked her twice and had another person attack her. Hazel didn't feel safe.

At three am, she gave up on trying to sleep, got up and put on her dressing gown, grabbed a blanket, and went into Camden's backyard. The border to their property was a river. She sat next to it, breathing in the night-air and looking at the stars and bright moon. It could have been perfect if it hadn't been for the fear and constant worrying. She heard someone approaching her but wasn't startled. The steps were from someone who wanted to join her, not hurt her.

A moment later, Namito sat next to her, putting his arm around her shoulders. "You couldn't sleep either?"

Hazel shook her head. "Every time I close my eyes, I see Dwight in front of me. What if he hired more people to come after me?"

"They will get arrested just like the last one."

"What if they attack one of you guys next?"

"We will be fine," he responded while pulling her closer. "I don't think anyone with ill intentions can use the court for it. Judge McGregor saw everything and will make sure that something like today won't happen again."

Hazel thought for a moment. It was quiet around, and they could only hear the rippling of the water nearby.

"Do you think I will ever feel safe again?" Her voice was calm, yet he could hear the sadness and despair.

"Oh, Hazel." He stood, helped her up too, and pulled her into his muscular arms. His heart broke for her. He wanted his happy, cheerful best friend back, and he would do what he could to get her to that point again. He wanted to hear her laugh and see her beautiful smile every day, and Dwight would not destroy that.

27
Final Threats

When Hazel stepped out of her room a few hours later, everyone was still asleep. Namito snored behind a door close by, and that made her smile. Hazel was about to close the door to her room when she noticed a letter on the floor. She picked it up, took it out of the envelope, and read.

Hazel,

You might think you are safe from me, but you will never be safe. Two more guys will be waiting in the courtroom for you today, and they will finish what Bradley wasn't able to do. Once they free me, I will come after you, and I will enjoy destroying your pureness and soul. Shall I tell you what I will do to you? First, I will beat you into submission. Then, I will slowly...

Hazel dropped the letter and ran down the stairs. She would not stay another minute in this town, and would never return to court to face that evil demon. She opened the front door and ran as fast as she could in the direction of the stagecoach station.

Alex Camden walked past her room a moment later and saw the letter on the ground. He picked it up and unfolded the paper.

Horror and disgust spread across his face when he read the written words. He looked up and realized that Hazel must have read it not long before him. He heard the front door open and close and rushed after her.

When he reached the front gate, he scanned the street and called her name, but she couldn't hear him.

She was quite ahead of him. Intense panic allowed her body to run in a way she had never run before. He followed at once.

Sterling Holden had stepped out of the hospital. He was about to mount his horse when he noticed Hazel across the street. Sterling called after her, but she didn't even turn around, just kept running toward the stagecoach station. He jumped on his horse and raced after her as fast as the morning traffic would let him.

As soon as he was next to her, Holden jumped off his horse and grabbed her by her arms. He turned her toward him.

"Hazel," he said with worry in his voice. "What is going on?"

"I... I can't... I am leaving," she stammered, emotions and breathlessness in her voice.

"What happened?"

"It doesn't matter, I am not staying." She tried to get out of his hold, but he held her firm.

"Hazel, stop." They heard Alex call her now and he reached them a moment later.

"Just let me go," she begged, pulled herself free, and was about to continue her run when Alex grabbed her around her waist and dragged her backward before turning her around and pulling her into his arms. Not a moment too late, or a stagecoach would have hit her.

"Let me go, please just let me go." She burst into tears, and Alex held her close.

"What happened?" Marshal Holden asked again, but this time he looked at Alex.

Alex held Hazel with one arm, pulled the letter out of his pocket, and handed it to the older man. Sterling Holden read it, and his expression changed from worried to pure anger. He clenched his fists, an intense fire burning in his eyes.

"He will pay for this. I promise that was his last threat to you."

Hazel dried her tears and lifted her head. Marshal Holden put his hand on her cheek and caressed her face with his thumb.

"Let's get her home," he said to Alex, who nodded in agreement.

They turned around and were about to walk back, but Hazel's body finally released the tension and stress that had kept her moving. Exhaustion replaced the tenseness, and the long run signaled she had reached her limit. Her legs gave out, and she couldn't hold herself up any longer. Alex steadied her body and lifted her off her feet.

"No, Alex, please put me back on the ground. You can't carry me back," she stammered and blushed.

"Hazel, you can't walk anymore. You just ran about two miles, and your body is still recovering."

"Put her on my horse, Alex," Marshal Holden said, jumping into the conversation. "I will join you guys as I have to speak to Harry, her father, and Robert Mitchell after the appearance of this letter."

Alex lifted her onto the saddle, and she held on to the saddle horn. She felt uncomfortable and embarrassed that she was riding, and the two men were walking beside her, but she had to listen to her body now. She had reached her limit and didn't want to lose consciousness again.

When they arrived at the house from the Camden's, Alex helped her off the horse. She made another step, but her legs gave out again, so Alex lifted her and carried her into the house, followed by Sterling.

Alex seated Hazel on the sofa in the living room and called a servant to get Dr. Sanderson. The physical exhaustion reached every inch of Hazel's body, and she was close to going into shock. Marshal Holden spoke to her, so she wouldn't collapse. Alex informed the rest of the household that they needed to meet in the living room at once.

No matter who walked in, as soon as they saw Hazel's pale and weary face, concern entered their eyes. Hazel closed her eyes and leaned her head back while Sterling and Alex explained the situation and allowed everyone to read the letter. Shock and outrage spread across the room.

"I will see Judge McGregor right away and will show him this letter. Something like that cannot happen again."

"How did that letter even get to Hazel's door?" Liz Camden asked.

"A boy delivered it, and one of our servants brought it upstairs, not knowing what it was," her husband explained.

"Harry," Sterling Holden said. "You need to talk to your servants and inform them that nothing, and I mean NOTHING, is to reach Hazel without at least one man in the house checking it first. I don't blame your servant, he didn't know better, but in case someone tries to get in touch with her again, it has to be caught before it reaches her."

"I agree, and I will speak to them right away."

"How did the raid go, Marshal Holden?" Hazel asked with a quiet voice without opening her eyes.

"We arrested everyone and freed the girls. They are at the hospital now. Unfortunately, two didn't make it. The abuse they had suffered was too much."

"How many girls were in the mine?"

"Twenty."

"What about Governor Deputy Reeves and the Senators?"

"They have been arrested or were killed. Not everyone cooperated and refused to surrender, so they ended up shot."

Hazel shook her head in sadness and defeat. How tragic that some people were so concerned about power and money that they didn't care how many lives were ruined and destroyed, including their own.

"May I have a moment alone with this young lady," Dr. Sanderson said as he entered the room. Hazel opened her eyes and gave him a weak smile. Everyone else left the room, and Marshal Holden took off to talk to the judge and show him the letter.

"Miss Buchannon, please look after yourself. Your body cannot take the emotional and physical stress and turmoil you are struggling with right now."

"I know. I am sorry I overdid it again."

"I don't want you to be sorry. I want you to give yourself the rest you need. For the remainder of this day, you have to rest and only rest. I promise you, young lady, if you are not listening to me as your doctor, I'll have your father tie you to your bed." His playfulness made her smile.

"What about the trial?"

"I will talk to Judge McGregor and let him know that you can't be present there today. Your health is more important right now."

"Thank you, Dr. Sanderson."

"She needs to rest. I will not allow her back in court. Facing that demon man again would be too much for her." The young physician spoke firmly and Helen and Liz nodded. "Please ensure she stays either in bed or on the sofa. I told her if she doesn't comply, I will have her father tie her down."

The two women smiled. Everyone in this house needed humor.

"We will make sure she gets the rest she so desperately needs," Liz Camden promised as they stepped back into the sitting room. Hazel gave her a weak smile.

"You will take your time and recover from all of this," Judge Thomas McGregor after entering the sitting room, followed by Marshal Holden, Harry Camden and the rest of the men.

"I excuse you from the trial until it is time for the verdict."

"Thank you, Judge McGregor," Hazel said gratefully, and he squeezed her hand.

"Marshal Holden showed me the letter you received this morning, and we'll use that as evidence. I don't think McKellar realizes that we have arrested the men in charge of white slavery, and the entire evil operation is being torn to pieces as we speak. Several of the girls kidnapped by McKellar and held captive in Walnut Creek have agreed to testify against him, and they'll join us later today. Mr. Buchannon, someone must always be with her. I believe this was the last threat to her because everyone associated with McKellar has either been arrested or will get arrested soon, but let's play it safe."

"We will stay with her," Liz Camden said, and Helen nodded.

"And so will I," Reverend Mitchell added and gave Hazel an encouraging smile.

"That's good," Thomas McGregor responded. "Hazel should always have at least one man around for protection."

"Let's have breakfast before you head to court," Liz suggested. "I instructed our servants to set the table, and everyone here is invited. Is Hazel allowed to be up for breakfast?"

"Thank you, Mrs. Camden, but I am not hungry."

"Miss Buchannon, remember what we discussed? You need to look after yourself, and that includes eating and drinking," Dr. Sanderson interjected.

Hazel nodded. "I will look after myself, I promise. I think the calmative you gave me earlier is working, though." She could barely keep her eyes open now, laid down, turned away from everyone, and fell asleep at once. She didn't even feel it when Liz put a blanket over her, and they all left the room.

Harry Camden and George Buchannon had barely sat down when two marshal deputies brought Gabriel McKellar into the courtroom. He scanned the room with his eyes, found Dave, Namito, and Alex sitting next to each other, but saw no Hazel. He grinned.

"Buchannon," he yelled across the room, "did you forget your daughter at home, or is she too scared of me to show her face?"

Namito and Dave clenched their fists, and even the well-tempered George had to hold himself back. Before he could reply, Thomas McGregor entered the room through a side door, and everyone stood. He had heard McKellar's comment, though.

He nodded to the audience, jury, and those who took part in the trial, and everyone sat down. Judge McGregor gave Gabriel a death stare.

"Mr. McKellar, let me be clear and direct with you, since that seems to be the only way you can communicate. Miss Buchannon is excused from this court for medical reasons. I am aware that you think highly of yourself and are convinced that this trial is only a joke, and that you'll get out of here in no time. I can assure you, though, that this is as serious as it gets, and you will get punished for all the crimes you committed. Oh and the two men you are expecting today who are supposed to free you, will not come. After yesterday's attack on Miss Buchannon, she took something from your friend and passed it on to us. You might recognize this piece of paper?" Judge McGregor lifted it, and Gabriel let out a quiet gasp.

"I thought you would remember this. Marshal Holden and his men started a raid across the country, arrested the men in charge, and are now finding everyone associated with these horrible crimes. Marshal Holden also freed the kidnapped girls they held captive in Walnut Creek. A few of them will join us later to testify against you."

For the first time since Gabriel McKellar had been caught and arrested, his expression changed from grinning to worry and concern. He had not expected such a turnaround.

"Your constant need for trying to torture Miss Buchannon has officially ended. Everything we find, like this letter, for example, will only be evidence against you, and we will let the jury read it when it is time to decide on a verdict."

"You have no proof that the letter is from me," McKellar snapped.

"Mr. McKellar, just because you didn't sign it doesn't mean we don't know who wrote it. You even referred to your arrested friend from yesterday and that you will finish what you started. The game is over for you."

Dr. Sanderson and a few of the hospital staff were called into the witness stand, one after another. Everyone testified about the same things and explained how bad Hazel's injuries had been, that she had been attacked a second time and shot into her shoulder as she tried to protect Reverend Mitchell. The audience gasped. Sheriff Baker and Judge McGregor confirmed the testimonies of Hazel's injuries.

"Miss Buchannon's back looked-liked she had been whipped. I have never seen such terrible injuries before, and I have seen a lot in my life. Treating another human being in such a degrading and evil way is demonic. Nobody should have to go through that. It doesn't matter if your skin tone is different, or you are a woman. Everyone deserves respect and fair treatment."

The audience clapped in agreement, but calmed down as soon as another witness was called.

Hazel slept all morning until early afternoon. After eating lunch, she asked if she could sit outside in the sun and enjoy the beautiful day. Helen, Liz, and Robert Mitchell told her she could, but Robert had to carry her out.

"Reverend Mitchell, this is silly, I had a lot of rest, and I am only walking through part of the house into the backyard." She was about to stand when he grabbed her and lifted her off her feet.

"Don't make me tie you to the sofa," he said with a growl in his voice to sound more intimidating. "Dr. Sanderson might have told your father to do that if you disobeyed his orders, but I can do it just as well." He looked into her eyes without blinking.

Hazel lowered her eyes for a moment and blushed. That was the same look her father gave her sometimes, and she hated it. It was a look of confidence and total strength and made her feel uncomfortable because she felt as if they could see right through her.

"Fine," she finally said with a sigh and rolled her eyes. "Before I let anyone tie me down, I'll let you carry me. It is still silly and unnecessary, though."

Robert Mitchell grinned at her, winked at Helen and Liz, carried Hazel to the backyard seating area, placed her in a comfortable chair, and looked deep into her eyes.

"Don't get any ideas, Hazel Buchannon," he remarked with his deep voice. "I'll carry you back inside too. Don't make me threaten you with more than tying you down."

She retorted with a playful scoff. "What is going on with you? I have never seen you so bossy."

"Bossy? You think I am bossy? Do you know what a bossy man does with a sassy young lady?" he replied with a twinkle in his eyes. He was about to grab her to throw her over his shoulder when she stopped his hands.

"No, please, Reverend Mitchell," she pleaded with a whining tone in her voice. "I am so weak, and I promised Dr. Sanderson I wouldn't overdo it. Besides, don't you remember the stab wound on my arm?"

He coughed to hide his smile, but almost laughed out loud when she changed her playful sass into drama and fake faintness.

"Now you remember your weakness and injury again, huh?" he mumbled, growling, but winked at her before he sat in a chair next to her.

"Didn't you want to go back inside the house?"

"I never said that," he replied with a raised eyebrow. "Why do you want me to go back inside, young lady?"

"I don't," she stammered and blushed again, "I assumed you would after you told me you would carry me back inside too."

"And then I decided I can't leave you out of my sight. Your sass made me rethink my plans."

"My sass?" Hazel glanced at him innocently. "Whatever do you mean, Reverend?"

He grinned. It was good to see her old self come out again. "I have taken the job of your protector for today, and I am taking it seriously. I bet the minute I turn my back on you, you jump off this chair and go for a swim in the river. I don't think so."

Hazel stared at him, speechless for a moment, contemplating what he had just said. He watched her eagerly.

When their eyes met, she burst into a fit of laughter, and he nodded amused. That was his Hazel.

"Hazel, you have a visitor," Liz Camden called out as she stuck her head through the door. Hazel tensed up at once. Her worry turned into a beaming smile when the door opened, and Russell Montgomery stepped out.

"Mr. Montgomery, what a pleasant surprise." Hazel was about to get up to greet her guest when Reverend Mitchell cleared his throat. She gave him a sly side glance but stayed seated.

"Forgive me for not getting up and greeting you properly, but my protector here doesn't allow me to be polite to people. I am lucky he lets me breathe on my own. You would think a man of his age would have learned by now how important manners are, but as you can see, bossing me around is more important to him than manners," she remarked with a straight face.

Reverend Mitchell's expression was pure shock, and he just stared at her for a moment. Before Russell Montgomery could say anything in return, though, Reverend Mitchell was next to her, pulled Hazel out of her chair, and threw her over his shoulder. Hazel didn't even know what was happening to her. He turned around and walked toward the river.

"No, no, please, Reverend Mitchell. Don't throw me into the water. Please, I promise I will keep my sass in check."

He took her off his shoulder and looked into her eyes. "I will hold you to that, Miss Buchannon," he replied with an amused twinkle in his eyes.

"Of course you do," she shot back with a straight face. "Let's return to our guest, shall we?"

He nodded, but before she could turn around and walk back to Russell Montgomery, Robert Mitchell picked her up and threw her back over his shoulder.

"Hey, put me down. What's gotten into you this time? I didn't give you any sass," she argued, but he kept on walking.

"I promised I would carry you, and I'll keep that promise."

Russell Montgomery grinned when Reverend Mitchell put Hazel back on her chair, and she rolled her eyes at him. He then greeted Russell with a firm handshake, and the two men seated themselves.

"What brings you here, Mr. Montgomery?" Hazel looked at him, and he squeezed her hand.

"Please call me Russell, Hazel. I think we are past the formalities."

She nodded.

Robert Mitchell almost gasped in surprise. He had offered her the same thing two years prior, but she couldn't make herself do it. Growing up around him and always calling him Reverend Mitchell was so part of her that she couldn't make herself call him by his first name. He had wondered why that was, but it made sense to him now. She had only known Russell Montgomery for a short while, so calling him differently would be easier for her.

"I am home after being away for business, but I wanted to check on you after hearing about what happened to you."

"How did you hear about it?"

"The newspapers have reported about it ever since your family brought you to the hospital in San Francisco, and they arrested Gabriel McKellar."

"The newspapers? Why do I not know about this?" Hazel gave Reverend Mitchell a reproachful glance.

"Your father handled it all, Hazel. Don't be angry with him. He spoke to Judge McGregor and Sheriff Baker after they had seen your injuries, and they told him it was the best way to get the word out and maybe get things rolling regarding changing the laws for women."

Hazel frowned, but Russell Montgomery agreed with her father.

"It was a good thing, Hazel. Really. So many men have come forward and have expressed their outrage that anyone would mistreat a woman. Men have stood up for women and threatened other men with serious consequences if they didn't stop beating and abusing their wives and daughters. The professors of the Institute in Salem acted and forced hearings to change laws, including who can own and inherit land. They are still facing a lot of resistance, but the beginning is done. You made that happen, Hazel."

"I did nothing."

"Yes, you did. You stepped up to the task of putting your foot down and making it clear you would not accept unfair treatment. I was highly impressed with you when you so fearlessly and determined argued with me the first time we met."

"You had one of your men carry me outside," she reminded him with a raised eyebrow, and he grinned.

"Yes, that's true. It had not much to do with you, more with my reputation. You are a force of nature and unstoppable. The way you fought for your right to take part in the examination convinced me you deserve a chance, and other women deserve that chance as well. I still believe you should be a lawyer."

Hazel smiled bashfully, but she knew he meant what he said.

"I know you didn't want the change to happen this way, Hazel," Reverend Mitchell said now. "None of us wanted for you to go through what you went through the past few weeks and months, but maybe this is a wake-up call America needs. The San Francisco and Washington Post reported about the white slavery raid, and it hit the citizens of San Francisco like an explosion. Everyone is talking about it, and everyone is talking about you."

"I don't want people to talk about me. I want people to change things, so everyone can feel safer and may do what they want to do. I know there will always be evil people who will terrorize another person, but if any of this will make people more willing to step up and not let unfairness happen so much, I'll see it as a good start."

28

Harrowing Nightmares

Since Russell Montgomery didn't have any commitments for the rest of the day, Liz Camden invited him to stay for supper. After everyone returned from court, they discussed the events that had taken place, shared the kidnapped girls' testimonies, and then moved on to more cheerful conversations. It was a great and pleasant evening, and even Hazel enjoyed herself. Marshal Holden was also a guest and brought laughter to the supper table.

Grateful, she didn't have to think about the trial so much; she let herself relax. It only lasted until evening. As bedtime approached, Hazel tensed up again and got quieter and quieter. Helen and Liz noticed it first and gave her worried looks.

Finally, Hazel couldn't stand the cheerful atmosphere any longer. She got up, told her goodbyes and goodnight, and left the dining room. She grabbed her warm shawl and stepped outside into the backyard to soak in the fresh air before heading to her room. Dave and Robert Mitchell followed her.

She leaned against a tree close to the river and tried to calm her anxious feelings. Tears entered her eyes, and she swallowed hard, so she wouldn't start sobbing. She heard the two men approaching her and automatically straightened her back.

Dave put his arm around her shoulders, and Robert Mitchell stepped next to her.

"Hazel," Dave said, worry and concern coloring his voice. "What is wrong?"

"I am scared," she replied.

"Scared of what? McKellar can't do anything to you. He is in prison, and Marshal Holden's men won't let him out of their sights."

"I fear going to sleep," she muttered, close to tears again. "I couldn't sleep last night because every time I closed my eyes, I saw Dwight in front of me. It is a sign of what is coming. I've had terrible nightmares as a child because of something I experienced, and it will happen again. The torture isn't over, Dave. Not for me. The actual torture is beginning now. I can distract myself during the day, but I can't control my dreams." Her voice was a trembling whisper now, and her body began to shake.

Reverend Mitchell pulled her into his arms. "It is okay, Hazel. Remember, you are not alone. We are here and will come to your aid whenever you need us."

Dave nodded in agreement.

"You need your sleep, too, though."

"Hazel," Robert Mitchell said and lifted her chin, so she had to look into his eyes. "We are in this together. You have gone through some serious tormenting and harrowing ordeals in your life, and we want to help as much as we can. If that means waking you up from a nightmare or comforting you in the middle of the night because of a horrible dream, we will do that. We love you, and loving someone means we are there for them no matter what. You do the same thing in return. When you jumped in front of me to take that bullet for me, I thought my heart would stop. Holding you so lifeless in my arms was the worst moment I ever experienced."

Tess rose and threw her off her back, but her foot got stuck in the stirrup, and she was now dragged behind her horse. She felt every rock and sharp edge on her back, leg, and shoulder, and her body burned like fire. He shot at her horse again, and Tess crashed to the ground. Tears streamed down her face when she realized she was about to lose her favorite and most beloved animal. Dwight pulled her on her back, and she fought him. She hit, kicked, and tried everything she could to break loose. When she couldn't get away from him, she became hysterical and started screaming for help. Why couldn't she get away from that monster?

George and Robert Mitchell heard when she became restless and rushed into her room. When George tried to calm her, she started fighting him. Both men held her down, so she wouldn't hurt herself. When she began screaming, they talked to her, but it wasn't until she woke herself up that she relaxed again. Hazel was covered in sweat, but fell back asleep at once. Her father and Robert Mitchell stayed by her side until they felt she would be okay for the rest of the night.

Dave stayed with Hazel the following day. He took her on a sightseeing tour through San Francisco and out for lunch. Many young women watched Hazel with envy of having such an agreeable looking partner by her side. They walked through the park when the afternoon approached and sat down on a bench next to the lake. Hazel was quiet again and couldn't help but think about the upcoming night.

"Try not to think about it, Hazel," Dave finally said and pulled her closer, so she could lean against him.

"I wish it were that easy, but it comes back when it gets closer to nighttime. I am so worried he will come after me again. He has done it before, he can do it again."

"We will not let that happen, and none of the marshals and deputies will let that happen. I promise you, McKellar will not get out of this without a serious consequence."

Gabriel McKellar was the first person called into the witness stand that day, and everyone could see he was eager to defend himself. His lawyer addressed him.

"Mr. McKellar, you heard many testimonies in the past few days, but the most accusing testimony during this trial was from Miss Hazel Buchannon. She accused you of several things and claimed you kept harassing her despite making it clear she was not interested in you. What can you tell the jury about this?"

"Everything Miss Buchannon said is a lie. She wanted me to notice her and kept playing with her looks to get my attention. I tried to ignore her beguiling playfulness, but she was so persistent, and man, I mean, have you seen her adorable lips?"

"Stay on topic, please," his lawyer rebuked him.

"Her father had me fired because they thought I was after her when, in reality, she was after me. Hazel encouraged me to meet them on the cattle drive, and I did. When she lured me into the little grove of trees, what was I supposed to do? A man can withstand temptation only for so long. I would have had my way with her right then, but that stupid cowboy interfered. Hazel freaked out as she didn't want her father to find out what she was like, and that's when things escalated."

"All of that is a lie, you evil demon," Namito yelled as he jumped up from his seat. Upset mumbling went through the audience because nobody believed the young man on the witness stand.

"Order, Order," Thomas McGregor scolded and slammed his gavel on the desk several times before everyone had calmed down again.

Gabriel grinned. George Buchannon, Robert Mitchell, and Marshal Holden were fuming, and Alex tried his best to prevent Namito from storming over to the criminal and giving him a beating of a lifetime.

"Mr. McKellar," Judge McGregor said now, "let me remind you that you are under oath. I recommend you stop telling your fairy tales. We know what happened. Several of the young ladies who testified in this trial shared the same or similar experiences. There is no reason for Miss Buchannon to make up a story."

Dwight only scoffed in reply. He was asked to return to his seat and sit next to his lawyer. Harry Camden called his son into the witness stand.

"Mr. Camden, you've worked for the Buchannon's for a while now. Has Miss Buchannon ever misbehaved? Did she throw herself at Mr. McKellar?"

"No. Hazel Buchannon is the opposite of Mr. McKellar's claim. She is virtuous and has high standards. Miss Buchannon had no interest in him and made that clear. She is honest and direct and would never pretend to be someone she is not. I heard him when he threatened Miss Buchannon after she rejected him the first time. He wasn't accustomed to rejection and was willing to do what it would take to make Hazel realize that. That's why we made sure he got fired right away. None of us felt it to be safe to have him around her any longer."

"But he followed you, anyway?"

"Yes. He attacked Miss Buchannon in the grove of trees, and when one of the Buchannon's ranch hands interfered, Mr. McKellar shot him."

"You saw how Miss Buchannon was dragged across rocks and sharp edges. You saw Mr. McKellar attacking her a second time after she had survived brutal injuries to her back, leg, and shoulder. What was he trying to do to her?"

Alex looked at his father, not sure what he wanted him to say. He seemed to be confused.

"Please tell this court what would have happened to Miss Buchannon if you, Mr. Tucker and Mr. Blake, hadn't arrived in time." He gave his son an encouraging nod.

Alex felt uncomfortable. This wasn't something that was discussed in public. He understood, though, what his father was trying to do. Harry wanted the world to know what would have happened to her if Gabriel McKellar had been successful. Harry Camden wanted to show the court how McKellar treated and tortured women. So far, every witness had only hinted at it, but nobody had said it out loud.

"Mr. Camden, please answer the question," Judge McGregor interrupted Alex's thoughts and gave him an encouraging nod. He, too, knew what Harry Camden was trying to do and agreed to such openness.

"Mr. McKellar wanted to violate her in the worst way possible. He not only wanted to humiliate and hurt her, but he wanted to take away her innocence and pureness. He wanted to ravish her."

Loud gasping and shocked mumbling went through the audience. Several of the female audience members lowered their eyes and turned red. Alex breathed through his teeth. This hadn't been easy for him.

"Thank you, Mr. Camden."

Namito was the last witness for the day and repeated everything Alex had shared. Since he had gotten Jeremy out of the grove of trees, he mentioned that as well.

Thomas McGregor adjourned the trial to the following day, and Gabriel McKellar was taken to his prison cell.

Hazel and Dave returned before everyone else came home, so Hazel stepped into their backyard. She loved Camden's garden. Being trapped in a big town for so long was not something she enjoyed, but their big yard gave her the feeling of freedom, the freedom nature brings.

Dave stepped out of the house and watched her for a while. She sat next to the river, lost in her thoughts. He knew she would start thinking about her upcoming nightmares again and wondered how he could distract her from those thoughts.

Namito wondered the same thing when he stepped outside after returning home. He, too, wanted to stop her from her depressing thoughts as long as possible. He saw Dave approaching Hazel and had an idea.

Hazel looked up when Dave stood next to her. He gave her an encouraging smile, but she was still lost in her thoughts and didn't react. Namito attacked him from behind and pushed him forward until Dave landed in the river.

Namito let out a hearty laugh when he saw Dave's shocked face. Hazel glanced around, stunned for a moment, before her shocked expression changed to amusement, and she burst out laughing. Dave gave Namito an understanding nod before giving Hazel a death stare.

"You are in hot water now, young lady," he growled at her, and Hazel jumped up and ran toward the house. He was faster, though, and had her in no time, turned her around and threw her over his wet shoulder.

"Dave, this isn't fair. Put me down right now. I wasn't the one who pushed you into the river."

"No, but you laughed at me when Namito pushed me in. Such sass and malicious joy is a sign that you would have done the same thing if you had been given a chance."

She squirmed around and hit his back with her fists, but he was unmoved. He carried her to the river and threw her in.

Robert Mitchell, George Buchannon, Alex, and Marshal Holden had just stepped out into the yard and watched, amused, what was happening.

Hazel climbed out of the chilly water. She watched Dave chasing after Namito to avenge the humiliation from before. Before Hazel knew what was happening, Namito hit behind her and used her as a human shield.

"Namito, stop that right now. I took my bath for the day, thanks to you. Let go of me, you two." She was caught in the middle, but ducked under their arms and stepped into safety as the two of them fell into the water. She burst into another fit of laughter when she saw their shocked faces, clearly stunned that she had gotten herself freed in time. Liz Camden came out of the house, carrying a large towel, and reached Hazel when the two young men were about to grab her again.

"You two should be ashamed of yourselves," she scolded with a twinkle in her eyes, and wrapped the towel around the young woman. "Getting this girl soaked and cold. If she gets sick now, I am holding you two responsible. Come with me, Hazel. We will get you warm and dry again." Liz had her arm around Hazel's shoulder and led her back to the house.

Hazel turned her head and stuck her tongue out at Dave and Namito, making the rest of the men laugh. When Hazel and Liz passed Reverend Mitchell, he gave Hazel a sly look.

"Didn't you say you would keep your sass in check?"

"Yes," she retorted without blinking. "I said I would keep my sass in check around you."

Robert grinned, and she gave him a wink and smile that would light up a room before following Liz Camden into the house.

Hazel fell asleep with a smile that night. Her heart was filled with gratefulness and not sad, fearful thoughts.

What are you doing here, Dwight? You are supposed to be in prison. 'I was in jail but got out.' He grabbed her and threw her on her hospital bed. Robert Mitchell stepped through the door, and Dwight lifted his gun and shot. Hazel thought her heart would break, and she jumped up and began hitting Dwight with her fists before Marshal Holden shot Dwight in his shoulder.

Hazel tossed and turned in her sleep. Tears ran down her cheeks, and she woke herself up when she let out a loud, painful sob. She sat up, covered her head with her hands, and cried. George, Helen, and Liz Camden came into her room, followed by Robert Mitchell.

"Honey, what's wrong?" her father asked, pulling her into his arms.

"I was too late. Dwight killed him. I wasn't fast enough," she said between sobs.

"Who did Dwight kill?"

"Reverend Mitchell. Dwight attacked me and pushed me onto my hospital bed, and when Reverend Mitchell came into the room, he shot him. I had no time to prevent it."

"Oh, Hazel, it was only a dream. You prevented it. You jumped in front of Robert Mitchell just in time. He is not dead. He is right here."

Hazel looked up, tears still dripping down her face. Reverend Mitchell took her hand.

"I am here. Nothing happened to me. It was a nightmare, nothing else." He caressed her face with his hand, and she calmed down. Helen and George helped her lay down, covered her with her blanket, and a moment later, she was deep asleep again.

Hazel woke up a few hours later, gasping for air. She couldn't remember her dream, but she had to get fresh air. She felt like she was suffocating. Hazel grabbed her shawl, ran down the stairs, and opened the back door toward the yard. As she stepped outside, she took deep breaths of air, but everything was spinning around her. She held on to a chair since she was close to hyperventilating and tried to calm herself.

"Hazel, are you all right?" Miles Camden stood next to her, a worried expression on his face. She tensed up.

"I am, I am..." she stammered, still trying to get her breathing under control again. "I don't know."

"Okay, I can see you are distressed. Try to breathe slowly. That's it. Slowly." He talked her through her panic attack until she felt better.

"What are you doing here? I thought you were visiting relatives."

Miles heard the concerned and hostile tone in her voice, but he understood. The last time they had seen each other, he had behaved terribly.

"I have just returned from Sacramento. Hazel, I am so sorry for everything. I am sorry I treated you so poorly and that I behaved so inappropriately. After reading the articles in the newspaper about what happened to you, I feel awful. I realized how much I was like McKellar, and I don't want to be like that."

"Thank you, Miles. I accept your apology. I am glad you can see things in the right light now," she responded weakly, and he held on to her arm.

"Do you want me to help you back to your room?"

She nodded. These nightmares and panic attacks took everything out of her. Miles walked with her up the stairs. They had almost reached her room when Namito and Dave came from the other side. They saw Hazel's pale and exhausted face, and Namito's calm expression changed.

"What did you do to her?" he snapped and was about to grab the other man by his shirt, but Hazel stepped between them.

"Calm down, Namito. I am okay."

"Good night, Hazel," Miles said now.

"Good night, Miles, and thank you."

They watched him walk back downstairs to the guest room behind the kitchen before Hazel looked at Namito again.

"Miles did nothing inappropriate. He helped me through a panic attack and apologized for his behavior on our ranch. He only brought me back to my room to make sure I was okay and he did not overstep the boundaries."

"He treated you awful last time we saw him."

"Yes, he did, and he even admitted that. I understand you are worried, but you have to trust me."

"Do you trust him?" Namito retorted, looking deep into her blue eyes.

"I don't know," she admitted, "but I will give him a chance because I feel he deserves one."

"You are a remarkable girl, Hazel Buchannon," he said with a big smile on his face.

"You think so?" she replied, amused.

"I know so. Now, let's go back to bed before the night is over. We could all use a little more sleep."

Trial proceedings continued the following day. Dave had to be in court that day, and Alex and Namito spent the day with Hazel. Liz and Helen went shopping and would meet the three young people for lunch at a French restaurant, one of the best restaurants in town.

When Alex, Hazel, and Namito stepped into the elegant building, many curious looks greeted them. Namito felt the judgmental whispering and glances they threw his way, and so he stayed behind the other two.

A young waiter approached them. "Sir, welcome to Toulouse. Do you have a reservation?"

"We have a lunch engagement with my mother. Mrs. Harry Camden."

"Oh, yes, of course. Mrs. Camden and her friend have arrived. May I take you and your beautiful wife to their table?"

Hazel just about had a heart attack, and her face was on fire at once. Alex grinned at her, trying to make her less uncomfortable, but before he could correct the misunderstanding, the waiter noticed Namito.

"Hey, you, OUT!" he snapped in mock-broken English.

Namito held his breath. Arguing with people like this waiter did nothing, and he had to stay calm because Hazel hated behavior like that. He watched her, and sure enough, her temper had reached the surface.

"How dare you treat another human being in such a rude and disrespectful way?" she raged and gave him a death stare.

"We don't serve savages here," the waiter replied with an arrogant tone in his voice.

"Savages? Did you seriously call him a savage? I demand to speak to the manager of this restaurant."

The restaurant owner stepped toward the small group. He looked uncomfortable, as he hated it when customers made such scenes.

"Is everything okay?" he asked politely and gave his waiter an understanding nod.

"No, nothing is okay," Hazel replied furiously. "Your waiter here refuses service to a paying customer, not to mention calling my friend names."

"We do not allow Indians in here," the restaurant owner responded with a nervous twinkle in his eyes.

"And why not?"

"We have our reasons."

"You do, do you? Would you care to share those reasons with us?"

"Miss, our reasons are simple. Savages like him tortured thousands of white people to death, murdered women and children, and killed soldiers. That is reason enough."

"Were you there when that happened?" she shot back, still fuming.

"No, but we heard enough of those stories and know they are true. Indians are a bunch of angry, aggressive, and violent savages, and they enjoy the shedding of blood and ravish women for entertainment only."

"It isn't necessary to become so detailed," Alex scolded now, his eyes dark and angry.

"How do you know that? How do you know that it was the Indians and not the soldiers and white people who started the murdering and acts of violence?"

"Miss, I don't think you have enough knowledge to discuss this with me."

"Oh, now you are smarter than I? This is outrageous."

Alex stepped behind her and put his hands on her shoulders to signal her, he agreed with her, but that she needed to calm down. Hazel breathed through her teeth.

The waiter stepped forward again. "The Indian can't eat in here, but you two can. May I take you and your wife to your table now?" he asked politely and stared at Alex. Hazel shook her head. Alex stepped next to her, looked into her blue eyes, and then toward the waiter.

"We will not eat here. A restaurant that treats customers so poorly is not a place where we want to be seen. Good day," he said and nuzzled Hazel toward the door before she could explode again.

"Wow, what a crazy person. This shows you what happens when you are not strict enough with your wife. He should give her a good beating, so she behaves as an obedient wife should," the restaurant owner mumbled to the waiter and shook his head. He noticed many eyes on him and was not happy. It made him angry when customers put his famous restaurant in such an unpleasant light.

"How can he treat you in such a horrible way?" Hazel snapped as soon as they were in front of the restaurant. "How can he talk to you in such a rude manner? I bet he has never even seen a real Indian before, and so, who does he think he is?"

Namito looked through the window and noticed that the door was still wide open, and the guests closest to the door listened in.

"Hazel," he began, but she interrupted right away.

"This is not okay, Namito. Nobody should be allowed to talk to you that way. You are my best friend, and none of these arrogant people know the giving and kind nature of Indians. Why doesn't anybody care about the truth? They persecuted Indians for years. The white man came here, took over the country, and began hunting Indians, chasing them away from the land they had been at first, killing thousands. The people in this restaurant don't know how vicious and brutal soldiers treated Indians. None of them were there when soldiers attacked peaceful villages and murdered women and children because they were Indian. They only see what they want to see. They judge all of you because of a few bloodthirsty tribes. Does it not matter to anyone that we took away everything from you and forced you into reservations where you are told what to learn and what to eat and are not free anymore?"

"Hazel," Namito said now and put his hands on her shoulders. Displeased mumbling came from the inside of the restaurant, but neither Alex, Namito, nor Hazel paid attention to it.

"That's precisely how it is. None of these elegant people have any experience with Indians, and they know nothing about the wars and struggles of the Wild West. They only hear of the suffering widows who lost their soldier husbands and the lies of the soldiers. You have a unique perspective because you were there when it happened. You experienced it firsthand."

Alex looked at them, surprised. He had never heard of that before.

"You were also raised differently and grew up on a ranch in the country."

"Pa, Alex, and Dave grew up in the big city and still treated you as an equal and an actual person from day one."

"Yes, they did, but they are caring, thinking men. Your father has allowed no one to tell him what he should think and believe, and Alex and Dave are the same. The rest of the family is too because that's just how you are."

"Is it that difficult to see past the differences? I mean, the same God created us. We might not look the same, might have different traditions and nationalities, but we are human. Why is it so hard for people to look for the common ground instead of looking for the differences?"

The restaurant guests, who still followed the conversation, had to admit she made critical and truthful points.

"It shouldn't be difficult to look for the common ground, but most people are not willing to change their thinking, or it scares them to be open to something new. Do you know what

I always admired about you? Your willingness to accept those around you no matter what. You might not always agree with everyone, but you will accept them as long as they accept you and your ideas and beliefs. That stood out to me the moment we met. You were like that as a child, and you are still like that. It is one of your best qualities and traits."

"I agree with Namito on that one," Alex said as he jumped into the conversation. "You are stubborn as can be and struggle to open up, but always willing to accept those around you, no matter their background or skin color." He gave her a kind smile, and she blushed.

To hide her feelings and embarrassment, she threw her arms around Namito's neck and gave him a heartfelt hug.

29

Closing That Chapter

Helen Buchannon and Liz Camden couldn't believe what they were witnessing. They had never seen such rude behavior in a restaurant before, and they were ashamed of the restaurant owner. After Alex, Hazel, and Namito had left, and they heard the owner's comment, they stood and headed for the door.

"Mrs. Camden, where are you going? Your food should be ready shortly."

"We will not eat in a restaurant that treats guests in such a disgusting way. We heard everything and saw how my son and his friends were treated, and we will not tolerate such behavior."

"Mrs. Camden, please." The waiter tried to hold her back, and the restaurant owner stepped closer again.

"Madam, you have to understand—"

"There is nothing to understand," she interrupted outraged as she directed her responses to the restaurant owner. "You, Sir, might want to think about your attitude toward women. If you believe a woman should always do as she is told and deserves a beating if she doesn't, I hope you are not married. You don't deserve a wife. Good day." Liz gave the two men an icy glare and followed Helen, who had already left the restaurant.

The owner stared at them, shocked. Could this day get any worse? It could. As soon as Liz Camden was outside, several other guests got up and left. Liz Camden was well known because of her husband's occupation and reputation, so many followed her example.

That wasn't the worst, though. A young man, seated right next to the door, had also followed the unpleasant exchange. He was one of the best journalists of the San Francisco Post. He, too, got up and followed Liz Camden out of the building.

"Hazel and Namito, I am so sorry about everything that just happened. I had no idea the owner had such a wrong, tedious attitude toward certain people. Let's go to the small café in the park. Harry and I are friends with the owner there, and he will not send you away."

The three young people went ahead, and Helen and Liz Camden followed at a slow pace.

"Hazel is a stunning and remarkable young woman. How is a girl like her not married?"

"Willamette Falls is a small town, and we live far out in the country. Hazel has always been independent, outspoken, and confident, and many young men in the country find that intimidating. Several of our cowboys have fancied her, but she has shown no interest. She doesn't care if a man is poor or simple, but it has to click. She needs someone who challenges her wit and stubbornness."

Liz smiled. "I would gladly accept her as a daughter-in-law. If it were up to me, she could marry one of my son's tomorrow. I love that girl. She has been through so much, and yet she keeps picking herself up. Not to mention how adorable she is when she is embarrassed. Did you see how she blushed when the waiter mistook her for Alex's wife?"

Helen nodded with a smile. "That caught her off guard."

"I also love her sweet temper and sass. The right man will never be bored." The two women chuckled.

"Mrs. Camden?"

"Yes?" Liz turned around and looked into the eyes of the young journalist.

"Forgive me for approaching you so unannounced, but my name is Derek Foster, and I write for the San Francisco Post."

"I am so pleased to meet you, Mr. Foster. My husband and I enjoy reading your articles. I love your honesty and directness."

"Thank you, Madam. I was sitting in the restaurant just now and witnessed the encounter between you and the restaurant owner. I want to write an article about the incident, but I heard the young woman and her Indian friend mention something from the past. Do you think your daughter would join me for an interview?"

"Oh, Hazel isn't my daughter. Not yet, anyway," Liz said and winked at Helen, who smiled.

"My apologies. I must have misunderstood the conversation. She is a determined and outspoken young lady."

“That she is. Hazel knows what she wants and will tell you if she disagrees with your stance on things.”

“Her words made me think, and I would like to hear more about her views and thoughts. I heard her talking to the young Indian afterward, and he mentioned something from the past. Something she experienced, and that’s why she understands Indians so well. Do you know what they were talking about?”

“No, I am sorry, but I have no idea. Maybe Mrs. Buchannon here can shed light on the mystery.”

“Wait, that young lady is Hazel Buchannon? The young woman who has been attacked and abused by the criminal Gabriel McKellar?”

“The very one, yes.”

“I must have an interview with her. Every journalist in the country is dying to meet her, but so far, we couldn’t track her down.”

“Well, she is living with us currently, so I am sure we can arrange something.”

“That would be wonderful. But pardon me, Mrs. Buchannon, I didn’t mean to ignore you. Do you know what Miss Buchannon was talking about?”

“I know what Namito was referring to, but neither my husband nor my step-daughter ever talked about it. I can only tell you that Hazel had nightmares for a long time after that experience, so it will not be easy for her to talk about it.”

“I will not pressure her into sharing anything she doesn’t want to share, but I would love an opportunity to meet with her.”

"I can't promise she will agree to an interview, but you are welcome to come by and meet her." Liz Camden gave him a friendly nod.

"Would tomorrow late morning be convenient for you?"

"I think so, yes. We have no fixed engagements."

"Wonderful. Please send my regard to your husband and have a good rest of your day."

"Thank you, Mr. Foster."

"Should we let everyone else know about our meeting with Mr. Foster?" Helen was a little hesitant.

"We should wait until today's article comes out tomorrow morning. It will be truthful and well written, but I want Hazel to see first-hand that he is an excellent journalist and writes the truth. I don't want her to feel obligated to talk to the young man."

Dave had shared his testimony about the incident and was released from the witness stand. Gabriel McKellar was called to the witness stand again.

Miles had joined his father and the rest of the group for that day's trial session. He watched his father fascinated and decided to study law. Miles was determined to bring his life back in order and stop the life he had been living all those years. He wanted to make a difference in people's lives, just like his father and even his brother did.

"Mr. McKellar," Judge Thomas McGregor addressed him, "we are reaching the end of this trial, and I want to allow you to defend yourself one last time before the jury goes into session. Choose your words wisely because this is your last chance."

"Why should I defend myself? I did nothing wrong, and I am not guilty. The girls tempted me, and I gave in to the temptations. They wanted what happened to them. Besides, why should I apologize for the way I treated a woman? That's what women are for, are they not? They are supposed to serve us and lie with us when we need them." He grinned at several female audience members.

Harry and George only shook their heads. Dave and Robert Mitchell looked disgusted by his comment, and Marshal Holden's expression communicated he wanted to murder the young man.

Loud mumbling filled the room now, and Judge McGregor had to use the gavel several times before it was quiet again. Miles felt as if he had just been slapped in the face. He was grateful for the wake-up call he had received because he had seen things a lot like Gabriel McKellar.

"Mr. McKellar, you do not understand life. What a pathetic and sad view you have. Women might not have many rights yet, but that doesn't make them stupid or less important. It should make us men step up and protect them in any way we can."

"Women are only on this earth for our amusement, pleasure, and to serve us. They are not worth anything, and we should be able to treat them any way we want. I bet these guys only rescued her because they wanted her for themselves. If they hadn't interrupted me, I would have had serious fun with that little tiger." He gave Dave a nasty smile.

"We heard enough. Hazel Buchannon is a fortunate young lady with men around who care about her. Men who stepped in when she needed help. Not every woman has such gentlemen in her life, and that is something we need to change. You don't even feel sorry for the things you did. The jury may now leave and start their deliberations. This trial is indefinitely adjourned."

"What a heartless, disgusting man," Dave said after they had taken Gabriel out of the courtroom.

"I am so glad you, Alex and Namito, got to Hazel on time. I don't even want to think about what would have happened if you had been a few minutes later." George still couldn't believe that men like McKellar even existed.

"There is a special place in hell saved up for that man," Marshal Holden commented as he stepped closer. "It will be my pleasure to get him there as fast as possible."

Hazel nagged everyone about the events of the day and didn't let loose until they told her everything. She was shocked.

"Why would he even say that? Who in her right mind would want to go through something so horrible? Girl or not, we want to be treated with respect and dignity, just like you men."

"The judge was aware of that and said something similar. The jury is now in session, and I am certain they will find him guilty of all charges," Harry Camden replied.

"And will he get locked up for the rest of his life?"

"That filthy swine deserves nothing but death," Marshal Holden remarked. "He will either hang or get shot and hopefully rot in the deepest depths of hell."

"Holden," Robert Mitchell rebuked him, pointing his head toward Hazel. She looked at the marshal wide-eyed, and everyone could see the disbelief spreading across her face.

"My apologies," Sterling mumbled. "I keep forgetting that we have ladies present."

"You can't possibly mean that?"

"Oh, I mean it, even though I shouldn't have said it so bluntly."

"If we kill him, we are just as bad as he is."

"He needs to be punished," her father said, jumping into the conversation. "He did many horrible crimes and deserves the consequences that will come for him now."

"I want him to be punished. I do, but what good does it do if we murder him? He gets away from misery and torment, while we have to live with these horrible memories for the rest of our life?"

"Oh, honey, he will not get away from anything. God is a just God, and he will judge the man in a way none of us ever could," Liz said now, and Helen nodded in agreement.

Harry Camden cleared his throat. "Judge McGregor is a fair and good man. He believes in second chances when he knows a person deserves another chance. McKellar is not one of those. He feels no remorse and will never change. He will continue to view women as less for the rest of his life and will use any chance he gets to torture girls. It is his joy. He is plain evil. Thomas McGregor knows that and doesn't want to put any more women at risk. This has to end now." He looked at Hazel kindly but with a firm expression. She nodded.

"Please excuse me." Hazel stood and went outside into the backyard. It looked like rain, and the wind was blowing pretty strongly. She leaned against a tree and breathed in the chilly air.

Alex stepped outside and just watched her for a while. It amazed him how adorable and gorgeous she was, and it didn't matter how sad, distressed, and sick she was. She always had that special something about her.

The newspaper arrived as the servants were getting breakfast ready. Everyone was seated in the drawing-room. Harry opened the paper and leaned back in his big armchair. His face dropped in surprise when he came across an extensive article about the restaurant's incident with Hazel, Alex, and Namito, but nobody had informed him about it. Derek Foster had repeated everything as it had happened. Even the conversation between Namito and Hazel in front of the restaurant.

Can we not use this as an example? Can we not see how arrogant and wrong our behavior is to judge another person by gender, status in life, or race? Why can't we look past our differences and see the human instead of what we don't have in common? I thought about everything she said. It was a wake-up call for me, and maybe we should do serious soul-searching and change our own opinions and views.

Harry looked over to Hazel, who was in a conversation with Dave and Namito. Everyone was talking to someone, and so he cleared his throat before he spoke.

"Hazel, I had no idea you are so famous?"

The young woman glanced at him with confusion. Her brows were furrowed.

"Why didn't anyone tell me that there was an incident at the restaurant Toulouse? Why do I have to find out through an article of the San Francisco Post?"

Hazel exchanged looks with Namito and Alex, but they shrugged.

"And you had a conversation with him afterward?" he asked as he addressed his wife. She nodded.

"Yes. Derek Foster followed us and asked a few questions. He wants to come by later and interview you, Hazel. He heard Namito mention the past, and would like to hear more about it."

"Why don't I read the article out loud, so you know what I am talking about?" Harry winked at Hazel, who still seemed confused.

As I was sitting at my usual table at the famous restaurant Toulouse, waiting for my lunch to arrive, a young man and woman entered. I noticed them right away because a young Indian followed them. Since Indians are not a sight we often see in San Francisco, I paid attention. As I found out later, the young man entering was Alex Camden, the son of Harry and Elizabeth Camden. With him was his fiancée, Hazel Buchannon, a beautiful young lady we have come to know and love due to the trial happening in our court right now.

Hazel gasped and immediately covered her face with her hands as heat crept into her face, her cheeks glowing with embarrassment. She wanted to hide in a hole. What was it with the people of San Francisco? Couldn't they ask before blurting out assumptions or, worse, printing it for everyone to see?

Alex's lips twitched as if he tried to hide a smile, but he gave her an encouraging nod and winked at her when she lifted her head again.

"Fiancé? You two are engaged?" George asked, wholly taken by surprise, and gave his daughter one of his famous dad-looks. Hazel didn't know where to look anymore, and her face felt as if she was sitting next to a fireplace. If only the ground would open up and swallow her right now.

"That is all a big misunderstanding. We are not engaged, George. I promise. The young journalist saw us show up together and must have assumed we were a couple. He should have asked first before printing it." Alex's attempt to reassure her father didn't seem very successful.

Helen and Liz exchanged a glance. "That might not be entirely correct," Liz said with a guilty expression on her face.

"Mom?"

"After we left the restaurant, Helen and I were talking, and I told her how much I would love for Hazel to be my daughter-in-law. I wasn't done with the conversation when Derek Foster approached us, and so when he asked me if you were my daughter, I responded, *not yet*. I should have pondered my words more, but thought nothing of it. Forgive me."

"We didn't expect him to misunderstand us," Helen remarked now, and they both gave her an apologetic glance.

Hazel didn't know whether she should laugh or cry, but she knew her face still hadn't returned to its natural color. She felt Alex's gaze on her, and the butterflies in her tummy were all over the place.

Miles, Dave, Namito, and Robert Mitchell had a hard time not bursting out laughing. Hazel's embarrassment was so adorable, and George's shocked expression too funny.

"You two are not engaged?" George was still not trusting this entire thing.

"Pa," Hazel tried to rebuke him, but he was too stunned to notice.

"We are not engaged, George," Alex said now. "I would ask for your daughter's hand before having it printed for all to see."

"Would an engagement between our children be such a terrible thing?" Harry asked now, amused by this conversation.

"It wouldn't be terrible at all. I would gladly accept Alex as my son-in-law. Hazel couldn't find a better husband, but I still would like to find out before everyone else. I mean, they haven't even started courting."

"Why are we still talking about this?" Hazel blurted out. Her face was a burning inferno now. "I am in the room and can hear you. I realize this might be a long shot, but believe it or not, this is embarrassing for me." She covered her face with her hands again and leaned forward, so she didn't have to look at anyone else. Everyone burst out in laughter, and Harry Camden pulled her into his arms.

"You would be my favorite daughter-in-law," he whispered into her ear and gave her a big grin. "All right, now that we have determined that Alex and Hazel are not engaged, what else did Derek Foster want?"

"He wants to come by later and ask you about something that happened in the past. Something Namito mentioned that you experienced, but nobody else has, and why you understand Indians so well."

Hazel's expression changed from embarrassment and smiling to despair and sadness. She locked eyes with her father, Robert Mitchell, and Namito.

"You don't have to tell us, but Derek Foster will ask you about it," Helen continued.

"Perhaps you should open up about the past, Hazel. It might help you move on once and for all. I know it is difficult to share those experiences and let people look behind the facade of the fakeness of some soldiers, but it might burst a bubble for many of the people reading it," her father said, his eyes resting on her daughter.

Hazel nodded, even though thinking about something that had shattered her heart into pieces was not something she wanted to do. If only she had never experienced it.

"I can't talk to you about it, but perhaps you can let everyone here know, Pa?"

"I will."

She gave him a thankful but sad smile and left the room to go to her favorite place in San Francisco, the Camden's backyard.

30

Excruciating Memories

As Hazel leaned against the tree next to the river, she closed her eyes and let memories flood into her mind, memories long forgotten but heartbreaking and unbearable. Tears ran down her face as an agonizing pain settled on her heart. Oh, how she wished she could scream it off her chest. How she wished she had never experienced such a dreadful event.

As she was getting more and more overwhelmed, Robert Mitchell stepped closer, clasped her hand, and pulled her into his arms. She began sobbing immediately, and he just held her. He knew what she was going through. It was one experience that connected them and created the warm and loving relationship they had. He held her tight, and she leaned against his chest, trying to deal with the agony of her heart.

It took Hazel a long time before she calmed down again. Reverend Mitchell did not rush her. He just showed her once again that he cared and was there for her. When she stopped crying, he lifted her chin and looked into her blue eyes.

"Do you want me to stay with you when Derek Foster interviews you?"

She nodded. Robert kissed her head, and they walked back toward the house when the door opened, and Namito and Derek Foster stepped out.

"Miss Buchannon, it is such an honor to meet you in person."

"It is a pleasure to meet you, too, Mr. Foster. May I introduce Reverend Mitchell to you?"

The two men shook each other's hands.

"Before we begin, I want to apologize to you. I should have checked the facts and not reported assumptions. I will correct that mistake in my next article."

"Thank you."

"Did Mrs. Camden tell you why I want to interview you?" he asked with a hopeful expression, and she nodded. "I intend to write something that will hopefully be a wake-up call for many. I want our readers to look into their hearts and be willing to change their views and opinions. Now, I don't want to pressure you to share something you aren't willing to share, but perhaps giving us a glimpse of your past can make a difference in someone's life."

"Is it okay if Reverend Mitchell and Namito stay? They can add anything I might miss or can't talk about since they are part of this too."

"Of course. May we sit down?"

Hazel nodded, and everyone took a seat.

"After my father moved to Oregon and bought the land for his ranch, he came in contact with the Kalapuya Indians who lived there. From the beginning, they had a great relationship. My father always believed that everyone should be treated fairly and with respect. The Indian tribe there was kind and helpful and not hostile. They helped each other. My father supported them in any way he could, and they helped him build up his ranch." A small smile appeared on her face, but was gone a moment later.

"Unfortunately, the soldiers kept changing, and pretty soon, we had soldiers there who made the lives of the Kalapuya's hell. My father and Reverend Mitchell did what they could to keep the tribe in the area, but the general and his men put more pressure on them. My father forced an agreement with a higher ranking officer in Washington and achieved the transfer from the general. The general was furious with my father, but a new company of soldiers arrived within the following days, and my father was to sign a contract with them. It would keep the soldiers away from the Indians and allow the Indians to stay in this area and take over part of my father's land. My father took me with him whenever he visited the Indian village, so I grew up with them being part of my life. My mother left us when my sister and I were only six years old, which crushed me on the inside. Namito's mother was one of the sweetest and caring women, and so she became a substitute mother for me. I loved her dearly, and Namito was like an older brother to me." Hazel smiled at her best friend, and he squeezed her hand.

"My father took me to the Indian village on the day of the contract signing. I was only eight years old. He went to the meeting place where he was supposed to meet the new military company, sign the papers, and then return to the village to pick me up again. I was playing with Namito and his sisters next to a river when we heard screaming, shooting, and fighting."

Hazel's voice trembled, and she stood and turned away from everyone. Reverend Mitchell stepped next to her and put his arm around her shoulders.

"Namito understood what was happening, grabbed my hand, and pulled me with him. His sisters followed us. He led us to a hollowed tree trunk and pushed me inside it. His sisters squeezed next to me, and there we sat for the next few hours. I was so scared, and it was difficult to hold back my tears, but I couldn't risk being found because that would have been the end for my Indian sisters for sure. I watched through a hole how the general pulled out a gun and pointed it at Namito's older brother. He killed him right then, no questions asked. Namito was also shot but survived this senseless massacre. I covered my ears and closed my eyes, but I still heard what was happening around us. My heart hurt so badly because these evil men were out there, killing my friends and Indian family. They murdered Namito's mom, and that ripped my heart to pieces."

Tears rolled down her face, and Robert Mitchell pulled her into his arms. She leaned against his chest and tried to calm herself again.

"It seemed like a long time until the soldiers were gone again. When it was finally quiet, my Indian sisters climbed out of the tree trunk and searched for their loved ones in hopes to find them alive. I couldn't make myself get out. I just sat there crying, not understanding why anyone would do something like that." Going through these memories, made her heart hurt just as much as it did during the massacre, but she forced herself to continue.

"I couldn't understand how anyone could have so much hate in his heart to murder other human beings in such horrific ways. Namito's mother was not far from the tree. They had shot her in her head."

Hazel's entire body shook, and it was hard for her to not have her sobbing turn into a crying fit. Robert held her close, and even Namito had tears in his eyes now.

He had seen none of it since he had been unconscious and didn't wake up until everything was over. He was shocked because Hazel had never talked about this to anyone after it happened, and so he didn't know she had witnessed everything so clearly.

Derek Foster was moved and horrified. He couldn't even imagine the horror this poor girl went through at such a young age.

Robert Mitchell realized she had reached the end of her experience and continued. "We met with the new sergeant, who was supposed to take over the post in Willamette Falls. Namito's father and his warriors made a pact with them, shook hands, and signed the contract. None of us knew what was happening at that moment in their beautiful village. When we returned with the new soldiers, those who had survived the vicious attack panicked and hid from us. The bloodbath and dead bodies in front of us put us in shock. We called for Hazel, but she didn't answer. Her father was petrified and searched the entire village in hopes his daughter was still alive." Reverend Mitchell's expression was fierce.

"I also began looking for her, but couldn't find her anywhere. Hazel finally came out of the tree trunk, saw the soldiers, and ran toward the sergeant. I still remember the poor man catching her trembling body, trying to comfort her while she hit him with her fists as hard as she could. 'Why did you do that? Why did you murder my friends?' She kept repeating those words between sobs until I reached her, pulled her away and into my arms. I have never seen her so upset before. She was crying so hard, I thought a few times she would pass out. The young sergeant was heartbroken and couldn't believe what the other soldiers had done, what the poor Indians had gone through, and this little girl had witnessed." He stopped for a moment and saw the disbelief on Derek Foster's face.

"As soon as her father saw her, he stopped his horse right next to us, jumped down, and pulled her into his arms. I've never seen him cry before, but at that moment, he lost it. Not only was he grateful that his daughter was still alive and unharmed, but his heart was broken from knowing what his friends had gone through." Reverend Mitchell swallowed, but continued.

"The sergeant called in his company doctor, and those injured received immediate treatment. Namito had a bullet stuck in his shoulder, and they operated on him right away. Her father instructed the young sergeant to report this massacre. Nobody wanted the general to get away with it. He promised that he would travel to Washington himself and demand from the President that this Indian tribe would have the protection from the military forever."

"That's why you want people to stop judging and looking past the outside, but focus on what's inside the heart?" Derek Foster asked as he looked at Hazel.

She nodded. "Yes. I never want to experience something like that again. I've pushed it out of my mind, so I wouldn't have to relive it again and again, but deep inside, it was still present. Thinking and talking about it brings back those horrible images from my past. I can still hear the screaming and crying from everyone there. I still hear Namito's sisters crying for their big brother and mother, and I don't think I will ever recover from this, but I want us as humans to get along." Hazel took in a deep breath.

"We need to learn from such horrible incidents. I only shared this because the truth needs to be out there. You can find evil people in every group, and so yes, there are bloodthirsty Indians out there, but we should never generalize and judge everyone by the evil-doing of a few. We are humans, created by the same God, and differences on the outside or in traditions and beliefs should not make us hate each other. We can be different and even disagree, but that shouldn't stand between us."

That night, Hazel had terrible nightmares again. She was not chased and attacked by Gabriel McKellar, but by the general and his soldiers. They had discovered her in the hollowed tree trunk. She couldn't see who it was, but someone grabbed her by her arms and tried to push her to the floor. She fought him with all the strength she had.

Miles had heard her distress when he walked past her door. He rushed into her room and tried to calm her down, but she fought him. He held her by her arms and spoke to her calmly, but she was entirely out of it. She pushed him away from her, jumped out of her bed and ran down the stairs and to the backyard. He followed her.

Alex, Dave, Robert Mitchell, Namito, and George stepped out of their rooms when they heard two people run down the stairs and followed at once.

Miles, who was worried she would run into the tree branches and hurt herself, caught up with her, but she continued to break loose. She was hysterical now, yet in a half-sleep trance, so no matter how much he tried to talk to her and calm her down, she didn't hear him as him but as someone in her nightmare. When George and the other men stepped outside, she again pushed Miles away and ran straight for the river.

Namito sprinted after her, followed by Dave and Alex. Miles reached her first, grabbed her around her waist, pulled her backward, and nuzzled her into Namito's arms.

"We have to get you out of here. The general will kill you," Hazel mumbled, holding on to him as if her life depended on it. Namito held her close, stroking her head.

"Nobody will kill me. It is a dream. Hazel, you need to wake up. It is just a dream."

Suddenly, a sharp wind blow slammed the door shut, and it startled everyone. It caused Hazel to wake up. At first, she didn't know where she was or what was happening to her, but they calmed her down and told her she had experienced another nightmare.

"I am so sorry," she stammered. "I don't mean to keep you up."

George pulled her into his arms now and held her. "It is okay, honey. This isn't your fault. You can't help those dreams, and we will always want to help you."

He led her back to her room and stayed by her side until she was asleep again. It broke his heart to see his daughter so fragile, exhausted, and pale, but he hoped that her nightmares would stop, eventually. She needed a good night's sleep.

Early the next morning, Harry Camden received a message that the jury had come to a verdict, and everyone was asked to go to court that afternoon. Hazel turned as white as a bedsheet when she heard she had to go back and see her tormentor again.

Everyone assured her they would stay by her side, but it didn't help her feel calm. After breakfast, she went back upstairs to take a nap. When Helen checked on her a few hours later to wake her up, so Hazel could join them for lunch, she found the room empty. Her bed wasn't used. Helen informed everyone, and they spread out, looking for her. Hazel was gone.

Hazel reached the public park an hour after she had snuck out of the house. She wanted to be alone, and she needed time to think things through and not have someone around her nonstop. Hazel knew she would get in trouble for sneaking out, but she had left a note on her dresser. That way, they knew she would join them later in court. As she closed her eyes and remembered everything that had happened to her over the past weeks, a kind voice brought her back to reality.

"Miss Buchannon?"

Hazel looked up and saw a girl in front of her who had been attacked by Gabriel McKellar. It was the girl who had gotten pregnant from his attack.

"Miss Walker, right?"

"Yes, Colleen Walker. But please call me Colleen."

"I am Hazel." They smiled at each other.

"May I sit down?" Colleen asked, and Hazel nodded. "I am glad I met you here and alone. I've been meaning to talk to you for so long, but never got the chance. I am so sorry about what happened to you. If only I had reported Gabriel to the sheriff when I had the chance, but wasn't brave enough."

"The sheriff wouldn't have believed you."

"Probably not."

"Besides, you were attacked worse than I was."

Colleen shook her head. "I don't think so. He was courting me for a while and was a kind and caring man. My parents liked him. I thought he was nice but didn't have actual feelings for him, and so when he asked for my hand in marriage, I declined.

My father wanted to force me into a marriage with him, but I refused. That night, Gabriel brutally attacked me. He came by the next day and asked again to marry me, pretending he was sorry for what happened the night before, making my parents believe I had wanted to lie with him. I yelled at Gabriel to get out and tried to explain to my parents he was lying and that he had forced himself on me, but they didn't believe me. My father was so angry, he belted me for an hour in hopes I would give in and marry Gabriel since I had disgraced the family. I continued to refuse him. When my father saw that no matter how hard he punished me, I still rejected him as a husband, he kicked me out of the house."

"Colleen, that is awful. How can you say I was treated worse than you?"

"Because Gabriel only attacked me once. Yes, I ended up with a child, but he didn't follow and torment me. It was my father who hurt me the most physically and mentally, and I haven't spoken to my parents since that day."

"What happened to you after they kicked you out?"

"I had a friend who let me live with her. She and her husband adopted my child after I had her. I didn't want to raise her by myself, and I knew I couldn't love her enough because of the circumstances, but they loved her from the moment they met her. She is two years old now."

"I am so sorry you had to go through that. My heart goes out to you." Hazel took Colleen's hand into hers and squeezed it.

"It is part of life. My father was a drunk, so I was used to him beating me when he got angry. It was a blessing when he threw me out because I was now free from his aggression and violence."

"Hazel, what a pleasure to see you all by yourself."

The young woman froze in terror and turned as pale as a bedsheet.

"Are you okay, Hazel?" Colleen grabbed onto her arm, but Hazel gave her a weak smile.

"Please leave now. Hurry, and don't look back," Hazel mumbled, her voice was trembling and there were held-back tears.

"But..."

"I will be fine, just leave."

Colleen heard the urgency in Hazel's voice, stood, and hurried away. She was determined to find help.

"What are you doing here, Reverend?"

"I was visiting family. As I walked through the park, I saw you sitting here. I figured I should at least stop to greet you," Jason Clark responded in a friendly voice.

"Well, you greeted me, now you can leave," she snapped and jumped to her feet.

"That isn't friendly, Miss Buchannon. Didn't your father teach you to be polite to men? Let's go for a brief walk, shall we?" He wanted to grab her arm, but she pulled herself away from him.

"Leave me alone." She turned around and hurried away, but he followed her, reached for her hand, and pulled her into his arms.

"I guess you didn't hear me, but I said you and I would go for a brief walk," he whispered into her ear. "Someone is dying to meet you."

Thinking he was talking about Gabriel McKellar, Hazel panicked. She kicked him against his leg, shoved him as hard as she could, and ran off the moment she was free.

Clark cursed under his breath. He wanted to follow her, but he knew with all those people in the park it would only draw attention to him, especially if Hazel called for help. When he saw two marshals entering the park, he slipped into the crowd and disappeared.

"Marshal Holden, quick please, Hazel Buchannon needs your help," Colleen gasped and stopped, trying to get her breathing under control again. He dismounted his horse.

"What? Why? Where is she?"

"We were in the park on that bench behind the big oak tree when a young man talked to her. She sent me away, but I could hear in her voice and see on her face how terrified she was. Please help her." Colleen was close to tears, and Marshal Holden nodded, mounted his horse, and dashed down the park path toward the direction Colleen had pointed.

Hazel ran as fast as she could. Her breathing became more and more unsteady, but she only cared about getting away from that man. She didn't stop until she saw the courthouse in the distance. She slowed down, but her unsteady breathing made her dizzy, and she gasped for air. Hazel stopped as the sudden panic attack made her hyperventilate.

Sterling Holden saw her and urged his horse to go faster. He stopped next to her a moment later, jumped off his horse and caught her the moment she collapsed. He lifted her and carried her to the courthouse and straight to the office of the judge. Thomas McGregor stood.

"What happened?"

"I am not sure yet. She collapsed as I reached her. She ran from the park to almost the courthouse."

"That is over two miles." Judge McGregor gasped as he looked at her exhausted face. His expression communicated concern and deep worry.

Hazel opened her eyes for a second and closed them again. Her head was still spinning. "What happened?" she asked, putting her hand to her head in an attempt to stop her dizziness.

"You fainted the moment I reached you," Sterling Holden responded.

"How did you know where I was?" She still had her eyes closed.

"I didn't. Miss Walker found me and sent me in the direction of the park bench you two had been sitting on. The courthouse came to my mind first, and so I went that way, and luckily, I did."

Her memory was back instantly. Jason Clark was in San Francisco. He had tried to abduct her again. Would he be able to free McKellar? Why was he here?

The two older men watched her, and they could see on her face that she panicked again.

"Miss Buchannon," Judge McGregor said, "breathe slowly. That's it. Take a breath and let it out slowly."

When she seemed to have calmed down again, Sterling Holden glanced at her with a serious expression on his face.

"What happened?"

"I... I am not sure..." she muttered, but both men knew she was lying.

"Hazel, you are not telling the truth," the marshal said sternly.

"I am sorry, but my family is worried about me. I should go." She opened her eyes and stood.

Marshal Holden grabbed her by her arms. "You are not leaving. You need to rest, and I want answers."

She avoided eye contact, but it was getting harder and harder to swallow the sobs that wanted to escape. Sterling Holden lifted her chin, so he could look into her eyes, and she burst into tears. She tried to get out of his hold, but he pulled her into his arms and gave her a fatherly hug.

"Why can't you just let me go?" she asked in between sobs, yet felt grateful for his comforting kindness at the same time.

"I know something bad happened. Miss Walker was beside herself when she reached me, and anxious about you. She said a young man spoke to you, and you sent her away. Who spoke to you, Hazel?"

"Please, Marshal Holden, let me go," she begged. "I am in enough trouble already." Her eyes pleaded with him, but he stayed firm.

"Who approached you?" he insisted and lifted her chin again, so she had to look at him.

"He is here, or he was. He... he... wanted me to go on a walk with him... he tried to force me to come with him... he said someone was dying to meet me," Hazel stammered, the sobs and fear restraining her voice.

"Who is here, Hazel?" Sterling Holden asked.

"Jason Clark."

The two men exchanged a glance. Neither of them had met him, but they had heard plenty about him.

Hazel grabbed onto Marshal Holden's jacket and looked up, despair and horror in her eyes. "Can he free McKellar? Are they both going to come after me now?"

"No. McKellar is well protected, and I trust my men with my life," Sterling responded firmly. "You have my word that McKellar will not come near you again."

"Thank you," she replied and stepped away from the marshal. A loud knock interrupted the awkward silence, and a moment later, her father, Reverend Mitchell, and Harry Camden stormed into the room.

"Hazel, thank goodness." George pulled her into his arms and held her. Hazel gave her father a weak smile. When her father let her go, Reverend Mitchell pulled her into his arms and hugged her before he lifted her chin and made her look at him.

"How could you do that, young lady? How could you leave the house without our consent and with someone for your protection? Why would you scare us like that?"

Hazel felt guilty. All three of them gave her a stern fatherly look, and she felt terrible. "I needed time to myself. I don't always want to have someone with me, and I just wanted to think."

"I understand, Hazel," her father responded, "but what you did was irresponsible. The white slavery threat might be over for now, but that doesn't mean there aren't people out there who could be dangerous to you."

She locked eyes with Marshal Holden, and he nodded.

"Hazel, would you wait outside, please? I have something to discuss with your father and the other two gentlemen."

She nodded, but her heart sank. The discussion with her father wasn't over. As soon as he would find out what happened, she would get in even more trouble. And Robert Mitchell was just as bad as her father. She was upset with herself because she knew better. Hazel had known before she left earlier that day, she should stay put. She ignored the warning feelings because she so desperately wanted her freedom and independence back.

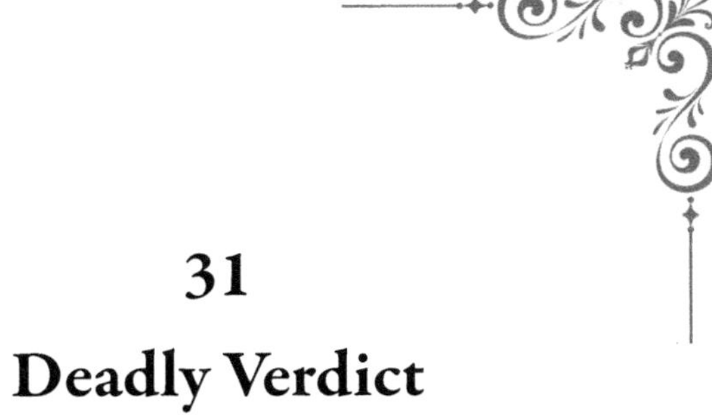

31
Deadly Verdict

"Hazel RAE Buchannon," Dave snapped as soon as he saw her sitting in front of the office of the judge. He grabbed her hard by her arms and pulled her off the bench. "Have you lost your mind? Why would you take off like that? You know you aren't supposed to do that."

"I know," she began, but Dave was so angry he interrupted her right away.

"Why are you playing with your safety? Are you trying to get yourself in more danger? Do you enjoy playing with the fire?"

Namito and Alex looked at him, shocked. "Dave," Alex began, but Hazel's pale face turned red with anger.

"Are you saying I am doing this deliberately? Do you think I want to be targeted?"

"It sure seems like it. My goodness, Hazel, I thought you were smarter than this. Haven't you suffered enough? All of us try to protect you as much as possible, but if you don't take these threats seriously, maybe we shouldn't try so hard."

Hazel couldn't believe her ears. Never in her life would she have thought to hear such hurtful words from Dave.

"I am sorry I'm making your life so hard and miserable. It wasn't my intention, I promise," she shot back, hurt and anger were coloring her voice.

"I never meant to become a burden to any of you. My apologies. How could I have been so thoughtless of becoming such a weight on your shoulders? Why didn't you let me die after Dwight attacked me? If protecting me has been such agony to you, why did you bother?" She pulled her arms out of his hold and hurried into the ladies' washroom.

"Dave, what on earth did you do? Why would you attack Hazel like that?" Namito snapped as soon as the young woman was gone.

"Do you have any idea what you did?" Alex asked, frustrated and upset.

"I am sorry. I didn't mean any of it. I was so worried about Hazel, and when I saw her, my feelings came tumbling out, and I blamed her even though I was so angry at myself that I hadn't found her earlier."

"You crushed her. Dave, you should have been the last person to attack her. She already felt bad and guilty. I know Hazel. She didn't leave to cause us grief; she left because she felt she was suffocating. Hazel loves her independence. Having to have a protector around her at all times, being trapped in a house full of people, and not being able to ride her horse was getting to her. Man, if it would change anything, I would beat sense into you. You ambushed her with that attack. Do you know how hard it was to fight for her trust? What you did wasn't just unfair, it was stupid," Namito raged, and Alex nodded in agreement.

Hazel went to the corner of the washroom, sank to her knees, and broke out in tears. The room was empty, and so she was able to let her emotions run wild.

Not long after Hazel had gone in, Shelly followed. She had been sitting in the courtroom by herself. Shelly hadn't heard every word, but she had heard that there was an argument between Hazel and Dave. She put her arm around Hazel's shoulders.

"Hazel, what's wrong?"

Hazel shook her head and continued to cry. Shelly knew those tears weren't just tears out of hurt, they were held-back-anger-tears. She stood next to Hazel for a while, but when Hazel didn't move, and her crying didn't stop, Shelly thought it was best to leave her alone.

As soon as she stepped out of the washroom, she stormed over to Alex, Dave, and Namito. "What did you guys do to Hazel?" Although she was usually shy, at that moment there was only outrage on her face.

"Why?"

"Hazel is in there, crying her eyes out. I don't know what you said to her, but I am not sure an apology can make it better." She glared angrily at Dave before stepping away.

George and the other men came out of the judge's office. George and Reverend Mitchell looked pretty shaken. Since the courthouse started filling up, it was time to go into the courtroom.

"Where is Hazel?" George asked, worry returning to his voice.

"She is in the ladies' washroom," Namito responded with another furious glance at Dave.

"Shelly, would you please go get her? The trial session will start soon."

The young woman nodded and disappeared. George and Harry went inside the courtroom and sat in their assigned seats. Everyone else sat in the row behind them, and Dave ensured an empty seat next to him.

When Shelly and Hazel walked in, Hazel ignored Dave and hurried over to the other side and sat between Robert Mitchell and Namito.

Reverend Mitchell noticed her swollen eyes and put his arm around her shoulders. "Are you okay?"

She shook her head. Before he could ask more questions, two deputy marshals brought in Gabriel McKellar. Hazel didn't look at him, but her entire body tensed up. What if Jason Clark was here too? She scanned the room until Robert Mitchell pulled her closer.

"He is not here," he whispered into her ear with his deep calming voice, and she turned her head to look into his eyes. "Marshal Holden will not let him come close to you."

Colleen Walker squeezed through the rows of benches until she sat behind Hazel. "Are you okay? Were you able to get away from that man? Did Marshal Holden get to you in time?"

Hazel nodded and was touched that the other woman was so concerned about her.

Judge Thomas McGregor entered the room, and everyone stood. He scanned the room for a second and gave Hazel a quick nod before everyone was asked to sit down.

"May I have the verdict of the jury, please?"

One of the jury members stood and handed Thomas McGregor a piece of paper. He read it before looking at Gabriel McKellar and his lawyer.

"Would the defendant please rise?" he called out and McKellar and his lawyer stood up. "Mr. Gabriel McKellar. The jury has found you guilty of all charges. I second that verdict."

"Of course you do. You have been against me from the start. What happened to the saying, I*nnocent until proven guilty?* You found me guilty before we even met," Gabriel snapped, but Judge McGregor wasn't faced.

"Your contempt and guilt-tripping will not work in this court. This room is filled with witnesses against you. Not only did you kidnap and abuse many of the women present here, but you ravished several others, killed a young cowboy trying to defend his boss's daughter, brutally attacked and injured a young woman, and harassed her. You paid someone to get you out of prison, so you can go after her again. You attempted to kill her more than once and shot her in the back."

"That was her fault. That bullet wasn't meant for her. I meant it for that clergyman over there who keeps meddling in my affairs."

"I stand corrected," Thomas McGregor replied with a raised eyebrow. "You attempted to kill her AND one of her protectors. Do you even realize what is happening here? Miss Buchannon not only survived your evil attacks and murderous actions," he said as he pointed at Hazel. "She risked her own life, so the life of another person could be spared. You should have the same integrity and heart. God created us, men, the way we are to step up and protect those who need to be protected and can't fight evil alone. He didn't create us so that we would abuse that privilege. It should be an honor for you to protect and fight for a beautiful woman. Why would you do the opposite instead?"

"Because that's what women deserve. They are weak and useless and can't do anything without us men, without running to us and crying for help."

Loud mumbling and angry gasps went through the entire courtroom. Even Gabriel's lawyer shook his head in disbelief.

"You are a fool, Mr. McKellar," Judge McGregor shot back. "Women are everything but weak. They fight for those they care about and will give their lives for them. Women shouldn't have to ask us for help; it should be a natural occurrence and reaction to step in and do our part. Helping and protecting doesn't make us less of a man. Do you even realize how much the women in our lives do for us? Standing up for them and keeping them safe is the least we can do, but we can never repay them for everything they do for us. You are alive because of a woman."

"I am *here* because of a woman. I am here because that wench over there ran to her protectors. She is just like all the other women out there, hiding behind a man for protection. She is nothing but a weak little girl."

Another gasping wave went through the audience. Hazel felt numb. Reverend Mitchell gently took her hand in his, trying to make her look at him.

Perhaps Dwight was right. Maybe I am weak? I should have fought this alone to prove that I could run a ranch as a woman.

"You are not weak, Hazel," Reverend Mitchell said now. He had watched her face and instantly knew what she was thinking. "Don't let that demon man get into your head. You are one of the strongest women I know."

She didn't even acknowledge she had heard him and continued to stare in front of her.

Thomas McGregor had watched her as well, saw the defeat and despair on her face, and could guess what went through her head.

"Hazel Buchannon is not weak. That girl is one of the strongest people I know. After you attacked her on the cattle drive, she could not run anywhere because of the severe injuries you caused. She survived because her family and friends looked out for her and took her to a hospital as fast as possible. Was her torment over? No. You went after her again and even threatened Miss Buchannon with a letter, after someone else did the dirty work for you. That girl has been through so much mentally and physically, and you wouldn't make it through half of it. You are a despicable human being, and I can't risk having you around any woman ever again. I now sentence you to execution through firing squad. The execution will take place tomorrow at noon in Alley Square, just outside of town. This trial is now closed." Thomas McGregor slammed the gavel on his desk, stood, and left the room.

Hazel jumped up and hurried out of the courtroom before Dave even realized she was gone. Robert Mitchell followed Hazel.

Judge McGregor had barely taken off his judicial robe when he heard a quiet knock. He opened the door to his office and was surprised to see Hazel standing there.

"Miss Buchannon, come in," he invited her with a kind smile on his lips, and she stepped inside the room.

"I am sorry to bother you, Sir, but if you have a moment I'd like to thank you for everything you've done for me in the past few weeks. Thank you for believing me."

He squeezed her hand. "You will never be a bother to me, Miss Buchannon. I am grateful we could give you justice, even though it doesn't make up for what you and the other women went through. The results of this trial will protect girls in the future, though. You are an outstanding young woman and never doubt the strength you have within you. Your example will hopefully lead men to do what is right and not only protect and provide for the women in their lives, but fight with them side by side so the laws will change in your favor. I believe this trial and the reports of the newspapers were an excellent start."

She nodded, and they said their farewell to each other. He watched her as she headed toward the front doors and couldn't help but smile. What a remarkable young lady she was.

Dave looked for Hazel as soon as the judge had left the room. Hazel was gone, and so was Robert Mitchell. He wanted to search for her, but everyone pushed their way out now, so it took him a while to get past the masses.

When Dave stood in front of the courthouse, he scanned the area, but couldn't see Robert Mitchell or

Hazel anywhere. He had felt awful ever since he had snapped at her. He shouldn't have said any of the things he said.

When Hazel walked out of the courthouse, she took a deep breath. It was over. The trial was behind her, and that chapter would be over for good after the following day. A burst of energy went through her. Since nobody was around, she jumped into the air, off the last step, and twirled herself around.

Robert Mitchell stood behind a tree and watched her, amused. Hopefully, this meant his energetic Hazel would come out more and more now that she had made it through this trial.

When she noticed her fatherly friend and realized he had watched her little joyful outburst, she blushed. He, however, grinned, spread out his arms, and she ran toward him. He caught her and twirled her around before putting her back on the ground and giving her a loving, fatherly hug.

"You did it. You made it through this trial and can now look forward again."

"I only made it because of you. If I had to fight this by myself, I would have given up a long time ago."

"I don't think you would have. Yes, you might have been defeated for a while, maybe it would have felt like giving up, but you are a natural fighter. None of us can make another person do something they don't want to do. Yes, we can encourage and even fight with the other person, but we have to do things ourselves. If you had wanted to give up, none of our attempts to keep you going would have worked. It came from deep inside your heart." He gave her a warm smile before he continued.

"I didn't make it up when I said you are not weak. I wasn't saying that to make you feel better. I believe it. You are a force of nature, and let me tell you something, it is normal to feel defeated. It is normal to be scared after all you have gone through, and everyone gets to the point of wanting to give up. You are not weak because you feel fear, defeat, and despair. To be honest, something would be wrong with you if you did not react to all of this. Satan doesn't go after weak people because he knows they are not a threat to him and are miserable. He goes after those who are fighters. He goes after those who get up again, no matter how hard he tries to keep them down."

"Thank you, Reverend Mitchell."

"You are welcome." He pressed a kiss to her forehead, and she gave him a beaming smile.

"Where have you been? I was looking everywhere for you," Dave blurted out as soon as she reached the house of the Camden's. Her happy and relaxed expression changed to anger and resentment.

"Oh, forgive me, I forgot to ask for permission to leave the courtroom," she replied, an icy fire replaced the usual warmth in her blue eyes. "It isn't any of your concern where I have been."

"Hazel, please let me explain."

"There is nothing to explain. You made yourself quite clear." She wanted to walk past him, but Dave clasped her arm.

"What is going on between you two?" Robert Mitchell asked, looking confused.

"It doesn't matter," Hazel replied. "Let go of my arm."

"I want you to listen to me. Please let me apologize."

"No." She pulled her arm out of his hold and rushed inside the house.

"What happened? I have never seen Hazel angry with you."

Dave explained the situation, and Robert Mitchell nodded with understanding.

"If you said that to her, no wonder she is upset with you."

"I didn't mean any of it."

"Making Hazel listen to you after her being hurt like that will not be easy. Don't worry, though, we'll figure something out."

Hazel spent the rest of the afternoon in her room. She had no interest in dealing with Dave. Around supper time, there was a knock at her door.

"Who is it?"

"Robert Mitchell. Can I talk to you for a moment?"

Hazel opened the door. "What can I do for you, Reverend?"

"Oh, Hazel," he sighed. "Don't you want to call me Robert, finally? You are not a child anymore."

"I know, but I can't make myself call you by your first name. You will always be Reverend Mitchell for me."

"Fine," he replied with another sigh. "Supper will be ready shortly, but Dave wants to talk to you before and explain why he said what he said."

As soon as he mentioned Dave, her expression changed to a pouting, stubbornness. Robert watched her, amused. He knew that expression so well. Even as a child she had pouted that way.

"I will not talk to him. He said hurtful and nasty things earlier, and I have no intention of listening to a flimsy apology."

"What if his apology isn't flimsy, but sturdy and exciting?" He looked into her eyes and saw an amused twinkle for a second.

"Reverend Mitchell, may I ask why you are getting involved in this? This has nothing to do with you. Why are you on his side, anyway? I remember you telling me as a six-year-old that you would always have my back." She raised an eyebrow, and Robert grinned.

"You would remember that in a moment like this. You think of these memories only when it is convenient for you."

"Hey, don't hate. It is not my fault that you can't remember the things you told me in the past. Should that concern me, perhaps? Maybe you didn't mean it." She gave him a provocative glance, and he coughed to hide his grin before he wagged his finger at her.

"Watch that sass, young lady," he shot back and gave her the stern fatherly glance she knew so well. She blushed but continued to look into his eyes.

"Fine, I will watch my sass, and you may inform Dave that I have no interest in listening to his pathetic excuse."

"Pathetic excuse? Those are serious judgmental words, Hazel. Perhaps I should have a word with your father. You seem to have forgotten his excellent parenting. A little more discipline might be necessary," he remarked with a straight face. Although she continued to blush, she was determined not to let him intimidate her.

"Please leave my father out of this. I am not a child anymore and will not be intimidated by your threats."

"Oh, you are too grown up now, huh? Perhaps I should teach you a lesson instead," he shot back, and his look became determined and confident. Hazel stepped backward.

"What do you mean?" she stammered as she retreated further into her room.

Robert Mitchell reached for her hand, pulled her closer, grabbed her by her legs, and threw her over his shoulder.

"No, no, Reverend Mitchell, I know what you are thinking, please put me down."

"A brief lesson in manners is what you need," he responded, unimpressed, and carried her out of her room, down the stairs, and into the backyard. Her father, Harry Camden, Alex, and Namito stood outside, talking, but big grins erupted on their faces when they saw Robert Mitchell with her over his shoulder.

"I swear, I will never talk to you again if you do this," she threatened, but he only grinned.

"At least then, I don't have to worry about your sass anymore."

She softly kicked against his chest and then started wiggling.

"Hazel Rae Buchannon," he scolded her right away. "Stop your wiggling at once. I don't want to drop you before we reach the river."

"Why do you care where you drop me? You are using your manly strengths against me, and that is unfair. This is deprivation of liberty or false imprisonment, and I demand to be released at once."

Robert Mitchell chuckled, while the men behind them burst out laughing. When Reverend Mitchell reached the river, he pulled her off his shoulder, but held her firm.

"You can't do this to me," she insisted and tried to break free, but he only lifted her off her feet.

"I can and will."

"Isn't there anything I can do to soften your demonic heart?" she asked sarcastically. Robert narrowed his eyes. "Stop looking at me like that."

"Why? Does it intimidate you?"

"Yes, it does. I hate that look. Pa looks at me that way too sometimes."

"Don't complain about our look, honey," she heard her father's voice in the background. "That's a look a father uses to teach his disobedient daughter manners."

"Reverend Mitchell isn't my father," Hazel remarked as she tried to avoid eye contact with Robert Mitchell now.

"I am as close to a father as anyone would be, and a sassy girl like you needs more than one man to teach her manners."

"Do men always have to stick together on these issues? I am outnumbered here."

"That is a good thing. Now, where were we?" Before Robert Mitchell could do anything, she threw her arms around his neck and held on to him with all the strengths she had.

"I demand at least a chance to get myself out of this unfair punishment," she said firmly and looked Reverend Mitchell into his eyes.

"Fine. I will not throw you into the river if you listen to Dave and let him explain and apologize."

Hazel stared at him. Everyone was silent now and watched her. She clearly contemplated his words before her eyes told him her decision.

"That is not going to happen," she argued, and stubbornness returned to her eyes.

"Namito," Reverend Mitchell called out, and the young Indian jogged over to them. "Lose her hands from my neck, and let's do this together."

Namito removed her hands, grabbed her under her arms while the reverend held her feet.

"This is unjust, cruel and shameful," she protested in vain before she flew through the air and landed in the outstretched arms of Dave.

Her shocked face resulted in loud laughter from the men around, and Dave gave her an apologetic glance. Torn between relief, anger, and resentment, she waited for Dave to say something.

"Are you now willing to hear me out?" he asked before he dropped her only to catch her right away again. Her heart just about stopped beating, and it took her a moment to calm her fast pulse.

"Speak." Her voice was cold and emotionless, but she noticed the mirth in his eyes when he realized that the threat of throwing her in the water had successfully made her willing to listen to him.

"I apologize for everything I said earlier. I didn't mean any of it. I only lashed out because I had been worried about you all day and was angry at myself that I hadn't found you. What I said was out of line, and it had nothing to do with you or that you left without letting us know. It was my failure to control my own emotions."

She turned her face toward Reverend Mitchell with a glance as if she were asking him what he wanted her to do now. He saw pure sass in her eyes.

"Don't make me come over there and drop you into the water myself."

"I didn't even say anything," she replied innocently.

"Your eyes spoke for you," he remarked, and turned toward the other men. "The sass is strong with this one."

Hazel bit her lip to stop herself from smiling and turned back to Dave. "I don't know what you want me to say."

This was payback. She wasn't mad at Dave anymore, but a little more guilt wasn't bad for him.

"Say that you will forgive me?"

"Do you think you deserve forgiveness?" she asked with a straight face and such seriousness that Dave was concerned he had messed it up for good. Robert Mitchell clearly saw right through her, though.

"Hazel!" he called out with a stern tone in his voice and a raised eyebrow.

She sighed dramatically. "My strict protector over there expects forgiveness. So, I guess I can forgive you."

Dave grinned and hugged her before walking back to the shore and putting her back on dry ground.

"Wise decision, young lady," Robert Mitchell said as he helped her climb the small embankment.

"What can I do? You seem to be thinking that I have to do as I am told, or I'll have to suffer severe consequences," she said calmly, her expression serious. Reverend Mitchell looked stunned.

"I guess free agency means nothing to you, and you will only grant it to those who obey you."

His shocked expression changed to playful confidence when he realized she had pulled his leg. Hazel turned around and made a run for it, but he had her in no time, grabbed her hands, and pulled her closer.

"Hazel's sass will not stop until she ends up in the river," her father remarked dryly.

"It sure looks like it." Robert stared into her eyes and was about to throw her over his shoulder again when Liz Camden called everyone inside for supper. "You got away this time," he mumbled as they walked back to the house. "Don't push your luck, though."

32
Execution of Justice

Hazel fell asleep with a smile on her face that night. She was grateful that cheerfulness was returning, and she had such remarkable people in her life. She loved that they were there for each other, but could let loose and just have fun.

Hazel did not have a nightmare that night, but a dark, gloomy feeling filled her chest when she woke up the following morning. As much as she wanted this to be over and McKellar getting punished, knowing he received the death sentence partially because of her made her sick to her stomach. Hazel realized it was because of his own doing and decisions, but she still felt terrible.

She was quiet during breakfast, and everyone watched her, concerned. When Helen noticed Hazel had hardly eaten, she felt the need to say something.

"Hazel, please eat. Your body needs nutrition so you can gain your strengths back."

"I am not hungry."

"Peanut," her father said now, "I understand you are worried about today, but Helen is right, you need to eat."

Hazel didn't even look at him but stood. "Please excuse me," she mumbled before hurrying out of the room. Robert Mitchell and George Buchannon exchanged a glance before getting up and following her.

Hazel was outside, leaning against the big oak tree next to the river. George and Robert stepped next to her.

"Are you okay, honey," her father asked, even though he knew she wasn't. Hazel shook her head.

"What is wrong?" Robert Mitchell asked now. "Are you worried about the execution?" Hazel stayed quiet. "Hazel, please tell us what you are feeling. Don't keep it inside."

"Robert is right, peanut. Let us help you."

"There is nothing you can do to help me," the young woman burst out. "You can't take away my worries and fears."

"No, but we might be able to ease those fears," Robert Mitchell responded. Hazel stared at him for a split-second before turning around to walk back to the house. Both men stepped in her way.

"We've been through this, Hazel," Robert Mitchell said firmly. "You can't run away from your problems."

"Watch me."

"Stop shutting us out. Don't you feel better when you confide in someone?" George squeezed her hand, and she nodded. "Are you scared of something?"

She nodded again. "What if the execution today doesn't happen or worse, Dwight manipulated the whole thing, and they only use fake ammunition, and he doesn't get killed? What if he escapes and comes after me again?"

The two men looked at each other, and George encouraged his friend with a nod to continue the conversation. Reverend Mitchell pulled Hazel into his arms.

"None of that will happen. Marshal Holden himself is taking part in the execution, and he will let nothing come in their way. I have known him for years. He will make sure that McKellar dies. If he has to load the guns himself, he'll do that. You have nothing to fear anymore. Gabriel McKellar's fate is set in stone."

Hazel glanced at her father, and he nodded. She lowered her eyes, but Robert Mitchell lifted her chin and made her look at him.

"That's not all you are worried about, is it?"

She shook her head. Tears entered her eyes now, and Reverend Mitchell pulled her tight into his arms.

"We will set you free once and for all. Clark will not get away with this forever. I promise you, Hazel, as soon as we are back in Salem, Marshal Holden and I, will do what we can to put a stop to that madman."

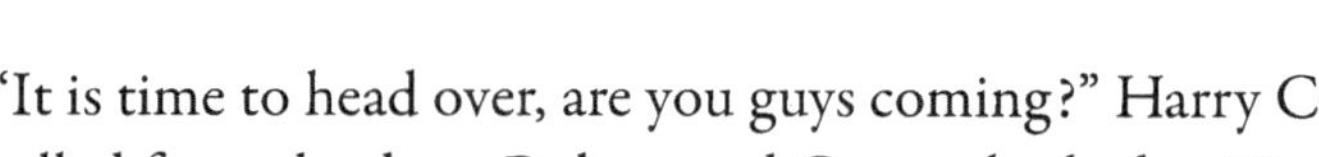

"It is time to head over, are you guys coming?" Harry Camden called from the door. Robert and George looked at Hazel, and she turned as white as a bedsheet.

"I am not going," she mumbled, and they nodded understandingly.

"I will stay with you, Hazel," Reverend Mitchell said, and they walked back to the house. Namito and Alex also stayed behind, as they had no interest in watching someone getting executed.

The Camden's, Buchannon's, and Dave reached Alley Square only minutes after leaving their house, since the Camden's home was on the town's outskirts. Many onlookers had gathered, and the area filled up momentarily. Judge Thomas McGregor joined the group a few minutes before Sheriff Baker and Marshal Holden, and their deputies, brought Gabriel McKellar. As they walked past everyone, McKellar saw the Camden's and Buchannon's, and looked around, obviously for Hazel. He grinned.

"Buchannon," he shouted across the street, "your daughter is still scared of me, huh? If she had cooperated better, we could have had so much fun with each other." He gave Helen a sleazy smile before Marshal Holden pushed him forward. Helen stepped closer to her husband, and he put his arm around her shoulders.

"What an evil man he is. Even a few minutes before his death, he still wants to torture Hazel."

Marshal Holden and one of his deputies placed McKellar against a fence. Sheriff Baker covered his head with a black bag, and everyone took a position. Dr. Sanderson and two other doctors from the hospital stepped closer, ready to confirm the prisoner's death.

Namito, Alex, and Robert Mitchell tried their best to cheer up Hazel, but she was an anxious wreck. She kept pacing the sitting room and watched as the enormous grandfather clock's pointer moved closer and closer to twelve.

Hazel knew she would be able to hear the shots. She wanted everything to be over and not have to worry about any of it anymore. Two minutes before noon, she was about to run upstairs when Robert Mitchell stepped in her way, pulled her into his arms, and gave her a fatherly hug.

"It's almost over. McKellar will not hurt you again."

She looked up and into his kind and understanding eyes when a moment later several shots were fired. Hazel tensed up, and tears entered her eyes. Reverend Mitchell held her close.

"You are free again. You can now move on and leave this terrible nightmare behind you."

"Thank you for always being there," she whispered, and he caressed her cheek with his hand. Namito pulled her into his arms next and bear-hugged her. She looked over her friend's shoulder. Alex gave her an encouraging and understanding smile.

Gabriel McKellar was dead. Dr. Sanderson and his colleagues stood and nodded to the onlookers, the judge, and Marshal Holden. A relieved sigh went through the square before people headed home again. Marshal Holden knew it was over and relaxed. His men moved the body, and he followed, deep in thought.

Colleen Walker breathed through her teeth. She watched the deputies carry away the body of the man who had caused her so much pain and grief. She was ready to move on and not look back anymore. Colleen felt grateful for the lessons she had learned, the freedom and strengths she had gained, and for the wonderful people she had met because of her trials. She thought of Hazel, and friendship and compassion filled her heart.

When the young woman looked up again, she saw a young man heading toward her. She smiled as she recognized him from the many court sessions she had attended.

"Miss Walker, right?" He looked down at her, and she blushed but nodded. "I am Miles Camden. I am so sorry for everything that man did to you and the other victims."

"Thank you, Mr. Camden."

"You seem to be content with everything, though. What's your secret?"

"It is the past, and I am ready to let go. I learned a lot in my life, and everything happens for a reason, even the bad things. We can't control what happens to us, but we can control how we react to it."

Miles looked at her, fascinated, and she felt bashful but continued to smile at him.

"Are you related to Harry Camden by chance?" she asked, and he nodded.

"Yes. I am his son."

"So, you know Hazel Buchannon?" Colleen watched him eagerly and he nodded again. "Please give her my regards and let her know that I hope we'll see each other again someday."

That same evening, Liz and Harry Camden invited Thomas McGregor and Marshal Holden over for supper. It was the last day before the Buchannon's and their friends would return to Oregon, and they wanted to get everyone together one last time. The friendships the horrible situation had created would last a lifetime, and they wanted to celebrate it.

It was a pleasant evening, and they parted ways with gratefulness and high regard for each other. Thomas McGregor promised himself and everyone that he would start fighting for better laws and more rights for women, and he was determined to see results soon.

Those who were leaving would travel together until Salem. Ted Burton had sent a telegram to George Buchannon and invited everyone for supper before they would continue their journey home the following day. Marshal Holden, his wife, and Robert Mitchell were included in the invitation. Hazel smiled when she heard that Russell Montgomery would join them as well, as he was in Salem for business.

The farewell the next day was heartfelt and warm. Hazel was beyond grateful for the kindness, love, and hospitality the Camden's had shown her and her family.

The journey was tiring, but everyone looked forward to returning home and leaving the bad things behind them.

"Hazel, it is wonderful to see you again. I am sorry you had to go through so many awful things. I wish I could have been there for you, but my business did not let me travel." Ted Burton pulled her into his arms and held her close.

"It is okay, Uncle Ted. I understand."

He caressed her cheek before letting her go, and then greeted the other guests. Hazel turned around and saw Ted's wife, Clara, standing close to her. She walked over to her and stopped in her tracks when she noticed an enormous bruise around her right eye and cheek.

"Aunt Clara, what happened to you?" she asked, not being able to take her eyes off the other woman. Clara smiled at her and hugged her, but before she could say anything, Ted stepped closer and put his arm around his wife's shoulders.

"She was cleaning the stairs, missed a step, and hit the banister hard. She was lucky it wasn't worse." He stroked her bruise and face and kissed her on the cheek.

Robert Mitchell and Marshal Holden stepped closer, and they could have sworn they saw her wince when Ted put his arm around her shoulders.

"That is an unusual wound for tripping and hitting a banister," Marshal Holden commented, and for a split-second, he saw anger flash in Ted's eyes. "Did you see a doctor, Clara?"

"Oh, it isn't that bad," she replied cheerfully. "I am clumsy sometimes, that's all." She squeezed Hazel's hand and followed one of her maids into the kitchen. Marshal Holden, Robert Mitchell, and even Hazel exchanged worried looks.

Hazel was about to follow Clara when Russell Montgomery was announced, and a moment later, he stepped into the entry hall. Hazel turned around, and he stepped closer and pulled her into his arms.

"It is so good to see you, Hazel. When Ted extended the supper invitation to me, and I found out you and your folks would be here too, I was determined not to let anything interfere with my plans. You look gorgeous."

Hazel blushed but continued to smile. "Thank you, Mr." she began before Russell lifted one of his brows and cleared his throat. "Russell," she finished with a playful sparkle in her eyes, and he grinned.

"May I introduce Mrs. Kendra Reeves to you?" he asked, and Hazel nodded before shaking the other woman's hand.

Kendra Reeves was the widow of the late Warren Reeves and a beautiful woman. She had dark brown hair, brown eyes, and a kind, engaging smile. Hazel watched Russell Montgomery and realized he adored her. Knowing that he had lost his wife several years before, Hazel's heart was happy. They were a beautiful couple and deserved each other.

The food was excellent, and the company exquisite. Hazel was seated between Reverend Mitchell and Marshal Holden, and across from her sat Clara Burton with George Buchannon and Alex Camden by her side.

"Aunt Clara," Hazel said as she looked at the woman across from her. "Where is Marianne? I was hoping I would see her tonight."

Clara glanced over to her husband, but he was engaged in a lively conversation with Katherine Holden.

"She is visiting relatives in Boston and is staying there for a while. My mother has been ill for some time, and Marianne is helping nurse her."

"I am sorry to hear about your mother," Hazel replied and smiled at her godmother.

"Does your daughter enjoy Boston?" Sterling Holden asked now, as he had followed the conversation.

"She loves it. She might never want to come home," Clara replied, and sadness colored her voice.

"Why wouldn't she want to come home?"

"It sounds like she met a wonderful young man and is falling in love with him."

"Wait, Marianne Burton, is your daughter?" Russell Montgomery looked at Clara with an astonished expression on his face.

"Yes, do you know her?"

"I do. Marianne has been courting my son Stewart for a few weeks now and is a lovely young lady."

"What is Stew doing in Boston?" Hazel asked curiously.

"He is doing an internship, but will be back for Christmas."

"Maybe Marianne won't be so far away, Aunt Clara. If she marries Stew, she will live in San Francisco."

"I hope my son proposes to her. She is a darling girl, and I am very fond of her." Russell nodded at Clara and she smiled proudly. "Ted," Russell called on the lawyer now. "This is excellent news. We might be related before we know it."

"So it seems," Ted mumbled with what seemed to be a fake smile, before he continued his conversation with Katherine Holden.

"I am so excited for Marianne. Stew is a wonderful young man, and Marianne will be in excellent hands if she marries him." Hazel's heart burst with happiness for the Montgomery's because both Stewart and Russell deserved true love and joy.

Saying goodbye to everyone that evening was hard for Hazel. She didn't know when she would see everyone again, and her heart ached when Robert Mitchell pulled her into his arms. She hated having to part from him.

Hazel tried hard to fall asleep after retiring to her hotel bed that night, but fear and worry snuck into her heart as she thought of Jason Clark, and how soon she would have to face him again.

33

Home Sweet Home

Before Hazel even had the chance to get up, the stagecoach door opened. Adam pulled her out and straight into his arms, just holding her tight. Hazel hugged him back and smiled.

"It is good to see you too, Adam," she said, and he put her on the ground.

"I am so glad you are okay. We were worried sick over here." He gave her another hug before he pushed her into Jackson's arms.

"Hazel, I am so sorry about everything. I should have never hired that evil demon."

"Jackson. This was not your fault. Nobody could have foreseen that. Please don't blame yourself for any of this."

He gratefully held her and was relieved she was back home, in his arms, and alive. Haven hugged her next and began crying. Having her sister back was a miracle, and she continued to sob for a while before she calmed down again.

Hazel breathed in the air during the drive back to the ranch. She had missed the smell, the beautiful scenery, and the people living there. It was good to be home, but as they got closer to the ranch, Hazel remembered that her beloved horse wasn't there anymore. Her heart ached. Oh, how she missed her beautiful companion and animal friend.

As soon as they reached their final destination, Hazel climbed off the horse carriage and hurried into the house. George turned to Dave, Alex, and Namito.

"Try to look after her in the next few weeks. She is not over this yet, and with her horse gone, she can't even go on a ride to escape her thoughts. Make sure you cheer her up whenever possible. She needs that more than ever now," he said, sighing, but they nodded.

"Jackson," George said as he turned to his foreman and friend. "We need to look for a new herd of wild horses. Hazel will fall into another depression if we don't get her a new companion soon."

"We took care of that," Jackson replied with a smile. "Caleb and I came across a big herd two days ago, and we caught most of them already. They are in the north enclosure next to the barn."

"You are a great man. Thank you. Now we have to give it time. Hazel will hopefully come across those horses soon, and maybe one of them is what she needs."

Hazel avoided the barn and stables. She had loved her horse Tess and missed her deeply. She wanted to ride so badly, but couldn't make herself do it.

A few days after their return home, she forced herself to go to her favorite spot again. It was the first time since Jason Clark had almost kidnapped her, but she was determined to not let those awful memories ruin this place forever.

Hazel sat on the bench below the Oak tree quietly and just listened. She heard the wind in the trees, slight waves splashing against the shores, the neighing of horses in the distance, and watched a duck and her five ducklings swimming across the lake.

Hazel was so far away in her thoughts, she didn't notice Namito, who had discovered her. He remembered George's words about cheering her up and had an idea. When Dave came around the corner, Namito walked over to him and shared with him his plan. Dave grinned.

Together, they watched Hazel. When she stood and started walking toward the house again, they hurried out of sight. Namito jumped into one of the water troughs, clothes and all, climbed out, grabbed a bucket, filled it with water, and ran after Dave.

Lost in her thoughts, Hazel walked back to the house. Suddenly, Dave sprinted around the corner. He grabbed her around her waist and hid behind her. Namito showed up only a moment later. He positioned himself close to Hazel and Dave and lifted the bucket. Hazel's eyes sparkled playfully.

"Namito, don't you dare," she scolded and watched him like a hawk.

"Dave deserves this."

"Maybe Dave does, but not me. I had nothing to do with this."

"I don't deserve it either," Dave argued and lifted Hazel in the air to cover himself even more.

"Hey, put me down right now. I am not your shield and don't want to be used as such. If you are not manly enough to take a punishment, hide behind a tree."

Namito and Dave both grinned, but the moment Namito splashed the water in their direction, Hazel freed herself, ducked, and it hit Dave full blast. Hazel burst out laughing and ran off as soon as she saw the look on Dave's face. He followed at once.

Haven and Alex stepped out of the house the moment Hazel tried to run inside. She collided with Alex.

"Careful, young lady," he said, grinning, while holding on to her, so she wouldn't fall backward. Dave came around the corner, and she hid behind her former teacher.

"Please, Alex. Keep Dave away from me."

"What did you do this time?" he asked with a raised eyebrow.

"I did nothing. He is in trouble with Namito, and they are trying to involve me in this childish nonsense."

Alex made eye contact with Dave, and the young vet nodded.

"Something tells me you are not innocent here," Alex remarked matter-of-factly. Hazel couldn't believe her ears.

"Seriously, Alex? I thought you at least would have my back, and believe me," she pouted as she looked around to find something she could use in her defense. Right behind her, next to the door, was an enormous rain barrel with an empty bucket next to it. The barrel was always in the shade, and that meant the water was nice and cold. She could barely hide her excitement.

"I'll always have your back when you're deserving of protection," he retorted and grinned at her.

"What happened to innocent until proven guilty?"

"Normally, I am all for it, but experience taught me that trouble with Namito and Dave usually means you are involved too."

"Is that so?" she asked sweetly. Alex nodded. Before Dave could come any closer, Hazel stepped backward, grabbed the bucket, immersed it into the water, and both men were soaked a moment later.

Haven, who had watched all that unfold, giggled. Hazel laughed heartily, but quickly disappeared into the house when she saw the mischievous grin on both men's faces. They followed her.

She was about to run up the stairs when Alex reached her, turned her around, grabbed her by her legs, and threw her over his shoulder. Hazel didn't even know what was happening to her. Dave stopped in his tracks when he saw that Alex had her, and turned around to look for Haven.

"Please, Alex, let me go. You can't be this heartless."

"You bet I can," he responded with a straight face, and continued his walk toward the lake. "Someone who gives me that much sass and dares to soak me with cold barrel water deserves a good consequence."

Hazel couldn't believe it. Alex had never taken part in these games, yet here she was hanging over his broad shoulder, with the prospect of being thrown into the lake. When he reached the lake, he put her back on the ground.

Hazel tried to break free, but Alex held her firmly. "Don't do this," she begged again, but he gave her a stern glance, which drove the heat into her cheeks. Before she could do anything else, he lifted her off her feet, and a moment later, Hazel found herself underwater. She pushed herself to the surface and saw the three men standing there with a big grin on their faces. Dave had Haven over his shoulder and threw her in a moment later. She screamed.

You will regret that, Hazel thought as she swam toward the shore. Alex and Dave gave her a playful smile, and both extended a hand to her to help her out. She grabbed both hands, pulled, and before they knew what was happening, the two men were also in the lake. Hazel giggled with delight and climbed out of the water. Namito burst into laughter, and even Haven grinned as she swam back to the shore.

Namito gave Haven and Dave a hand and pulled them up again. Hazel extended a hand to Alex. He grinned at her as she pulled him up and hugged her a moment later. Her heart skipped a beat.

Haven and Hazel had trouble falling asleep that night. Both were on cloud nine and hyper and giddy. Hazel still couldn't believe that Alex had joined in the teasing that day, but her heart beat faster when she thought of him and how much he meant to her.

Hazel woke up early the following morning. She decided to go on a walk before it was getting too hot to be outside. She got dressed and quietly left the house. Haven was still asleep, and she assumed everyone else was as well.

She enjoyed the fresh breeze as she walked along the lake and toward the horse enclosures. Birds were chirping, she saw a few deer running across the path and came across a skunk family, which made her hurry ahead. She felt no desire to get sprayed, no matter how cute they looked.

Suddenly, she heard the neighing of a horse, and it sounded almost like her horse, Tess. Hazel followed the sound and reached the north enclosure a moment later. A brand-new herd of wild horses was there, and the neighing came from a beautiful dark brown mare in the middle of the herd. She was gorgeous, and Hazel was drawn to the animal at once.

Alex, Namito, and Dave had seen Hazel leave the house and followed her. They watched her reach the horse enclosure and stepped closer. George Buchannon and Jackson Harrison watched the young woman from the barn and held their breath. Would Hazel pick her new horse?

"Come here, beautiful," Hazel called to the horse as she climbed on the fence and held her hand out. The mare watched her suspiciously but came closer. She sniffed Hazel's hand before making a few playful jumps. Hazel pulled an apple out of her pocket and held it out to the horse. The animal came closer again and took the apple so softly from her that Hazel smiled. What a beautiful creature. She petted the horse's head and neck and observed the mare, but the animal's ears were straight up, no hostility.

Dave grinned. "That looks like love at first sight."

Alex and Namito nodded, and they watched fascinated how this new friendship developed right in front of their eyes.

Hazel let the horse sniff her more before she went to the enclosure where they broke in the horses. She grabbed a halter and went back to the mare. She climbed on the fence and tried to put the halter on, but the horse was not ready for it and rose with her hoofs high in the air. Hazel jumped off the fence and retreated, but continued to talk to the animal to calm her down again.

As soon as the animal had calmed down, Hazel offered her fresh hay, which she found next to the enclosure. When the horse took it, she petted her head and neck. She tried to put on the halter again, and this time, the horse let it happen.

Hazel clasped the rope attached to the halter and led the animal into the empty enclosure next to it. She removed the rope and watched the wild animal run around with so much happiness and joy, it made her heart happy. Hazel wanted that horse. She wanted it to be hers and hoped that her father did not have plans for this herd yet. When the horse calmed down again, she came over to Hazel. Hazel sat on top of the fence and let the animal come to her. The mare greeted her with a gentle push, and Hazel continued to pet her.

Hazel took her time and did not rush the animal. When the horse started grazing right next to her, she decided it was time to see if the mare would let her stand next to her without a fence between them. George and Jackson held their breath. Dave, Alex, and Namito stepped closer again.

Hazel climbed off the fence, softly talking to the animal. The mare watched her come closer, but did not run away and didn't signal any aggression toward the young woman. Hazel was in heaven. She was right next to the horse now and petted her gently and lovingly. The animal sniffed her head and back and let out a relaxed blow. Hazel giggled.

The five men stepped next to the fence and watched what would happen next. They smiled.

Hazel hadn't noticed them yet, but the mare had. She became nervous and chomped with her hoofs. Hazel glanced around and saw Namito climbing on the fence, and that made the animal more uneasy. She rose. Before anyone could react, the horse was back on her feet and ran toward the three young men.

During the rising of her legs and lowering them again, one hoof hit Hazel on her shoulder and pushed her to the ground. Hazel watched as the wild animal rushed toward the young men, and they all jumped backward and away from the fence. George and Jackson were about to open the gate to get to Hazel, but the horse turned and ran toward them. They, too, stepped back.

Hazel smiled when the horse trotted back to her, but the men held their breath. Jackson drew his gun.

The young woman lifted her hand toward the animal, and the horse sniffed her head and back again. When Hazel stood, the horse didn't move an inch. Hazel leaned against the beautiful animal and nuzzled her neck.

"Wow. I have never seen a wild horse do that. The horse was protecting her from us." Jackson was stunned. None of the men dared to step closer again, and waited for Hazel to leave the enclosure.

Hazel stayed with the horse for a few more minutes until her burning shoulder was getting too painful. She returned the horse to the other enclosure, removed the halter, and stepped backward.

As soon as everyone was sure the horse couldn't see her anymore, the five men jumped into action. Hazel sat on a tree trunk and held her bleeding shoulder.

"Is it bad, Hazel? Let me see your wound," Dave said. "We need to get Dr. Harper for this, but it doesn't look too concerning."

"You were fortunate," her father said, his eyes on his daughter's face. "That could have ended badly."

"Yes, it could have," Hazel admitted, "but none of this was my fault. I did everything the way I was taught, and if you hadn't overreacted, nothing would have happened."

As soon as her shoulder had healed, she started working with her new horse. She had named her Montana. The pair were inseparable. Montana was easy to work with despite her feisty temper. Montana continued to protect her. No matter who came near her, if that person felt like a threat, he better knew how to run.

34
An Unforgettable Dance

Willamette Falls organized a dance every year to celebrate the end of the summer. It was a big event and exciting for young people, since it allowed young men to invite the lady of their hearts to be their date for the evening.

Two weeks before the big dance, Hazel heard a knock at the door. She ran down the stairs and opened.

"Adam, what are you doing here?" Hazel smiled and hugged him.

"This young lady here was on her way to your ranch, and so I told her I could drop her off."

"Welcome, come on in, you two," Hazel responded and smiled at the girl. She was pretty, with dark brown curly hair and brown eyes. She seemed shy but stepped inside despite her nervousness.

"Is Shelly around, Hazel?" Adam asked now, but Hazel shook her head.

"No, sorry. She is in Portland with Helen and Haven to sell her finished dresses. Is it important?"

"No. I just wanted to see her."

"Aww, young love," Hazel teased, and he gave her a nudge.

"Is my brother here, at least?"

"Yes, he is. You will find him in my father's office."

"Great." Adam walked through the living room and toward the office door and disappeared.

"Now, what can I do for you, Miss...?"

"Claire, please just call me Claire."

"Claire it is," Hazel said, still smiling. "Please have a seat. So, what brings you here?"

"You," Claire replied shyly, and Hazel looked confused.

"Do we know each other?"

"Not in person, no. But I heard so much about you and your sister Haven. I am supposed to give you this." The girl handed her an envelope.

To Hazel Buchannon

"Why are you handing me a letter?"

"Because... I...," Claire stammered. "This is so difficult to explain."

"Is the letter from you?"

"No. The letter is from my mom... and your mom... Abigail."

Hazel gasped for air. Everything around her spun, and she hyperventilated. Dave, who was walking down the stairs, was by Hazel's side at once. He put his arm around her and steadied her.

"Breathe slowly, Hazel. That's it. Slowly."

"I can see this is a tremendous shock for you. I am so sorry," Claire muttered.

Jackson, Adam, Brenna, and George entered the room now and greeted the guest. Hazel was still in shock, and so Dave stayed by her side.

"Welcome to our ranch. May I ask who you are?" George asked and gave her a welcoming smile.

"I am Claire Stannings, Abigail's daughter."

Everyone stared at her, stunned. Nobody had expected that.

"How is your mom?" George asked, and tears entered Claire's eyes.

"She died last week. Mom handed me a ticket for the stagecoach before she died and told me to come here and hopefully stay with my sisters, well, half-sisters. I am sorry, I should have never come here. I thought mom had contacted you."

Hazel finally found her voice again. "Please excuse me for a moment," she mumbled, removed Dave's arm from around her, and rushed out of the house. Dave and Adam followed her.

Claire sank back in her seat, covered her face, and sobbed. Not knowing how to handle the situation, George did what he thought his girls would need in a moment like this. He took Claire's hand, pulled her up and into his muscular arms. She didn't resist him and cried against his chest.

Hazel had reached the bench next to the lake and broke out in tears. Adam stepped next to her and pulled her into his arms. It took the young woman a long time before she calmed down again. Her emotions were all over the place as she had not expected such news.

When her sobbing stopped, Adam sat on the bench, pulled the girl next to him, and put his arm around her shoulders. Dave sat down as well.

"Do you want me to read the letter to you?"

Hazel nodded. Dave took the envelope, opened it, and read.

My beloved Child,

So many times have I started this letter, and yet I never could make myself finish it. My heart is breaking for you because I caused you unbelievable pain over the years. I only have a short time left on this earth, and I want to tell you what I should have told you a long time ago.

I am truly sorry I left you and your sister and that I wasn't a good mom to you both. I didn't love your father, and I missed my late fiancé. You two looked so much like George. It was the feeling of being trapped that made me run away from my family and problems. I know I hurt you, but I want you to know that it had nothing to do with you. I loved you, but I hated my life and felt like I would never be happy there. When I ran off, I considered taking you two with me, but George loved you girls so much, I couldn't do that to him.

After I divorced your father, I married a wonderful man, and a few years later, Claire was born. She is a sweetheart, and I love her dearly. I tried to be the mother to her, I should have been for you and Haven. I failed you, and I won't be around to make it up to you, but hopefully, Claire will bring us closer again.

I often wanted to come back and talk to you, but I couldn't make myself do it. I was scared, ashamed, and worried. George wrote to me how much you were missing me and how much you were suffering, but I couldn't face you, not after what I had done. I don't expect your forgiveness, but I hope one day you will understand me at least a little. I am not saying it was right what I did, it wasn't.

Please look after Claire. She has nobody now, and I worry about her. You were always so strong, determined, and stubborn. I am sure you turned out to be a fighter and a beautiful young woman.

Love,

Mom

Hazel's eyes welled with tears, and Adam pulled her tight into his arms. Both men felt for her. They hoped this would be the closure she needed to move on and leave the past behind her.

When Hazel calmed down, Dave squeezed her hand. "Will you be okay?"

Hazel nodded. "Yes, but that's a shock I have to digest for a while. I didn't hear from my mother for over fifteen years, knew nothing about Claire, and suddenly, I have a half-sister and this letter."

"I understand this might feel like a slap to the face, but perhaps it will help you move on and let go of the pain and hurt."

"Maybe. I just wish my mother would have told me in person."

"Perhaps it was better this way," Adam remarked. Hazel looked at him.

"What do you mean?"

"Your mother loved Claire, and it sounds like she was a wonderful mother to her. If your mom had come back, you might have met her with resentment and hostility. This way, Claire can help you get to know the real Abigail."

"That's true."

They sat there quietly for a few minutes before Dave broke the silence. "So, you were stubborn as a child, huh? That explains a lot." He grinned at her.

"Oh, you have no idea how hard-headed she was," Adam replied before Hazel could even say anything. "This girl is the queen of stubbornness."

"Hey!" She gave both of them a sly look, which made the two men laugh.

Claire stayed with the Buchannon family. Everyone loved her right away. She had a sweet and kind personality. Haven was shocked when she returned home, but Claire was part of the family right away. Since the girl had just turned thirteen,

George asked Alex to stay on and not leave at the end of the year as planned. That made Hazel happy. Her feelings for the young man had not subsided, but had grown stronger, and Hazel didn't want to see him go.

A week before the dance, Todd Holden showed up at the Buchannon ranch and asked George if he could speak with the adults of the ranch. George called everyone into his office.

"The dance is just around the corner, and with Clark still being around, I talked to my father, so we can keep Hazel as safe as possible."

"I am not going to the dance," she replied, fear and panic in her voice. "I don't want to see that man ever again."

"It is important that you go."

"What? No. I will stay here with Claire."

"Hazel," Todd said. "If you stay here, you might be at an even higher risk of getting into the hands of Jason Clark."

"Don't you understand? He scares me. I don't want to see him. I am not going, and you can't make me," she snapped, jumped off her chair, and was about to rush out of the room when Dave and Alex stepped in her way.

Todd clasped her arm. "Listen, Hazel. I understand how hard this is for you, but we need to get to him finally. We want to get him away from you once and for all. My father thinks this would be an excellent way to take some of Clark's power away from him."

"How are you going to do that?" George asked curiously.

"At first, my father thought I could start courting Hazel and take her to the dance, perhaps even announce our engagement. When we thought about it more, we realized I wouldn't work for that. Clark would most likely not believe it if she was suddenly in a relationship with me, especially since we haven't even courted yet."

"The idea overall is not bad, though," George commented, and Jackson nodded. Hazel's expression had changed to shock.

"No, it isn't," Todd agreed. "Dad and I think it will work, but we need the right person at Hazel's side. Someone who would not seem suspicious and could play her fake beau well."

"Excuse me," Hazel interrupted with a raspy voice. She was bright red and clearly uncomfortable. "I don't want anyone to play my boyfriend or, worse, fiancé. That is dangerous. What if something happens to him?"

"Hazel, this is an excellent way to get Clark out of the way. If you have a man in your life, the demon reverend will have to act. This will put him under a lot of pressure because he has to act before you are married," Jackson commented, and everyone else agreed.

"I was thinking, instead of me asking Hazel to be my date and play her fiancé, I will ask Haven. That way, I am still associated somewhat with the family, but not with Hazel. Now, who would be a suitable match for Hazel?" Todd looked at the other men while trying to hide a grin and winked at George.

"Namito and Dave are like brothers to her, so they are out of the question," Jackson thought loudly.

"Yep, that wouldn't work. It has to be believable."

"Alex." Todd and George said at the same time, and Hazel thought her heart would stop.

"Sure, I do it. We will pull off a believable couple, right, Hazel?" he said with a confident grin and winked at her. "We already did that in San Francisco without even trying."

Hazel couldn't believe what was happening here. She felt her cheeks burst into flames, her heart beat like a drum, and she just wanted to hide in a hole.

"That's right, you two pulled that off," her father remarked now. "Say, does the San Francisco Post ever make it to Willamette Falls?"

Todd shook his head.

"Does anyone have a copy of the said newspaper?"

"I have one," Dave replied. "After that wonderful unexpected announcement, I bought a copy."

Hazel rolled her eyes.

"We can make that work to our advantage," Todd said now.

"But how?" Jackson asked. "Nobody reads the San Francisco Post here, and if anyone does, they will have the next article too. Derek Foster wrote a retraction the following day, didn't he?"

"Yes, he did," George interjected, "but we can still make that work."

"The article was written weeks ago. How could we turn that to our favor?" Jackson looked confused.

"Easy," Todd replied. "This happening weeks ago works out great. We could cut out that part of the article and have Helen carry it in her purse. She could share with other town folks how exciting this event was and how it surprised them."

"You want me to lie to people in town?" Helen asked with a raised eyebrow after following the entire conversation, half amused, half concerned.

"We will explain it to everyone once Clark is arrested. What do you think, Hazel?" Todd turned to her, catching her off guard, but she recovered quickly.

"Oh, you actually want my input?" she replied dryly and raised an eyebrow. Her face was still glowing with heat.

"Sure, we want your input. You have to play your part believable and convincing. You need to make sure you look in love with him," Todd shot back with a straight face. Hazel's face was on fire.

"We can make it work," Alex said now, trying to take the attention away from Hazel, so she could relax again and not be so embarrassed anymore. "What will we tell our closest friends and relatives? Will we tell them this is fake?"

"No. Only the people in this room can know this isn't real. Everyone else must think it to be true. We don't want Clark to find out, or things can get dangerous and serious fast. After it is official, you two have to act like a couple, even here at home. I don't want Brenna, Haven, or Claire to become suspicious, and your cowboys have to think of it as real as well."

Hazel shook her head. Her heart was about to jump out of her chest, not to mention the many butterflies in her stomach. Here she was, having to pretend she was in love with someone she was truly in love with, and had to make it believable enough that even her twin sister would believe it. She had only one thought in her head: Bring it on.

George and Helen asked Todd to stay for supper, and he did. Since it was such a beautiful evening, they ate outside on the front porch. Before Todd left that evening, he asked Haven if she would be his date for the dance, and she accepted.

A few cowboys walked past the house at that moment, and Hazel noticed how Caleb winced, and his expression changed from smiling to despair. She couldn't believe it. He was in love with her sister.

Alex followed Todd's example and formally invited Hazel to the dance. She blushed again but accepted it with a smile. Brenna, Haven, and Claire looked surprised, but they were excited for Hazel to have such a kind and handsome date. Hazel was terrified to see Jason Clark again, but she wanted that part of her life to be over.

On the day of the dance, Hazel, Haven, and Brenna made themselves as pretty as possible. Helen's stepmom arrived early to look after Claire while everyone else was gone, and Helen helped the older girls get ready.

Alex watched Hazel with a fascinated look when she came down the stairs. She looked gorgeous in her light blue dress. Her hair was up, and her blue eyes sparkled. She blushed when she saw him in his evening attire but tucked her arm under his before they left the house together. Haven already sat next to Todd, who had come to pick her up.

Since Todd wanted Alex and Hazel to stand out, George insisted on them using the one-horse carriage instead of riding with the family. Hazel had reached a point of just playing along, since none of her objections had changed anything. Alex helped her into the carriage, sat next to her, and off they went. After driving quietly for a while, Alex looked at Hazel.

"How do you feel about all this?"

"Honestly? I am relieved I have you by my side, but I am scared to see Clark again. What if he does something to you or anyone else in the family? I don't want to be the cause for more heartbreak."

"Hazel," Alex said and gave her an encouraging smile. "Don't worry about anyone else. We will be fine. We must get you away from that man for good. You deserve to be free and happy, and I will gladly do my part." He winked at her and smiled. Hazel lowered her eyes and breathed in the warm evening air.

"We have almost reached Willamette Falls. Should I put my arms around your shoulders now?" He grinned when he saw how embarrassed she was, but waited until she nodded in agreement before he put his arm around her shoulders and pulled her closer. She leaned against his chest, making the farce of a couple in love complete.

Curious and surprised eyes followed them as Alex drove the carriage into town. Mrs. Brenton and the other ladies stared.

After Alex stopped the carriage in front of the hotel, he got out and offered Hazel his hand. She stood. Before she could climb down, however, he lifted her in the air, held her there for a moment, lowered her into his arms, kissed her cheek, and put her on the ground. Hazel looked up at him, cheeks bright red, but a beaming smile on her lips.

Dave and Namito had just arrived. They dismounted and looked over to Alex and Hazel.

"Are you sure those two are not an actual couple?" Namito whispered to his friend, and Dave grinned.

"They sure are outstanding actors."

As Alex offered Hazel his arm, two eyes watched them with fury and hate. Jason Clark stood on the opposite side of the road and couldn't believe his eyes. That was not part of the plan, and something had to be done about it, and fast.

Adam stood next to Hank Thompson and his wife Caroline when Alex and Hazel entered the hotel.

"Alex, Hazel. I just heard. Congratulations. You two make a beautiful couple," Caroline exclaimed enthusiastically and pulled Hazel into her arms.

"I didn't even know you two were courting," Adam remarked and raised an eyebrow.

"We wanted to keep it quiet for our family's sake. Plus, Hazel has gone through so much this past year, we felt it was best not to make it official yet."

"Your parents know, then?" Adam asked in a suspicious voice, which made Hazel uneasy and nervous. Alex pulled her closer.

"Yes, they do. We made it official for our families while in San Francisco."

"So when are you two getting married?" Adam continued his interrogation, and Hazel started to get angry. Why was he making this so difficult? Why was he the one causing such a scene?

"We haven't decided on a final date yet, but sometime before Christmas."

"That is only a few months away."

"It is, but I always wanted to be a December bride, and Alex is willing to go with it," Hazel remarked, successfully keeping the irritation out of her voice. "Will you excuse me for a moment? There is someone I need to greet." She squeezed Alex's hand and ran toward the door as Robert Mitchell, Sterling, and Katherine Holden entered.

Robert caught her with his arms and twirled around with her before putting her back on the floor. He then pulled her into his arms for the traditional fatherly hug.

"Reverend Mitchell, Marshal, and Mrs. Holden, what are you doing here?" she asked with giddy excitement, and they smiled at her.

"We thought we would surprise you. Congratulations on your engagement to Alex Camden. I hope he knows what of a treasure he is getting by marrying you," Marshal Holden remarked sheepishly and winked at the young woman.

"I sure do," Alex responded as he stepped behind Hazel and wrapped his arms around her.

"Who is officiating the wedding?" Robert Mitchell asked, also winking at Hazel. So Reverend Mitchell knew too.

"Would you do us the honor, Robert?" Alex responded right away. "Hazel wouldn't want anyone else marrying us, and Salem isn't that far away."

"It would be my pleasure. I'll talk to Bishop McDonald as soon as I get back, but I am sure he will have no issue with such a joyous occasion."

Hazel tensed up as soon as she saw Jason Clark enter. Her entire body froze on the spot, and her breathing became unsteady. Alex turned her around, away from the young reverend and pulled her tight into his arms before leading her to their table, where the rest of the family was seated.

Robert Mitchell and the Holden's joined them a moment later, and Hazel relaxed again. Strong and protective men surrounded her, so hopefully, that would keep her safe.

It was a wonderful evening. When the band was playing, Hazel and Haven were on the dance floor. Todd was a true gentleman and made Haven feel like a princess. The rest of the men were attentive to Hazel. Every time Jason Clark seemed to walk in her direction, someone asked Hazel to dance. She was grateful.

When she was dancing with Reverend Mitchell, she noticed Dave standing in a corner, not being his usual self. He had kept away from the dance floor most of the night.

Robert Mitchell watched Hazel and realized she was not paying attention to him or the dance. "Miss Buchannon," he called her out a moment later, and his deep voice communicated that she was in trouble. She looked up, and he gave her a stern glance.

"Yes, Reverend Mitchell?"

"Has your father not taught you how rude it is to dance with someone and not pay attention to them but watch other people instead? Have you heard anything I just said to you?"

Hazel lowered her eyes with a guilty expression on her face. Robert grinned, amused, but turned serious as soon as she looked up again.

"I did not, sorry."

"Do you know what the punishment is for not paying attention to a dance partner?" She shook her head. "The punishment is a waltz, just you and your dance partner while everyone else is watching."

Hazel gasped. She hated it when she had to be the center of attention. When Reverend Mitchell stopped, clasped her hand, and started walking toward the musicians, she held on to his arm.

"Reverend Mitchell, please don't do that. I promise I will not be rude again."

He eyed her like a hawk, contemplating how he should continue, but decided she was punished enough.

"Fine, but you better keep your promise."

When the musicians took a break, Hazel walked over to Dave. He was standing still by himself next to a window.

"Hey Hazel," he said, lost in thought.

"What's going on, Dave?"

"What do you mean?"

"Oh, come on. You are not yourself tonight, hardly danced, and seem to be upset. Anything you want to talk about?"

He shook his head. Hazel looked up at him and saw him glancing over to Haven and Todd. It clicked at once.

"You know what? You should march over to my sister, ask her to dance, and propose," Hazel burst out with a big sassy smirk on her face, taking her directness to a whole new level. Dave's mouth dropped,

"Excuse me?" he finally gasped when he found his voice again.

"You heard me. I have been watching you all night. You stare at Haven with the look of a man in love."

"Hazel," he began uncomfortably, but she interrupted him.

"Are you jealous of Todd?"

"Young lady," he scolded her now and gave her an intimidating glance. "You better watch that sass."

That was her friend Dave. He was back to his humorous self, and now she only had to push him a little further.

"What sass? I am trying to boost your courage, so you become my brother-in-law. Now, if you are still too scared to approach her, I'll have your back."

"What do you mean?" he growled at her.

"Nothing much. Just assisting you in something that needs to be done. I'll get Haven and distract Todd. Be right back," she declared giddily and was about to turn around when Dave grabbed her and threw her over his shoulder. "Put me down, Dave. You should save your energy for the proposal to my sister," she teased.

"That's it." He walked out of the ballroom, out of the hotel, and went straight for a watering trough.

"No, no, Dave, stop, please. I am wearing a new dress."

"You should have thought about that before giving me so much sass."

"I was only trying to help to lighten things up again. You seemed so down, and I want you to be happy."

"Ha, ha," he said, grinning, but took her off his shoulder.

"You love her, don't you?"

He nodded. "It is so strange. I only saw Haven as a friend until Todd picked her up today, and I saw her dancing with him all night. I am not a jealous type, but I couldn't stand watching them together."

"Well, what are you waiting for, then? Claim your bride," Hazel responded with a smile and watched him run back to the hotel. Her heart made a happy jump.

“Finally, I was hoping to catch you alone.”

Hazel felt the blood drain out of her face. “Get out of my way.”

“No, you’ll come with me right now and finish this once and for all. We have no time to waste.” He grabbed her wrist and pulled her closer. Hazel flew into a panic at once.

“Leave me alone. I will not go with you, not now, not ever.” She tried to pull her arms back, but he only held her tighter and covered her mouth with one of his hands.

“Your time has come to become mine,” he whispered into her ear as he pulled her away from the people, the buildings, and into the darkness.

35
Fatal Jealousy

"Hazel, wake up."

"Honey, please wake up."

Hazel didn't want to open her eyes. She heard what the voices said to her, but it seemed so far away. She felt numb, exhausted, and dizzy. What had happened? She couldn't remember anything.

"Peanut, please wake up. Can you hear us?"

I don't want to wake up. Let me rest longer. I am trying to remember what happened to me.

"Do you think she can hear us?" Dave glanced around, worried. Gordon Harper rushed into the room and asked everyone to leave. He examined Hazel, checked her heartbeat, lungs, looked into her eyes, and felt her pulse. After what seemed an eternity, Dr. Harper allowed everyone back in.

"What happened to Hazel?"

"We don't know yet. Shelly and Haven found her next to the woman's washroom, and she was unconscious."

"I was outside with her before. We spoke, and she encouraged me to do something I should have done a long time ago," Dave remarked and gave Haven a beaming smile. "I ran inside to look for Haven. Suddenly, Hazel was gone, and then the girls found her next to the washroom."

"Is she okay?"

"She seems to be. Her vitals are normal. She is waking up. Someone must have sedated her."

"Sedated her with what?" Helen looked scared.

"I smell chloroform on her. The person behind this must have spilled a little."

Hazel gasped. The last thing she remembered was Dave leaving and Jason Clark threatening her. Where was he? He had told her, the time had come to become his. What happened between that moment and now? How did she get to the woman's washroom?

Hazel's breathing steadied itself, and she opened her eyes. Dr. Harper was by her side at once.

"How are you feeling, Hazel?"

"Not sure," she mumbled. "Tired, confused. Where am I, and how did I get here?"

"That is a big mystery right now. Do you remember anything?"

She nodded and shared with them what happened to her after Dave had left.

"Where is Clark now?" Reverend Mitchell asked and looked around. Hazel tensed up.

"I found him at the church. He, too, had been sedated and woke up when I entered. He couldn't remember anything either." Todd Holden gave his father a meaningful glance, and Sterling nodded.

"Okay, that's creepy," Adam said now and looked beyond worried. "Someone must have seen Clark trying to abduct Hazel, had chloroform with him, sedated both, and dropped them off at different spots?"

Marshal Holden nodded. "So it seems. I mean, it is a good thing someone intervened, but unsettling that said person had something only doctors can get their hands on."

"I checked my chloroform supply after returning from the church, and nothing was missing. Whoever did this, must have gotten it from somewhere else."

"What are we going to do now?" Alex asked, his expression somber.

"I suggest you take your *wife-to-be* home and let her rest," Dr. Harper responded. Alex nodded.

Wife-to-be? I am engaged to Alex? When did that happen? Hazel thought, confused, but then she remembered it was just fake.

"I believe this evening is over for us," George said now, and everyone nodded. "Thank you for everything, Todd. I excuse you from taking my daughter home. Recent events have changed things."

Todd grinned, and so did everyone else in the room.

"Did I miss something?" Hazel asked innocently, even though she had a good idea of what they were talking about. Haven rushed to her side and hugged her sister.

"Dave and I are engaged, Hazel. He loves me." Haven's eyes were beaming with happiness and love. Her giddy excitement made Hazel smile.

"I told you it would happen. I knew he would come around, look past your shyness, and see the beautiful girl who was there the entire time."

"Wait, you knew this would happen?" George asked, stunned.

"I assumed it, Pa. I recognized Haven's feelings for Dave right after he first arrived, and my gut told me they belong together. Today, when I noticed Dave's feelings had changed, I just gave him a little push."

"A little push? Ha. I don't think anyone could have been more blunt and direct."

"You are welcome," she responded with an enormous smile on her face and winked at her sister.

"All right, folks," Dr. Harper said now, "let's get this girl home."

When Hazel attempted to get up, everyone stared at her as if she had lost her mind.

"What do you think you are doing?" Reverend Mitchell asked with a raised eyebrow. Hazel blushed, but she wasn't speechless.

"I am trying to get up, so I can walk out of this room and get on a horse or carriage, so I can return home," she replied dryly, and looked straight into his eyes. Reverend Mitchell stepped closer.

"You better watch that sass, Miss Buchannon, or I'll encourage your fiancé to give you much-needed discipline."

Hazel turned bright red but was clearly determined to withstand his threats. "My *fiancé*," she said, emphasizing that word, "would never discipline me. He loves me too much, right, honey?"

Alex coughed to hide his grin. The way she challenged Reverend Mitchell was priceless, and everyone in the room burst out laughing. Robert Mitchell pulled her up and into his arms.

"I am so glad you have your humor back. I missed that ...yes, even your sass."

Hazel smiled.

"Now, you are not walking out of here, Hazel. Alex can carry you," Dr. Harper commented, and her father, Robert Mitchell, and Helen nodded.

"I am not injured, though," she argued, but Alex had already lifted her off her feet.

"And we want to keep it that way, my dear," he said and placed another kiss on her cheek before he carried her outside.

Caleb approached Haven as soon as he saw her the following morning. Haven and Hazel were sitting on the porch talking.

"Haven," he snapped. "Are you courting, Sheriff Holden?"

Haven looked at him, stunned and surprised. "No, of course not. Todd only invited me to the dance."

"Good. I don't want you to court anyone else. We've known each other long enough now, and it is time that we start courting."

"Caleb," Haven began, but he didn't let her finish.

"Tonight, I am taking you out to dinner," he decided, and Haven made eye contact with her sister, completely overwhelmed. She had never seen the quiet young man so aggressive and unpleasant.

"Wait a minute, Caleb," Hazel interjected, irritated. "You will not tell my sister what she can or cannot do. You have no right to boss her around."

"Haven does not know what is best for her. Women can't decide on their own."

"Oh yeah?" Hazel snapped and jumped off her chair. "We made decisions just fine until now. Who do you think you are to tell us otherwise?"

"I want to marry Haven and will ask for her hand later."

"Caleb, please," Haven began again, but he brushed her off.

"You stay out of it."

"Okay, that's it. Caleb Norton, you are way out of line. I will not let you mistreat my sister, and you have no right to talk to us in such a degrading and disrespectful manner. How dare you snap at her and tell her to be quiet? This is her life, and she gets to decide what she wants to do with it. For your information, she is engaged. She accepted a proposal last night."

"Haven, is that true?" he barked, anger and irritation coloring his voice. Haven only nodded. She did not like that side of him and felt intimidated and scared. "Who is it? Did you get engaged to the sheriff?"

"It is none of your business. Haven got engaged to someone she loves and who loves her and treats her with the respect she deserves. You better watch your tone now, or I'll have you fired."

"You are no threat to me, Hazel Buchannon. Worry about your own unsafe life. You never know when Reverend Clark might show up again."

Haven broke out in tears. "Oh, Caleb, what is happening to you?"

"Shut up, Haven. Your tears do not affect me," he shot back, coldly, before turning to Hazel again. "I'd be careful if I were you. Clark can be anywhere."

Hazel swallowed hard. Was Caleb the reason Jason always seemed to know where she was? Her heart beat faster, and she turned as white as a bedsheet.

"That is enough, Norton," Alex remarked angrily after stepping out of the house. He had been in the middle of teaching his students but had heard the argument through an open window.

"What is it to you? You have no say here."

"I am Hazel's fiancé."

"Oh, really? Since when? Are you marrying her to take over the ranch when her father is dead? Are you one of those men who marry a rich girl out of convenience?"

"Shut your mouth, Norton. If you don't leave this minute, I'll remove you personally, and I can guarantee you, your employment here is over."

Caleb scoffed, but turned around, and left.

Before Alex could say or do anything, Hazel hurried away. Alex was torn between wanting to comfort Haven, who was still crying, and following Hazel. When a moment later, Dave and Namito came around the corner, he went to find Hazel.

Hazel sat on her bench and burst into tears. Was Caleb Norton a traitor? Her heart was hurting, and yet she was still so angry at how he had spoken to her sister. Would her sister be safe after this argument? Who could she trust still?

Her thoughts went to Jason Clark, and her breathing became unstable. She had to get away from here. It was too much. Every time she had collected herself and things looked better, something happened again. Maybe if she left for good, her family would be safe? Perhaps she could stay with her uncle in Sacramento for a while. She would send him a telegram from Salem, but she had to leave at once before anyone could stop her. She wiped away her tears, straightened her back, stood and turned around only to run into Alex.

Hazel looked up, startled, but lowered her eyes at once. Alex had seen the distress in her eyes, though.

"Where are you going?" he questioned her right away and tried to make eye contact again, but she didn't look at him.

"I am going for a ride," she stammered and tried to walk around him, but he stepped in her way and grabbed her by her arms.

"You are thinking about running away, Hazel. And I won't let you do that."

"I don't know what you are talking about, Alex. I just need fresh air."

"You are outside right now. Isn't that fresh air enough?"

"Why are you bothering me? Shouldn't you be inside with your students?" she snapped defensively, and he smirked.

"I am where I am needed," he shot back.

"Well, I don't need you. I want to be alone right now." She tried to get out of his grip, but he held her firm.

"Hazel. Reverend Mitchell told you several times now that you can't run away from your problems."

"I am not running away from my problems. I don't care what happens to me. I don't care if I die, but everyone in this family is in danger because of me," she burst out and tears shot into her eyes.

Alex pulled her into his muscular arms and held her despite her resistance. She sobbed against his chest. Once she had calmed down again, he lifted her chin, so she had to look at him.

"Listen. I understand that you worry about us, but you need to worry about yourself too. If you run away now, Clark wins."

"He will never let me go. No matter what we do and try, he gets away." Hazel's voice was full of despair.

"No, he doesn't. We are getting to him now. Our engagement threw him over the edge. He would have never tried to kidnap you last night if things had been the same. He is running out of time and is making mistakes. We also know now that Caleb is involved with him somehow. Caleb is obsessed with your sister, and that she is engaged is making him show his true colors."

"But shouldn't we report him to Todd?"

"Definitely. As soon as your father gets home, we'll tell him everything."

When George and Jackson found out what had happened, they were furious. They rode into town and reported the incident to Todd Holden. Todd reacted quickly and searched the area, located Caleb, and arrested him. Everyone on the Buchannon ranch was more than relieved.

A few days after the dance, and unpleasant situation with Caleb Norton, Hazel, Claire, Haven, and Brenna went on a picnic. They picked one of Haven's favorite spots, right next to a canyon. It was a beautiful day, and the girls were happy and cheerful. Haven and Claire weren't that big on riding, so they took a horse-carriage, and Hazel and Brenna rode on their horses.

Todd kept Jason Clark under constant watch, so Hazel knew they were safe. Their picnic spot was on their land, but she took one of her father's guns with her, just in case. Mountain lions and snakes were all over the place, and she was an excellent shot.

They reached the canyon after an hour. Haven and Hazel put a blanket on the ground, the picnic basket on it, and the girls sat down. Since it was warm that day, Hazel picked up the reins and walked the horses to a small stream.

Suddenly, a powerful feeling told her to return to the other girls. She listened to that feeling and turned around at once. She had barely tied Brenna's and the carriage horse to a tree when she heard Haven gasp with fright and terror.

Hazel turned around and there was Caleb with Claire in his hold and a gun to her head. The girl looked at her older sister in horror. They stood next to a few rocks, and behind them was the cliff.

"Caleb, let her go," Hazel said quietly as she grabbed her father's gun from the saddlebag and stepped closer. "She has nothing to do with this, don't make things worse for yourself."

"Ha," he scoffed with hatred and disdain. "It can't get much worse anymore."

"How did you get out of jail?"

"That wasn't hard. I have an excellent lawyer in Salem, and he bailed me out."

"Let Claire go."

"No way ...and if you come any closer, I'll kill her," he snapped and Haven broke out in tears. "I'll let her go if you marry me, Haven."

Before Haven could even reply, Hazel answered for her. "She will never marry you. Now, let Claire go. I'll switch places with her," Hazel mumbled, not leaving her sister out of her sight.

"Always the brave big sister, huh?" he mocked her, but Hazel didn't care what he said to her. Her heart was racing and the fear she felt nearly took her breath away. Caleb and Claire were too close to the cliff's edge, and Hazel was still several feet away.

"Last chance, Haven," he barked again as he turned to the other young woman. "You either marry me right away, or your sister here is dead."

"Caleb, don't do this. Please let her go." Haven stood up too, tears streaming down her face.

"You know what, I don't believe you will marry me even if you agree right now." He jerked Claire backward, holding her with one hand over the cliff.

"Caleb, don't be a fool. Claire is innocent. Please pull her back to safety. We will let you go, if you promise not to harm her." Hazel was getting hysterical, but kept her voice calm.

Suddenly, a rattlesnakes' loud rattling sound broke the silence, causing everyone to be alarmed. Right next to Caleb, two rattlesnakes had appeared between rocks and they felt threatened. He pulled Claire away from the cliff, but that was the moment one of the snakes shot forward to attack, and he jumped out of the way. Claire lost her footing and fell backward.

"NOOOOOOOOOOO." Hazel screamed in deep pain.

Caleb stared at the cliff. For a brief moment, he felt anguish when he realized what had just happened. He was torn between hurrying back to rescue Claire and going for Haven. His jealous heart decided for him, and he sprinted toward Haven.

Hazel lifted her gun and shot him in his shoulder and leg. He was thrown to the ground, moaning in pain. She ran over to him, ripped the weapon out of his hands, and threw it far into the canyon. Montana sensed the danger and rushed toward Caleb, who was attempting to get up. The mare attacked him with her hoofs, causing him to fall backward as he was trying to get away from the horse. He hit his head on a rock, and passed out.

"I'll get the sheriff and doc," Brenna yelled in shock, mounted her horse, and raced toward town.

"Haven, go get Pa and the others," Hazel shouted at her sister, but Haven was on her knees, sobbing.

"HAVEN. GO, GET HELP!" Hazel bellowed forcefully, and her sister finally reacted, ran to the other horse, and dashed toward home moments later.

"Claire, please hold on," Hazel mumbled under tears, grabbed the rope from her horse's saddle, tied it to a tree next to the cliff, and began climbing down. Her sister was on a drop-off about thirty feet below her. The rope wasn't long enough, so Hazel had to climb part of the mountain wall to get to the girl. During the climb, she received several gashes and deep cuts, but nothing stopped her.

When she reached Claire, the girl was still breathing, but Hazel saw at once that she would not survive. She had several broken bones, and the blood running from her mouth showed that she was bleeding internally. Knowing she had to stay strong for her sister, Hazel laid next to her, took Claire's hand into hers, and stayed there until the girl stopped breathing. Only then did Hazel curl herself into a ball, broke out in tears, and cried and cried and cried.

When the tears finally stopped, she turned herself on her back and allowed the black cloud of hopelessness and giving up, wash over her.

36
Shattered into Pieces

Haven shouted for help long before she reached the ranch house. Everyone around came running, fear on their faces. Haven jumped off the horse and threw herself into Dave's arms, and explained what had happened between sobs. Horrified, the men saddled their horses, and George shouted at a few of his ranch hands to follow with a wagon and bring everything they might need for a rescue.

They got to the canyon almost simultaneously as Sheriff and Marshal Holden, and Robert Mitchell. The Holden's and Reverend Mitchell had already taken their seats in the stagecoach when Brenna reached the town. As soon as they saw the distressed, hysterical girl, they knew they had to help. Todd handcuffed Caleb and sent him back to jail with his deputies.

George leaned over the cliff and saw Hazel next to Claire, not moving. He thought his heart would stop as he kept calling her name, but there was no reaction.

Namito, Todd, and Alex tied ropes together and climbed down the steep wall. When Alex reached the drop-off and noticed that Hazel was still breathing but was utterly apathetic, he sighed, relieved, and gave George a sign that she was alive. Namito and Todd covered Claire with a blanket and called to everyone on the cliff to send down a stretcher.

Once the cowboys reached the spot with the wagon and a wooden cot, George, Jackson, and two cowboys lowered the stretcher down to where the other three men were.

"Hazel, it is time to climb back up," Alex mumbled, but she only shook her head. "Please, we have to treat your wounds and injuries."

His sweetness made her tear up again, but she only rolled herself to the side. Since Hazel wasn't going anywhere, they sent Claire's body up first. They put her on the cot, covered her with the blanket, and used a few ropes to tie her body to the stretcher to prevent her from falling.

George and Jackson pulled up the cot, and Namito and Todd climbed beside it to keep it from getting stuck.

Hazel watched as they pulled up Claire's body. She whimpered her sister's name the entire time. When the cot reached the top, Alex lifted Hazel, tied a rope around him and her, and they were pulled up as well.

George tried to pull his daughter into his arms, but she sank next to the cot, bursting into tears again. It was heartbreaking to watch, and no matter how much they tried to get her away from there, she clung to her sister's body.

It was Reverend Mitchell who managed to lift Hazel, carrying her away. Hazel leaned against his chest, crying. Her heart was shattered into tiny pieces, and she was confident it would never heal again.

The funeral was the following day, and they buried her in the small cemetery on their ranch, which was only for family. Reverend Mitchell did the service, and he tried to make it hopeful and heartwarming. Hazel remained expressionless throughout the entire funeral but stayed behind at the cemetery when everyone left. As soon as she was by herself, she laid herself next to the grave and burst into tears again.

Helen stood on their porch and looked worried into the distance. Everyone else was still in the house, but Hazel hadn't returned, and it was getting cold and dark.

"She still hasn't come back yet?" Robert Mitchell asked when he and Alex stepped next to Helen. She only shook her head.

"I'll look for her," Alex remarked with concern. Hazel wasn't stable and could snap any moment now.

"I come with you," Reverend Mitchell replied.

Hazel thought about everything that happened over the past year. She had fought, but for what? She had nearly lost her life, and had been physically attacked and assaulted. None of that mattered because it had been her and nobody else. But this last incident changed everything. Her beloved sister died because of her. Yes, Caleb wanted to marry Haven, and Claire's death had been an accident, but he had worked with Jason Clark, and this had been another way of trying to break her. It worked. She was willing to give herself up now.

Her fighting spirit had finally cracked, and she had no energy left. Hopelessness had won. She had to give herself up to keep the rest of the family safe. She left the graveyard, mounted her horse, and rode toward Willamette Falls.

Alex and Robert Mitchell felt more and more uneasy as they dashed toward the cemetery. It was almost dark now, and when they reached the graveyard's fence, Hazel was nowhere to be seen. Alarmed, they turned their horses around and tore toward the town.

Montana sensed Hazel's hopelessness and that she was about to do something dangerous and wrong. The horse became unsettled and restless, making it hard for Hazel to calm the nervous animal. Montana rose several times, and her loud neighing echoed through the cold, darkening dusk.

"Steady, Montana, steady." Hazel tried to sound calm, but the animal was not listening. It was as if some unseen energy spooked her.

"Did you hear that?" Robert Mitchell asked, and they stopped their horses for a moment. Alex nodded.

"That was Montana, and she sounded distressed."

"Let's go," Robert shouted and kicked his horse on its sides.

When Hazel saw two men coming toward her, she tried to get Montana to go, but the horse stopped in her tracks. Before the young woman could get out of the saddle, Alex was next to her, pulled her on his horse, and stopped next to Reverend Mitchell. Hazel tried to resist both of them, but Alex lowered her straight into Robert's arms.

"Why can't you two just leave me be? Why do you always have to interfere?" she mumbled with tears in her eyes and tried to loosen his grip, but he held her firm.

"Because we love you, Hazel. We will not let you give up."

"I can't do this anymore, I can't, I can't," she burst out and started hitting Reverend Mitchell's chest with her fists. "Just let me go. Leave me be. It is of no use."

Robert talked to her until she broke down and stopped resisting him. He pulled her tight into his arms and held her.

"Keep fighting. You can't give up. Your mission on this earth is not fulfilled, and you are needed here."

"For what? For losing loved ones? For seeing my sister killed? She didn't deserve any of that, and it is all because of me."

"No, it isn't. Hazel, *listen* to me. None of this was your fault. None. You are not to blame. Satan got a hold of Clark and Norton's heart, and they only listened to him. They chose their actions, but will have to face the consequences."

"I failed. I failed everyone. My mother asked me to look after Claire, and she died. I didn't protect her."

"You are the best sister anyone could wish for. You have a heart of gold. You protected Haven when you were in that hotel room in Salem and made sure she was hidden and safe. It was you who jumped in front of me and took the bullet when McKellar tried to shoot me. Haven told me you tried to convince Caleb to let Claire go and take you instead. You did everything you could, but God has different plans sometimes. He wants us to have agency, and that includes evil people. They get to choose too, and He accepts their decisions. Sure, he could interfere and stop awful things from happening, but if He only allowed good decisions and stopped us from making terrible choices, we wouldn't have free agency. Now, let me repeat this: *You are not to blame*. Everything that has happened to you these last months was not your fault. Others made terrible choices, and they will have to answer for it. You are the victim here. Don't allow anyone, including Satan and his followers, to make you feel like you did something wrong. Promise me you will keep fighting. Promise me you will not let the dark feeling win."

She nodded and leaned her head against his chest. He was right. She couldn't let Clark win.

The next few weeks were filled with wedding preparations. Dave and Haven wanted to get married in November, and after Namito proposed to his love, they decided to have a double wedding.

Hazel threw herself into work and accompanied her father and Jackson on their business trips to Portland and Salem, and other areas. She didn't want to think about the changes ahead. Her heart ached when she thought about Alex leaving. Now that Claire was gone, he was scheduled to leave for San Francisco a week before Christmas, right after Brenna's sixteenth birthday.

The two couples asked Reverend Mitchell if he would marry them, and he agreed.

George and Hazel attended several official meetings to change the laws, and Hazel was asked to address the council every time. She realized, even though the lawmakers were moving in the right direction and some laws were about to change, the struggle was far from being over. Laws were essential and would change a lot for women, but the everyday fight for acceptance and equal treatment would still exist.

She was willing to face those struggles. Taking over her father's ranch was her dream, and it was worth fighting for. Hazel visited Claire's grave whenever she had the chance to remind herself not to give up and stay true to herself.

After Alex and Robert Mitchell had come after her, she had promised herself that she would never let herself get to that point again. No matter what happened, she would fight through it. Hazel realized that she had no control over certain things and had to take and accept life the way it was. Everything happened for a reason, and maybe sometime in the future, she would understand why things turned out the way it did.

As the wedding approached, Hazel did what she could to keep herself busy. She didn't want to think about Dave and her sister, leaving. Sure, they would only be a few miles away from them, but it wouldn't be the same anymore. As a married couple, they needed time alone, and even though she understood, she already missed them.

Haven was a beautiful bride, and her beaming smile was contagious. Hazel watched her sister with tears in her eyes as she walked down the aisle of the church. Her heart was overflowing with happiness. Since Haven and Dave were leaving for their honeymoon early the following morning, George had asked Helen's brother if they could use the big ballroom of the hotel for the wedding reception. It was a beautiful evening, and the two couples looked happy and beautiful.

Saying goodbye to her sister was difficult for Hazel, but Haven was in excellent hands and had a wonderful husband by her side. She also had to say goodbye to Reverend Mitchell again, and no matter how many times she saw him, the farewell part was always hard for her because it meant Jason Clark was still around and not her fatherly friend.

As Hazel stood by herself watching the stagecoach leave, Alex, Todd, and Adam noticed Jason Clark eyeing her. Alex walked up to Hazel, wrapped his arms around her, and gave her a radiant smile.

"How are you feeling?"

"I'll miss them. Beaver Creek without my sister and Dave will just not be the same."

"No, it won't, but at least we have each other," he remarked before leaning down to her, pressing a kiss on her cheek. She blushed at once.

"So, when are you two love birds tying the knot?" Todd asked as he and Adam stepped closer.

"I spoke to my parents, and since they want to celebrate Christmas with us, we were thinking of having the wedding on December 20th."

Hazel watched Jason Clark out of the corner of her eye and noticed how tense he got. The three young men saw it too.

"Does that mean you start your honeymoon after Christmas?" Adam asked as he jumped into the conversation and watched Hazel with a grin as her face turned into a burning inferno. Todd grinned as well.

"Would you two stop making my girl blush," Alex scolded playfully and pulled her into his arms, so she could hide her heated face from them. Adam and Todd burst out laughing.

"HARRISON," Clark shouted when the other young man entered the church. "Where have you been?"

"I had stuff to do, Clark. Believe it or not, but I am a busy man."

"I can't believe Hazel is engaged. I thought at first it was a joke, but since they keep up their affections and talk about a wedding, I have to take it seriously now. Damn it, what are we going to do?" He punched one of the church benches.

"Not sure that there is anything we can do."

"Yes, there is, but we have to act fast. The guy who wants her will travel for business at the beginning of December and wants to stop here. Hazel needs to be in our hands so I can hand her over, and marry her off before she marries Alex Camden."

"That shouldn't be a problem. Do you know the exact date when he will pass through Willamette Falls? It has to happen in one day and quickly. Otherwise, we risk having her rescued before he gets here."

"True. I'll contact him and let you know when I know."

37

Trapped By The Devil!

Hazel had barely put flowers on Claire's grave when she heard a horse come closer. She turned around only to see Adam jump off his animal and run toward the cemetery fence.

"Adam, what is happening?"

"Marshal Holden returned to Willamette Falls and arrested Jason Clark. They finally have enough evidence against him. Reverend Mitchell is with him, and they want to meet you at the church before they return to Salem."

Hazel's eyes lit up at once. "Does that mean Reverend Mitchell will return for good?"

Adam nodded. "We have to hurry, though, since the stagecoach leaves in about two hours, and they would like to see you before they leave. Marshal Holden needs to ask you a few more questions about your experience with Clark."

Hazel followed him to the horses, mounted Montana, and together they tore toward town.

When they reached the church, Adam helped Hazel off her horse, and they hurried inside the building.

"Reverend Mitchell? Marshal Holden?" Hazel called out, but nothing happened. She turned around to look at Adam. "Do you think they already left?"

He shook his head.

"No, they haven't left. How can anyone leave if they aren't even here?" Jason Clark stepped out of the darkness and walked toward Hazel. She turned as white as a bedsheet.

"I thought they arrested you."

"Is that what you told her, Harrison?" Jason raised an eyebrow.

"I had to tell her something," Adam replied and grinned.

"You are the other traitor?" Hazel cried out as she stared at him in shock and disbelief. Adam's expression changed from kind to disdain. He grabbed her arms.

"Yes," he sneered. "Clark offered me a lot of money a while ago, and since I want to expand my business, I figured that would help me a great deal."

"So you lied to us this entire time? You pretended to be like family and sold me out?" Hazel was furious. As scared as she was, her temper reached a boiling point. The hurt she felt because of his betrayal was stronger than her fear.

"Yes. My stupid brother and Shelly were always willing to share information, and I passed it on to Clark. It is wonderful when people are so trusting," he replied, grinning, but Hazel exploded and shoved him away from her.

"You are a disgrace and a filthy coward. I am ashamed of you. How can you do that to your brother and us?" She began hitting and pushing him, and her outrage got worse and worse, which made the two men laugh. Adam finally wrapped his arms around her and held her. She continued to rage and kick, but to no avail.

"Okay, Harrison. Let's take that little beast to the hunting cabin before her protectors get here."

"NOOOOOOOOOOOO, STOP. Someone help me please," she screamed and continued to fight the young man holding her, but he covered her mouth and dragged her outside toward the horses.

As soon as Montana sensed that Hazel was in trouble, she went straight for Jason. Adam tried to force the young woman on his horse, but she kicked herself free and ran as fast as she could toward town.

"Don't let her get away, Harrison," Clark shouted out of breath, still trying to get away from the aggressive horse.

Adam sprinted after Hazel and had to wrestle her to the ground before he had her under control again.

"Adam, please don't do this to me. I thought we were friends." Tears were rolling down her cheeks now, but he remained unfazed.

"You should save those tears for later. I am sure your upcoming marriage will give you enough to cry about."

Hazel bit her lips and swallowed her tears. Adam stared into her eyes and could see wounded pride, despisement, and resignation.

"Here, tie her hands together and gag her," Jason yelled out and threw the items to Adam. The young reverend was still getting attacked by Montana. Before Adam could gag her,

Hazel whistled. Montana stopped chasing the clergyman and neighed.

"Go, run home, and get help. Quick, GO." As if the horse had understood every word, she rose into the air and tore toward the Buchannon ranch. The two men laughed.

Adam and Jason didn't know that Hazel had practiced that exact drill with Montana ever since she found out how protective the horse was of her. So, no matter how amusing Adam and Jason Clark found the situation, Montana was up for the task of getting help.

Jason heard voices and looked around the building. "Sheriff Holden and his deputies are walking toward the church. I'll keep them distracted, and you take her to the hunting cabin. I'll follow as soon as I can."

Adam nodded, lifted Hazel on his saddle, and climbed behind her. He kicked his horse in the sides, and they rode off into the forest. Hazel felt defeated. She was determined not to give up, but the fact that she had trusted Adam, and he had betrayed them in such a horrible way, hurt. The horse moved forward slowly and quietly, and Adam was silent too.

When Hazel saw an old-looking dark hunting cabin in the distance, she panicked, and this time she hyperventilated. Her breathing became more and more unsteady until Adam stopped the horse, pulled her down, and took off the gag.

"Breathe slowly, calm down, that's it."

As soon as Hazel felt her breathing was normal again, she began fighting him, but he held her tight. She tried to get away from him until she had no energy left. She broke down crying.

Adam glanced around, and when he saw he was alone with her, he pulled her into his arms, despite her resistance.

"Hazel, listen to me. I'm sorry I have to put you through this. I am not betraying you or my brother, but I've been working undercover for Todd and Marshal Holden by pretending to help Clark, so we could defeat him. Marshal Holden, his deputies, and several others are in these woods, waiting for the right time to take over and attack," he whispered into her ear.

Hazel looked into his eyes to verify the truth, but his eyes told her he was honest.

"This is a trap. I am not sure what else will happen, but we will end this today."

"So, can you hide me somewhere now?"

He shook his head. "You need to play along. We have to catch him with evidence."

"No, please, Adam, don't leave me alone with him." Her entire body began trembling, but he grabbed her and dragged her with him.

"We will intervene as soon as we can, be brave."

"I can't, please, I can't. Just let me go," she begged, and it took her full strength not to burst into tears again. Her fear tore on his heart, and it was tough for Adam to continue, but he had to stay firm.

"Listen, I don't know what will happen once I take you into the cabin. In case we are not back fast enough, and you have a moment to yourself, check the room's wall. Here is a key," he whispered and dropped it into her dress pocket. "I was able to turn part of the wall into a hidden trapdoor when Clark was in San Francisco. The keyhole is on the left side of the fireplace. It isn't a big trapdoor, but it will be enough for you to get out. Just make sure you lock it again from the outside, so Clark doesn't know what happened to you."

She nodded, even though she shook with worry and fright. He pulled her into the dark cabin across the front room, opened another door, and pushed her into the room. She heard the key turning and him walking away.

For a moment, she just stared at the door. Suddenly, she heard a noise behind her. She turned around, and her heart skipped a relieved beat before she threw herself into his arms.

"Uncle Ted, what are you doing here? I am so happy to see you." Her body was still trembling, so he pulled her next to him onto the room's only furniture, an old dirty bed. He put his arm around her shoulders, and she leaned against his chest.

"Did you come with Marshal Holden and Reverend Mitchell?" she asked, but Ted Burton shook his head. "We need to get out of here before Jason Clark shows up."

"You don't need to worry about Clark, Hazel." He stroked her arm and kissed her on her head.

Hazel scanned the room and noticed the only light came from the fireplace. The room had no windows and no furniture except the bed and a shelf on the other side of the room.

Ted lowered his hand down her arm, kissed her cheek, went down to her neck, and placed his other hand on her knee, pulling up her long skirt.

Hazel froze for a second before she pushed him away from her and jumped to her feet. It finally dawned on her. He wasn't there to rescue her, he was the one who wanted her. Clark was nothing but a distraction.

"You are my godfather," she snapped, and looked horrified and disgusted at the same time.

"Yes, I am," he replied, giving her a nasty grin, "but that doesn't mean I don't have needs."

"You are disgusting."

"I am a man, and you are a beautiful girl." He stepped closer and wrapped his arms around her body, burying his face into her hair and slowly kissing her neck, which tensed up her entire body. She felt sick to her stomach. "I have been fantasizing about you for a long time, and tonight you will be mine."

Hazel wiggled herself free. Her hands were still tied so that she couldn't defend herself properly. "I will never be yours. You are a filthy, immoral old devil."

He grabbed her by her arms and pulled her so close, she could feel his breath on her face and neck.

"Oh, you will be. Clark is taking care of the sheriff, and if your father shows up, he will be taken care of too. Clark will marry us, and we will celebrate our wedding night here."

"Let me—"

"And don't worry," he whispered into her ear creepily before she could continue. "I'll make sure your first night is unforgettable. I promise to be gentle if you are a good girl."

Hazel's anxiety level shot through the roof, and bile rose to her throat. "Why are you doing this? What about Auntie Clara?"

He scoffed with disdain. "Clara is a boring old hag now and doesn't fulfill my needs anymore. I've been enjoying a few young girls these past few years before selling them off to other men in need."

Hazel's mind worked quickly when she remembered Clara and her eye injury.

"So you gave Auntie Clara that black eye?"

"She wasn't cooperative and disobedient. Don't worry, though, she was used to it. That wasn't the first time I had to beat her into submission."

"Why me? All those years, you've been like an uncle to me. Why would you think of me in such a sick, evil way?"

"You are a beautiful girl, and I love your temper. It will be fun to tame you and do as I please with you. I also want your father's ranch, and I figured it would look better if I had his daughter as my wife."

"You can't have more than one wife."

"I can if I don't tell any of the authorities, and if there are issues, I can always divorce Clara."

"My father will never hand over the ranch."

"He has no choice. The signature I got from him last year will be used for the special Will I have created and our marriage certificate. Your Pa will not survive for much longer. As soon as he shows up here, I have him killed." They heard voices outside, but before Hazel could scream for help, Ted was next to her and covered her mouth with his hand.

"I do feel sorry he has to die, but nobody lives forever, and his time is up just sooner than expected."

"*No*," she shouted as she pulled herself out of his embrace and hit him with her tied hands. She shoved him harder and harder. He finally grabbed her and threw her onto the bed.

"Let me be clear with you," he said through gritted teeth. "You can either calm down, and we wait until we are married, or I'll take you right now. The choice is yours."

She looked at him with hatred and disdain. "I will never be yours, and I will not go down without a fight. You might be stronger than me and can make me submissive to a point, but my soul will not be tamed or intimidated."

"You fear your own shadow and have been a scared little girl ever since this entire thing started," he spat out.

"Just because I feel fear does not mean I can't fight you. Of course, I am frightened and scared, but I am still me."

"I have to admit, you have been putting up a good fight, which makes it so much more endearing to tame you," he remarked as he looked her up and down while lustfully licking his lips. "I thought you would crack eventually, at least after Caleb killed your sister."

Hazel gasped in shock and horror. "You know about that?"

"Sure. Norton asked me for advice, and I told him he needed to do what it takes, even if it meant scaring you with wanting to kill Claire so you stubborn girls would finally break. Unfortunately, it happened as an accident, but that's life."

Hazel jumped off the bed and went forward to attack him, but he grabbed her again.

"I warned you, Hazel. I told you what would happen if you didn't calm down, but that will make this so much more fun." He pushed her backward and onto the bed, but before he could throw himself on her, she kicked him with so much force into his chest he flew back, hit his head on the edge of the shelf, and passed out.

Hazel breathed through her teeth, and swallowed her tears. She had no time to cry, but had to get out of there. The young woman stood, hurried to the wall next to the fireplace, and felt the wall until she found the keyhole Adam had mentioned. She fumbled for the key, got it out of her pocket and into the hole. A moment later, the trap door opened.

Hazel noticed that the porch went around the entire cabin, and so she rolled herself out of the hole, closed the door, and locked it before moving herself to the edge of the porch. She sat quietly for a moment and listened. When it remained silent, she jumped into the leaves beneath her.

A loud snapping sound was heard, and Hazel broke down, moaning in pain. Her left foot was stuck in a metal bear leg trap, and it hurt immensely. She tried to open it, but it was too strong and heavy. She was lucky it hadn't snapped her bones, but there was no way she could escape now because the trap was attached to a long chain wrapped around a tree nearby.

Hazel burst into tears. It wasn't just the pain, but the hurt inside and the frustration of being stuck. After a few minutes, she tried to open the trap again, but nothing. She looked around and thought she saw a few more traps near her, but none of them were chained to a tree, just held by a metal spike hammered into the ground. Why did she end up in the one that would not let her escape? She reached for a large stick and placed it above each trap she could see. The metal snapped loudly each time.

Suddenly, she heard her godfather rage inside the cabin. Hazel's blood froze with fear and horror. He yelled her name and broke open the door toward the front room. Hazel panicked and tried even harder to open the trap, but it didn't budge. Tears of anger and defeat entered her eyes again, and she just wanted to scream the pain off her chest but realized she had to stay quiet.

Hazel was so concentrated on breaking free and trying to calm her nerves, she almost jumped out of her skin when two arms came around her. Her heart just about stopped beating before she screamed and broke out in hysterics.

"Shhh, shhh," a deep voice said. "It is okay, Hazel. It is me, Robert Mitchell." With a quick movement, he cut the ropes around her wrists, and she threw her arms around his neck and broke out in tears.

"It is okay, I am here now. It is okay," he mumbled and stroked her hair and back.

All her emotions came tumbling down now, and her sobbing pivoted into a crying fit. His heart hurt for her, but he held her tight in his arms to signal her he was there, and she wasn't alone. It took a while until she could get control over her crying. When her sobbing was almost non-existent, Reverend Mitchell removed her arms from around his neck.

"I need to get you away from here." He tried to lift her, but she burst into tears again when the trap buried itself deeper into the flesh of her leg and foot. Robert hadn't seen the trap until that moment and gasped in horror before he apologized.

"I've tried to open it myself, but nothing happened," she cried, and he squeezed her hand.

"I'll give it a shot," he responded, and looked around to see if there was a long and robust enough tree branch he could use.

"Please be careful. There were three more traps around me, and who knows how many more are in this area." She looked around with fury. Anyone who used traps like that to hunt animals was not only a coward but a demon. Killing an animal had to happen quickly and with as little pain as possible. Those traps tortured them to death.

Robert Mitchell stood and found himself a long, thin tree branch with leaves on it. He used that as a broom to see if there were any more traps close to them. He found two more, but that was it. Robert had barely found a big, sturdy branch and knelt next to Hazel when they heard yelling from the front.

"Where is she?"

"I locked her in the room with you, how would she escape? You were in there the whole time," Adam's angry voice replied.

"Did she maybe take the second key from you?" Clark said now.

"I had the key in my pocket still."

"How could you have not seen her escape?"

"She kicked me so hard I hit my head against the shelf and passed out."

"Did you check under the bed?"

"How stupid do you think I am? Let's spread out, and we better find her."

Hazel flew into another panic, but Robert took her head into his hands and looked into her eyes. "I am here, you are safe now. Marshal Holden and the other men are around too. Ted Burton and Jason Clark will not hurt and torture you anymore."

He tried to open the trap but couldn't do it either. He would need at least one other person. Hazel was getting cold and shivered. It was time for her to get inside again.

"Of course, you end up in the arms of your fatherly protector," Ted scoffed with hatred and disdain. "I guess your father will not be the only one who will die today."

"Shut up, Burton, and stop your empty threats. The only thing we will witness today is your arrest."

Ted lifted his gun.

"Burton, where are you?" George Buchannon shouted from the front. "Release my daughter at once, you pathetic coward."

Ted turned around with a grin.

"PA, NO." Hazel yelled as she tried to get up, only to be pulled down again by the trap. "I need to get out of here, he will kill, Pa."

"Marshal Holden is there too. Your father will be fine."

"Drop that gun, Burton. The game is over for you." Marshal Holden looked at him firm, pointing with his head at the other men around them.

"I will never surrender myself," he responded with an arrogant scoff, lifted his gun, and was about to fire at George Buchannon when a shot from a deputy knocked him off his feet.

"As much as I would like to kill you," Sterling Holden spat out as he looked him up and down, "the bigger punishment for you is to rot in jail for the rest of your miserable life."

"I have no intention of going to prison," Ted remarked, lifted his gun to his chest, and fired a shot.

"Hazel," George said as he came around the cabin, jumped off his horse, and hurried over to her. She threw her arms around his neck and broke out in tears again.

"We need to get her out of that trap," Robert commented and pointed at her foot.

"Who on earth uses awful things like that?" Jackson snapped while dismounting his horse.

"A man without a heart and soul," Adam remarked as he came around the cabin, followed by Namito, Alex, and Todd Holden. The deputies had already arrested Clark and were taking him and the body of Ted Burton back to Willamette Falls.

"Okay, let's open that torture tool and get Hazel to a doctor," Marshal Holden said when he knelt next to Hazel. She finally calmed down, but braced herself for the pain to get worse when they freed her foot and leg.

"I'll hold her." George grabbed her under her arms and held her tight. Todd found an old ax behind a pile of wood. He used that to split open the trap, while Robert Mitchell and Sterling used a thick wooden tree branch to open the trap further. Hazel whimpered in pain, but was free a moment later. She was grateful that the boots covered most of her foot. It wasn't enough, though, to adequately protect her foot, not to mention that part of her lower leg was severely injured. George lifted her and carried her to her horse.

"Montana," Hazel exclaimed excitedly, and the animal came closer and sniffed her hand. "Did she get you guys?"

"Yes, she did," Jackson said, smiling. "She neighed and threw a tantrum until we were on our horses and followed her."

"Good girl," Hazel said and petted the horse's neck before her father placed her on the saddle.

"Let's get you to Dr. Harper."

"Hazel, you need to stop coming in here with such serious injuries. One might think you are trying to out-hurt the boys," Gordon Harper teased, and Hazel grinned.

"I'll try to do better, I promise," she replied with a twinkle in her eyes. Dr. Harper removed her boot and sock. It looked painful, and her foot was now swollen and bruised, which made it hurt even more.

Hazel held her breath, but couldn't help the tears from entering her eyes. He cleaned everything, covered her foot and leg with healing ointment, and bandaged it up, so the lotion would stay in place.

When Dr. Harper was done, he gave her a warm hug. "Are you okay besides that?" he asked and looked into her blue eyes.

She nodded. "Just shaken."

"I can imagine. Shall I let your father come back in, Hazel?"

"Can't I get up yet?"

"No, I want you to stay here and rest for at least another hour."

"How are you feeling, Hazel?" George asked as he stepped closer, and the other men followed him into the examination room.

"Good thing, this is such a big room," Gordon Harper remarked dryly, and everyone grinned.

"I want answers," Hazel responded without skipping a beat and looked at the men in the room. "Did you all know this would happen today?"

Everyone nodded.

"Jason Clark told Adam that Ted Burton would travel through Willamette Falls today, and so we planned our trap around that information," Todd said.

"So you used me as bait?" She looked at her father, Adam, and Todd pouting, and irritation spread across her face.

"I am sorry, honey. We didn't want to put you through all of that, but it was the only way to end this."

"Who sedated Clark and me?"

"Adam and me," Todd said apologetically. "Dad brought chloroform with him when he came from Salem."

"And why didn't you arrest him at that time?"

"Dad and Reverend Mitchell already had a hunch that Ted Burton was involved and didn't want him to get away. We needed Clark to get Burton."

Hazel nodded. That made sense. "How did Clark know where to find me in San Francisco? I mean, he found me in a busy park."

"Caleb has relatives there, and one of them followed you around whenever you left the house of the Camden's. The day Clark arrived, he met with that person, and that's how he found you."

"How did Clark end up working for my godfather?"

"Clark got into trouble in Salem. He harassed a girl and cornered her one night, but she escaped. She has two older brothers, and when they found out what Clark did and tried to do, they went to the church and beat him up. Since there was no evidence against Clark, the two brothers ended up in jail for assault. Burton bailed them out and promised the girl's family that Clark would get transferred somewhere else if they would not press charges. The girl's father agreed," Reverend Mitchell replied now.

"Were there any other girls he went after?"

"Yes, but they were too scared to go against him, as Burton kept sending them anonymous threats. I hope now that Burton is out of the picture, they will be willing to be a witness in court."

"So why didn't Bishop McDonald do anything but transfer him away?"

"After the incident with the girl, nobody knew there were more girls who were harassed by Clark. We thought it was only that one girl, and it would stop when he was gone. Burton was delighted when he found Clark and realized the young reverend could help him carry out his deepest desire. When I found out Clark had gone after you, I started working with my church members in Salem and discovered the truth slowly."

A knock at the door, made everyone turn around. The person entering made Hazel gasp. "Auntie Clara?" She had not expected to see her. "I am sorry about everything." The young woman lowered her eyes as she teared up again.

"No, sweetie, you have nothing to apologize for, you did nothing wrong."

"But you lost your husband because of me."

"No, Clara lost her husband because of himself," Robert Mitchell corrected her, and Clara nodded.

"Please have a seat, Clara," Gordon Harper said now and placed another chair next to Hazel.

"Do you know each other?" Hazel was confused.

"Oh yes," Clara responded with a smile. "I grew up in a little homestead along Beaver Creek and met Gordon when he started as a young doctor here. Jackson and I grew up together."

Jackson nodded. "I wanted to marry her when she was old enough, but that devil father of hers married her off to Ted Burton."

Clara nodded. "He was a drunk and always wasted the little money we had to buy more alcohol. When my father was about to lose our homestead, he met Ted Burton in Willamette Falls, who was visiting George. Ted offered to pay the debt if he could have me as his wife. I was only sixteen years old."

"Oh, Aunt Clara," Hazel said, compassion and sadness coloring her voice.

"It is what it is."

"Did he always punish you when you didn't listen to him?"

"Not in the beginning. He was sweet and a true gentleman, but I realized how obsessed he was with beautiful women and that it was my job to please him whenever he felt the need. After several years, I felt used and hated how he ordered me around all the time. My father had done the same thing."

Everyone in the room shook their head.

"When I finally had enough and refused to obey him, he showed his true face and beat me so badly I thought I would die. I realized that moment my life would never change, and I had to learn to live with it."

"Men should not be allowed to use violence against women and children. Why doesn't the law prevent that?" Adam remarked angrily.

"Because many men like to feel powerful and show those who aren't physically stronger than them that they are in charge," Robert retorted.

"It is because they can't control their temper and emotions. Men seem to lash out with violence when they don't get their way. It is like watching children who haven't learned yet that you fight with words, not with your fists."

"You have a remarkable understanding, Hazel," Gordon Harper said, impressed. "That's precisely how it is. If they can't hurt or threaten you with words anymore, they will hurt you physically."

"Did he ever touch Marianne and your boys?" George asked now and looked at Clara.

"He tried, but I did not want them to go through the same things I had to as a child, and always took it for them. Our boys moved out early, and when Marianne got older, and he saw how pretty she was, he was after her. Marianne was terrified of her father, and to protect her, I sent her to my sister in Boston, who is taking care of our mother. I told Ted that my sister needed help with my mom, so he wouldn't become suspicious, but I wanted to protect her from him. I'm so sorry he went after you, Hazel. Never would I have thought he would do that, even though I found out he was involved with white slavery."

"You found out about it?" George looked at her, shocked.

"After you left when you came back from San Francisco, Robert, and Sterling visited me a few days later and told me they knew he was abusing me. They asked if they could search the house and his office, and I permitted them. They found several bills and letters about his immoral and sinful activity."

"He pretended to help young girls and women when they came to him, asking for legal help to get them away from their father or other abusive people in their lives. Since they didn't have any money, he made them pay it off in a *different way*," Robert Mitchell said through gritted teeth. "If they refused, he threatened to take them back to their abuser. After they *paid off* their debt to him, he didn't let them go, though, and sold them to other men."

That hit Hazel like a punch in the guts. He would have used her the same way. Everything around began spinning. The voices were far away, and she felt the blood drain from her face. She felt sick to her stomach. Something inside her screamed that she needed to get out of this room and away from this conversation as fast as possible. She jumped off the examination table and the sharp pain of her leg and foot injury took her breath away. Blackness closed in on her. As she reached for something to steady her, her legs gave out and she lost consciousness.

As soon as Hazel fainted, all the men reached out, but it was Robert Mitchell, who stood closest to her, who caught her and laid her back on the table.

"Please, leave the room now. It is too much for her presently," Gordon Harper said and was by her side at once. They nodded and left.

"What happened, and where is everyone?" Hazel asked when she woke up again.

"You fainted, and so I sent them outside to wait in front of the clinic. Hearing those things right now is too much for you. You are not stable after what you went through. You need to rest now."

She nodded, still exhausted and pretty shaken. Just the thought of the things her godfather had done to other girls drove tears into her eyes, and she covered her face with her arm so that Dr. Harper wouldn't notice. He had seen it, though, and squeezed her hand.

"Let it out, Hazel. It is okay to cry and feel scared and overwhelmed. Yes, the threat is over, but you went through horrific ordeals and torture for months. That is not something you can just move on from and pretend it didn't happen."

"Can they come back inside? It comforts me," she whispered, and he nodded.

"Yes, but they need to keep the conversation light and positive. But first, let me move you over to the settee over there. You need to sleep. Take this, please. It will help you calm down and put you to sleep."

She downed the medicine, and he led her across the room and helped her lay down. He covered her with a blanket and left the room to call everyone else inside. Hazel was asleep before he reached the front door.

When they noticed that Hazel was sleeping, George, Jackson, and Robert Mitchell sat across from her and whispered to each other. Gordon Harper went to another treatment room to continue working.

"Do you think I could ask Clara for her hand in marriage? I know her husband barely died, and she is supposed to mourn for a year, but he wasn't a good man."

"Clara mentioned she wants to move back to Beaver Creek when everything is settled in Salem. Both her sons are lawyers in Portland. She said her oldest son would take care of selling the house and everything she doesn't want anymore, and then open a bank account in Willamette Falls for her," Robert replied.

"Do they know what Ted was like?" George was still in shock. How could he have been so wrong about a person?

"They knew he was abusive toward their mother, but Ted only beat her when they weren't around. She contacted them when Sterling and I wanted to meet with her and came down for that. So now they know everything, except what he did and tried to do to Hazel." Robert clenched his fists, sighed, and gave Jackson an encouraging smile.

"I think asking Clara to marry you if you think she is ready is okay. Yes, tradition calls for her to mourn for a year, but I am certain once words get out about what Burton was like and what she went through during her marriage with him, people will not condemn her for it. As long as her children are okay with it, I see no reason to wait."

"Clara's sons mentioned that they are hoping for her to find a good man to live with for the rest of her life, so she wouldn't just know abuse and mistreatment."

Hazel moved, and they went quiet and watched her, but she didn't seem to be awake.

She was with her back to them, and so they couldn't see that she had her eyes open and was now listening.

"One thing that makes me sad about ending this horrible ordeal for Hazel is that Alex and Hazel are back to normal now. I hate to see their fake engagement to be over. They are such a wonderful couple."

"And they did a remarkable job faking their affections, if they even faked it. Shouldn't we try to convince them to get married after all?" Jackson looked at the other two.

"We can't interfere. Alex already has a new job lined up for when he returns to San Francisco."

"Do you know how Hazel feels?" Robert asked now.

"I have no idea. She's never been open with her feelings, especially the feelings she might have for a young man. I thought she was in love with Dave for a while, but obviously I was wrong. With Alex, who knows? Even though I would love to have him as a son-in-law."

"Is that so?" Reverend Mitchell responded with a grin. "You didn't seem too thrilled when David Foster announced their engagement in the San Francisco Post."

"That had nothing to do with Alex. It was the shock of hearing of the engagement through a newspaper article. If Alex came to me and asked me for my daughter's hand, I would say yes in a heartbeat."

"Hazel's embarrassment was priceless, though. I have seen that girl blush a lot in my lifetime, but that moment beat the other times, hands down," Robert remarked with a massive grin on his face. They chuckled, and Hazel blushed again when she thought about that moment.

"One thing is for sure, though, I'll miss Alex when he leaves. Watching him with Hazel these past few weeks was refreshing and wonderful. None of their engagement felt fake. Their whole interaction seemed honest and real." George sighed.

Tears entered Hazel's eyes, and she had to fight hard, so she wouldn't make any noise and let the three men know she was awake.

It was very real for me, and I'll miss him more than anyone can imagine.

38
Joyful Hearts

With Jason Clark in prison and Ted Burton no longer being a threat, Hazel felt like she could enjoy life again. However, with all the changes that had taken place, it wasn't that easy.

Her sister and Dave returned from their honeymoon, but she only saw them occasionally. Brenna was close to graduating and kept herself busy, and Namito and his wife spent all their spare time with each other, so she didn't see them much either. Hazel missed her sister, and she missed her friends. Alex tried to spend time with her, but she didn't want to fall any deeper into a black hole and kept her distance since he was leaving soon.

Clara Burton moved back to Beaver Creek within a week. She asked her son to take care of everything, and so when Robert Mitchell moved back to Willamette Falls, she joined him. Clara wanted to start fresh and stayed at the hotel in Willamette Falls until a small house would become available. She didn't want any of her old furniture and decided to either order what she needed or buy what she could find in the general store of Willamette Falls.

Jackson and Clara spent time with each other and started courting. After the Salem Times printed the entire story, everyone in Willamette Falls and Salem had nothing but compassion and understanding for her.

Hazel was happy that Clara and Jackson had each other now, and worked toward a wedding. They decided to wait until spring to tie the knot, but it gave both of them something to look forward to.

As Alex's departure day came closer, the weather changed too, and they had a few snow days. George purchased two sleighs for the long winter, a small one and a larger one, so they weren't stuck if emergencies occurred. Plus, with Haven living just outside of town now, he wanted to visit her.

A week before Alex's departure, George called Hazel into his office. It surprised her to see Jackson and Robert Mitchell there, but she was always happy to see her favorite reverend.

"I have something important to share with you," George began with a serious expression on his face. "I contacted Harry Camden, and he is making Robert Mitchell your godfather."

Hazel's eyes lit up for a split-second before she turned serious again. "And you didn't feel the need to discuss such an important matter with me? I mean, I understand that you had to decide what was best for me when I was a child, but now that I am a grown woman, shouldn't I have a say too?"

All three men looked at her, stunned, and their mouths dropped.

"I thought you would be happy to have Reverend Mitchell as your godfather."

"It has nothing to do with being happy, but with you deciding without even asking for my opinion. Besides, is it smart to choose another older gentleman for such an important task? I mean, choosing someone of your age to look after me when you pass on is somewhat ironic, don't you think?"

Jackson and George were speechless, but Robert Mitchell raised his eyebrow to signal her to be careful.

"Maybe we can ask Adam to be my godfather," she suggested, still with a straight face. "He is young enough to outlive you guys, and I am sure he would gladly take over the role of a guardian if it becomes necessary."

"Hazel," Reverend Mitchell said now with a growl in his voice and gave her a look that made her blush. "Your sass is way out of control, young lady."

"Is it? I don't think I said anything sassy."

"You said nothing, sassy?" her father asked now. "What about calling us older gentlemen?"

"That's not sassy, but a fact," she shot back with a grin on her face. "I mean, you have to admit you are not exactly twenty anymore."

"No, we are not, but I wouldn't call us old either."

"I never said you are old, I said older."

"Just be aware that older gentlemen can still teach sassy young women manners," Robert remarked and narrowed his eyes to look more intimidating.

She smiled sweetly. "Of course, I am aware. Luckily for me, the weather is too cold to be thrown into the lake or one of the water troughs."

"There are plenty of ways to punish you. We don't need a lake for that," Reverend Mitchell retorted and stepped closer with a confident grin on his face, which made her blush again.

"I understand. Anyway, are we done here, Pa?" she asked, trying to get herself out of this uncomfortable situation.

"We are, if you have no objections to who your godfather will be," George commented.

"I told you what my objections were. You should have discussed that with me before making any arrangements, but since decisions have been made, I will agree to it."

"Oh, you will, will you?" George replied dryly and gave her his strict father-look.

"I don't think it is fair of you to stare at me like that," she complained a moment later. "Three men against a girl?"

"A girl who still gives said three men sass, despite her being on her own," Robert reminded her.

"So, what is your biggest concern about having Robert as your godfather?" her father continued.

"Not a concern per se, but some hesitation."

"How so?"

"Well, for starters, he constantly complains about my sassiness, yet he pushes it out of me with his sarcastic and challenging comments."

"I push the sass out of you?"

"Yes, you do. Perhaps you three should ask yourself why you are so quick to threaten me with punishment. Could it be that my fast-thinking wit is hurting your manly pride, and you have to prove to yourself and those around you that you can still keep up physically with the younger generation of men?"

Hazel grinned from ear to ear and stepped away from them and toward the door. Before she could make her escape, however, Robert was next to her and threw her over his shoulder.

"My point exactly," she remarked and winked at her father, who had to cough to hide his smile.

"What are we going to do with her?" Jackson asked before turning to George. "I see what Mrs. Brenton was on about last year. You were not strict enough with Hazel. I suggest we throw her into the enormous pile of dung heap to teach her a lesson."

"A nice cold pile of snow will do too," Robert responded with a straight face and walked out of the room. The other two followed. When he opened the front door and walked toward one of the big snow piles next to the barn, she wiggled.

"No, please, don't throw me in there. I'll keep my sass in check now."

"You promised me that before and yet, the sass still keeps flying out of your mouth." He took her off his shoulder and dropped her right away. She formed a few snowballs and threw them at the three men, which they returned in a heartbeat before lifting her and returning to the warm house.

Those silly times made life bearable and fun again. It was important that they kept their humor alive and reminded each other that being a loving family also meant sass and teasing, as long as it wasn't used to hurt a person.

Brenna graduated with excellent grades. To celebrate her accomplishments and say goodbye to Alex, Helen and George invited everyone for the last get-together the evening before Alex's departure.

Hazel had stayed away from him most of the week. She had thrown herself into work at the office by going through paperwork and looking through the inventory. She didn't want to think about him leaving because she loved him more than ever, and this goodbye would break her heart.

The evening had arrived, and Dave and Haven, and Namito, his wife, Clara, and Reverend Mitchell, joined them. Hazel loved having everyone together, but her heart ached, and she kept fighting her tears all night. When she couldn't take it anymore, she said a quick farewell to Alex, excused herself, put on her coat, and left the house.

She went to the barn first, grabbed a few blankets, and hurried over to her favorite spot, even though it was cold. She sat on two of the quilts and covered herself with the last one. It was a beautiful, crisp night. The moon was out, she saw stars over her head and noticed clouds moving in, which meant it would snow soon. She loved the smell in the air before a snowstorm and breathed in deeply.

"Hazel, why are you out here?" a voice said behind her.

"I needed fresh air, that's all."

Namito sat next to her and put his arm around her. "Are you sure it is nothing else?"

"I am feeling down with all of you here," she admitted after a brief pause.

"I thought you love it when we are all together."

"I do, but tonight it is reminding me of how lonely I am, and that makes it difficult to enjoy."

"Oh, Hazel, why do you think you are lonely? You have all of us, and we love you."

"I know you love me, but things are different now. You are married and spend most of your time with your wife, Alex is leaving, Pa and Helen have each other, Jackson and Clara will be married soon, and Dave and Haven are gone too."

"We are not that far away, though."

"No, but our get-togethers are a lot less now."

"Why can't you just be grateful for the times we are together?"

"I am grateful. Please don't think I am not. I love being with you all. I am happy for all of you too, and I want you to spend time with your other half or future spouses, but it makes me miss you. Can't you understand that?"

Namito squeezed her hand. "I can understand. Change as this has always been hard for you because you feel your family is falling apart. Reverend Mitchell is back, though, and that should make you happy."

"I love that he is back, but he is busy too and can't always spend time with me. I appreciate the time I have with him, though. I just wish Dave and Haven lived on the ranch still. I miss them both so much."

Namito gave her a sideways glance. "Shouldn't you be over Dave by now?"

Hazel stared at him confused, her mouth fell open. "What are you talking about?"

"Oh, don't give me that," he responded. "Do you think I have forgotten what you told me in San Francisco?"

"What did I tell you about Dave?"

"Come on, Hazel. When we came back to San Francisco for the trial and visited you at the hospital, you said—"

"Whoa, stop right there," she interrupted, feeling uncomfortable. "I said nothing about Dave. That was all you. You had it in your head that I was in love with Dave, and well, since you are so hard-headed about stuff sometimes, I let you believe it."

"Let me believe it? Hazel, you can't fool me. I remember how you greeted Dave, and a moment later, Alex and—" he paused and stared at her wide-eyed. The shock was evident on his face.

Alex couldn't focus on the conversations around him. He had to talk to Hazel. Leaving without speaking to her was impossible, so he put on his coat and went outside. He knew where he would find her.

"You've been in love with Alex this whole time?" Namito asked as he shook his head. Hazel nodded. "Why didn't you say anything?"

"I needed time to come to terms with it myself. I was glad you thought I was in love with Dave because that way, I was able to think things through."

"So, during your fake engagement—"

"... I was in love with him," she finished his sentence. "None of that was fake for me. At times, I thought he felt it too, and it broke my heart when the time was up, and he would leave."

Not showing himself, Alex let out a sigh of relief. He hadn't meant to eavesdrop, but maybe this was meant to be. He knew what he needed to do now.

"Do you know how he feels?"

"No. Sometimes I thought Alex's feelings were real too, but I couldn't quite tell."

"Hazel," he said, now, "you need to tell him before he leaves."

"No, I don't need to do that."

"He can't leave like that, maybe he loves you too?"

"And what if he doesn't? I can't make myself vulnerable like that. This is hard enough."

"He might have the same feelings for you."

"Yes, perhaps, but most likely not. It is not like Alex is shy. He could have shared with me how he felt, but he didn't."

"How many opportunities did you give him? You keep your distance as soon as things get difficult. Maybe he wanted to talk to you but didn't because you pushed him away."

Alex had to agree with that. He had been longing to talk to her, but he didn't know how to approach her because she was so distant again.

"I do that for my protection, Namito. It hurts to see him go. I don't want him to leave, but I also don't want to push myself on anyone. Do you know how hard it is when you feel like crying all week, especially tonight, but have to pretend you are fine? Losing him is one of the hardest things in my life." Tears ran down her cheeks, and she jumped up.

"Just talk to him. Maybe your story can have a happy ending too. All of us were hoping for you to get together. Your fake engagement felt so real. It seemed like you two belong together."

"It felt like that to me too, which makes it even harder for me now."

"Then go. Find him and tell him how you feel."

"No, I am sorry I can't," she muttered under tears, turned around, and was about to run back to the house when she saw Alex close to them. "Alex?"

Namito turned around, grinned, and then stood up and walked away to give them privacy.

"Hazel, I need to talk to you."

"Alex, if you heard all of this, don't worry about it. It is nothing." She tried to walk past him, but he stepped in her way.

"This is not nothing, and we need to talk before I leave."

Hazel swallowed the tears. He was close enough for her to throw her arms around his neck, and that gave her butterflies, something she didn't need at that moment.

"Alex, please don't make this more difficult. We already said our goodbyes." She tried to walk past him again, but he pulled her into his arms.

"I love you. I want to marry you and spend the rest of my life with you. You are the most wonderful and beautiful woman I ever met, and I am not leaving you."

Hazel looked at him in shock, not sure what to say.

"After the incident with Claire and seeing you so broken and hopeless, I realized how much you meant to me and that my heart is yours and yours alone. When we had to pretend to be engaged, it felt so right and made me happy. I saw in your eyes that this entire thing wasn't as fake as we made it look. I believe everyone around watched us, hoping for us to become a real couple. I wanted to talk to you so often, but I didn't want to put that on you while we were still trying to end things with Clark and Burton. I promised myself I would speak to you right after, but you withdrew from me and pushed me away, and I wasn't sure if that meant you didn't feel the same way or were protecting yourself. Something told me earlier that I shouldn't leave without talking to you. So, when I came looking for you and heard what you and Namito were talking about, it made me the happiest man alive."

Hazel continued to stare at him. Was all of this real? Had he said he loved her and wanted to spend the rest of his life with her? As it began to snow, Hazel found her voice again.

"Alex, please don't tease me, don't joke with me. Is all of that true?"

He smiled and took her head into his hands. "Yes, it is. My heart is now and forever yours. I could burst with joy, knowing that you feel the same way. I love you, Hazel Buchannon."

Her heart skipped a beat, and a beautiful smile lit up her face. He let go of her face, stepped backward, went down on one knee, and looked deep into her blue eyes.

"I love you more than I can ever express. You are a dream come true, and I want to have you by my side for the rest of forever. You are the most beautiful girl I ever beheld, and I never want to let you go again. Hazel Rae Buchannon, will you marry me?"

Hazel blinked a few tears away before she nodded. Alex jumped to his feet, grabbed her around her waist, and lifted her in the air, twirling around with her.

When he put her down again, he leaned down, capturing her lips with his for a passionate kiss. Hazel's heart skipped several beats at that moment, and the butterflies in her tummy turned to elephants. Oh, how she loved that man.

"I have something for you," he whispered into her ear as they stood next to each other, enjoying the quiet snowfall. He pulled a beautiful but simple ring out of his pocket and put it on her finger. She was speechless for a moment before giving him a side-ways glance full of sass.

"I thought you didn't know how I felt about you. Do you just carry an engagement ring with you wherever you go?"

He laughed heartily before pulling her into his muscular arms. "Isn't that the way every man does it?" he shot back and grinned. She looked up at him and blushed.

"It was my grandmother's ring, and my mom gave it to me, years ago, so I would be ready when the time came. Do you like it?"

Hazel nodded. "I love it. It is beautiful."

He kissed her again, and they walked back to the house.

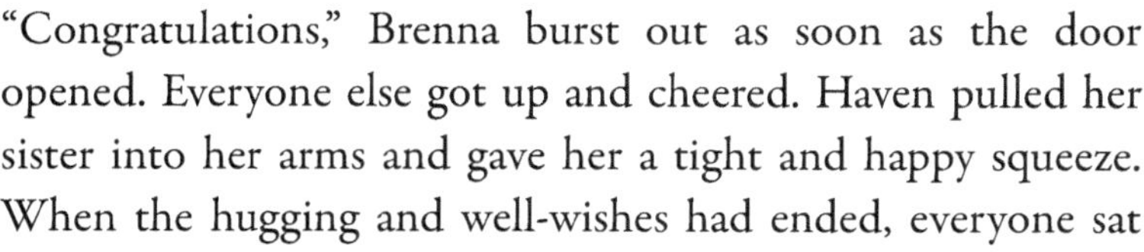

"Congratulations," Brenna burst out as soon as the door opened. Everyone else got up and cheered. Haven pulled her sister into her arms and gave her a tight and happy squeeze. When the hugging and well-wishes had ended, everyone sat down again, and Alex pulled Hazel close, with his arms wrapped around her.

"So, what's the plan now?" George asked with a content smile on his face.

"I would like to ask you officially for the hand of your daughter. May I have your permission to marry her?"

Everyone stared at George, and he gave his daughter and future son-in-law a serious, thoughtful glance as if he had to consider it.

"Hmm, I don't know. Are you sure you are up for it? That one has a lot of sass in her, you might want to think about it more before making a final decision."

Alex grinned, while Hazel narrowed her eyes and gave her father a death stare.

"I am sure I can manage. If Hazel's sass gets too bad, I'll bring her to you so you can discipline her."

Hazel rolled her eyes but blushed. Robert Mitchell grinned, amused.

"In that case, you have my permission," George responded with a big smirk on his face. Hazel leaned over and kissed her father on his cheek.

"So, shall we have the wedding the day you already planned for?" Robert Mitchell asked with a playful sparkle in his eyes.

"I normally would say yes, but we have to give my parents the chance to get here for the wedding. Today is December sixteenth' and we have to inform them about a change of plans and ask them to come here instead."

"How about December twenty-second? I'll send a telegram to them first thing in the morning and invite them to Beaver Creek for Christmas. Should we surprise them with the engagement or mention it in the telegram?" George looked at the young couple, and they thought about it for a moment.

"It would be fun to surprise them," Alex said finally, "but we have to figure out a way to invite them without them becoming suspicious."

"How about two celebration reasons? To celebrate Brenna graduating and getting together with all our friends and loved ones to show our thankfulness for the blessing of stopping the demons that tortured Hazel for so long," Helen said.

"That is an excellent idea, honey," George responded. "With the day set, we can invite all our other friends as well and make it official. If there is anyone specific you would like to invite, don't hesitate to let me know."

"And don't you worry about a thing, Hazel," Helen remarked now. "Haven, Brenna, Shelly, and I will plan and organize everything, right girls?"

The three young women nodded.

"I'll get started with your wedding dress tomorrow," Shelly promised with a big smile on her face. "I saw wedding gown material at Mr. Bennett's general store when I checked last week, and I don't think anyone has bought it yet."

"Just tell us what you want for your wedding," Haven added.

"I have nothing specific in mind. Being with you for that special event, and having our relatives and friends there, is all I need. I leave it in your capable hands." Hazel smiled and kissed her fiancé on his cheek. He smiled at her.

George sent off the telegram invitations the following day, and Harry Camden replied quickly, letting them know that they would arrive in Willamette Falls December twenty-first.

Hazel was nervous and excited, yet her heart couldn't be happier. Alex was secretive during the following few days, and she only saw him in the evenings, but it made everything so much more exciting.

Hazel and Alex went to pick up his parents together. It was a beautiful winter day, and the fallen snow covered the trees and land in a winter wonderland. Hazel snuggled up to her fiancé, and they reached Willamette Falls a while before the stagecoach arrived. Many greeted the young couple with enthusiasm and excitement and told them how much they were looking forward to their wedding.

Alex grinned.

"Why are you smiling like that?" she asked innocently, yet watching him curiously.

"I just remembered that I have to talk to your step-uncle about reserving us a room for our wedding night."

Hazel turned bright red, and he pulled her into his arms with a chuckle. "I am excited about our wedding and look forward to our future together," he said quickly to help her over her bashfulness, and kissed her right then.

"How are we going to tell your parents the news?"

"We can leave it up to my mom. She has a sixth sense for those things. Just don't let her scare you off when her excitement takes over," he replied, grinning. "Mom can become like a little girl when her happiness boils over."

"No way, not your mom," Hazel said with pure disbelieve in her voice.

"Wait and see."

"Alex, Hazel, it is so good to see you again," Harry Camden said as he climbed out of the stagecoach and before helping his wife down the steps.

"Hi Dad," Alex responded, and they embraced each other for a warm father-son hug. Liz hugged Hazel, and then Miles climbed out of the stagecoach and behind him...

"Colleen? Colleen Walker? What are you doing here?" Hazel smiled big and hugged the other young woman as soon as she reached her.

"Miles and I are getting married next spring. We got engaged yesterday."

"That is so exciting. Congratulations to you both. How did you meet?"

"We met at the execution of McKellar actually and, well, kind of fell for each other," Miles responded and gave Hazel a hug and kiss on her cheek.

"Now, now, don't get too cozy with each other," Alex interrupted with a grin and gave his brother a welcoming hug. Suddenly, Liz squealed and pulled Hazel back into her arms. The young woman didn't know what was happening to her.

"You two are engaged?"

"Engaged? What are you talking about, Liz? They haven't said a word, yet." Harry looked at her as if she had lost her mind.

"Look, Hazel is wearing my mother's ring," she blurted out and lifted Hazel's hand into the air before squealing some more. Hazel glanced at Alex, and he nodded.

"Told ya," he mouthed to her.

"Yes, Mom, we are engaged," Alex said now. "I proposed to her a few days ago, and we are getting married tomorrow. That's why we had to change our plans and asked you to come here. We are celebrating the other things as well, but this get-together is mostly for our wedding."

Liz jumped up and down and kissed and hugged Alex and Hazel. When Hazel was free again, Harry pulled her into a fatherly hug.

"You have no idea how happy that makes me. I have been hoping and praying for this ever since we met you."

Hazel was truly touched.

39
"Till Death Do Us Part!"

The big day had arrived. Hazel and the other women left early for Willamette Falls to get ready for the hotel's big event. They would meet everyone else at the church later that day. Hazel looked stunning in her simple but elegant wedding gown. Shelly had outdone herself. She knew what style Hazel liked, and so it fit her perfectly.

Haven styled her sister's hair and added a veil. When Hazel stepped out of the room and Liz and Helen saw her, they couldn't hold back their tears. George felt the same way when he saw his beautiful daughter and had to swallow several times to keep the tears from coming. Everyone was ready, and they hurried ahead to the church. George hugged his daughter and looked deep into her eyes.

"Ready?"

"As ready as I ever will be," she responded with shaking hands. "Why am I so nervous?"

"It is part of being a bride or groom. I am sure that Alex is just as nervous."

"Let's hope he'll be there and won't stand me up."

"No way. Alex is absolutely and unconditionally in love with you. He will not leave that church until you are Mrs. Alex Camden," her father said, grinning, watching his daughter blush. He kissed her on her cheek. "Let's get you to the church."

The church was packed. Everyone invited was there. Russell Montgomery and his brand-new wife, Bishop Steven McDonald, and even Stewart Montgomery and Marianne Burton, as well as Judge Thomas McGregor, had come to be part of Hazel's wedding.

Alex couldn't stop looking at the bride when George walked her down the aisle, before placing her next to him.

Robert Mitchell looked at her fascinated. Seeing her get married was touching and special to him. He remembered when he met her for the first time. She was such a feisty little girl, yet so heartbroken and sad. Having this strong-willed beautiful young woman in front of him, who was about to make a covenant with God to marry this outstanding young man, made Robert's heart swell with pride and thankfulness.

She deserved this. She had earned this more than anyone after the struggles and heartache she had gone through. Knowing she had found such a special young man, made him happy beyond imagination.

"I now declare you husband and wife. Alex, you may kiss your bride." Reverend Mitchell said with a grin, and Hazel lowered her eyes, but her now-husband lifted her chin and gave her a sweet and gentle kiss.

It took the newlywed couple a long time before they could make their way to the hotel to continue the celebration. Everyone wanted to hug, kiss, and talk to the young couple. Harry and Liz hugged the bride together.

"From now on, you call us Mom and Dad," Harry said and kissed her on her cheek. Hazel only nodded, since she had a big lump in her throat now.

They celebrated the young couple until late at night. Finally, Alex indicated that it was time for them to leave. They said their farewell, and Alex climbed on the carriage, helped his wife up, and they waved at everyone as the guests threw rice at them.

"I thought we would stay here at the hotel," Hazel remarked, confused, but Alex only grinned. He clicked his tongue, and the horse started walking.

"I have a surprise for you," he said, and Hazel glanced at him curiously. "Well, a surprise from Helen, your father, Jackson, and me."

"Is that why you were gone so much this week?"

"Yes."

Hazel moved closer to him, and he put his arm around her shoulders. They smiled at each other and continued quietly. The moon was bright and made it easy for them to see.

When they reached their destination, Hazel couldn't believe her eyes, and she jumped out of the carriage before Alex could help her. He was about to scold her, but she was already walking toward the building.

"That's Pa's old hunting cabin. It looks entirely different."

"That's right. This is our surprise. Your father started renovating it after we got back from San Francisco. At first, he thought of giving it to Haven and Dave, but when Dave bought the house in town, he continued with the work for his retirement. When our sudden engagement happened, he changed his mind and said, we can stay here as long as we want," Alex responded, and Hazel grinned happily.

"...or until our family grows," Alex whispered into her ear with a smirk, knowing quite well what would happen to her face. He turned her around, leaned down, and pulled her so tight against him, she gasped. Before she knew what was happening, his lips pressed against hers, and he kissed her until she was breathless. He pulled his head back.

"Do you want me to show you everything?"

"Yes, please."

He took her to the stable first. It had only been a tiny open shed, but was now a small stable. It fit two horses, a cow and had room in the middle for chickens.

"This is incredible. I love it," Hazel burst out and smiled when she saw Montana in there and a cow from the ranch. The chickens were already asleep. Behind the stable was a barn filled with hay and straw, and on the other side of the cabin was another shed filled with firewood. Hazel was stunned.

When they walked toward the front porch's steps, Alex grabbed his wife and lifted her off her feet. "I have to carry you over the doorstep. It is tradition."

Hazel smiled, and so he carried her inside the cabin. She looked around, but it was too dark to see, so he made her close her eyes until he had lit several candles and started the fire.

The room looked so different. It was not a hunting cabin anymore, but a beautiful little home. A settee was placed in front of the fireplace, a dining area on the other side, paintings beautified the walls, and when Hazel walked through another door, she ended up in a tiny kitchen with an actual stove and oven. Everything was stunning, and it was beautiful and clean.

Alex had left again and brought the horse into the stable. He locked everything and closed the shutters from the outside before returning to the cabin.

Hazel walked into the bedroom and was just as amazed. The old broken apart separate beds had been switched with new beds pushed together. The room had a small stove to keep the room warm and a closet filled with their clothes.

Next to the bedroom was a washroom with a door attached to the outhouse. The washroom had a bathtub and could quickly be filled with water heated in the kitchen, bedroom, or living room.

"Do you like it?" Alex asked after locking the front door.

"Like it? I love it."

"I did the last touches this week. Haven, Helen, and Shelly made the curtains for our windows. I added a few more decorations and furniture."

"It looks lovely. I never expected this. It feels like we have our own little home."

"This is our own little home," he replied as his brawny arms came around her, and he looked deep into her eyes. "I love you so much, Hazel."

"And I love you."

He picked her up again, gave her another passionate kiss, carried her into the other room, and closed the door.

Hazel was sitting on the steps of the front porch and soaked in the surrounding beauty. The snow was covering everything, Beaver Creek was frozen, and her heart was happy. Alex walked out, sat behind her, and wrapped his arms around her.

"You love it here, don't you?" She nodded, her eyes sparkling in the sunlight. "Let's warm up inside," he said, pulled her to her feet, and returned to the cabin and snuggled up in front of the fireplace. He pulled Hazel on his lap.

"So, we won't see everyone until tomorrow night?"

"I doubt it. I bet my mom has been bugging my dad all morning that she wants to see us and our cute little home, and we might even get more visitors than just my parents."

"But we are on our honeymoon," Hazel replied with a playful sparkle in her eyes, which made him kiss her.

"Let's just hope they won't stay long."

"Alex," she began scolding him, but he only grinned at her.

"We can always ask them to leave."

"That is rude. We can't do that."

"There is one more way to let them know we need time alone, by only hinting at it."

"And how will we do that?"

Instead of answering, he lifted Hazel off his lap, jumped to his feet, and twirled her around. Hazel smiled at him. Suddenly, he leaned her backward, which caused her to gasp in shock. Before she knew what was happening, Alex pressed his lips onto hers and kissed her with so much passion, it took her breath away. When he let go of her again, she had to collect herself for a moment. He grinned at her.

"What do you think, will that do the trick?" He watched her amused, and sure enough, as soon as she realized why he had kissed her that way and what he was trying to say, she blushed.

"No way. You can't do that," she stammered, and he chuckled.

"I am only teasing you. I enjoy kissing you like that, but it isn't a kiss to share around guests." He grinned when he saw how embarrassed she still was and just held her close.

"Good. I am not sure what my father would do if he saw you kissing me like that," she remarked dryly.

"Who says he doesn't kiss Helen like that?"

Hazel's face was on fire at once, and Alex let out a hearty laugh. He pulled her tight into his arms.

"Maybe we won't get any visitors," she finally said.

"I am telling you, my mom is odd with these things. She has been hoping for years that Miles and I would get married. She wanted daughters more than anyone, and so this is a dream come true for her, especially since Miles and Colleen will get married in a few months."

"I better check the kitchen to make sure we have something to feed potential guests."

"You mean more than the left-overs from our wedding yesterday?"

"Yes, exactly. And it was so kind of you, good sir, to serve such a tasty breakfast to me this morning."

"It was my pleasure. Having such a beautiful wife makes serving wedding left-over for breakfast easy," he replied and winked at her, which made her giggle. "Don't worry, though, we are all set and have plenty of food," Alex said with a grin. Before she could say anything in return, he grabbed her by her hand and threw her over his broad shoulder.

"Hey, what is that for, Mr. Camden?"

He carried her into the kitchen, put her on the floor again, and gave her a sassy grin. "I wanted to make sure you wouldn't get tired on your way to the kitchen."

"Ha-ha, very funny, Sir." She gave him a side-way-glance, and he swept her up into his arms and kissed her again. When he let her go, she checked the ice box, cupboards, and shelves for food, and sure enough, they had plenty. There was flour, sugar, eggs, milk, and anything else they needed.

"Wow, you did an excellent job preparing this place."

"It wasn't just me. Haven and Helen did most of that."

"I am still impressed, Mr. Camden."

Being distracted by his beautiful wife, Alex stepped backward and fell over an open cupboard door. Hazel burst into a fit of laughter, but one stern look from him, and she hurried out of the kitchen and sat on the settee before he was on his feet again. As soon as he reached her, he pulled her into his arms to kiss her thoroughly, when there was a knock at the door.

He sighed. "I was afraid of that. I bet those are my parents. They always have the best timing," Alex said while rolling his eyes, and Hazel grinned.

"Shall we pretend we aren't here?" she whispered in return, and Alex laughed out loud. "Yeah, well, I guess we can forget that now." Hazel raised an eyebrow and gave him a playful look.

"They wouldn't believe it even if I had been quiet as a mouse." He went to the door and opened it wide. In came his parents, George, and Helen, Reverend Mitchell and Miles and Colleen. Hazel greeted everyone with a smile and a hug and asked them to sit. Since the settee and chairs weren't enough seats for everyone, Alex pulled his wife on his lap again.

"You guys know we are on our honeymoon, right? Honeymooners don't entertain company."

"Sorry, Son, but you know your mom. She's been annoying me all morning about a visit here, and when I gave in, everyone joined us.

"This is such a beautiful little home. I love it. It is so charming and perfect for a young married couple," Liz exclaimed and looked around curiously.

"You are welcome to check out the entire place, Mom." Alex didn't have to tell her twice. Helen smiled and glanced at Hazel.

"How do you like this place?"

"I love it. Pa, you did such an outstanding job with it. I hardly recognized it. And I love the touches you made to this place and the food you stored here for us, Helen. Are you two sure you are okay with us living here for now?"

"I am sure, and not just for now. The cabin is yours," George responded and squeezed his daughter's hand.

"As long as it is just you two, you should be fine here. Once you give us grandchildren, you might have to move, though, but you can always come back here with your husband while we babysit for you," he continued and winked at Alex and a blushing Hazel.

"Oh, yes, grandchildren. I can't wait to be a grandma," Liz called out from the bedroom, and everyone chuckled.

"Mom. We got married yesterday, don't start bugging us about grandchildren already." Alex shook his head.

"I have never seen your mom like that. It is so cute," Hazel said now and watched her mother-in-law check out the washroom next.

"I am glad you think so, my love. Dad, Miles, and I don't see it as cute anymore."

"This place is so adorable and lovely," they heard Liz's voice once again in the background, which made everyone chuckle again. Hazel was confident that Christmas with her mother-in-law would be fascinating.

The sitting room of the Buchannon ranch was filled with the people she loved. Hazel looked around, and her heart beat faster when she remembered how special they were to her. Here they were together, celebrating the birth of Jesus Christ.

Conversations were light and joyful and Hazel snuggled up to her husband as she got lost in her thoughts.

She thought about the many struggles she had gone through this past year and how grateful she was for each person present. She loved them unconditionally. They were her family.

Love, not just blood, binds a family. This past year had taught her how badly some people treated their blood. But nothing could ever destroy a family connected by love. Such bonds were more robust than anything in the world.

As Hazel looked around the room, her eyes stopped at a picture frame her grandmother had made for her father. It was his favorite passage from the bible. 1 Corinthians 13.

It was what they had and were still working on and what kept this unique family together, even if it required daily work. Keeping love alive means hard work, the willingness to forgive, and strong faith in God and Jesus Christ. Hazel wanted that love with her forever.

She closed her eyes and recited the words in her mind. A strong, warm feeling testified to her, it was the truth and that the people in her life were there for a reason.

Hazel knew she still had difficulties ahead of her and would have to face the trials of Jason Clark and Caleb Norton, but she wasn't scared anymore because she knew justice had won, and she wasn't by herself. She was also more determined than ever to fight for more rights for women and others who were mistreated. Everyone deserved respect, and she would do what she could to make that happen.

The End

Epilogue

"Mrs. Camden, I understand you are raising awareness, so the laws in our different states and territories are being challenged and changed. You want women to have the right to own land and inherit the land from their fathers. The Territory of Oregon has just changed their laws in your favor, but why are you pushing for more laws."

"Because women are still mistreated. A father and husband can do whatever they please with their wives and daughters. Countless women and girls are getting beaten every single day. Abuse of any kind is wrong. You are physically in advantage. Why not use it for good and protect those in your care instead of hurting them?"

"Women should be submissive to their husbands and need to be obedient. If they are not, there will be consequences."

"Wife beating is wrong," Hazel snapped and gave the council member in front of her an angry glance. "Beating your children is wrong. Why can't you understand that?"

"Men were put on this earth to be in control of everything."

"No, that's not true. Tell me, Sir, are you married?"

"Yes, I am."

"Does that mean you believe in abusing your wife and children by beating them with your hand?"

He looked at her, flabbergasted and shocked, and didn't know what to say.

"Mrs. Camden, it isn't our job to tell a man what he can and cannot do in his own house," another council member interjected.

"Yet you have no problem telling women what they can and cannot do. Don't you see how hypocritical that is?"

"A woman has to do as she is told—"

"Yes, yes," Hazel interrupted impatiently. "A woman has to be meek and submissive. I know. Do you gentlemen believe in God and the scriptures?" All of them nodded. "Then let me ask you this: Where does it say in the bible, you can beat your wife and mistreat her? I remember what God told Adam when he made Eve. In Genesis 2:18 it says:

And the LORD God said, [It is] not good that the man should be alone; I will make him a help meet for him. A help meet, not a slave. God created us so we would complete each other. We should be equal in mind and treatment even though we are different in other ways. It also says in 1 Peter 3:7:

Likewise, ye husbands, dwell with [them] according to knowledge, giving honor unto the wife, as unto the weaker vessel, and as being heirs together of the grace of life; that your prayers be not hindered. [1]

Giving honor to your wife, and being heirs together, doesn't sound like it is okay to mistreat your wife."

The council members looked at each other, shocked and stunned. That young lady had an exceptional understanding of the scriptures and was wise beyond her years. They didn't know what to say.

"You said earlier that a wife needs to be obedient and submissive, and when she isn't, a husband can punish her. Do you think beating helps her be submissive and obedient, or is it fear of the punishment? Women and children might be obedient after a punishment, but fear makes them that way, not because they want to be or because you made them change. Threatening and hurting a weaker person is nothing you should be proud of. Yes, they are afraid of you and will most likely do as they are told, but that makes them prisoners in your house and their skin. They don't respect you, they fear you. Respect is earned, not given, and many men still have to learn that lesson in this life."

Afterthought

Wife-Beating was a frequent and regular practice in the 1800s. It took a long time before it was made illegal. The book "Victimization of Women" says: "Official disapproval against battering was more characteristic of the late 1800s and early 1900s. Three states passed laws punishing wife-beating with the whipping post: Maryland (1882), Delaware (1901), and Oregon (1906)..." [2]

Some states started early, others eventually followed, but it wasn't until 1920 that wife-beating was made illegal nationally. [3]

---

[1] https://kingjamesbibleonline.org/Bible-Verses-About-Helpmeet

[2] *https://books.google.de/books*[1]

---

1. *https://books.google.de/books?id=9tNoaQ7YJEgC&pg=PA40&lpg=PA40&dq=when+was+wife+beating+against+the+law+in+Oregon+1800s?&source=bl&ots=cvwgUgH9sG&sig=ACfU3U3rYClKGwX9hhxodo8hDn4aFcPDIA&hl=de&sa=X&ved=2ahUKEwixnJadlozoAhVFKuwKHdrMA9UQ6AEwAHoECAcQAQ#v_43ec3e5dee6e706af7766fffea512721_onepage_6cff047854f19ac2aa52aac51bf3af4a_q_6cff047854f19ac2aa52aac51bf3af4a_f_43ec3e5dee6e706af7766fffea512721_false*

[3] https://google.com/search (wife beating)

Did you love *Not Without A Fight*? Then you should read *Healing the Orphaned Heart*[2] by Rebecca Lange!

[3]

All Rose ever wanted was the love of her father – not his money or prominence, just his love. After her mother's early death, her father was all she had left. But, instead of reaching out to her and giving her the love she so desperately needed, his grief and pain made him pull away - leaving her to the care of his servants and staff. She grows up into a beautiful, headstrong, feisty, yet serious young woman, but no matter how hard she tries to ignore the emptiness in her heart, it was still there. Terrified to meet the relatives she hadn't seen since she was five years old,

---

2. https://books2read.com/u/bx1gqk

3. https://books2read.com/u/bx1gqk

she makes the journey alone. She quickly realizes that her late father's wealth - and with that, her dowry – made her a target for journalists and men everywhere. Will her family welcome her with open arms, or are they taking her in because they have to? Is a man worthy of her love out there, or does everyone only care about her wealth?

Read more at https://rebecca-lange-books.square.site.

About the Author

Rebecca was born and raised in Germany and lived there until 2002 when she served a mission for her church in Scotland. She is a member of the Church of Jesus Christ of Latter-day Saints. Together with her husband and two sons, Rebecca currently resides in Utah.

A romance lover at heart, Rebecca has been writing stories since her teenage years and decided to become more serious about them in the summer of 2012. In February 2013, Rebecca published a little cookbook, later a trilogy, and from there followed nearly a dozen stories, such as the one you just read. She is always working on several romance suspense novels and novellas.

If you liked the story, please consider leaving a review.

Read more at https://rebecca-lange-books.square.site.

www.ingramcontent.com/pod-product-compliance
Lightning Source LLC
LaVergne TN
LVHW020646110826
845149LV00012B/1922

* 9 7 8 1 9 5 7 0 8 9 2 6 3 *